Praise f...

"The follow-up to a... nd on this magical ne... tic and entertaining ch... ate and integral to the novel as the elem... ad- ers will anxiously await the next opportunity to dwell in this delightful town."　　　　　　　—Kings River Life Magazine

"Annabelle's feline familiar is featured heavily and is given a delightful personality. The mystery moves nicely and is given a very satisfying ending. I look forward to seeing what Anna- belle, Alistair, and her magical crew get mixed up in next."
　　　　　　　　　　　　　　　　　　—The Qwillery

"Great story, strong characters, lovely setting, fun familiars, as well as a great mystery and a ghost or two . . . I hope you will love this one as much as I did!"
　　　　　　　　　　　—A Cup of Tea and a Cozy Mystery

Praise for *A Familiar Tail*

"This intriguing first installment of a new series is populated with wonderful characters and has a twisty plot that will keep you turning the pages. If forthcoming novels are as tantalizing as this one is, this series should land on every- one's must-read list!"　　　　　　—ReadertoReader.com

continued . . .

"Much like *Bewitched*, the feline in this one is a blast, and Annabelle is perfect when it comes to magical thinking and doing in New Hampshire. It will be more than fun to follow her journey for a good, long time to come."

—*Suspense Magazine*

"Anna is so genuinely likable, the dialogue so cleverly written, and the plot so compelling, that readers will enthusiastically follow her adventures and eagerly await their next chance to enter her world. Continual twists guarantee that readers will be as surprised by the truth as Anna, and the wit and confident writing by the author will cement her place on the list of must-read paranormal mystery series."

—Kings River Life Magazine

Berkley Prime Crime titles by Delia James

A FAMILIAR TAIL
BY FAMILIAR MEANS
FAMILIAR MOTIVES

Familiar Motives

A Witch's Cat Mystery

DELIA JAMES

BERKLEY PRIME CRIME
New York

BERKLEY PRIME CRIME
Published by Berkley
An imprint of Penguin Random House LLC
375 Hudson Street, New York, New York 10014

Copyright © 2017 by Penguin Random House LLC.
Penguin Random House supports copyright. Copyright fuels creativity, encourages
diverse voices, promotes free speech, and creates a vibrant culture. Thank you for buying
an authorized edition of this book and for complying with copyright laws by not
reproducing, scanning, or distributing any part of it in any form without permission.
You are supporting writers and allowing Penguin Random House to continue to
publish books for every reader.

BERKLEY is a registered trademark and BERKLEY PRIME CRIME and the B
colophon are trademarks of Penguin Random House LLC.

ISBN 9780451476593

First Edition: October 2017

Printed in the United States of America
1   3   5   7   9   10   8   6   4   2

Cover art by Irina Gamashova-Cawton
Book design by Kelly Lipovich

To Blueberry, who is the Original

❧ I WANT TO be really clear about a few things. I do not habitually hide important information from my friends and family. I do not eavesdrop on other people's conversations, especially from under tables, and I don't run out on parties to which I have been invited as the guest of honor.

Unless it's really important.

My name is Annabelle Amelia Blessingsound Britton. That's a lot by normal standards. When you belong to an old New England family, though, it's part of the standard package, along with the native stubbornness and a reluctance to pronounce the letter *R*.

I'm also an artist. And a witch. That's a little less standard.

In fact, I found out about the witch thing only when I moved to Portsmouth, New Hampshire. I had always known there was something . . . different . . . about me. I have a—well, call it an unusual ability. I pick up on the emotional vibrations associated with dramatic events that happen inside a house or building. If something happened in the past, like a death, or something is coming in the future, like a

wedding or a birth, I will know about it as soon as I walk
into a room, whether I want to or not. If the emotions surrounding the event are intense enough, they will flood right
through me. The stronger they are, in fact, the stronger my
reaction will be. That reaction can include breaking down
or passing out.

This doesn't happen all the time, thankfully, or I wouldn't
be able to walk into the Circle K without losing my mind.
But, while I've lived with what I call my "Vibe" since I was
a kid, it was only recently that I found out it's rooted in a
long, secret family history of magic and magic workers that
includes my sweet and innocent-looking grandmother.

I was still trying to get used to that.

My Vibe was not the cause of today's headache, however.
Today's problems were purely the fault of my cat, Alistair,
and the fact that I had to take him to the vet.

Alistair was a facet of my Portsmouth life I was still
getting used to. He had been living on his own for months
before I arrived in town, and he was still a part-time outdoor
cat. That meant he really needed a checkup, whether he
wanted one or not.

Trips to the vet can be challenging for any cat owner.
Many otherwise loving felines will find creative ways to
resist the simplest medical procedures. But when you're an
apprentice witch and your cat is also your magical familiar,
there're some added levels of complication. Especially when
your familiar has the ability to (literally) vanish into thin air.

Fortunately, I had an ace up my sleeve. Despite the occasional outbreak of witch-hunting, there are still fair a
number of magic practitioners scattered around New
England. Portsmouth, for example, is home to a witch cop,
a witch bookstore owner, a witch bed-and-breakfast propri-
etor, and even a witch housekeeper. So I wasn't entirely
surprised to hear we also have a witch veterinarian.

"Ramona Forsythe has been taking care of Max and Leo
for years," Julia Parris told me. Julia is the leader of my
coven. She's also my mentor and the human partner to a pair

of miniature dachshunds. "She knows Alistair very well. She can handle him."

I hoped so. Because here I was, walking out of New Hampshire's truly impressive November cold into the cheerful green-and-blue-tiled waiting room of the Piscataqua Small Animal Clinic with an (entirely empty) kitty carrier in one hand and my fingers crossed. The carrier was strictly for appearances. I mean, it would look a little strange to come to a cat appointment without a cat. But Alistair had vanished the second he saw it.

The assistant at the reception counter wore scrubs covered in rainbow-striped cats and a name tag reading JEANNIE. I gave her my name and my cat's name and made sure to set the carrier on the floor so she wouldn't see someone was missing from this conversation.

She was still registering my arrival when a woman leaned out of a door labeled ROOM 3.

"Anna?" she asked. "I'm Dr. Ramona Forsythe. I've been expecting you and Alistair." She held the door open and motioned me inside the bright, antiseptic-scented examination room.

Dr. Forsythe was one of those short, round women whose cheerful competence tends to mask a steely core. Her chestnut brown hair was just starting to go gray. She wore a white coat and green scrubs and certainly didn't look much like a modern-day witch. As she closed the door, though, I felt a slow prickling begin in my fingertips. This, I was beginning to learn, was the sign of active magic happening somewhere close.

"Nice to meet you, Dr. Forsythe," I said as I set the empty kitty carrier on the stainless steel exam table.

"Please, call me Ramona," she said. "And it's great to finally meet you. I was so glad when I heard Alistair found a new partner. We were all worried about him after Dorothy died." She squinted inside the carrier. "I see he still doesn't like vet visits, though."

"Um, no."

"Well, don't worry. This is the room we keep for our *special* patients." She winked and gestured to the walls. Now I could see what I'd thought was a wallpaper border was actually a carefully painted pattern of knots and stars. I might be new to the practice of the "true craft," but I could recognize a ceremonial circle when I saw one. Eventually anyway.

Ramona adjusted the door so it was open just a crack. "Go ahead and call him."

Alistair, being my familiar, cannot be kept away from me, except by strong, focused magic. He can appear in an attic, a deep basement or the locked bathroom when I am taking a shower, and he has done all of these. The flip side of this is he has to come when I call, something he considers an affront to his feline dignity.

I would be hearing about this for days.

I let out a long, slow breath and reached down inside to gather my personal energy.

"Alistair," I called to thin air. "Come on, Alistair."

Nothing happened.

"Try these." Ramona opened a drawer in the examining table's pedestal and pulled out a bag of K.T. Nibbles. Clearly, Ramona was familiar with my cat and his habits.

I took the bright green bag and shook two treats out into my palm. Attitude Cat, the famous black-and-white spokes-feline, glowered up at me as if she resented being used for our nefarious plans.

Come on, Anna, focus. "Alistair!" I called again. "Nibbles!"

And just like that, my big gray feline familiar was sitting on the examination table. I held out the nibbles and he stretched his neck forward to take one. Ramona slapped the door shut, closing the room, the circle and the spell contained in the painted border. A prickle of fresh magic shot up from my fingertips to my elbows.

Alistair's head snapped up.

"Merow!" Alistair shook himself, but nothing happened. He lashed his tail and put his ears back. Still nothing. "Meerr-ooowww!"

"Sorry, big guy," I told him. "But it's for your own good. Finish your nibble." I held out the remaining treat. Alistair grumbled deep in his throat, but he did take it.

I won't say Alistair exactly cooperated after that, but he didn't exactly fight either. He just sort of melted onto the table as if he thought that if he flattened himself out far enough, Dr. Forsythe wouldn't be able to pick him up. This did not faze Ramona one bit. Ignoring Alistair's glowers, grumbles and general bonelessness, she efficiently weighed him (twenty pounds—wow), took his temperature (normal), checked his ears (clean), and palpated his tummy (big, soft) and other places (pass, citizen). I held him down for the shots and winced with him.

"Well, Alistair here is in very good health." Ramona scratched him behind the ears. He did not look mollified. I put another couple of nibbles on the examination table. He ate them both, without taking his eyes off me. Oh, yes. I'd definitely be hearing about this for a very long time. "He also seems to have made a full transition to bonding with his new partner."

Alistair's previous partner had been Dorothy Hawthorne, one of the founding members of the guardian coven that I now belonged to. In fact, Dorothy was responsible for a lot of my life in Portsmouth. Her magic had helped bring me here; her cat had helped keep me here. Her former cottage had become my home once I really did decide to stay. I didn't actually own the house. That belonged to Frank Hawthorne, Dorothy's nephew and the publisher of the local paper, the *Seacoast News*.

Ramona beamed at me. "Do you have any questions, Anna?"

"Actually, I did. It's about his diet. He won't eat cat food." Unless there was nothing else available. In the whole county.

"That's not a surprise. A lot of familiars prefer to eat what their partners do. But that doesn't mean it's a good idea. In fact—" A knock on the door interrupted her.

"Dr. Forsythe?" Jeannie, the receptionist, called from the other side of the door. "Kristen and Ruby are here."

Ramona glanced at her watch. "Oh . . . shoot, that's right. I'm sorry, Anna. I'll just be a second."

I gathered up Alistair, and Ramona slipped out into the waiting room. I swear for a minute I felt him begin to dissolve in my arms, which was very weird. As soon as the door snicked shut, though, he was back to being solid, and highly annoyed.

Alistair flowed out of my arms and under the visitors' chair.

"Fine." I sighed. "Be that way."

"Merow," he answered. He also flattened down in a clear attempt to become one with the floor tiles.

"Kristen," I heard Ramona say out in the lobby. "Hi. I'm sorry. I thought you weren't coming until two."

"I wasn't," answered another woman. "But, well . . . some stuff has come up, and I needed to bring Ruby over early."

The exam room door had a narrow glass window above the handle. In an effort to show my indifference to Alistair's sulks, I drifted over and looked out into the lobby. Ramona stood with a slender young woman in a black knitted hat and green parka. She had no carrier with her. Instead, one mittened hand held a bright red leash. A black-and-white cat sat beside her on the reception counter, calmly washing its whiskers.

Must be nice. I squinted at the unusually mellow cat. It was a longhair and had one black ear and one white ear, which, along with the blotches on its face, gave it a kind of checkerboard look.

In fact . . . I blinked. I also looked at the bag of K.T. Nibbles on the counter by the sink. The cat out there, Ruby, was a dead ringer for the famous K.T. Nibbles spokesfeline, Attitude Cat.

"Merow?" Alistair poked his head out from under the chair.

"Nah," I murmured back. "Couldn't be."

"I've got a meeting with some of the PR people," the woman, Kristen, was telling Ramona. "You would not *believe* the stuff they've got us deciding on. I mean, T-shirts were one thing, and the toys, but now it's greeting cards, and they want to do an Attitude Cat coloring book . . ."

I looked at Alistair. I looked at the Nibbles bag. Attitude Cat looked back. "Maybe it could."

"I told you, you should hire an assistant," said Ramona.

"Or three," agreed Kristen. "Pam kept insisting she had it covered, and I believed her." She reached across and rubbed her cat under her black-and-white chin. "And now here we are."

"Merow." The cat, Ruby, rolled over on her back and swished her tail a few times.

Alistair and I blinked at each other. This was Attitude Cat? The famously aloof and never-to-be-pleased feline who stared with indifference at every kind of food, toy, or snack that did not come from the aisles of a Best Petz store?

"You're just tired, Kristen," said Ramona. "It's been a roller-coaster ride for you, and now you've got to go take care of your mom."

This, I realized, was eavesdropping. It was rude. I should move away from the door and pay attention to something else. I should check my e-mail on my phone or read the warning posters about heartworm and feline leukemia. Really. I should. Right now.

Out in the lobby, Kristen shook her head and said something I couldn't hear. Ramona touched her arm. I thought I saw Kristen wince.

"Can you hang on just a second?" Ramona asked Kristen. The vet walked briskly back toward our room. I jumped back from the door so it wouldn't look quite so much like I'd been listening in.

"Anna, I need to ask a favor . . . ," Ramona began as she opened the door.

This time Alistair was ready for both of us. He darted straight past Ramona like a bolt of fat gray lightning and vaulted up onto the counter beside the black-and-white cat.

"Oh, good grief!" I muttered. "He's gone fanboy. Sorry," I said to the woman, Kristen, as I scurried over to attempt to retrieve my familiar. "He's, uh, friendly."

Fortunately, Kristen just laughed. "I can tell."

"Kristen Summers, this is Anna Britton." Ramona performed the introductions. "And the ladies' man here is Alistair."

"Hi." Kristen and I shook hands. Alistair pushed his nose toward Ruby. Ruby lifted her chin and looked away in cold disdain. Oh, yeah. This really and truly was Attitude Cat. Even Alistair seemed taken aback. His hesitation gave Ruby a chance to jump down onto the floor.

"Your name sounds familiar," Kristen said. She was a few inches taller than me, and a few years younger, with tawny skin and rich brown eyes. She wore her dark brown hair in a long braid down her back. "Did we meet somewhere? And if we did, I'm sorry I forgot . . ."

"Don't worry about it," I told her. "We haven't."

Down by our shins, Alistair nosed Ruby, who turned away from him. He circled around her.

"Do not be that cat, big guy," I muttered. "Take no for an answer."

Alistair promptly plumped himself down and started washing his hind leg.

"I really am sorry," I told Kristen. "He just doesn't know when to quit."

"Don't worry about it. Ruby can take care of herself." Then Kristen snapped her fingers. "I remember now! You're a friend of Valerie's, right? Valerie McDermott?"

"That's right." My yard backed up onto the garden of McDermott's Bed & Breakfast, which Valerie ran with her husband, Roger.

"That's how I know your name. She's talked about you. How's the new baby?"

"Sweet and perfect, with a very healthy set of lungs."

"I keep meaning to call them, but everything's just been so crazy . . ." As if to prove Kristen's point, a phone rang from deep inside her purse.

"Sorry." Kristen pulled out a brand-new smartphone to check the screen. She hit a button and scurried to the other end of the reception room. "Hello?" she said into the phone. "No, not a good time."

Dr. Forsythe dug both hands into the pockets of her white coat and watched as Kristen turned her back. She was frowning hard, and she didn't seem to realize it. *Something is going on.* The thought popped into my head before I could stop it. I immediately told myself to quit speculating. As a witch, you're supposed to be attuned to the natural energies that came from the world around you, including the people. The side effect of this was that sometimes you—okay, *I*—thought I could tell more about a person than I actually could.

"Merow," said Alistair.

"Quiet, cat," I muttered.

"Sorry?" Dr. Forsythe shook herself. "Did you say something?"

"Nothing important," I told her.

"Yes, yes," Kristen was saying into her phone. "But I've got to call you back, okay? 'Kay, thanks." She hung up and turned back to us. She smiled as she came back to the counter, but that smile was tense. Ruby purred and flicked her tail back and forth. Alistair nosed her neck. The purring stopped.

"Attitude Cat Enterprises never sleeps," Kristen said, trying to sound casual, but her voice was strained. "Listen, Ramona, are you sure you're good with this?"

"Oh, absolutely," said Ramona, but like Kristen's, her voice was strained around the edges. Alistair and I looked at each other. These two definitely wanted to have a serious conversation, but not in front of us. We should go away. Now.

"Great," Kristen was saying. "I've got her bed and stuff in the car. I'll just . . ." Kristen gestured toward the glass doors and froze. "Oh, no."

We all looked, cats included. Outside, a woman in a checked overcoat was striding across the parking lot. She opened the clinic door like she was trying to yank it off its hinges.

"You pathetic thief!" she shrieked.

❧ 2 ❦

🐾 "WELL, GOSH. HI, Cheryl." Kristen's voice was bright, brittle and entirely unhappy. "I take it you got my message?"

"No, actually, I didn't." The woman, Cheryl, stalked forward. She had a impressive stride, especially considering the height of the heels on her designer boots. But then, it was clear this was a woman who knew the value of making an impression. Her pale face was perfectly made-up, and I suspect had been adjusted in a few other ways. Her checkered coat was fifties vintage with black velvet cuffs and a broad collar, and her perfectly bobbed, perfectly dyed blond hair was covered by a brimmed felt hat. The handbag was at least as designer as the boots. She wore chunky silver-and-turquoise earrings, and the bracelets on the wrists of her black gloves were that hypertrendy Aldina brand that you could customize with about a dozen different baubles dangling off each, like upper-class charm bracelets.

Kristen was not the only one less than thrilled to see this woman. Ruby pressed her fluffy belly down flat against the floor and made a warning noise deep in her throat. In response, Alistair yawned and stretched and plumped himself down between Ruby and the new arrival.

Cheryl stared at this unexpected piece of feline chivalry. "Who are you?" she snapped at both me and my cat.

"Anna Britton," I told her. "And this is Alistair. Sorry. He's got no manners."

The look Cheryl gave me indicated she didn't think I had much in the way of manners either. I smiled apologetically, but this time, I didn't pick him up.

"I left you a message," Kristen said to Cheryl.

"You would say that, now that I've caught you trying to hide my property!"

Jeannie, the clinic assistant, poked her head out from the main treatment area, looking in to see if she was needed. Ramona waved her away. Jeannie ducked back so quickly, I suspected she was glad to be elsewhere.

"And you . . . !" Cheryl turned on Dr. Forsythe, and Ramona clutched the counter like she was going to break a chunk off. "How much did she pay you to help her little scam?"

"There is no scam!" Kristen threw out both hands. "Nobody's trying to hide anything, Cheryl!"

"Except the fact that you're a thief!"

"Merr-oww," muttered Alistair. I nudged him with one toe. He scooted sideways out of reach. At the same time, I slid my hand into my purse so my fingers curled around my wand. Yes, I have a wand, and I carry it with me. It's not as magical as what you see in the movies or the Harry Potter books, but it does help with focus and control, like in situations when I might need to help exert a healing or calming influence, around a person, or maybe a cat.

"Cheryl." Ramona mustered a professional smile and gestured toward the rear of the clinic with the hand that wasn't hanging on to the counter for dear life. "Why don't we all go back into the office? We can sit down and straighten this out."

"There's nothing to straighten out!" Cheryl shouted. "I've got a court order." She yanked a sheaf of papers out of her purse. *"She"*—she flapped the papers toward Kristen—"is not allowed to take Ruby *anywhere* without notifying me! And you . . . !"

"I'm not taking her anywhere," snapped Kristen. "Ruby is boarding with Dr. Forsythe for a few days."

"So you were planning on hiding her!" shouted Cheryl triumphantly.

Ruby jumped up on the counter, her leash trailing down behind her. From there, she leapt straight into Kristen's arms. Alistair, down by my ankles, gave a warning growl. His tail lashed back and forth.

Don't even think about it, big guy.

Now I did pick him up. He didn't like it and I felt his claws press ever so slightly against my sleeve. I was going to be dishing out a lot of tuna and nibbles later.

"Cheryl, there's no scam, and nobody's hiding Ruby," said Dr. Forsythe firmly. "She'll be staying with me, at my home."

"My mother is in the hospital," said Kristen through gritted teeth as she stroked Ruby's back. "She needs surgery. My sister can't get out until Tuesday. I've got to be there. I sent you an e-mail. I didn't know if you'd gotten it, so I wrote everything down. I was going to leave all the details at your attorney's office." Kristen cradled Ruby in the crook of one arm and fished an envelope out of her purse.

Cheryl snatched the letter out of Kristen's fingers and skimmed it. I kept one eye on her, but I was really watching Ramona. Her face wasn't pale anymore. In fact, it was flushed red.

What is going on with you? I wondered. I cradled Alistair in the crook of one arm while I kept the other hand on my wand. Working any kind of spell without prior preparation is not easy, but there are some small things that can be done on the fly, including conjuring a calming atmosphere.

Of course, as an apprentice, I wasn't supposed to do any kind of magic without permission or supervision, but Ramona was a senior witch and standing right here, so I was in the clear on this one. I tried to breathe deep and exude an air of calm.

Absolutely nothing happened.

Well, almost nothing. Ramona did glance at me and quirk one eyebrow. I blushed.

Fortunately, Cheryl and Kristen were too busy to notice any of this.

"I'll be showing this to my lawyer," Cheryl announced. "Expect the call. You as well." She shook the papers at Dr. Forsythe. "This is *not* in the court order. Maybe you stole Ruby out from under me, but I'm getting what's mine—"

This was too much for Kristen. "You are not touching Ruby!" she snapped, and the force of the exclamation tightened her arm around her cat. Ruby squeaked, jumped down to the floor and whisked under one of the chairs, the red leash scraping against the tiles. Alistair immediately wriggled himself free from my grip so he could drop to the floor and galumph after her. "I swear, Cheryl, if you don't cut this out, I'll . . ."

"You'll what?" sneered Cheryl, a little too obviously pleased that she'd gotten Kristen to lash out. "What are you going to do once your record's splashed all over the papers and the Internet? Huh? And when the judge hears the whole sordid story?" She smirked. "Or your mom and your sister and . . . ?"

"I've made up with my family. Maybe you should be working on that, and leave me and Ruby alone!"

Ramona caught my eye again and let out a long breath. I picked up the hint, tightened my grip on my wand and deliberately slowed my own breathing down. In my mind, I began a silent invocation.

In need I call, in hope I ask, an' it harm none . . .

This time, the familiar prickling ran up my arms, and I felt Ramona's influence boosting my own. Below us, Alistair started purring like nothing had ever been wrong. He circled Kristen's ankles once, and then again.

Slowly, but perceptibly, the tension between Cheryl and Kristen began to fade. Kristen eased back, and so did Cheryl, although much more slowly. Alistair circled Kristen's ankles again. Ruby cocked her head and managed to look mildly impressed. Alistair licked his chops. That's my cat. Charm all the way. Literally.

Kristen rubbed her eyes. "I'm sorry, Cheryl. Really. I should have called. I know. Take the papers to your lawyer. You can call if there are any questions, okay?"

"That sounds fair," murmured Ramona. The prickling in my fingers sharpened slightly, and in my mind I repeated my invocation. "Don't you think, Cheryl?"

Cheryl's jaw worked itself back and forth a few times, but she did take the envelope. "You will hear from us," she muttered.

"I'll be waiting." Kristen sighed.

The two women glared at each other. I felt their anger struggle against the soothing aura of Ramona's (and my) magic. Cheryl frowned hard and looked like she was about to say something. Ramona smiled and I smiled and Alistair purred, and a faint breath of warm air that could easily have been a draft curled around our shoulders. Cheryl turned away on her designer heels as smoothly as a ballerina doing her best pirouette and clicked out the clinic door.

❧ 3 ☙

🐾 THE DOOR DIDN'T slam, but we all winced anyway. Ramona's mouth moved, and I felt more than heard her breathe the words that dispersed the spell.

So mote it be, I murmured under my own breath as I released my own energy and focus.

"Meow," added Alistair. Ruby groomed her tail assiduously.

"Sorry about that." Kristen sighed. "I really didn't mean—"

"It's not your fault," Ramona told her before she had to say any more.

"Isn't it?" Kristen muttered. I couldn't tell if she was angry or just too tired for words.

"Of course not!" Ramona assured her.

"Um . . . I take it there's a problem between you and . . . ?" I asked, because I am very good at stating the obvious.

"Cheryl. Congratulations, Anna." Ramona chuckled, but there was no humor in it. In fact, she sounded just as tired as Kristen. "You've just stepped straight into one of Portsmouth's weirdest property disputes."

Alistair inched just a little closer to Ruby. Ruby yawned, got up and walked around to the other side of her owner. Alistair batted at her leash. She ignored him.

"Cheryl and I used to be . . . roommates." I caught the hesitation in Kristen's voice and in her eyes. "We found Ruby in the laundry room of our apartment building. You should have seen the poor little thing." Affection softened Kristen's voice and her expression as she looked toward her cat, who was rubbing up against her ankles. "Just a bundle of fur and nerves." She picked Ruby up. Alistair plopped back on his hindquarters, immensely disappointed.

"A couple of months after we found her, Cheryl, well . . ." Kristen rubbed Ruby's ears restlessly, trying to choose her words. *Trying not to say too much,* I thought.

"Meow," said Alistair, which sounded a little too much like encouragement to be entirely comfortable.

"We started to argue about money . . . and things," Kristen was saying. Ramona nodded sympathetically. "She was threatening to throw me out because I was broke, and I . . . well, I was broke. I offered to try to figure something out, asked her to give me time to find a new place. Then Cheryl ran out on us." Kristen pulled a face. "I woke up one morning, and she was just gone. The rent was overdue and I couldn't even pay my share, let alone the whole thing. But I'd seen a sign for this contest at the Best Petz store, a kind of audition for local cats. The top prize was a few hundred dollars cash and a chance for your cat to be in a commercial." She flashed us a chagrined smile and Ruby squirmed and let herself be put down on the counter.

"Merow," said Alistair, and I could see him getting ready to leap up beside her. I nudged his hindquarters again. I also ignored the look of mortally wounded feline dignity he leveled at me.

"Anyway, I figured, what the heck." Kristen shrugged. "And it turned out the camera loved Ruby, and the rest is . . ." She scratched Ruby under the collar. "Well, it's history. It's also contracts and lawyers and agents and trademarks and merchandising and a whole lot of other stuff that makes me regret not having a business degree."

"So, what happened?" I asked. Alistair was pacing around by my ankles and stepping on my feet, hoping I would pick him up. I ignored him. "I mean, if Cheryl's the one who left you and Ruby, she can't exactly claim that Ruby is her cat."

"Well, that's the problem. She's finally found a lawyer she can convince that *I'm* the one who left and that I took Ruby with me when I did."

"Ouch."

"Yeah," said Kristen. "Ouch. And I've got no proof and no witnesses, but then neither does Cheryl, which it turns out is not as much help as it should be."

"Because it makes the whole thing a she said, she said?"

"And what she says"—Kristen jerked her chin toward the door—"is that I stole Ruby and should give her back."

"Along with some of the money?" I guessed.

"Along with a whole lot of the money," agreed Kristen.

"Meow," announced Alistair loyally. Ruby started grooming her front paw. The rest of us stood together in silent sympathy. Sympathy, and more than a little quiet scrambling to find something meaningfully supportive to say.

Jeannie peeked out from the back again. Ramona beckoned her back to her chair at the reception desk. Jeannie sat, flashed us all a nervous smile and started typing vigorously, while pretending not to pay any attention to what was going on in front of the counter. Again, the exhaustion in Ramona's eyes and the pallor of her face struck me. I was dying to ask her what was wrong. What was it about Cheryl's visit that had upset the vet so badly? I found myself wondering if she was closer to Kristen and Ruby than she'd let on so far. They must be good friends if she was cat-sitting, right?

Of course I couldn't ask, for a lot of reasons, starting with the fact that while this was all happening right in front of me, it remained absolutely none of my business.

"Well, I'm no expert, but I would think a judge would

find the timing all awfully fishy," I said, more to fill the silence than anything else. "I mean, Cheryl has everything to gain by lying about what happened between you."

"Yeah, well, there's a problem," said Kristen. "I have some . . . stuff in my past that might make a judge less willing to listen to my side."

"Oh," I said, which was not the best answer, but it was the only one I had at the moment.

"Yeah, 'oh.'" Kristen smiled in that tired sort of way people do when they really hope they can trust you. While this fresh silence was stretching out, Alistair jumped up on the counter, meowed and head butted my wrist.

I glanced at my watch. "Jeez, I'm sorry. I've got to get going. I've got a whole bunch of errands to run before the party tonight."

"Oh, right," said Ramona, and I know I did not miss how relieved she looked to be able to change the subject. "The unveiling is today, isn't it? Anna's an artist," she told Kristen. "She's done some artwork for the Midnight Reads bookshop, and she's got one of those new adult coloring books coming out."

Alistair head butted my wrist again. I scratched his ears to let him know I wasn't ignoring him.

"Best of luck," Kristen told me. "And despite everything, it was good to meet you. Tell Val I said hi and I will call soon."

"Sure thing." We shook hands and smiled. Kristen picked up Ruby and draped her against her shoulder so Ruby was looking back at us as they walked out the glass doors. Alistair drooped visibly.

"And here I thought you were stepping out with Miss Boots," I muttered as I scratched his ears. "Or did Colonel Kitty agree to take you back?"

Alistair washed his whiskers like he didn't hear a word I said.

"Well," said Ramona, too briskly, I thought. "Shall we finish up?"

"Sure," I said uncertainly and scooped up Alistair to follow her back into the examination room.

But once she closed the door and I set Alistair down on the table, Ramona just stood there with her hand on the knob for a minute.

"Anna, I'm about to tell you something." She spoke softly and quickly, like she needed to get the words out before she changed her mind. "And I'm speaking as a friend and a sister practitioner."

"Um, sure, Ramona."

"If you're thinking about a coloring-book deal, or anything like that, with the Attitude Cat people, don't."

I hadn't been, until she mentioned it. Now, though, I opened my mouth to ask *Why not?* but from out in the lobby we heard the sound of people and at least two quarreling dogs entering the clinic.

"We'll talk more later." Ramona smoothed down her lab coat and walked out of the room without looking back.

"Wow. Okay," I said to the door.

"Merow," agreed Alistair. He also, somewhat to my surprise, let himself be put into the carrier and taken out into the lobby. I gave my credit card to Jeannie and signed the receipt. Ramona was smiling at an old woman with a pair of shih tzus on gold leashes. She also stepped back to let a man and a little girl clutching a cardboard box walk past her into another examination room. She didn't even look up at us.

Something is going on, I thought. Then I thought, *It's nothing to do with you, Anna. You've got a party to go to and books to draw and there's the matter of Thanksgiving coming up. You are planning on spending quality time with your family; oh, and trying to find some way to tell them all you're a witch. That's more than enough to be juggling right now.*

This was all very true and perfectly reasonable, and it almost worked.

Almost.

❧ 4 ❧

🐾 "ANNA!" JULIA PARRIS made her way through the crowd of guests as I walked into the bookstore. "There you are!"

Julia Parris owned Midnight Reads. She was a tall woman about my grandmother's age with long snow-white hair and a figure best described as zaftig. She always carried herself with immense dignity, even though she did have to walk with the help of her black cane. She had a taste for dramatic clothes and tonight was wearing a floor-length black velvet dress covered by a long jacket of gold and silver lace.

"Sorry I'm late," I said as I shook icy rain off my scarf and hat. "I had trouble finding a parking spot. Hi, guys." Maximilian and Leopold, Julia's minidachshunds, scampered up to sniff my ankles, bark, wag and generally make sure I was who I was supposed to be. I reached down to ruffle the dogs' ears, because, well, dachshunds. How can you resist?

As Gabrielle, Julia's newest sales assistant, came to get my coat, Julia cast an appraising glance over my appearance, which included gently chattering teeth. "Wine or coffee? I suspect coffee."

"Please." I rubbed my hands together. I grew up mostly in Connecticut, so it's not like I'm a stranger to rough winters. New Hampshire, though, was teaching me a few things.

"I'll get you a cup. You circulate." Julia handed me a name tag to clip to my red cardigan so people would know who I was. "A number of my guests have been waiting to talk with you about the paintings."

Julia moved off toward the snack tables that had been set up next to the wine selection. I took a deep breath and faced the crowd, putting on my best professional smile.

Not only is Julia a great witch and a great teacher; she knows how to throw one heck of a party. Midnight Reads bookshop was full to the brim with people there to enjoy wine and snacks, new books, used books, and, oh, yes, some new paintings by a local Portsmouth artist. Even without my magical Vibe going, I was instantly warmed by the cheerful, chatty atmosphere.

While tables and open shelves dominated the front of Midnight Reads, a set of older, library-style shelves waited up a short flight of stairs. When I first saw them, they'd been plain wood labeled with section names: MYSTERY, PSYCHOLOGY, HISTORY, ROMANCE, ETC. (Literally. Julia kept a section of otherwise unclassifiable books for the adventurous reader.)

Those shelves were now decorated with my artwork. I'd taken popular editions of some of the titles and re-created their covers on the ends of the bookshelves, both the ones that faced the doors and the ones that faced the comfortable sitting area at the back of the store. I'd layered and framed the painted covers carefully, so that the effect (I hoped) was like looking down on inviting piles of books, so you could decide which one to pick up next. The mystery section had probably been my favorite to paint. I love those old noir-style covers from the forties and fifties with the damsels either in distress or vamping in doorways.

While I sipped the coffee Julia brought me, people began coming up to talk about the paintings and to express anticipation about the new coloring book. I admit it, I enjoyed all the warm greetings and friendly faces. In fact, as I made my way through the shifting knots of people, beaming and shaking hands, I was amazed at how many of those friendly faces I recognized, even though I hadn't been in Portsmouth for very long.

"They do look fantastic." Sean McNally came up beside me. Sean had gotten off of his usual bartending shift at the Pale Ale to supervise the wine service for the party and, incidentally, advertise the drinks selection from that historic Portsmouth tavern. "And so, by the way, do you."

"Thank you, sir," I murmured. I may have preened, just a tiny bit. Since I was a guest of honor at this little shindig, I had dressed up more than usual. This involved unearthing my only black pencil skirt, my black tights, and the bright red cashmere cardigan my grandma B.B. had given me as a Christmas present last year. I had also wrestled my unruly brown hair into a French twist. "You're looking pretty good yourself."

Sean was lean and tall, with a neatly trimmed beard, an easy smile and more than his fair share of Irish charm. As usual, he dressed in his slightly vintage style, which today included a pin-striped vest over a bright blue shirt and char-coal gray tie.

"Maybe I can sweep the guest of honor away afterward?" he suggested softly.

Sean and I had been on our first date just last week. Nothing huge. Just dinner (a very good dinner) and a movie (Sean did not balk at going to see a romantic comedy, and I promised we'd go see the latest superhero extravaganza next time). We'd talked and we'd laughed and the twinkle that seemed to always lurk in the depths of his blue eyes was proving a strain on my resolve to take this very, very slowly. After all, my last relationship had ended when a blond nineteen-year-old from Vegas showed up on my doorstep looking for my then boyfriend. That kind of thing can make a girl a little hesitant when it's time to jump back into the dating scene.

"You should be careful," I murmured out of the corner of my mouth. "Your boss is watching."

"What am I watching?" Martine Devereux strolled up to us both. Martine is a tall African American woman with dark brown skin. She looked resplendent in her scarlet chef's jacket. She is the head chef at the Pale Ale and has been my best friend since forever. In fact, my original reason for coming to Portsmouth was to visit her. I'd planned to stay for only a couple of weeks, but things got, well, just a little complicated.

"Thanks for being here, Martine," I told her as we exchanged a quick hug.

"Can't stay. Full house tonight, but I wanted to check out the grand opening." She nodded toward my paintings. "Nice job, Britton. You're taking the town by storm. Enjoy it. Oh, and, hey, great cheese muffins," she added over my shoulder to Roger McDermott, who was behind the snack table, refilling a tray of miniature treats. "You ever want a job, you come see me."

"Thanks, Chef." Roger beamed. "That's a real compliment."

Roger was my neighbor and was married to one of my coven sisters, Valerie McDermott. Together they ran McDermott's B and B. Valerie handled the business end, while Roger was in charge of maintenance and food. I had to admit, he'd outdone himself with the selection of minicupcakes and savory muffins on display. He grinned over the heads of the crowd toward Val, who was standing in the far corner talking with some other members of the coven, Shannon Yu and her sister Faye. Allie Paulson was there too, gesturing grandly about something. The dramatic was pretty much Allie's home territory. She ran a housekeeping business, as well as a book-and-tour group for those who loved gothic romances and mysteries. Trisha Robinson stood in another corner. Trish was a freelance computer programmer and would, if you gave her more than two glasses of wine, start explaining how computer programming and spell casting are essentially the same thing. She makes a surprisingly good case. The stocky man in a linen sports coat beside her was probably her boyfriend, the one who worked at MIT in the communications lab and was going to make the Internet obsolete. I had informed Trish that if he took away my ability to watch cute cat videos, I would never forgive either of them. She made faces at me.

In fact, about the only member of the guardian coven missing from the party was my grandma B.B. Grandma had gone back down to Sedona, Arizona, to pack up her apartment. She was reversing the usual American senior migration pattern to move back up here and become Julia's roommate. She'd be back before Thanksgiving, but given the amount of stuff there was to pack, probably not much before then.

The thought of Thanksgiving threw cold water on my glowing spirits. I was just settling into my identity as a witch, which meant I was also just starting to tell people that's who I was. I hadn't told my family yet, though. I didn't like to think I was stalling, but I was. Especially when it came to telling my father. Grandma had said that the one time she'd tried to talk to Dad about her magic, he'd gotten so angry he'd threatened to cut her off from her grandkids.

If I was going to come out of the broom closet, I was going to open a whole very large can of worms over the roasted turkey and cranberry relish.

This, however, was a problem for another day.

Sean gave me a grin and quick touch on the shoulder before heading back to man the wine supplies. I smiled back, and looked around for something distracting. Fortunately, Valerie noticed I was at a loose end and edged her way through the crowd.

"Nice turnout," she remarked. Val is a small, freckled, strawberry blond woman with a stubborn streak that you'd never guess waited behind her sunny face. Her baby daughter, Melissa, had inherited Val's coloring and, I suspected, something of that stubbornness. Although, again, you'd never know it if you saw the newest McDermott sleeping on her mother's shoulder, her tiny fist pressed against her mouth, like it was now.

"Julia throws a good party." I whispered in that way you do around a sleeping baby. I smoothed down one of Melissa's soft strawberry curls. I'd been designated an adopted aunt. Which was, of course, very nice, but I had made it clear, I wasn't going to be one of those people who go overboard about that kind of thing. I certainly had not gotten into the habit of buying cute little stuffed animals or infant clothes at the drop of a hand-knitted strawberry cap. Those pink footie jammies with the Picasso-style cat on them were strictly a one-time event. Except for the yellow ones with the Monet water lilies and the green ones with the bit of *A Sunday on La Grand Jatte* and the . . .

Yeah. Well. Okay. Moving on.

"I met a friend of yours today," I said to Valerie. "Kristen Summers."

"Really?" Surprise widened Valerie's eyes, followed fast by a faintly worried look.

"Yeah, I had to take Alistair to Dr. Forsythe, and Kristen was there with her cat."

"Oh." I knew I did not imagine the relief in Val's face or her voice. "What did you think about our local kitty celebrity?"

"Well, for one thing, I think you never told me you knew Attitude Cat."

"Well, I think you never asked," Val shot back with a grin. "Besides, I try to respect their privacy."

"Then you may need to warn Kristen that Alistair might just have a crush on Ruby."

"Anna, you are going to have to have a talk with your familiar." Val made a face. "And, yes, I did just say that. Witch life is strange."

I nodded in agreement and swirled my coffee. "I met Cheryl too."

"Cheryl Heathe? Oh, no, wait, it's Cheryl Bell now. Was Kristen still there?" I nodded, and the worry intensified behind Val's bright eyes. "I bet that was interesting."

"'Interesting' is one word for it." I looked into my almost empty coffee cup, searching for subtlety. I didn't find it. "Sounds like those two have a lot of history. Or maybe those three?" I added. "If, you know, you count the cat."

Valerie cocked her head at me and rocked in that slow little side-to-side dance parents do to comfort sleeping babies while standing (relatively) still. "Anna? Is this you fishing for gossip?"

"No. Just"—I gestured toward the gathering—"making party small talk."

"Uh-huh." If I didn't know better, I'd have sworn my coven sister doubted me. "Well, how about this for small talk? Do not get involved. This isn't just a dispute between old roommates. It's a huge mess, with serious money at stake and lawyers aimed and ready to fire."

"You know, you're the second person to tell me to not get involved with Attitude Cat," I said, and took another sip of coffee. "You'd think I have reputation or something."

"I wonder how that happened?" Val murmured. I ignored her.

"I just feel kind of bad for Kristen. Cheryl seems like a pretty hard case."

"Not answering."

"Sure you're not." I grinned and leaned closer. "Not even a little?"

"Nope," said Val firmly. "Not going to enable you. Oooh . . . look, there's a new Sandra Boynton board book! Come on, baby girl." She cooed at Melissa, who shifted in her sleep and tried to stuff her fist a little farther into her mouth. "Mama wants to go look at some pretty pictures."

"Coward," I muttered at Val's back.

"Something wrong?" This came from Kenisha as she moved away from the wine table to stand next to me. Kenisha Freeman is another of my coven sisters. An athletically built African American woman, Kenisha is the only witch cop in New Hampshire. She has rich brown skin and a sprinkle of dark freckles under both eyes. Tonight she wore an electric blue silk blouse and beaded jeans. Her red- and auburn-streaked hair had been pulled into a pair of braided loops at the back of her head. "You don't look really happy to be here."

When you're a witch cop you become uncomfortably good at watching people.

•

"It's nothing," I told her. "Val thinks I'm becoming a Nosey Parker."

"You?" Kenisha said blandly. "Well, dang, girl. There's some real news. Should I call Frank over at the paper?"

While I was still fumbling for something suitably witty to say back, that familiar prickling began in my fingertips.

"Hey, Anna." Kenisha lifted her chin, like she'd just caught an unpleasant smell. "Is it just me, or . . . ?"

"It's not just you." Val came over to us, shifting Melissa from one shoulder to the other. "I can't tell what it is, though."

I bit my lip. Then I saw Max and Leo scrabbling up the stairs that separated the two halves of the store. The dogs made a beeline, or at least a dachshund-line, for the back of the shop. A lightbulb went on in the back of my mind.

"I think I know," I said. "'Scuse me."

Smiling and doing my best to act casual, I slid through the crowd, up the three steps and between the shelves to the rear of the store. The sitting area here had overstuffed couches and armchairs in front of a fireplace, all tailor-made for browsing on a lazy afternoon. There was also a door that led to Julia's cramped and book-piled office. I followed the dachshunds inside. A window looked out onto the alley. It was closed, of course, because while it might be a little stuffy in the store, it was nowhere near stuffy enough to open the windows onto New Hampshire's November.

On the sill on the other side of the glass, Alistair paced urgently back and forth.

❀ 5 ❧

🐾 "MEROW!" ALISTAIR SCRABBLED at the window latch. Max and Leo yipped urgently and pawed at the desk, craning their necks to get a look at the cat outside the glass. Midnight Reads was magically warded by Julia herself. This meant that the bookstore was one of the few places Alistair couldn't just pop into whenever he felt like it.

I undid the latch and shoved the window open. Alistair and a blast of frigid wind flowed inside. But instead of leaping into my arms or demanding attention, my cat snaked between the dachshunds and straight under the desk.

"Merow!" My familiar hugged the floor, his tail lashing and his eyes so wide I could see the whites. "Merow!"

I stared. What on earth was the matter?

"It's okay, big guy." I squatted down, carefully, because of the narrow skirt and high heels. "Come on, Alistair." I held out my hand. "It's all right."

Alistair made a growling sound low in his throat and scrunched back farther. Goose bumps prickled down my arms, and the hairs on the back of my neck stood up. I was still getting used to my empathic connection to Alistair, but even I could tell what was happening. My familiar's agitation was strong enough to communicate itself to me.

I swallowed and told myself to calm down. Myself wasn't listening. Something was really, truly, deeply wrong.

"Uhh . . ." I looked back over my shoulder toward the shop and the crowd where I was supposed to be mingling and signing up preorders for my coloring book. "Crud."

"Yip!" Max slipped past me and darted under the desk. I tried to grab him, but I was too late. Crud, again. With Alistair so freaked-out, was there about to be a full-on cat familiar versus dog familiar fight?

But Max just started licking Alistair all over his face. Much to my surprise, Alistair tolerated this behavior. Now I knew something was up.

"Anna? What's happening?" Julia stepped into the office just in time to see Leo duck under the desk with Max and Alistair, wagging and whining.

"I don't know, but—" I barely got the words out when Alistair, who was clearly done with the canine commiseration committee, leapt into my arms.

"Ooof!" I caught him but also toppled onto my backside. "Hey, hey, easy. Ummm . . ."

I didn't have the chance to get any further. Alistair climbed up my chest, over my shoulder and around my neck so he could launch himself from me to the desk to the open window, and vanish.

Max and Leo came out from under the desk to snuffle at Julia's ankles and bark urgently, wagging their whiplike tails.

"Everything okay in here?" asked Kenisha from behind us.

Julia and I both turned, me a little awkwardly since I'd gotten up only as far as my knees. Kenisha stood on the office threshold.

"Yes, I noticed something's up," Kenisha told Julia. "So have Val and the rest of the coven. Are you guys okay?"

"Yes, but Alistair isn't." Julia bent down and scooped Max up in the crook of one arm. He licked her face and wagged and whined some more. "Yes, yes. All right," she whispered at him. "We see. We see."

I grabbed the edge of the desk and pulled myself to my feet. "I've got to find Alistair. I've never seen him this upset."

"Not alone," said Julia flatly. "Whatever is happening with Alistair, it is clearly serious, and it could be dangerous."

The hairs on the back of my neck stood up a little straighter.

"Don't worry, Julia. I'll go with her," said Kenisha. "It will look strange if you and Anna are both gone." She nodded back toward the shop and the ongoing party.

"Uhh . . . ," I began. Julia frowned. Kenisha just folded her arms and turned her best cop glare on me.

"Anna, from what you're saying, your familiar is boss-level freaked. With all the things that have gone wrong around you recently, you need real backup. Wherever you are going, I'm going with you."

"I wasn't going to argue," I said quickly.

"That's because you're smart," said Kenisha. "Let's go."

FOR A MOMENT, I actually considered sneaking out the back door. I am not proud of this. But it would have been easier than walking out through the party, bundled up in my good coat, very obviously hurrying away early. Sneaking out back, I could explain later. Out front, I had to explain now.

And by now, I meant right now. Sean was not the first one who noticed me heading for the door, but he was the first one who excused himself from his conversation to come over and touch my elbow.

"Everything okay, Anna?"

"Uh, something's come up," I said lamely, as if my coat and gloves hadn't made that much clear.

Sean glanced toward Kenisha in her down parka, who had already marched past us looking very pointedly over her shoulder at me as she went to stand by the door.

"Something . . . business related?" he breathed.

"Yeah." Sean and I had talked. If we were going to date and . . . well, whatever we might eventually end up doing, I was going to be honest with him about my epically complicated life. He deserved to know what he was getting into. Plus, he'd seen Alistair's Cheshire cat imitation, so I really had no choice but to tell him about the magic.

"Do you need someone to go with you?"

"Kenisha is," I told him, and he looked a little disappointed. He cared. It was sweet. The problem was, I didn't know if I was ready for his concern. Which was not his fault, but I couldn't help it.

"Will you call?" he asked.

"Promise," I agreed.

As a reward for giving the right answer, I got a smile and a peck on the cheek. I tried not to blush. I failed.

Outside, I found Kenisha standing beside my battered red Jeep, talking into her cell phone. It had stopped raining, but the wind off the river stung my cheeks and cut right through my coat. I shivered. Suddenly, the skirt and pumps were not feeling like such a good idea, fleece tights or no fleece tights.

If Kenisha felt the cold, she didn't show it. But then she had on a parka, a shearling cap, thick gloves and motorcycle boots. She held up one finger to signal for me to wait while she listened to whoever was talking on her phone.

I looked around optimistically for Alistair but didn't see him. Worry knotted itself up in the back of my mind. I dug into my purse to find my wand. The touch of the carved wood under my knitted glove soothed me, at least a little.

Kenisha shut off her phone.

"We've got no reported disturbances," she told me. "Do you have any idea where Alistair's gone?"

"None." The hitch in my voice surprised me, and that knot of worry tightened.

"It's okay. Try calling him."

I screwed up my focus and my nerve. "Alistair? Alistair, come on, big guy. You're freaking me out here."

Nothing. Not a flash of a blue eye or a twitch of a whisker. My heart banged against my ribs.

"He's not there, Kenisha," I whispered. "He's not . . ."

"Easy, Britton." She rested a hard hand on my shoulder. "We will find him."

"How?" I said, and the word came out a lot closer to a squeak than I wanted it to.

"Oh, right." Kenisha motioned for me to unlock the Jeep. "I never told you my specialty, did I? I'm a dowser."

Generally speaking, the magic we practiced in the guardian coven was a group effort. For the invocations and spells to be effective, and safe, different sets and levels of energies had to be woven together. This required multiple practitioners, as well as a sacred space defined by a circle, or at least an altar. But as a witch practiced and perfected her craft, she usually found out she had a particular, personal talent that she could call on at will. I had my Vibe. My grandma B.B. could read palms. Julia was a summoner, meaning she could bring people and things and powers together.

"I thought a dowser was somebody who could find water," I said to Kenisha as we both climbed into the Jeep. I turned the key and started up the heater, on high.

"I can find water, but I can find other things too."

"Good talent for a cop," I said, and immediately wished I hadn't. Kenisha had definite views about mixing magic with law enforcement. That she was willing to put her talents to use now added another loop to the worry knot inside me.

"Um . . . so, what do we do?"

"You stay quiet and give me a minute." Kenisha buckled her seat belt. Then she pulled her black gloves off and laid them in her lap. Resting her hands on the dashboard, Kenisha let out a long, slow breath. I felt her gathering her personal focus. I reached down to the side door compartment where I'd tucked my evening bag and pulled my wand out. I breathed deeply too, just like I had when I helped Ramona raise a calming influence. I also stayed quiet. I did want to support Kenisha; I didn't want to throw off her concentration. Tapping magical energy is an internal process, nothing like the light show you see in the movies. It's all about feeling and focus.

Kenisha's eyes closed and her mouth moved as she whispered an invocation to the elements and the spirits, asking for help and blessing. The prickling in my fingers intensified, and I felt an abrupt internal shift, as if a door had popped open in the back of my mind.

"Drive," said Kenisha.

I threw the Jeep into gear and drove.

6

❧ I'D THOUGHT THAT Kenisha would be giving me detailed directions about where to go. This was not what happened. Kenisha barely spoke at all. At the same time, I remained intensely aware of her presence and everything else—the depth of the cold darkness around us; the way the wind off the river buffeted my Jeep; the sparkle of the fresh snowflakes that swirled down past my headlights. It was like all my senses had been opened wide.

Every now and then, Kenisha raised her hand, pointing toward the left or right, but I would already be working the wheel and the stick shift. I was also driving with a precision that I knew was not naturally mine, as if I was channeling the officer sitting next to me.

This was not at all out of the question.

It also would have been more than enough for my overloaded nerves to deal with, but before we'd gone a mile from Market Square, I felt something else.

Alistair. Between one heartbeat and the next, I knew exactly where my cat was.

I couldn't see it, like a vision, which was probably just

as well, because I needed my eyes for red lights and stop signs. I just knew, in the same way I knew that I was in the Jeep with Kenisha sitting beside me.

So when I saw the apartment buildings overlooking the river mouth, I knew we'd reached the right place without Kenisha even having to point. I pulled into the small parking area and straight into the visitors' spot that was, by some miracle, waiting empty right beside the front door. This tended to happen when there was another witch in the car. One of these days I was going ask about it. I had a feeling my coven sisters were holding out on me when it came to traffic magic.

Now, however, was not the time.

Kenisha blinked hard and took a few deep breaths. She wasn't the only one. I needed a minute of my own to try to dial my awareness back down to something like normal levels.

"You ready?" Kenisha asked, pulling on her gloves.

I grabbed my purse. I had no idea what was going to happen next, but I wanted my wand and my phone with me when it did. "Ready."

We both climbed out into the yellow sodium light of the parking lot. The sign out front of the buildings read RIVER-VIEW CONDOMINIUMS. For once there seemed to be some truth in the apartment advertising. Nothing but a short, boulder-strewn beach and a low stone wall separated the condos from the black-and-silver stretch of the Piscataqua. The pseudo–Cape Cod–style buildings had decks and balconies facing the river that were carefully staggered so each unit could have its view without an overhanging shadow.

A gust of wind hit me right in the face and started my eyes watering, but I ignored it. Alistair was in there. I knew it. He was waiting for me, and not at all patiently.

Okay, okay, I thought, a little desperately. *Cavalry's here.*

That could not possibly have been a real *meow* I heard in the back of my head.

Even though Kenisha was on high alert, she walked toward the nearest building with a smooth decisiveness you could have mistaken for nonchalance. She climbed up the steps to the concrete porch and tugged on the door. It was locked.

"Recognize anybody?" She pointed at the column of black intercom buttons. Some of them had names taped up beside their unit numbers.

I squinted. There was a light shining down onto the porch, but it was pretty dim. "No . . . Oh, wait." I touched the name beside the buzzer for Unit 2B. R. FORSYTHE. My brow furrowed. "Alistair's vet is Ramona Forsythe."

Under what possible circumstances could my cat have voluntarily come to the vet's home? Then I thought about how upset Ramona had been when Cheryl Bell stormed into her clinic. A chill that had nothing to do with the wind cut through me.

"Right." Kenisha moved her hand toward the buzzer.

"Wait," I stopped her. "I need a second."

I made sure I had my wand securely stowed in my coat pocket. I also whispered my own invocation.

In need I call, in hope I ask, to stand in the protection of the Light.

Kenisha had to deliberately call on her abilities as a dowser. My Vibe, though, was less patient or predictable. It could hit me anytime and anywhere. Because of this, the first thing Julia taught me was how to raise a set of magical shields so I could block, or at least blunt, any mental and emotional invasion.

I repeated my invocation three times, all the while picturing myself surrounded by a shimmering curtain of positive energy—blue and green and gold like the aurora borealis, because I am an artist and everything must have color.

When I felt my shields were firmly established, I opened my eyes again and nodded to Kenisha.

I did not let go of my wand.

Kenisha pushed the buzzer labeled R. FORSYTHE, and we waited, but not for long. Through the glass door, we saw a young man with black-rimmed glasses, wearing a thick striped scarf around his neck, come trotting down the stairs with a cardboard box braced against his hip.

He held the door for Kenisha and we walked right in. Easy-peasy. Kenisha's jaw shifted.

I didn't get a chance to make any remark about the building's lack of security, though. The second the door swung closed, a Vibe slammed up against my shields.

Anger. Burning anger, and desperation and fear and . . . and . . . and . . . My shields buckled, and I staggered. My back banged against the wall.

Oh.

Oh, no.

"What is it?" asked Kenisha.

My mouth moved, but no sound came out. I knew this feeling, with all its cold horror and heartbreak. I willed myself to focus and to shove my shields back into shape. But I couldn't think. I couldn't breathe. I hurt. I was cold. I couldn't see. I was surrounded by anger, anger and greed, and . . . I hurt, I hurt . . . I was . . . I was . . .

Oh, no. Oh, no, no, no!

Kenisha yanked her phone out of her purse and hit a speed-dial number. I had a feeling she undid her concealed-carry pouch as well.

"Stay here."

Kenisha did not run. She walked calmly up the single, short flight of stairs and down the hall with her smooth, alert grace. No hurry. Nothing to see here.

I leaned my head against the wall and tried not to be sick. Impressions slid through my shields like a draft through a cracked windowpane.

How could she do this . . . the greedy little so-and-so . . . you promised me!

I'm getting what's mine!

Don't make me do this! Don't make me!

It's mine! I deserve this! It's mine!

"Dr. Forsythe?" I heard Kenisha knock on the door. "Dr. Forsythe, it's Kenisha Freeman. I'm a friend of Julia Parris's."

But it wasn't Ramona who answered.

"Merow!"

Alistair.

Despite my heels and my narrow skirt, I was up the stairs, down the hall and through the unlocked door before I could even think about what I was doing.

It was a nice apartment, small but airy and very modern. The living room had a vaulted ceiling and a stairway to a half loft that was a sleeping area. The light was on in the kitchen, and the smell of burned coffee hung everywhere. It was also freezing cold. The river's arctic wind blew through a set of open glass doors. Alistair was on the balcony railing, pacing back and forth like only a cat can. Scattered snowflakes settled on his twitching ears.

"What part of *stay here* did you not understand?" demanded Kenisha.

"I . . . *Oof!*"

Alistair blipped off the balcony railing and reappeared right in my arms. He was trembling and trying to bury his face under my right arm.

"Easy, big guy, easy . . . oh . . . shoot . . ." My shields shivered and strained. Anger, greed and desperation swirled around my head harder than the November wind.

"Do *not* move. Stand absolutely still." Kenisha stepped swiftly, lightly, across the room to the bleached-wood balcony.

"Somebody's dead," I croaked.

"No sh— sugar, Sherlock." Kenisha looked over the railing onto the rocky beach. "And I'm betting it's Dr. Forsythe."

7

❧ KENISHA WAS RIGHT. It was Dr. Forsythe. She sprawled facedown beside a pile of tumbled boulders under her balcony.

The police—the rest of the police—were there so fast, Kenisha barely had time to give me my orders. She did, however, grab me by both shoulders and look me right in the eye, in case I might not be paying attention.

"We have got no reason to be here," she reminded me. "If anybody asks, you say Dr. Forsythe was watching Alistair and you were scheduled to pick him up after the bookstore party. I'm with you because you were going to drop me off home afterward."

"Meow!" Alistair was on the kitchen counter, pacing back and forth like he had out on the balcony rail.

"Is anybody going to believe that?" I asked Kenisha.

"Meow!"

"No," Kenisha told me. "But we'll worry about it later."

"Meeerrrroooowwwww!"

"What?" I spun around. Yes, I was demanding answers

from my cat. And because this was me and Alistair, I was kind of expecting them.

Alistair jumped off the counter and trotted over to the trio of blue plastic food bowls that had been put down next to the dishwasher. For a moment, I thought he was complaining because they were empty, but then I stopped.

"Oh, cr . . . ud." I spun around. Nothing. I saw nothing new, anyway. I bit my lip and started toward the stairs leading to the loft.

"Stop!" bellowed Kenisha. I froze, one foot still in the air. I resisted the urge to put my hands up.

"This is a potential crime scene! You do not move," she growled. I nodded. I did, however, set my foot down, carefully.

"Now, what is it?" Kenisha asked through gritted teeth.

"Ruby," I told her, which only made her frown harder. "Attitude Cat. Dr. Forsythe was watching her while her owner is out of town."

"Wait." Kenisha made the time out sign with both hands. "Dr. Forsythe was babysitting Attitude Cat? *The* Attitude Cat?" And that made it official. Absolutely everybody knew about Attitude Cat.

"Her real name is Ruby and her owner, Kristen Summers, had a family emergency. Her mother was in the hospital for surgery. Dr. Forsythe was boarding her . . ."

"Merow!" agreed Alistair.

"And now she's missing?" If Kenisha asked this question a little more to Alistair than to me, that was perfectly understandable.

"Who's missing?" asked a man's voice.

Kenisha and I both turned to see Detective Pete Simmons standing on the condo threshold, with a trio of uniformed cops right behind him.

Alistair vanished. For once, I couldn't blame him.

WHAT FOLLOWED WAS a whole lot of hustle and bustle.

I was hustled down to where the police cars and the ambulance were pulled up in the parking lot, their red and blue lights flashing. A lot of people in blue uniforms, both cops and EMTs, bustled up the stairs and around the building. They unrolled spools of yellow tape or stood and talked with the people bundled in parkas and pajamas who gathered around holding cell phones up to their ears, or over their heads. A lot of different people were both hustling and bustling around between them, writing a lot of different things down. Everybody's breath steamed in the sodium lights.

Including Pete Simmons's. Pete stood with me and Kenisha by his unmarked car, completely ignoring the freezing wind. I'm sure the huge, furry, Russian-style hat pulled down over his thinning hair helped. I wished I had one.

Kenisha told Pete how we had been let into the building, complete with a description of the young man with his black-rimmed glasses, his striped scarf and his cardboard box. She went on to say how we'd found the condo door unlocked (she discreetly omitted my Vibe) and walked in to find Dr. Forsythe dead beneath her balcony and Ruby missing.

When we explained who Ruby was, Pete let out a long, low whistle.

"Were there any signs of a struggle?" he asked. "Human or animal?"

I glanced down. Alistair had reappeared under the yew bushes outside the condo building and was now watching me with almost as much skepticism as was the detective in the furry hat.

"No," I said.

"Not that I was able to ascertain," agreed Kenisha.

Alistair blinked and vanished. I suppressed a grumble of irritation, but not fast enough. Pete saw and decided to go from studying Kenisha to studying me.

"I'm sorry about this, Ms. Britton." Pete had the kind of dark and drooping eyes you normally saw in a middle-aged basset hound. It made you inclined to think he was perpetually anxious and mostly harmless. This was a mistake. "I know you've just had a shock, but I have to ask. Why did you come out here tonight?"

"Dr. Forsythe was watching Anna's cat, Alistair," said Kenisha before I could get my mouth open. "She was giving me a lift home from the bookstore, and we'd stopped to pick him up."

Pete nodded and noted this down, somehow without once looking away from me. "Where is your cat now?"

I swallowed. "He's in my Jeep." I had to work to keep this from sounding like a question. "I didn't want him to get in the way," I added.

Pete looked at Kenisha, who nodded. He glanced at my Jeep. I looked too, but not before I mentally crossed my fingers.

Alistair, bless his furry little familiar heart, lay curled up on the dashboard, clearly visible in the blinking blue and red lights from the surrounding emergency vehicles. I hoped Pete didn't notice me let out the breath I'd been holding.

Pete wrote something else down, carefully. I tried not to squirm.

"So, Ms. Britton, your cat was fine but you saw no sign of the other one . . . what did you call him?"

"Her. Ruby. Attitude Cat is a stage name." Yes, we were having this conversation. Pete didn't even pause in his note taking.

"And how did you know Ruby was supposed to be there?"

"I met her owner, Kristen Summers, when I took Alistair to the vet."

"The balcony doors were open when we entered the premises," said Kenisha briskly. She was entirely back on duty. "The cat might have gotten out that way."

"Sure, sure, sure," murmured Pete. "I'm just wondering. Probably a cat with that kind of . . . what would you even call it?"

"Star power?" I suggested.

Pete shrugged. "I'll go with that. It's going to make her valuable."

"You think somebody *stole* Ruby?"

Pete considered what he'd just written. "Probably not.

Probably she just got out the open doors and went home. But . . ." He paused and shrugged.

He didn't need to finish. *But,* he was thinking, *if somebody had wanted to steal Ruby, they might have had to do it over Ramona's dead body.*

I glanced down toward the bushes again. Alistair was back, hunkered down flat against the frozen ground, claws out, tail lashing back and forth.

Oh. No.

I gave Kenisha the tiniest possible nod and her face clouded over. I knew what she was thinking. We should let Pete know he was on the right track, but how? You can't tell a detective you might have a witness to the theft and the murder when that witness is a magical cat.

I was beginning to sympathize with Kenisha's resistance to mixing magic and law enforcement.

Fortunately, neither one of us had to come up with an answer right away, because just then a tiny blue Miata barreled into the parking lot and stopped an inch shy of hitting my Jeep's bumper. Before I had time to do more than wince, a woman jumped out.

"What is going on here?" she shouted.

I was half expecting Cheryl Bell, but this woman was much taller and professionally tanned. Her long neck was wrapped in a shimmering patterned scarf, and a felt cloche hat covered her blond hair. She wore a fur coat that, to my eye at least, looked real. A purse with clunky gold hardware bounced on her shoulder, and black leather boots encased her fashionably slender calves.

She strode right up to Pete. "I was told something was wrong and I needed to get over here."

Pete nodded as if this was only to be expected. "And you are?"

"Pamela Abernathy, Abernathy & Walsh, and . . ." She dug into her purse, probably looking for a business card and probably on reflex.

"Is that a law firm?" Pete asked.

"No, we're public relations." The wind gusted hard and she slapped one leather-gloved hand over her cloche before it tumbled sideways. "Please, Officer . . . ?"

"Detective," Pete corrected her. "Peter Simmons. Is your firm connected with the Attitude Cat campaign?"

"That's right. I . . ." She stopped rummaging and lifted her gaze, taking in the lights and the cops and the EMTs fully. "What is going on here?"

Pete didn't answer. Instead, he asked, "It's not exactly office hours. Do you live here?"

"I got a phone call. I was told something might be wrong with Ruby—that is, Attitude Cat—and that I should check in on her."

Pete's notebook was back out and his pencil was poised for action. "Who told you this, Ms. Abernathy?"

"It was a voice mail," she said softly. "I didn't recognize the number."

"May I see your phone?"

Ms. Abernathy reached into a side pocket on her designer purse and started to hand over her phone but at the last minute snatched it back.

"I . . . um . . . no," she said quickly. "I think I'll need to talk to our attorney first."

"Oh, sure, sure, sure," said Pete. "And of course normally, I'd agree that would be a smart move, and perfectly within your rights. But just now, it might hamper our ability to find her."

"Find who?"

"Ruby," said Kenisha. "I'm sorry to tell you this, Ms. Abernathy, but Attitude Cat is missing."

Pamela Abernathy blinked at Kenisha and Pete and me. Then, without a noise, she crumpled to the ground.

8

THE LAST TIME somebody passed out in front of me was in college, and then there had been an injudicious amount of alcohol involved. Somehow I doubted that was the case this time. Pam Abernathy had heard Attitude Cat was missing and fainted from the shock.

Wow.

Fortunately, we had a raft of EMTs right on the spot. With professional speed, they bundled Ms. Abernathy into the back of the ambulance and did . . . emergency medical things. I couldn't see exactly what, because of the shifting crowd of blue backs and shoulders around her and because I stepped (okay, jumped) back to get out of the way.

While I was getting myself out of the way, though, I noticed Pamela's phone lying on the frost-browned grass where she'd dropped it. Nobody, not even Pete or Kenisha, seemed to be coming back to pick it up.

I bit my lip. I looked toward my Jeep. Alistair was nowhere to be seen. I hoped Pete didn't take it into his head to check up on the whereabouts of my cat.

I looked down again. The phone, which Ms. Abernathy

did not want the police looking at, was still there. Right on the grass, where somebody might step on it. Which would be a shame. It was a nice phone. Brand-new, slender, with a big screen.

I stretched out the toe of my impractical black pump and nudged the phone a little farther back from the sidewalk. It was also a little closer to me. This, of course, was pure coincidence.

I looked around for Pete and Kenisha. They were both talking with other officers near the open back of the ambulance where the EMTs were helping Pam Abernathy.

I looked at the phone.

I didn't really plan on touching it. And I wouldn't have. Except it buzzed. And buzzed again.

It was too much. I stripped off my glove, snatched a Kleenex out of my purse, used it to carefully pick the phone up and touched the Accept button. Because you can't get smartphone buttons to work through gloves, but you can through a Kleenex. No, I won't tell you how I found that out, and no, I don't recommend this as a lifestyle choice. Especially when it's not your phone and there are police around.

"Hello?" I whispered.

"Thank God!" shouted the voice on the other end. The connection snapped and sizzled so badly, I couldn't even be sure if I was hearing a man or a woman. "Pam . . . hear me now? . . . the heck . . . are you . . . out there?" I was getting only about every third word. "What happened . . . the vet? All good?"

"What?" I croaked.

"The vet! The vet!" Silence cut in and cut out again. ". . . happened with the vet?"

"Um . . . ," I breathed. "There's a problem."

"What? We gotta bad connection! I . . . Damn. That's mine. Call you back." The call and the voice cut off.

I looked up. Kenisha was looking right at me. Now Pete was standing at the back of the ambulance, saying something to the revived Pamela Abernathy. I couldn't hear Pete, but I did hear Pam's response.

"Where's my phone?" she demanded. "Where is my *phone!*"

Kenisha very deliberately turned her back on me. I very deliberately let the phone slip out of my fingers.

"Where did you have it last, Ms. Abernathy?" Pete asked.

I raised my hand like I was in third grade and wanted a turn to speak. With my other, I pointed to the ground. Kenisha hurried over and scooped the phone up. Our eyes met. It will come as no surprise to anybody that I looked away first.

"It's right here, ma'am." Kenisha handed the phone to Pamela, who snatched it and shoved it back into her purse without even looking at it.

Somewhere, something else was ringing. I pulled my phone out just long enough to see that (a) it wasn't mine and (b) it was midnight. The witching hour. Just a couple of weeks earlier, I'd stayed up late with my coven to celebrate this exact time. It had been beautiful under the bright full moon and I'd felt filled with wonder. Tonight, the moon was hidden behind heavy clouds, and all I felt was that this particular hour had really gotten away from me.

I shoved my phone back into my purse and my hands back into my pockets. I probably could wait in the Jeep. Start the engine and turn on the heater. Call Julia. And Sean, I added, feeling a little guilty.

Kenisha walked over to stand beside me. She looked tired. But then, I'm sure I did too.

"Okay," she said, sighing. "Looks like we can—"

Before she got any further, a uniformed officer pushed open the condo building's door. "Detective! We need you up here."

Pete hurried to the door. Kenisha muttered something under her breath.

"We can what?" I asked.

Kenisha set her jaw. "The *only* reason you get to stick around here is that I need a ride home."

Because none of the police officers—who were all her friends and colleagues—could give her one? In a surprising display of common sense, however, I kept this question to myself.

I eased myself back into my Jeep and started the engine to get it warmed up. Alistair was definitely gone. I couldn't see him or sense him.

"Where are you, big guy?" I whispered, but this time I got no answer.

I drummed my fingers impatiently against the steering wheel and thought about the phone call and that frantic voice exclaiming about the vet. I thought about Dr. Forsythe and how instantly I'd liked her when I met her (just this morning? really?) and how good she'd been at handling Alistair. I closed my eyes because I didn't want to remember everything I'd felt in Ramona's apartment. I also didn't want to be so certain that whatever had happened to Ramona, it wasn't just an unlucky fall. But there was no getting away from it. Ramona Forsythe had been killed. Her murderer had been filled with so much anger and so much greed, he or she had left some of it behind in the apartment.

And now Ruby was missing. And there was that phone call.

A sketchbook and pencil lay on the passenger seat, because I always have a sketchbook and pencil with me somewhere. I flipped open a fresh page and scribbled down what I could remember of that brief phone conversation I wasn't meant to hear. I was putting down the final period when Kenisha yanked open the door, sending a fresh blast of cold air into the Jeep.

I looked at her grim expression. "Should I ask?"

"No," she answered as she climbed inside and slammed the door. "And you know you shouldn't."

"Right," I agreed. "And I know I shouldn't show you what I wrote down on this sketch pad that I am asking you to hold, because I don't want to toss it in the backseat, because some very valuable drawings might get wrinkled."

"Just so we're clear on that." Kenisha finished buckling her seat belt and took the pad. But she didn't look at it.

"Are we going home now?" I asked.

"Yeah. We are."

"Okay." I buckled up, put the car in gear and eased us out onto the street. Kenisha drummed her fingers on the pad.

"I don't suppose you remembered to write down the phone number?" she asked.

I winced. "No. Sorry. But it was a New York City area code. I recognized it."

"Well, that's gonna narrow it down," she muttered.

"Sorry." I stopped at the red light and wished I had something more I could say.

"This is going to be in the papers tomorrow," she said. "And all over the Internet."

"Yeah, well, that happens with a murder," I answered, and wished I didn't feel quite so queasy.

Kenisha worked her jaw back and forth a few times. I watched the debate going on inside her. Was she going to ask or not? She knew I'd gotten a very strong Vibe. The problem was, asking about it would run up against the line Kenisha drew between her job and her magic.

"You're sure it was a murder?" she said finally.

"Yes. I am."

She nodded. "So am I."

I kept my eyes on the road, and I waited. I knew what I wanted to say, but none of it would make things any better. Kenisha clearly needed some space to make up her mind.

Eventually, she did. "There was something wrong in there."

"You mean besides—"

"Besides the obvious, yeah." She stared straight ahead, but I could tell she wasn't seeing anything through the windshield. "There was something wrong in that apartment, but I didn't have time to figure out what it was." She drummed her fingers on the sketch pad again. "And before we left, Dr. Forsythe's phone rang."

I waited.

"It was Kristen Summers."

"Kristen?"

"Yeah. She says she was checking her voice mail and

she'd gotten a call saying she ought to call Ramona and check on Ruby."

"What?" I am very proud of the fact that I did not jerk the wheel or slam on the brakes or do anything else stupid right at that moment.

"She said it came while she was on the plane, so she had her phone turned off and didn't get it until she landed."

"Did she say who it was from?"

"She said she didn't recognize the number or the voice. So," Kenisha went on grimly, "that's two phone calls, both saying that people should check on Attitude Cat."

"Is it just me, or does that sound like . . . ?"

"We got a cat-napping as well as a murder?" said Kenisha. "Oh, yeah, it sure as heck does."

🐾 9 🐾

🐾 I SLEPT LATE the next day.

This was not surprising, considering that it was one a.m. before I actually pulled my Jeep into my own driveway. Even then, though, I couldn't go straight to bed, no matter how much I wanted to. I absolutely had to call Julia.

She answered on the first ring. "Anna, I've been waiting for you. Tell me what's happened."

Since this was Julia I was talking to, I knew any attempt to soften the blow would only make things worse. "Ramona Forsythe is dead."

Julia was quiet for a long time. "She was murdered," my mentor said at last, and it was not a question.

"Yes."

More silence followed, and when Julia spoke again, her words were filled with a flat, hard rage that I hope I never hear directed at me. "Who did this to our sister?"

"They don't know, and I don't know," I told her. "I got a Vibe, a strong one. Somebody was there when she died, but I couldn't get a handle on . . ." I had to stop and swallow. "On who it was."

"Tell me everything, from the time you left the shop. I take it this was what had upset Alistair so badly?"

"Yes," I said. Then I told her how Kenisha had used her dowsing ability to find where Alistair was, and how we'd gotten inside the building and found Ramona dead and Ruby missing. I explained about the phone calls and the appearance of Pam Abernathy. Julia listened silently. I could picture her expression, still and steely.

"I will have to think about what you have said," she told me. "And I will need to speak with Kenisha. We cannot let the death of one of our own go unanswered."

A chill ran up my spine. This was not a conversation Kenisha was going to want to have. "Um, Julia, I think Kenisha's going to be a little busy for a while. Maybe—"

"Thank you for calling, Anna. We will speak again in the morning."

My mentor hung up before I could mention that it already was morning. I stared at my phone for a while. I rubbed my forehead and stared some more. Then I dialed another number.

This time I got voice mail.

"Hi. This is a recording of Sean McNally. If this had been an actual Sean McNally, you would not now be getting directions to leave a message." Then there was the beep.

"Hi, Sean," I began. "Sorry about—" There was a click and the sound of fumbling and rustling.

"Anna?"

"Oh, hi, Sean. Sorry. I didn't mean to wake you up . . ."

"Bartender, remember?" he said, and I could hear the smile in his voice. "This is practically lunchtime for me. I'm glad you called. Is everything okay?"

I'm pretty sure I'd been planning on telling a small but reassuring lie. Now that I had Sean's voice in my ear, though, I couldn't go through with it.

"Umm . . . no," I said, and gave him a slightly edited version of the story I'd told Julia.

Like Julia, Sean listened until I was finished without interrupting.

"Are you all right, Anna?" he asked when I'd finally run out of words.

"Yeah. I think so." I ran a hand across my hair, which was badly windblown but still crispy from all the spray I'd put in it to try to hold the twist in place for the party. "Mostly."

"Do you want me to come over? Or call Valerie for you or something?" he added quickly. Because Sean knew I was still coming off a bad relationship and because he was a gentleman. Which was lovely and considerate, and it made me smile.

I suddenly realized I did want him to come over. A lot. I wanted to see his smile and his twinkly blue eyes. I wanted to tell him everything that had happened and to hear what he had to say about it.

I jumped back from that feeling like Alistair from a bathtub full of cold water.

"Thanks," I said, and even though he couldn't see me, I mustered a smile. "But I'll be fine. Strong, independent artist girl here, remember?"

"Never doubted it for a minute. Will I see you tomorrow?"

"It's already tomorrow."

"It isn't tomorrow until you've actually been to bed."

I rubbed my face and tried not to chuckle. "And this is, what? How bartenders keep time?"

"Yep. So. See you tomorrow?"

"Definitely." And I meant it. I might be frightened of how much I meant it, but that didn't change anything.

"Get some sleep."

"You are not the boss of me. And you too."

We said good night and I went upstairs, and, unusually, I left the light on in the hall while I changed into my pajamas and climbed into my bed. I lay awake for a long time, listening to the wind under the eaves. My house sighed and creaked and settled, in the slow, punctuated rhythms I was getting used to. *It's all right,* it seemed to be saying. *You can sleep. I'm on watch.*

Which was of course purely a trick of my imagination.

At least, I was pretty sure it was. On the other hand, the cottage had belonged to my predecessor in the coven, Dorothy Hawthorne. Dorothy was not only a powerful witch; she had a wicked sense of humor. I blinked toward the framed movie photo I kept on the wall—it was that scene from the movie *The Wizard of Oz* where the Wicked Witch of the West is skywriting SURRENDER DOROTHY.

Dorothy had died before I arrived in Portsmouth, and I'd helped her nephew, Frank, prove that her death had been a murder. My stomach curdled. I really was not at all sure how I felt about being in the middle of yet another mystery.

It's all right, whispered that voice in the back of my mind again. I might not entirely agree, but I felt obscurely better anyway. I rolled over, pulled the covers up to my ears and went to sleep.

WHEN I DID finally peel an eyelid open, the ancient digital clock at my bedside read 9:30. For a morning person like me, this was classifiable as a crime against the whole day.

I threw back the covers and shoved my feet into my sheepskin slippers so I wouldn't have to put them on the floorboards. I love my cottage. It is dramatic and beautiful and snug, with an amazing spiral-patterned garden out back. It's also a hundred years old. During that time, it's developed some quirks, including a persistent draft across my bedroom floor. Both Sean and his father, Old Sean, had turned their attention to it, but neither one of them had been able to track down the source. Old Sean had started to openly speculate that it might be all in my head. My coven sister, Allie Paulson, though, assured me it was just that the house was just cranky, and while it loved me, it also liked to make sure I was paying attention.

I didn't actively doubt her, but I had decided I was going to put this assessment on the shelf with all the other things I needed to get used to.

I showered, dried, brushed what needed to be brushed

and changed into flannel-lined jeans and a fleecy sweatshirt
with the words NEW ENGLAND GIRL: WARMTH IS OVERRATED
on the front. I had shuffled all the way downstairs to my
kitchen before I realized what was really wrong. I turned
around in a circle.

My familiar was nowhere to be seen.

Normally, Alistair would have slept on my pillow or my
stomach, and he would be right here, right now, complaining
about the fact that I hadn't gotten his breakfast fast enough
or was unreasonably trying to make him eat kibble instead
of scrambled eggs or tuna fish.

I looked automatically at Alistair's food bowl. That was
empty. I was sure I'd filled it before I left for the party, so
he'd been here at some point.

My snug, lovely, reassuring cottage suddenly felt discon-
certingly empty.

I told myself it was nothing. I mean, Alistair might be
magical and highly intelligent, but in all the ways that
counted, he was entirely a cat. He came and went as he
chose. I was just rattled by last night's events. Discovering
a body had that effect on a person, with or without a possible cat-napping thrown in.

I started the coffeemaker. Ever the optimist, I looked in
my fridge to see if I had anything edible. My grocery shop-
ping is a highly irregular activity and my cooking skills
nonexistent. Today, though, I was in luck. I found some
bagels and cream cheese and peanut butter. I pulled them
all out, because I am all about the healthy breakfast.

I popped two bagel halves into the toaster. Alistair still
wasn't anywhere in evidence. *No worries,* I told myself.
*None at all. There's an explanation. He might be out with
Miss Boots, or chasing that rabbit out in the garden that
will not get the message.*

I filled his bowl with the last of the Best Petz Kitty Kibblez and rattled it.

"Alistair? Breakfast!"

No answer. No big gray cat popped onto my windowsill
or strolled in from the living room.

I put the bowl down. "I got half a can of tuna," I tried. Still no answer.

Now I was worried.

"Come on, big guy," I muttered. "This is not okay."

And still no answer, at least not from my familiar. My toaster, on the other hand, popped. I spread the bagel halves with cream cheese and peanut butter, set them on the table in my breakfast nook and went to get the pot of coffee and a mug.

I sat down and stared at my breakfast. The house was too quiet. My head was too full. I missed my grandmother. I wondered how much longer it would take her to pack up her things in Arizona and move up here. I'd offered to go with her, but she insisted she was *more* than capable, thank you *very* much. Emphasis hers. Grandma B.B. spoke in italics.

I missed Valerie too. Most mornings we wound up sitting together in my kitchen or hers. I didn't immediately reach for the phone, though. Early November was the break between the leaf-peepers and the winter tourists and sports season. This meant it was a slow few weeks for the B and B, but not for Valerie and Roger themselves. They needed the time to repair and restock, not to mention continue the major project of readjusting their lives around little Melissa. Roger was also in the middle of planning a total blowout Thanksgiving Day feast for his family, which included about twenty people flying in to meet the baby. By the time he was done, there wasn't going to be an unrelished cranberry or unbaked pumpkin left on the whole East Coast.

The thought of food reminded me that there was somebody else I needed to call. Martine. In fact, I probably should have called her last night. I gave up on my bagel for the moment and dug my phone out of my purse.

This was when I found out I also had fifteen voice mail messages, and most of them were from Valerie. My thumb wavered between buttons before I decided on the phone call. Val's messages had waited all night. They could wait two more minutes.

I hit Martine's number and waited while it rang.

"This better be good, Britton," announced Martine after the third ring. "And it also better be about why you left the party last night."

"I don't know if 'good's' exactly the word," I told her. "But otherwise, yeah."

"The sound you hear now is me being patient."

Actually, the sound I heard now was the bang, clatter and shout of a restaurant kitchen in the middle of lunch prep. But I figured I didn't need to mention this. I took a deep breath and got ready to tell the whole story about what happened to Ramona again. Of course, that was the moment Alistair chose to pop onto the kitchen counter.

"Gah!" I remarked.

"Britton?" shouted Martine in my ear. "Anna? Are you all right?"

"Yeah, sorry. Alistair's been . . . gone all morning. He just, uh, got back."

My cat twitched his whiskers and jumped down to his food bowl. He sniffed dubiously at the Kibblez.

"You snooze, you lose," I muttered.

"I beg your pardon?" said Martine.

"Sorry, I was talking to Alistair. It's the Best Petz stuff." I lifted the bag to show him. "Look. Ruby likes it."

Alistair put his nose in the air and stalked away into the living room.

"You do not need me on the phone to talk to your cat." A distinctly dangerous note had crept into my friend's voice.

"Sorry. You remember that one time when you told me if I didn't call you right away when . . . certain kinds of stuff . . . happened, you'd stop talking to me?"

"Yeah?"

"This is me making sure you don't stop talking to me."

"You're coming over here. Now."

I agreed that I was, because Martine's tone did not encourage argument. I hung up. I turned around.

"Alistair!"

My cat looked up from the half of *my* peanut butter and

cream cheese bagel he was busily licking. "Merow?" he asked, clearly confused by my reaction.

"And just where were you all night, young man?" That was when I realized I had both hands on my hips and was glowering. At my cat. For an answer, Alistair blinked at me, his blue eyes as wide and innocent as any Disney cartoon's.

"Merp?"

I sighed and pinched the bridge of my nose. Alistair went back to his breakfast, which used to be my breakfast.

"Cats," I muttered.

"Merow," agreed Alistair.

❧ 10 ❧

🐾 MARTINE HAD TOLD me to get over to the Pale Ale. Valerie and the rest of the coven needed to hear about what had happened to Ramona. Fortunately, I was going to be able to kill two birds with one stone, or at least one phone tree.

Less than half an hour later, I was sitting with a substantial portion of my coven around a table in the private dining room at the Pale Ale.

Martine's restaurant is the kind of place the guide books and tourism Web sites label a landmark. The boxy, slate-roofed brick building has stood on its Portsmouth street corner since colonial times. Martine got the head chef job last spring. Since then, she's been busy turning the historic tavern into what she calls a locally sourced, nose-to-tail, farm-to-table "experience." She spends her off-hours going through the oldest cookbooks she can find, looking for recipes. The results were pretty amazing, such as the walnut cake in front of us and the mugs of spearmint and comfrey tea that we were all hunching over instead of coffee.

"We" meant Allie Paulson and Trish Robinson, as well as Val, with little Melissa on her shoulder. Allie had arrived shortly after Val and the baby. The fact that Allie owned her own housekeeping service gave her a certain amount of flexibility during the workday. Right now, she had the sleeves of her white blouse rolled up to her elbows and looked ready to physically move anything or anybody who might be even thinking about getting in her way.

Trish, in the meantime, was bravely trying not to sneak peeks at her smartphone.

Shannon and Faye Yu were both on shift over at the hospital and so couldn't be there. Kenisha wasn't there either, which didn't surprise me. When you are a cop in a small department, a murder and potential cat-napping will tend to make you kind of busy.

But Kenisha wasn't the only person still unaccounted for.

"Have you heard from Julia this morning?" I asked Val between bites of Martine's walnut cake, which was taking the place of the bagel Alistair had appropriated. "I tried, but I only got voice mail."

"I got hold of her just before I left," said Val. "She said she was fine."

"She would, wouldn't she?" murmured Allie.

"I don't know when I've ever heard Julia say anything else." Trish turned her phone over a couple of more times. "Whether it's true or not."

"She did promise to call back." Val patted Melissa on the back, but she also looked anxiously toward the door. I found myself wondering what else Julia had said to her this morning.

"And she knows we're all here," I added. "I called her too."

"Funny, so did I." Allie drummed her blunt, strong fingers on the table so hard I was surprised she didn't leave dents.

Trish turned her phone over again.

That was when Martine pushed through the door from the kitchen. "Okay, things are holding steady in there." She dropped into one of the empty chairs and poured herself a mug of hot tea. "So, Britton, what have you got yourself into this time?"

With that, and some additional cake and tea, I told them all about finding Ramona dead and Ruby missing. I added a description of Pam's arrival, and, after some hesitation, the phone call I'd listened to, as well as the one that had come to Ramona's phone from Kristen Summers. My coven sisters and my friend, and even baby Melissa, listened with various expressions and exclamations of surprise and disbelief.

When I finished, a thick cloud of silence settled over all of them. Well, almost all of them.

"Ppppbt," said Melissa. She had this way of puckering up her mouth that made me feel like she wanted to talk to the management, because this ride was not quite what the brochure promised.

"Ah, ah, manners," said Val, giving the baby a little bounce. "Sorry, Anna, it's not you. She's been gassy all morning."

"Aww, that's okay, isn't it, bubby?" I touched her button nose. Fussing over the baby was a lot more comfortable than thinking about Ramona's death, or why Julia hadn't shown up yet.

"Mmm-ma-mmm. Ppppbt," Melissa answered.

"You're going to have trouble with that one." Trish chuckled and turned her phone over one more time. "She definitely knows her own mind."

"It's an independent streak," retorted Val loftily. "Just like her mommy. Right, peanut?"

"Pppbut-um," said Melissa, and to emphasize the point she shoved her fist into her mouth.

"Val, do you know if Julia and Dr. Forsythe were close at all?" I asked.

"Not really," Val told me. "Dr. Forsythe was from one of the old families, but she was never part of any coven. She always said if she was going to take care of people's familiars, she needed to stay . . . neutral."

"Why neutral?"

Val's face crinkled up in disbelief, but she quickly smoothed the expression away. "I forget how new you are around here."

"You may, however, have had the opportunity to notice us witches do not always get along," said Allie blandly.

"And some of those arguments go waaaaaay back," Trish added with a grimace, and a thumb hovering restlessly over her phone's screen.

"Well, I mean, I know about the feud in the sixties." That feud, in fact, was why Grandma B.B. had left Portsmouth in the first place.

"Tip of the iceberg," said Trish. "Like, sinking-the-*Titanic*-sized iceberg."

Allie nodded in agreement and flicked a strand of dark hair back over her broad shoulder. "There are at least half a dozen different covens up and down the seacoast. Once you get down to Salem, that number increases pretty drastically." Salem, Massachusetts, is Grand Central Station as far as the witch community is concerned, even after all this time. "Those covens, unfortunately, have bred a whole set of ongoing quarrels."

"Family fights are the worst kind," said Martine. "Doesn't matter who's in the family." She might not be a witch, but working in restaurants gave you a front-row seat when it came to watching people.

Val nodded in agreement and cuddled her baby a little closer. Like me, Allie had a magical family. Val and Trish, though, did not. They'd both come to the true craft on their own. Some hereditary witches considered people like Val permanent outsiders, or, worse, thought they never should have been taught the true craft. This little difference of opinion could make things awkward at the intercoven potluck.

No, I don't know that we actually have intercoven potlucks, but you get the idea.

"Anyway," said Allie. "Ramona decided since she was a veterinarian and had a duty to care for all the familiars, she couldn't be seen to be favoring any of their human partners, so she never joined any coven."

"Ramona and Julia always respected each other, though," said Trish. "And Dorothy was always one of her biggest boosters. In fact . . ." She turned her phone over again. "I'm surprised Frank Hawthorne isn't here."

"He's probably way too busy," said Val.

"Really?" I admit, I hadn't thought about Frank before Trish mentioned him. I plead the fact that my morning, not to mention the night before, had been kind of eventful. Now that his name had come up, though, I was surprised I hadn't at least gotten a phone call from him. "I mean, I know it's news, but—"

"*News?*" Allie's jaw dropped open. "It's a tsunami!"

"Anna!" exclaimed Val. "I told you to turn on the TV! I left you about a billion messages."

"Erm . . . ," I started, and then I decided that wasn't going to go anywhere useful. Anyway, Val was already on her feet, shifting her hold on Melissa. "Martine, do you mind?"

Martine waved us toward the main dining room, and we all followed Val (with Melissa smiling over her mom's shoulder and trying to grab a chunk of her ponytail). There was a screen over the antique oak bar, but it was turned on only during major sporting events. This mild concession to the twenty-first century came from Martine's recently discovered enthusiasm for baseball, which, of course, had nothing to do with the fact that her new boyfriend was an athletic trainer for the Red Sox.

Martine pulled the remote out from under the bar and hit the Power button. A news channel with a toothy blond guy front and center flickered into life. To my surprise, the Piscataqua Small Animal Clinic was framed in the background.

"Coming to you *live*, from Portsmouth, New Hampshire, where the shocking murder of a local veterinarian coincides with the disappearance of America's most famous cat . . ."

Martine pressed the Change Channel button. Another toothy blond appeared, female this time, and this time standing in the middle of Market Square.

". . . we're still trying to get you all the details on the shocking murder and disappearance of the world-famous Attitude Cat. So far no ransom . . ."

Martine hit the button again.

". . . calls coming into tip lines from all over the country from people claiming to have seen Attitude Cat, but no ransom demand . . ."

And again.

". . . we've got a clip here of Attitude Cat . . ."

Again.

". . . the *stunning* disappearance of Attitude Cat. While the nation waits breathlessly to hear of any ransom . . ."

"Wow." Trish's thumbs danced across her smartphone screen. "It's all over the Web, too. Tops all the lists and stuff."

"So, yeah," said Allie. "Frank is probably a little busy right now."

"Yeah," I agreed. I admit, I was more than a little surprised. "I mean, I knew the cat was famous, but . . ." I couldn't finish. I was thinking again about Ramona and the anger and the greed I'd felt inside her home. Not to mention the phone calls to Ruby's owner and her publicity representative. No wonder everybody was waiting for a ransom demand.

And then there was that other one, to Pam Abernathy's cell phone. The one I could only partly hear but that was asking if everything was good with the vet.

Val saw my troubled expression and laid a hand on my shoulder. "It's okay, Anna. Kenisha and Pete will find out who killed Dr. Forsythe."

"*We* will find out," said a voice behind us.

❧ 11 ❧

🐾 A WITCH AND her familiars walked into a bar. But one glance at Julia's stony face and none of us felt like making a joke.

Julia wore a long black coat with billowing skirts and a shoulder cape trimmed in black velvet. Her scarf was amethyst and her hat was black shearling wool with an amethyst pin on the turned-up brim. She looked like a cross between Marlene Dietrich and Mae West come in from the cold. It was a sight to make even Martine hesitate, which was something I hadn't witnessed since high school.

"Uh, Ms. Parris, your dogs . . ."

Max and Leo were with Julia, of course. Max wore a green sweater and booties, and Leo was fetchingly decked out in red.

"Oh, yes," said Julia as she stripped off her gloves and removed her hat. "I apologize. Max. Leo. Wait by the door."

The dogs yipped and scampered back past the hostess station. They both hunkered down by the door, heads up and ears pricked.

I was suddenly, painfully aware that Alistair had not yet

put in an appearance. Well, I told myself, he knew how Martine felt about animals in her restaurant.

Martine looked like she wanted to say something, but from somewhere in the depths of the kitchen came what I can only describe as a mighty crash. This was followed by a whole lot of rapid-fire Spanish, most of which you would never be taught in high school. Martine groaned and darted through the kitchen door, leaving us witches to file back into the private dining room.

"Pppbbbttt," announced Melissa.

"Uh, Julia?" Trish said as the door swung shut behind us. "Maybe I misheard, but it sounded like you said *we* were going to find out who killed Dr. Forsythe?"

"I did." Julia settled down onto one of the banquettes and folded her hands on her walking stick. "We are the very at least going to help. There are some things that need to be ruled out, and which Kenisha cannot address in her official capacity."

Allie looked at Julia carefully from under her dark brows. "You mean magic?"

"Yes, that is exactly what I mean."

"But . . . you can't believe that a witch had something to do with Ramona's murder," whispered Val.

"It is a possibility," said Julia grimly. "There are signs."

"What signs?" breathed Trish. She was looking a little green around the gills, and frankly, I couldn't blame her.

"Ramona's home was warded against evil influence," Julia told us, and we nodded. All of us had wards around our homes. "When I was there this morning, the wards were shattered. Not just breeched, but shattered."

"You could tell that?" I said, impressed. I mean, I could sense magic, but not with that kind of nuance.

"Of course I can't," said Julia, sounding a little like my first-grade teacher.

"But . . ."

"Max and Leo can."

Oh. Of course.

Val shifted Melissa uneasily from the crook of one arm

to the other. "Ramona would have felt the wards break, wouldn't she?" Wards are like psychic burglar alarms. The person who set them can tell if they're even challenged, never mind actually broken.

"She certainly should have been able to," said Julia. "Unless she was magically prevented."

"Or unless they were broken after she died," put in Allie.

"Or were deliberately broken by the murderer to get Ramona to come back home to . . ." Trish didn't finish, but she did turn her phone over a few more times.

"Any of these could be true," agreed Julia. "That is why we need to know more. We must make sure that Ramona's death was not caused by someone using the true craft."

"But . . . but . . . *how*?" The idea that someone would, or even could, use magic to commit a murder seemed to be raising Cain with my powers of rational conversation. The magic I'd learned so far had been about influencing probabilities and energies, cleansing and clarifying. I'd broken a couple of small objects, either accidentally or on purpose, and I'd conjured some visions of various kinds. But nothing in the books or the lessons I'd been given even talked about enchanting people directly. I'd started to think that was, well, something out of a fairy tale.

"It is not something we discuss," Julia said grimly. "Perhaps, considering the circumstances under which you came to your practice, I should have broached the subject earlier." Julia is not one for revealing facial expressions. But when she's really upset, her language gets increasingly formal, as if she were building a fortress with her words. "However, yes, it is possible to use the true craft to exert a strong influence over others, and that influence can be highly detrimental."

"Do you mean we can really use magic to force a person to . . . hurt themselves?" I looked around the table, but no one looked back. Allie was studying the tabletop. Val rocked Melissa slowly, her face uncomfortable and crestfallen.

I swallowed, hard. Images of dolls with pins sticking out of them rose in my mind. I pushed them aside immediately.

First, because thanks to my acquaintance with Martine and her Haitian family, I knew enough about the religion of vodun to know that "voodoo dolls" were pure pop-culture invention, and second, because . . . well, frankly, because I just plain didn't want to think about it. Not with the image of Ramona sprawled on the rocks filling my mind.

"We can't make a person do something that goes directly against their nature," Julia said. "No matter how powerful I might be, Anna, I could not make you hate your grandmother, or Valerie abandon her family; not for long, anyway. But"—she lifted one finger in case any of us were getting ready to interrupt; we weren't—"if someone is, for example, attracted to another and wishes that feeling to be reciprocated, an unethical practitioner can push that other person into experiencing lust or some other emotion that could be mistaken for genuine affection."

Love potions. She was talking about love potions. And she wasn't done.

"If a person is angry, hatred can be inflamed. If a person is sad, they can be pushed into depression. If a person is genuinely depressed, then . . ." Julia stopped. She didn't do anything so obvious as swallow, but she clearly needed a moment to collect herself.

I thought about the rocks under the balcony.

"I thought Ramona only lived on the second floor." Allie broke in on my thoughts, and I was grateful. "You'd have to jump from a lot higher up than that to kill yourself."

"We don't know she fell from her own balcony," said Julia. "I saw the police up on the roof this morning."

"Do you seriously think a witch, one of *us*, could have . . . used magic to force Ramona to commit suicide?" said Val.

"It must be considered."

"No," I said.

Julia turned to me, her glare absolutely icy. "I beg your pardon, Anna?"

"The Vibe I picked up in Ramona's apartment was really strong," I said. "My shields were up," I added hastily. I didn't want Julia to think I'd been careless. Really careless, anyway. "She wasn't killed long-distance. Somebody was there in the apartment with her."

No one doubted me, not even Julia. They all knew what my Vibe could do, especially when the emotions trapped in a place were intense.

"That leaves another possibility," said Julia.

"Oh, no," breathed Val.

"You don't think . . . ," said Allie.

"It couldn't be." Trish blanched.

I raised my hand. "Ummm . . ."

"Someone might have used the craft to influence the murderer," said Allie, more to the bottom of her teacup than to the rest of us. "Somebody used a spell to inflame their anger or their greed, and made them mad enough to kill."

❧ 12 ❧

🐾 I FELT THE blood drain out of my face. "That's . . . that's . . ."

Wicked. Evil. Foul. Wrong. Bad. Really bad.

"Yes," said Julia, as if she could read my thoughts, which I'm sure she couldn't. Reasonably sure, anyway. "It is as great a transgression as any practitioner of the true craft can commit."

"But what about the threefold law?" I asked. "If they used their magic to hurt somebody, it'd come back on them. They'd have to know that, wouldn't they?"

The threefold law is the first and last principal of the true craft. It's even carved on my wand, in Latin no less: WHAT YOU SEND OUT INTO THE WORLD RETURNS TO YOU THREE-FOLD. It means that the good you do comes back to you, increased. So does the bad.

I looked around at my coven sisters for reassurance. They all suddenly seemed to be very busy studying other parts of the room.

"Unfortunately, a witch's urge toward self-justification can be as strong as anyone else's." Julia's voice took on a ragged edge. I got the feeling she might be remembering something specific, and specifically bad. "However desperate the act, usually the witch feels she, or he, was driven to it, and that whatever it is, it is forgivable, perhaps even laudable."

"And if Ramona was killed by magic, or if magic influenced the murderer?" asked Allie. "Then what?"

"Then we will act," said Julia firmly.

"And just what are 'we' going to do?" inquired a new voice, and it did not sound at all happy.

We all looked up. Kenisha stood in the doorway with her arms folded and her grimmest expression tightening her face. She was back in uniform, and clearly back on duty.

"Kenisha," said Julia. "I did not expect you could be here. How are you doing?"

Kenisha decided not to answer that. "If you're having secret meetings, you shouldn't all park your cars right out front." The glance she shot me was particularly sharp, and I cringed inside.

"It's not secret," said Allie.

"Then why didn't I know about it?" Kenisha snapped.

This shocked me, badly. I mean, I had just thought Kenisha couldn't be there because she had to be on duty. It never crossed my mind that she hadn't been told we were getting together.

"That was my decision," said Julia. "I didn't want you to feel conflicted."

"Too late." Kenisha pulled out a chair and sat. "So you might as well tell me what 'we' are planning." She settled back, very clearly getting ready to wait as long as it took.

I wished Alistair were there. I needed a friend to hold on to.

"Julia says the wards on Ramona's apartment were shattered," Val told Kenisha. "There might be magic involved in her murder."

Kenisha let out a long breath of air. She reached out a hand and touched Melissa's damp little fist. Melissa grabbed hold of her finger immediately and held on.

"Kenisha," began Julia. "I respect your boundaries, but this is time . . ."

"No." Kenisha bit the words off. "It isn't time for anything. Lieutenant Blanchard is all over this one."

"Uh-oh," murmured Trish, and I agreed. We all did.

Michael Blanchard (Jr.) was Kenisha's superior officer, and he was . . . a difficult man. People said he was a good police officer. Well, some people said that. He did, however, have definite ideas about what kind of a town he thought Portsmouth should be, and life could become noticeably trickier for those people he decided did not fit.

It could also become trickier for those people on the force he decided were not getting with his particular program.

"If Blanchard catches any of you messing around with this case, he's gonna have an excuse to . . ." Kenisha bit her lip. "Sorry. This is my problem. Not yours."

"It is ours. We're your sisters," said Trish.

"Has Blanchard got a suspect he likes?" I asked, which was the closest I could get to changing the subject.

"Not yet, but he will." Kenisha spoke softly. She was suppressing so much emotion, I wondered where she found the strength to hold it all inside. I moved to reach out to her. But the tiny headshake Val gave me stopped me.

"Has there been any movement at all this morning?" asked Trisha.

"That you can tell us about," I added quickly.

"Yes, of course," said Trisha. "Like, you know, a ransom demand or anything? It's all over the news that Ruby was cat-napped."

Kenisha made a face. She also clearly made a difficult decision. "No," she told us. "No ransom demands. That we know of." I wished she hadn't been looking so closely at me when she said that. But then, after the stunt I pulled with Pam Abernathy's phone, I suppose I kind of deserved it.

At the same time, I couldn't help thinking this was really strange. After two anonymous calls warning two different people they should be checking on Ruby, you'd expect a ransom demand. As much as you could expect anything in this situation.

"Kenisha," said Julia. "Let us work with you. I swear, we will go no further than to try to discover if magic had a role in Ramona's death."

"And if it did?" asked Kenisha.

Julia didn't answer, but she clutched her walking stick so hard that even from where I sat, I could see her knuckles turned white.

"Julia?" said Allie quietly. "There's something else. Have you heard anything from the rest of the Forsythes?"

Julia shook herself and turned to answer. "I spoke with Wendy this morning. They are all extremely distraught, as you can imagine."

"Are they okay with us stepping in?"

A world of tension and history weighed down that question. I looked to Trish and then to Val. Neither of them seemed at all interested in looking back.

Terrific. Even more terrific was how Julia seemed to be undergoing some internal struggle.

"I will of course be speaking further with Wendy," she said finally. "And with Marjorie before any decisions are made."

"So you'll put your plans on hold to talk to another family but not to me," said Kenisha softly.

"That's not—" began Julia.

"No, course not." Kenisha slowly got to her feet and walked out.

13

I WAS THE first one on my feet and out the door to the main dining room.

In the restaurant foyer, Kenisha yanked her uniform jacket off the coat peg. Max and Leo watched her pull it on and zip it up but for once did not come scampering over to sniff, snuffle or yip.

When I saw the look on Kenisha's face, I couldn't blame them.

"Are you okay?" I asked, which wasn't really what I wanted to say, but they were the only words I could manage.

I half expected a brush-off. Heck, I half deserved one, but Kenisha just sighed.

"I don't know." She dug her hands deep into her pockets. "This is just such a massive cluster . . . mess," she corrected herself. "We've got so many TV crews around you'd think it was an election year. Blanchard is having the time of his life being interviewed every five minutes. Pete's trying his best to keep his head down and actually get some kind of evidence together, and now it looks like we got a witch who . . ." Kenisha stopped. "When I joined the force, I told myself I didn't have to worry. This would never happen. No modern-day witch would actually . . ." She stopped again. "You've got no idea what kind of power and effort we're talking about here. I'm not sure any of us even *could* do what Julia's talking about."

"She seems pretty sure, though," I said.

"Yeah, doesn't she? The problem is, Julia doesn't realize . . ." She stopped.

"What?"

Kenisha glanced around to make sure we were alone. No one else had come out of the private room. It was just me and Kenisha, and the unusually subdued Max and Leo, here in the foyer. No one else had followed us from the back room, not even Val.

I wasn't sure what to think about that either.

"Julia's overreacting, Anna," breathed Kenisha. "And it's because of Dorothy."

The soft words went straight to my heart and squeezed. Dorothy Hawthorne had led the guardian coven until her murder. She and Julia had been close in that complicated way you get when you've known someone your whole life.

"I know she never talks about it," Kenisha said, "but she's carrying a ton of survivor's guilt. She missed the fact that one of her oldest friends was in trouble. And now here's this mess with Ramona. It's opened the scars, and she is not thinking straight."

"You can't . . ."

Kenisha turned and looked at me. This wasn't her on-duty glower or her skeptical glance. This was something more distant, sadder and much, much colder. "Can't I?" she whispered.

She might have added something else, but Max chose that moment to yip. Kenisha started back, every muscle in her body as tense as if she'd just heard a shot.

"I gotta go," she muttered, grabbing her hat. "Listen, Anna . . ." She took a long breath. My neck muscles tensed up just watching the slow and careful way she turned to face me. "I never in a million years thought I'd have to say this, but . . . Julia's not wrong. If there was magic involved . . . I have to know, but I can't be caught . . . doing anything about it."

I nodded.

"I'm not asking you to do a full-on Nancy Drew," she said. "In fact, that is absolutely off the table, you understand?"

I nodded again.

"But if you and Julia and the others . . . if you find out that magic was directly involved with how Ramona got killed, I need to know, okay?"

"You could go back and tell them that yourself," I suggested.

"No," she said flatly. "I . . . It's complicated. And I do gotta get back to the station. Take care of yourself, Britton."

"Kenisha . . ."

She didn't stop. She pushed her way out the door and strode away into the November morning.

"You too," I murmured.

"Yip?" Max wagged at me.

"Yap!" Leo snuffled at my boots.

"Not now, guys," I said, and because they were dogs, not cats, they actually paid attention and settled back down by the door.

Julia never did talk about Dorothy's death. I did not like the idea that Julia's ideas about Ramona's death were being driven by her pain. Can you put something extremely mildly? Because I had just done it. But at the same time, I had to admit, Kenisha might be right.

I was still staring out the windows when Valerie came out of the dining room, her arm looped through the handle of Melissa's car seat, which she affectionately referred to as "the baby bucket."

"How's Kenisha doing? I didn't want to come out before. She doesn't like to be crowded."

"She's upset." My hand pressed against my purse, like I could feel my wand through the side. I wanted something to hang on to. "I've never seen her like this."

"I have, but not for a long time." Val reached down to tuck Melissa's traveling blanket in a little more firmly. "She's a veteran, did you know that?"

"Um, no." But it did explain how Kenisha would be so quick to recognize Julia's survivor's guilt.

"She was in Iraq, and she came back in a bad way. Finding the true craft pulled her part of the way out; finding the police pulled her out the rest. It let her feel like she was doing some good with all her combat training. I've always been afraid there'd be a day when the two were in conflict."

"They're not in conflict," I said. Not really. Not yet.

"May it stay that way," whispered Val. "So mote it be."

"So mote it be," I agreed. Because the alternative didn't bear thinking about.

Before either of us had a chance to say anything else, the swinging door behind the bar opened and Sean backed in, his arms full of plastic containers, which were in turn full of lemons and limes, all sliced and ready for those who might like a cocktail with their lunch. It made me very aware that the tavern's main dining room was pristine and still. All the white cloths and wineglasses were in place. The hostess was at her station. The curtain, metaphorically speaking, was ready to go up. It was time for us to leave Martine to her show.

Of course, Sean saw me standing there with Val and raised his eyebrows. I gave him what I hoped was a reassuring smile. In response, he made a small gesture with his chin, asking me whether he should come outside so we could talk for a second. I shook my head at him to signal that he should stay at his post. He was on the clock, after all. Sean held his hand up to his ear and mouthed, "Call me?" I nodded again. He gave me a thumbs-up and a smile that did pleasantly fizzy things to my blood, and headed into the back, probably for more fruit and bottles of something tasty.

Val took in all these little details, despite the fact that she had appeared completely fully occupied with getting little Melissa into her hand-knitted strawberry cap (yes, okay, I did get her one) and trying to pull the matching booties (totally not guilty of those; they were Allie's work) onto her amazingly squirmy feet.

"So, how's that going?" Val asked brightly.

"Amm-ppt-mm!" added Melissa.

"Now is not the time," I murmured.

"Probably not," Val agreed. "So, how is that going?"

Of course, Trish and Allie managed to come for their coats and hats just in time to overhear this little exchange. Which for some reason they found highly amusing, even when I narrowed my eyes at them. That only made them grin wider. Clearly, I was going to have to work on that steely glower of mine.

But then Julia emerged, walking slow, and nothing felt amusing anymore. She had her hat back on her head and carried her gloves in her hands. I won't say we all fell back, but there was a much broader path around her than usual. Max and Leo, of course, had no sense of occasion. They both bounced to their feet, wagging like they wanted to shake their tiny behinds loose.

"Yes, all right," she said to them. "I understand." She bent down to ruffle their floppy ears. One of her gloves slipped from her fingers.

I hurried over and picked it up.

"Julia . . ." I handed it back to her. "Are you sure we should get involved in this?" There were all kinds of things I wasn't saying, of course, but I didn't need to. Julia could read them all in my expression anyway.

"Normally, I am in agreement with Kenisha," she said, softly but firmly. "Law enforcement should handle this matter and we should not attempt to interfere, but there is a place for us, for you, Anna, in this. We cannot neglect or ignore it, if for no other reason than we owe it to Rachael."

"Rachael?"

"Ramona's daughter."

"Oh. I didn't realize." My heart squeezed just a little in sympathy for this young woman I'd never met. I lost my mother to breast cancer. It was the worst thing that had ever happened to our family. At least we'd known it was coming and had some kind of chance to get ready for it. I couldn't imagine how it would have been to just wake up one day and find out she was gone.

"Rachael is also one of us," Julia said. "Although we would of course support her in any case, I believe it increases the imperative." She pulled her glove on and smoothed it over the back of her hand. "I will speak with Wendy Forsythe and make sure she knows what we have discovered thus far. Then we will decide what to do to gain justice for our sister."

Which, needless to say, was exactly the kind of talk that Kenisha had been afraid of, especially coming from Julia. Especially now.

And she wasn't the only one.

14

WHEN I GOT home, Alistair was curled up on the window seat, enjoying a rare November sunbeam.

"Merow?" He opened one blue eye as I tossed my keys and my purse on the sofa.

"Well, I'm glad one of us is having a relaxing morning," I muttered as I dropped down beside my stuff. It had taken me more than half an hour to navigate the normally calm route from Market Square to home. Portsmouth had been flooded to the brim with news trucks and their attendant crews. They were blocking traffic, setting up lights, interviewing bemused passersby. I must have counted fifteen networks represented, and I'm sure I saw a few T-shirts for blogs and podcasts. And all this on top of the fraught meeting with the coven at the Pale Ale.

"I don't suppose you considered I might need some moral support?" I asked my cat.

Alistair yawned and for good measure stretched out both front paws, spreading his claws and toes.

"Uh-huh. That's a big help."

In response, my familiar thudded down off the window

seat and padded across the floor. He jumped up straight into my lap and put his paws on my chest so he could press his big furry head under my chin. He also started purring like a miniature cement mixer.

"You big faker," I told him, carefully, so I wouldn't inhale cat hair. "You're not fooling anyone."

"Merow?" He cuddled closer. "Merp?"

Alistair might have been a big faker, but I was clearly a big softie. "All right, all right." I sighed and scratched his ears. Alistair purred and curled up in my lap, and pretty soon I couldn't remember why I was feeling so crabby at him. "All is forgiven," I told him. "Besides, we've got bigger problems."

"Merow?" Alistair lifted his head and one ear twitched. If I didn't know better, I would have sworn he was concerned.

I thought about Julia and Kenisha. I thought about the huge gulfs that had opened between what I could do, what I wanted to do and what I ought to do.

There was something else, too, something perfectly normal and entirely important that the events of last night and this morning had almost pushed out of my head. I seized on it now like a lifeline.

"Okay. I've done what I can this morning. It's time to get back to the paying work."

Alistair cocked his head, managing an expression somewhere between doubtful and contemptuous. But that could have just been because I was about to remove my warm lap from under his furry belly.

"You remember work, right?" I asked. "That thing that keeps a roof over our heads and food in your bowl?"

Alistair vanished.

"Fine," I muttered and got to my feet. "See if I care."

I MEANT WELL; I really did. I went upstairs to the spare bedroom I'd converted to a studio. I checked my e-mails. I sat down at my brand-new (to me) drafting table and looked over the work I'd done yesterday for the coloring book. It seemed pretty good, even to my hypercritical eye, which was a relief. There are days I manage to convince myself I couldn't draw a straight line with a ruler and a set of directions.

The theme for the book was inspired by my practice. Not that I was going to say this to anyone outside my immediate circle. That far out of the broom closet I am not. But in the ritual magic of the true craft, each direction has associated colors as well as elements. I took that idea and worked it into the repeating theme of a compass rose. I liked the idea of using the symbolism of guidance and direction. I hoped it not only would interest the colorers but would help people who might be looking for stability and calm in their lives.

I'd said this to Julia. She'd said I was beginning to think like a witch as well as an artist.

I sharpened a pencil. I opened my pen case. I stared at the page and the half-completed circular pattern of elaborately interlocking flames and sunbursts.

Right. Okay. Time to get to work.

I needed this. Never mind the rent and the other bills that this book would cover; I needed to take a step back from the meeting this morning and the events of last night. I was jittery, itching to take some kind of action, but I couldn't. There was too much I didn't know yet, and if I wasn't careful, I might make the situation worse. Besides, Julia had promised that none of us would do anything beyond finding out if a witch had been involved in Ramona's death, and I had no idea how on earth one did that. At least, not magically.

But magic wasn't always necessary to find hidden things.

Stop it, Britton, I told myself. *You heard what Kenisha said about the full-on Nancy Drew routine. Stick to your knitting. Or your drawing.*

I faced the table again. A white news van rumbled past outside my window. I muttered something my grandmother wouldn't have wanted to hear and reached up to pull the curtains shut. And I froze.

There was nothing I could do.

Except.

Maybe there was something somebody *else* could do for me. Us. Ramona. And Kristen. And Kenisha. And Ruby.

I laid my pencil on the tray.

"Alistair?" I said to thin air. "Come on, Alistair, it's really important this time."

I started to count to ten to allow for feline sulks. I'd gotten to nine before my familiar appeared on the daybed I kept for guests.

I reached into the drafting table drawer, where I stashed useful things like erasers, X-Acto knives and the spare bag of K.T. Nibbles. Ruby's aloof black-and-white face looked back at us.

"I got a job for you, big guy." I shook out a couple of nibbles into my hand.

"Merow?" Alistair eyed me and the treats suspiciously.

"I need you to look for Ruby." I added another nibble to the little pile. "Maybe ask some of your friends?" Not that I believed Alistair actually talked to the other cats in town. I mean, we did not live in a Disney movie. Except, I kind of did. And he was magic.

Alistair combed his ears, and I felt a sudden creeping reluctance from nowhere I could define.

"Anything at all might be happening to her. Please, big guy."

"Merow." He dropped heavily off the bed and came over to nose my hand, the nibbles and the bag. I shook out one more treat and tried to ignore the feeling I was being blackmailed. He jumped up on my lap and graciously agreed to take the treats.

"Help me, Alistair," I said. For good measure, I scratched his ears. "You're my only hope."

My familiar blinked at me. He licked his whiskers and vanished. I chose this to mean that Alistair, Feline Extraordinaire, was on the job.

"Right. Okay. That's done." I made myself take a deep cleansing breath and face my table and my partially completed page. "Now I will begin working hard and staying out of trouble. Really. Here I go." I picked up a pencil. "Really."

Except there was maybe one more phone call to make without interfering. I mean, I needed to check up on my friends at a time like this and make sure they were okay. It shouldn't make any difference that the friend in this case was my landlord and a newspaperman.

Right? Right.

I pulled my phone out and hit Frank Hawthorne's number. I wasn't all that surprised when I got his voice mail.

"Hi, Frank. It's Anna," I said when the leave-a-message beep sounded. "I was just wondering—" But what was I really wondering? If he'd heard anything about the murder yet? Or if there'd been any kind of ransom demand for Ruby? Or if there was a New York City connection of any kind, I added, thinking about the phone call to Pam and the area code it had come from. Maybe I should ask if he had any clues about what had really happened to Ramona, or Ruby, or if he'd heard which direction Blanchard was looking in. "—if you'd call me," I finished, which was more than a little lame. I hit the End Call button before I could start stammering.

Right. Okay. That's it. I picked my pencil up, again, and faced my half-completed page, again. Work was good. Work would help me focus. It would soothe away some of my aching worry and curiosity. I had done everything I could for now. Anything more would be reckless. If Lieutenant Blanchard caught me doing anything he could label sniffing around, Kenisha would be the one who got in trouble. I could not, for example, walk over to Val's and ask if she'd heard from Kristen Summers, or try to get her to talk about her old friend. That would be both pushy and unproductive.

So why was I heading downstairs to pull on my jacket and my battered rubber boots to get ready to squish through my garden and across the back lawn of McDermott's B and B?

Because you're hopeless, I informed myself as I grabbed my knitted cap with the rainbow pom-pom. Myself didn't bother to argue.

❧ 15 ❧

🐾 "HI, ANNA." ROGER pushed open the door to the B and B's big commercial kitchen. "I thought you might be coming by."

A cloud of warmth and the scent of baking bread enveloped me as I stepped inside. Roger wore a blue apron with the words BEING THE CHEF MEANS NEVER HAVING TO SAY YOU'RE SORRY on the chest and was wiping his hands on a dish towel. Baby Melissa was curled up in her bouncy seat on the dining room table, fast asleep and looking peaceful and adorable. Several cooling racks of perfectly browned whole-grain bread shared the table with her.

"Val's in the back," Roger told me. "Would you take the pumpkin bread with you?"

"Thanks," I said, for both the directions and the basket of sliced bread, which smelled fabulous. I also headed to the kitchen's rear door.

McDermott's B and B had started life as a Georgian-style mansion. It was a big orange brick residence with graceful rooms, narrow hallways and steep stairs. Roger and Val had put a lot of work into restoring and refreshing its grand parlors and bedrooms, but there wasn't anything to be done about the narrow halls. Not even the one that had been built in the 1930s to connect the main house with what used to be a groundskeeper's cottage but was now Val and Roger's private apartment.

Since they spent so much time in a place decked out to invoke the nineteenth century (enhanced, of course with comforts like cable, Internet and central heating), Val and Roger could be forgiven if they went a little ultramodern in their own home. But both of them loved comfort almost as much as their daughter and each other. So the furniture was all either overstuffed or vintage, or both. The pictures on the walls were either of Roger's family or soothing land-scapes and artsy black-and-white photos. Valerie's family was nowhere in evidence.

Valerie herself was curled up an oversized burgundy armchair, talking on the phone. It turned out I wasn't going to have to ask if she'd heard from Ruby's owner. I could hear it for myself.

". . . It's a huge mess. I'm so sorry, Kristen." Val paused and listened intently to the voice coming through the handset. "Yes, it's true. I'm so sorry, but the police do think Ramona was murdered. Have they called you yet? Uh-huh . . . Wow. Yeah."

Valerie glanced up, saw me and beckoned for me and the bread basket to come in. "No. They don't know anything yet. The police are doing their best, believe me. I just wanted to make sure you were okay." While Val listened to the answer, I sank onto the sectional sofa as surreptitiously as I could, setting my basket on the coffee table.

"It's okay, I understand," Val went on into the phone. "You're not babbling. You're upset." Another pause. "Of course we can. But you should probably know, the town's swarming with cameras and stuff. They're probably camped out in front of your place. Do you want to stay here for a few days? Of course it isn't any trouble. We're actually closed down this week while we redo the floors, but you can stay in the house. And don't worry, we'll have Ruby back and this whole mess cleared up way before Thanksgiving." Val paused again. "This is me you're talking to, Kris. I know exactly how bad this is, and I would never feed you a line. We will figure this out."

Kristen's answer lasted a long time.

"Okay," Val said. "Yes. See you soon." She hung up the phone and blew out a very long sigh.

"Hi," I told her.

"Hi," she answered, smoothing her curling bangs back from her forehead. "Come on in. Have a seat. Coffee?" She lifted up the carafe on the round table beside her chair. Val had given up caffeine while she was pregnant. Now that she was nursing, she was still on a fairly limited intake and was determined to relish every precious drop.

"Thanks." I mean, who was I to leave a friend to drink alone?

Roger's coffee was as good as everything else he made, and we both took long, appreciative swallows.

"How's Kristen?" I asked, even though I already had a pretty good idea.

"Not good," Val answered. "You may have noticed that the world's kind of exploded over Attitude Cat going missing. About the only good thing is Kristen says her sister was able to go out to Minneapolis earlier than she thought, so Kristen's on her way back now. We'll pick her up from the airport. Maybe having her stay here will throw some of the media off the scent." Val made a face into her coffee. "Kris says her phone has been ringing nonstop. Her PR people and Best Petz are handling most of it, but she's still taking a lot of . . . stuff."

"That's hard."

"The hardest part is she's beating herself up. She's afraid Ramona might have been killed trying to keep—whoever it was—from stealing Ruby."

"Has she had a ransom demand yet?"

"No. Nothing," said Val. "It doesn't make sense! Why would somebody call Kristen saying there might be something wrong with Ruby and then not follow it up with a ransom demand?"

"Maybe whoever called Kristen and Pam wasn't the kid-napper. Maybe it was someone who knew the kidnapping was being planned and was trying to tip them off."

"Maybe," said Val, but her heart wasn't in it. Then a thought struck her. "Or maybe, you know, Ruby got away. I mean, she's a cat. She's not going to stay somewhere she doesn't want to be. Now whoever tried to steal her *can't* make the ransom demand, because they can't prove they've got the cat!"

Which was a real possibility. So real, in fact, I was em-barrassed I hadn't thought of it myself.

"Well, for what it's worth, we might have an answer soon," I said.

"Oh?" Val arched her brows.

"Don't 'oh' at me like that. I didn't do anything. I just asked Alistair to look for Ruby."

Val stared at me. "That's a really good idea," she said. "The sooner this is over, the less time there will be for anybody to really start digging." Her voice was unusually grim.

"You mean into Kristen's past?" I asked.

"What have you heard?"

"Nothing, really. She said something about it when we met at the pet clinic, after she had her argument with Cheryl." I paused. "But Cheryl made a huge deal about how she was going to tell everybody Kristen was a thief."

"She would," muttered Val.

"So you know Cheryl Bell, too?"

"Oh, yeah, I know her." I won't say Val's words dripped poison, but they definitely leaked some intense dislike.

"And Kristen's past, whatever it is . . . Is it serious?" For the record, I was not prying. I was encouraging. Val clearly needed to talk. I was her friend. Encouraging her was part of my job.

"It's pretty serious," said Val. "We . . . She stole some purses, wallets, stuff like that. Sold some credit cards and other things that did not belong to . . . her."

I did not miss that "we," and I did not miss the way Val

was much more interested in helping herself to a piece of pumpkin bread than she was in looking at me.

"Was that how you met Kris?" I asked.

Val shook her head, but then, more slowly, she nodded. She tore the bread in two and ate half in three large bites. "I don't know why it's still so hard to talk about this. It's just . . . it is." She started reducing the piece of bread that remained in her hands to crumbs.

"You don't have to say anything you don't want to," I said, and I tried to mean it.

"Yeah, actually, I do." She crumpled her napkin around the crumbs. "Because you're going to find out eventually. I just hope the whole world isn't going to find out with you."

I waited. Val picked up her cup and studied her coffee and then her comfy living room with its scattered baby towels and toys. I could tell she was thinking about Roger and Melissa.

"You know . . . ," she began. "Well, no, you don't. My family . . . I came out of an abusive home."

"Oh, Val. I'm sorry."

She shrugged. Her face had gone so hard and sad, I almost didn't recognize her. "When I was sixteen, I decided I'd had enough, and I ran away. I was on the street for a while after that. I started stealing because it was better than some of the alternatives. Plus I had this sweet freckled face, and it let me get away with . . . just about anything." She made her eyes go wide and blinked up at me, suddenly looking absolutely innocent and more than a little scared.

"I met Kristen in Cleveland and we teamed up. It was safer as a pair, not to mention easier. She'd play lookout and I'd . . ." She waved her hand. "Grab whatever wasn't nailed down too tight. It was an awful life. We tried to go straight a few times. We'd get jobs, mostly hotels and restaurants, where they didn't ask too many questions and were willing to pay under the table. But, you know, when that's what you're doing, the money's awful, and the managers cheat you . . . and so we kept on stealing, usually from the guests. Then we'd skip town and set up someplace else."

Even I can occasionally recognize when it is time to keep quiet. Now was definitely one of those times.

"Eventually, we drifted into Boston, and, well, we wound up having to get out of town kind of quick." Val turned the cup in her hands, looking at it from a fresh angle.

"Should I ask why?"

"Kristen got arrested," Val said. "And then she skipped out on bail."

"Oh."

"Yeah, 'oh.' She got a good lawyer, and it got cleared up. But, you know, it did happen, and it's a part of the public record." Val took a long swallow of coffee. "Anyway, when we were trying to figure out where to go next, Kristen told me she had a friend in Portsmouth who'd let us crash with her, and so we came here."

"Was the friend Cheryl?" I asked.

Val nodded. "She even had a real spare room. Things were pretty good, so we stayed. And then . . ." Val paused and I watched a slow flush creep up her throat. "Then I tried to steal Dorothy Hawthorne's purse."

"You're kidding."

"Nope. Right on Market Square. When you're a pick-pocket, little old ladies are usually your best marks. Usually," she repeated with a rueful headshake. "She caught me, of course, or rather, Alistair did. I thought I'd be going straight to jail.

"Instead, she took me back to the cottage, gave me a cup of tea and a long talking-to and . . . Well, I got out of there as fast as I could, and I figured that was that. Just another do-gooder. Except, after that, all of a sudden I couldn't snatch a darned thing. Not a purse, not a wallet, not a piece of bubblegum from the candy store. Nothing. Every time I tried, I'd trip or get distracted, or my hands would start shaking. It was spooky." She shivered.

"Did Dorothy put a spell on you?" I asked incredulously.

"Not on *me*, exactly, more on what I was doing. Doomed me to failure. She started following me around, too, and talking and talking and talking. It took a while, but eventually I started listening. I started learning about the true craft, and after that, my life really began to turn around. I moved out of Cheryl's, took some legit jobs at the motels by the highway and got my GED at night school. Dorothy helped me get my business loan to open the B and B, and then I met Roger, and the rest is history." She took a deep, shuddering breath. "So, now you know."

I did. I also leaned over and squeezed her hand. "It's okay, Val. It's over and done with. You're safe now."

She smiled gratefully, and her eyes were shining with unshed tears.

"Thanks, Anna. The problem is, I'm really not."

ᗘ 16 ᗖ

❧ "WHAT DO YOU mean?" I asked.

As an answer, Val picked up the remote control and aimed it at the TV. She hit a button and the screen blinked on to show a talk-show set with two people seated on a couch while an immaculately coiffed blond spokeswoman leaned toward them from her armchair.

One of the two people was Pam Abernathy, dressed in a severely tailored navy skirt suit. The other was a slim white man with rich dark hair just starting to go gray around the temples. He wore a dark suit and a red power tie. Every inch of him screamed "lawyer."

". . . And that's why I was so glad for this chance to explain our position," said the suspected lawyer smoothly. "Mrs. Bell would have come herself, but she is home by the phone. She didn't want to miss the possibility of news regarding the health and welfare of her beloved Ruby, who the whole world knows as Attitude Cat."

"So, it is true that Cheryl Bell claims that Ruby is her cat?" inquired the spokeswoman.

"Ruby is her cat," Lawyer Man answered. "Cheryl rescued

Ruby when she was just a kitten, abandoned in a laundry room. Cheryl sat up with her, night after night, feeding her milk from an eyedropper while her then roommate, Kristen Summers, was out on the town with her friends. Cheryl . . ."

"Cheryl skipped out on her rent," interrupted Pam Abernathy, "leaving Ms. Summers stranded and in dire circumstances, along with the cat you are claiming Mrs. Bell loved so dearly."

"That's right, Pam." The spokeswoman gave Pam an encouraging smile that could have lit whole city blocks. "You and Kristen Summers—who, I should remind our audience, is the CEO of Attitude Cat Enterprises—you say it was Cheryl who ran away first."

Pam's answering smile was thin and razor-blade sharp. "I have no doubt Cheryl had more than a few late nights after Kristen brought Ruby home. She was a pretty famous party girl during and after her marriage. But let's consider this." Pam crossed her ankles and leaned in. "This baseless lawsuit came only after Cheryl got a whiff of the millions that Ruby and Kristen earned. If Cheryl was so very concerned about the welfare of a beloved pet, why didn't she take Ruby with her when she ran away to Manhattan? Why was it Kristen who, looking for a way to meet her personal obligations, took Ruby to the initial audition? And why . . . ?"

"And why are you ignoring Ms. Summers's criminal record?" shot back Lawyer Man. "Or the criminal gang she associated with?"

Val slapped her hand over her mouth. I snatched the remote out of her hand and hit the Power button to shut the TV off.

In the other room a phone rang, followed by some clattering and banging from the kitchen. Val glanced toward the door.

"It'll be okay," I told her. "This hasn't got anything to do with you."

"I know, I know." But there was a little hiccup behind Val's words. We could hear Roger's voice on the phone, but not what was being said. Worry furrowed her forehead.

"Were you still living with Cheryl and Kristen when they found Ruby?" I asked.

Val shook her head. "Kristen told me what happened, but I'd moved out by then, so I didn't actually see any of it. I was trying to talk Kristen, well, both of them, really, into going straight with me." She pulled another slice of Roger's pumpkin bread out of the basket and took a bite. "Kristen wanted to, but Cheryl . . . Something was going on with Cheryl. Kris said Cheryl was in some kind of trouble, and she was going to stay and try to help if she could."

"They must have been close," I said finally.

"I don't know about that." Val brushed a few crumbs off her knees. "I don't think Cheryl really got close to people. She always struck me as somebody who was going to find the angles and work them."

Which made this lawsuit perfectly in character, then.

"What ended up happening?"

Val shook her head slowly. "They had some kind of a blowup, but the few times I asked about it, Kristen just clammed up."

"Was it about Ruby?"

"No. That much I'm sure of. But Cheryl vanished pretty quickly after that and left Kristen hanging. That was when she took Ruby to the audition and . . ."

"The rest is history?"

"Yeah." Val sighed. "And like history always does, it's come on home." She glanced toward the doorway. "That was the house phone that rang," she muttered. "Not the B and B phone. Who . . . ?"

"Roger knows, right?" I asked. "About your past?"

"Of course he knows!" she snapped. "Do you think I could have married him without telling him?"

"You'd be amazed what people forget to mention when they're stupid in love," I said.

"Speaking of in love . . ." Val leaned forward so her elbows were on her knees.

"Which we weren't," I said quickly.

"You brought it up."

"I was being reassuring!"

"So we're not going to talk about you and Sean?"

"No, we are not," I told her firmly. "We are going to talk about Kristen, Cheryl and Ruby and you."

"Oh, all right." Val flopped back in the chair with an exaggerated sigh and a mischievous grin. I frowned at her. It had no visible effect whatsoever.

I knew what she was doing, and I understood why. She was worried and she needed a distraction. I might even have humored her, if she'd picked some subject besides my social life.

Fortunately, I wasn't the only one who realized Val was having a rough time.

"Knock, knock." Roger shouldered his way through the living room door, carrying little Melissa, who was now wide-awake and thoroughly wriggly. "We thought you might need some cheering up."

"Awww! Come to Mama, sweetie." Val cradled the baby in her arms, but she was looking at Roger. "What was the phone call? And don't say 'nothing,'" she added quickly.

"Reporter," Roger answered.

Val blanched, which, considering how pale she is naturally, was a really impressive sight.

"Someone's found out I knew Kristen and Cheryl."

Roger nodded. "I told him where to go."

"You probably shouldn't have done that."

"Yeah, well, I'm impulsive that way." He put a hand on her shoulder. "We're going to need to start that cuss jar. I'm afraid Missy may have heard some bad words from Daddy."

Missy blew a bubble. "Ahm-mmm-am," she told us, and grabbed a fistful of Mommy's T-shirt. Val adjusted her hold and extricated her shirt.

"Have you thought about talking to Frank?" I asked them. "I mean, he is a journalist. He should be able to tell you what to expect from the reporters and how you can handle it."

"It's not a bad idea," said Val to Roger. But Roger waved this away.

"It'll blow over," he said.

"So will a hurricane," she answered. "That doesn't mean you don't close the shutters and bring out the sandbags."

"Mh, ppbbbtt!" added Melissa, with a wave of her chubby fist for emphasis.

Roger sighed. "Yes, dear," he said as he leaned over to kiss his daughter and then his wife.

"Love you too," murmured Val.

Probably there would have been more along those lines. Melissa, however, decided that this display of parental public affection had gone on long enough and let out a very healthy howl.

"Oops." Val gave me an apologetic glance. "Somebody's hungry."

"I was just leaving. I need to get some work done." I got to my feet. "Hang tight, Val. We're all here for you." I paused. "Um, I don't suppose you've heard from Kenisha?"

"Not yet." Valerie hoisted Melissa onto her shoulder, which was not where she wanted to be, and to make sure we all knew that, she let out an earsplitting shriek. "I was going to wait until she was off shift to call."

"Good idea."

I gave Val a one-armed hug, which caused a delay Melissa most definitely did not appreciate. She turned bright red and wailed at the injustice of it all.

I left to let Val get on with the important business of feeding her baby. But as I paused by the kitchen's back door to gather up my coat and gloves, Roger stopped me.

"Anna?"

"Yeah?" I answered, tucking my hair into my knitted cap.

"Val said . . ." He took a deep breath. "Val said there might be magic involved in this mess."

"No one knows anything for sure," I told him. As reassurance went, it was pretty weak. Okay, it was very weak. I didn't even need to see Roger's expression to know that.

"It'll be okay," I told him firmly. "Do you really think Julia would let anything bad happen to any of her people?"

Roger chuckled. "No, I guess not."

I made myself smile and keep my mouth shut. Julia was shocked. Julia would calm down and be her normal self in no time. We'd gather the whole coven and we'd solve this like we always did—together. Roger did not need to hear about what had happened at the Pale Ale. He had enough to worry about.

"When's Kristen coming in?" I asked.

"Tomorrow morning, early."

"You'll let me know if there's anything I can do to help, right?"

"Of course. Oh, and this is for you." He handed me a heavy cloth bag. The yeasty smell of fresh bread rose from inside. "Thanks, Anna."

We said good-bye and I headed off across the back lawn toward the gate in the fence. Just a few weeks earlier, our gardens had been a riot of fall color. Now that was all washed away. I trudged through a landscape of damp grays and browns, cradling the warm bread close to my chest. The wind blew hard around my ears. I was so lost in thought, I barely noticed.

I'd promised to stay out of this. I was supposed to limit any poking around to figuring out if magic was involved in Ramona's death, and, okay, hoping my familiar could play pet detective. But everything I'd just heard, in person and on-screen, had knocked me off-balance. If my friend's past was dredged up, it could make real trouble for her and her family.

How was I supposed to just stand back and let that happen?

❧ 17 ❧

❧ THE OFFICES OF the *Seacoast News* took up the second floor of a converted warehouse near Market Square. It might be first thing on a Sunday morning, with the late November sun just starting to put in an appearance, but the sound of ringing phones filled the narrow stairway.

Under normal circumstances, I would not expect to find Frank or anybody else in his office this early on a Sunday. But everything I'd seen on TV and on the news Web sites after I left Valerie's the day before proved conclusively that these were no longer normal circumstances.

Well, that and the fact that I'd been woken up at two a.m. by somebody cruising up and down the street out front with their high-beam headlights on and leaning out the window and hollering, "Ruuuubbbbyyyy! Heeeerree, kitty, kitty, kitty!"

Alistair had attempted to burrow under my pillow. I had attempted to join him.

When I pushed the door open onto the *Seacoast News* exposed-brick-and-scuffed-wood space, everybody was either on the phone or on their computers, flicking through

Web sites and social media sites as fast as they could point and click.

"Sorry, Anna." Maria covered the mouthpiece on her phone to talk to me. "The chief's in an interview." When I'd first met Frank, Maria had been a summer intern. I guess that had worked out all right, because summer was a distant memory and she was still here.

"Would it be okay if I waited by his desk?" I asked.

The light on Maria's old industrial beige phone flashed. At the same time, another phone on another desk rang. "Yeah, sure, I guess." There was another flash and another ring. "Hey!" Maria shouted. "One of you big strong men could pick up a phone!" Before any of them could answer, she stabbed the button on her own phone. "*Seacoast News*, how can I help you?"

I did my best to fade away. Clearly, it had already been a long morning for everybody.

Frank did not have a corner office. He was the paper's editor in chief, not to mention its publisher, and chief cook and bottle washer. All that power and responsibility earned him a space in the back of their open loft. His battered desk was piled with papers, leaving just enough space for the monitor, keyboard and another of the old office phones like the ones Maria and her coworkers were all talking into, that is, the ones who weren't on their own cell phones and head-sets. A poster-sized black-and-white photo of legendary journalist Edward R. Murrow hung on the wall beside a framed copy of the front page of the first issue of the paper.

I couldn't see Frank, but I heard him. His voice drifted over the secondhand cubicle dividers that had been set up to create a kind of conference room.

". . . But do you have any evidence that Ms. Summers organized Ruby's disappearance?"

"Her record speaks for itself," said a second, familiar voice.

Cheryl Bell.

My eyebrows shot up in surprise. Apparently Mrs. Bell had decided to leave no news outlet untapped.

"Yes, we'll be checking into that," Frank answered patiently. "But it would be helpful if we had something more to go on. Any threats? E-mails? Any indications that she meant to pursue matters outside the lawsuit?"

I didn't mean to eavesdrop. Really. I just couldn't help hearing. Okay, I could have stepped away, but Maria and the rest of the staff were clearly under a lot of strain, and I didn't want to risk disturbing the office any more than I already had by getting in anybody's way.

Yes, that's my story, and yes, I'm sticking to it.

"Well, I'm sure I'm not supposed to say this." Cheryl's tone oozed with smooth confidentiality. In my mind's eye, I saw her leaning forward, smiling to let Frank know she was giving him a scoop. "But if you contact Lieutenant Blanchard at your local police department, you'll find that Kristen Summers is *definitely* on their radar screen." There was a pause so pregnant it was going to have kittens any second now. "In fact, I'm surprised you haven't already done so. It can't be every day such a massive story like this lands right in your lap."

A phone rang. And another. A staffer rushed past. So, of course, I had to step a little closer to the divider to get out of the way.

"You can be sure we'll be following up from every legitimate angle," said Frank. I could picture his polite, professional smile and his clenched jaw. "Again, it would help if you could provide some anecdote or incident, or actual evidence . . . ?"

Which was just about enough for Mrs. Bell. "You're the reporter; that's your job!" she snapped. "I told you my story, and if you can't be bothered . . . Well, I can see why this is such a small paper." There was a rustle of cloth, and the crown of a black hat appeared over the top of the dividers. "If you'll excuse me, Mr. Hawthorne, I have an *important* brunch meeting at the Harbor's Rest I simply can't be late for."

A split second later, Cheryl appeared in the doorway in all her black-and-white vintage glory. I smiled, and she frowned, clearly trying to place me. If she did, she gave no sign. She just lifted her chin and stalked right down the middle of the loft like she was walking down a very chilly catwalk.

Frank also appeared in the doorway, watching her leave. He was definitely not a happy camper. I was used to Frank looking rumpled, but today he looked like he hadn't been to bed at all. There were circles under his blue eyes, and his waving black hair stuck out in all directions. He dressed more like a college professor than anything else, favoring slightly worn sports jackets, some with patches on the elbows, and khaki pants and button-down shirts. Today's jacket was corduroy of a cut and vintage that hadn't been in style since I was in middle school, and it looked like it had been under his bed since then. He had a tie on too, but it hung loose around his neck.

"Good morning, Anna." Frank raked his fingers through his hair, making even more of it stand up on end. "I've been expecting you."

"Darn. I hate being predictable."

He flashed a small grin and gestured for me to follow him into the conference area, which I did. Frank dropped into a chair at the Ikea table and glowered into the empty paper cup that I was sure had once held coffee. Frank was an Olympic-level caffeinator.

"Tough news day?" I asked.

"You could say that." Frank put the disappointing cup down next to his mechanical pencil and the yellow legal pad full of sprawling notes. Unfortunately, Frank's handwriting is as bad as any doctor's, even without his highly personal and eccentric abbreviation style, and I couldn't read a darn thing. Not that I was trying. Really.

I was in fact not trying so obviously that Frank flipped over to a blank page to remove all temptation. "Please tell me you haven't come all the way across town to offer me fresh insight on the Attitude Cat disappearance."

"Um . . . no?"

"Thank goodness for that, anyway."

From the other side of the dividers, a fresh chorus of telephone rings split the air. This time we heard some of those big strong men's voices answering. Clearly, Maria had made her point.

Frank tossed his cup into the wastepaper basket by the wall. "I've never heard it like this. We've got school board and zoning board and town council meetings going on right now. They're discussing issues that are going to directly affect this city and people's lives. On top of that, a genuinely nice person has been murdered, and what are people demanding to hear more about? The missing cat."

"Everybody loves a cat story," I said.

Frank's face twisted. "And all of them think they know something. Half of those calls"—he waved toward the main office and the jangling telephones—"are going to be Attitude Cat sightings, with and without questions about a reward. The other half are going to be cable talk shows looking for local color and s . . . stuff. And Mrs. B . . . Bell there is sitting square in the middle looking to cash in."

I almost remarked that he seemed to be developing a serious stammer, but I decided against it. "I'm sorry," I said.

"It's just that there's no sense of proportion!" He looked over the divider toward Ed Murrow, presumably pleading for patience.

"Maybe people get so worked up because it's something they can care about that's . . . uncomplicated."

"Maybe," he muttered. "I don't know. But. You are here and you want to talk." He was clearly trying to rally both spirits and patience.

"Erm . . ."

"Not about the cat, right?"

"Only kind of not about the cat."

"I should've known. Okay, what's up?"

"You know they're treating Ramona Forsythe's death as a murder."

"My money's on Mrs. Bell." He glowered at the chair I assumed Mrs. Bell had occupied. Then he rubbed his face. "Sorry, Anna. I didn't mean that."

"I know," I told him. "The thing is, I was there. When they found Ramona."

Frank sat up straight, as instantly alert as if he'd just gotten a fresh shot of espresso. "Nobody's mentioned that." He reached for his pencil.

"Have they mentioned that Kristen Summers is an old friend of Valerie McDermott?"

"Oh." Frank flipped open a fresh page on his notebook but didn't move to write anything. "Yeah. Well. That was going to come out. Not from me," he added.

"Val's really worried," I told him. "Her whole reputation is at stake, and the business with it. I was hoping you might be able to . . . give her some advice on how to handle the media?"

Frank blew out a sigh. "Unfortunately, the media's not all she's got to worry about. I'm assuming you accidentally overheard my talk with Cheryl Bell there?" He didn't bother to wait for my answer. "She was right about one thing. Lieutenant Blanchard is looking at Kristen Summers for theft, and maybe for murder."

"Theft? What does he think she stole?"

"I haven't found out yet, but apparently something's gone missing from Ramona Forsythe's apartment."

"And they think Kristen . . . how? She wasn't even in town. She was on her way to see her mother in the hospital."

"In Minneapoplis. Yeah. At least, she was supposed to be," Frank corrected me. "She says she was. But you know, people don't always tell the truth."

"You can't possibly think any friend of Valerie's—" I began, but Frank cut me off.

"You were the one who came in here worrying about her old record."

Yes, I was, wasn't I? Darn me anyway. I folded my arms. "This is a mess."

"Yeah," he agreed.

"I don't suppose there's been a ransom demand yet?" I asked.

"If there has, the police aren't saying anything to us." Frank looked at me, way too closely and way too carefully for comfort. "Why?"

I shrugged casually. Okay, I jerked my shoulders up and down in an attempt to shrug casually. "It's just that the only reason to steal Ruby would be for the money, right? So, either they're going to hold on to her hoping for a reward, or they're going to make a ransom demand."

Frank considered this. "And if there wasn't one, either Ruby got away from the . . ."

"Cat-nappers?" I said, so he wouldn't have to. Frank was, after all, a serious journalist and clearly was not thrilled at the idea that he might be forced to put the term "cat-nappers" into print.

"Yeah. Right. Them."

"Frank . . ." I hesitated. I told myself I wasn't really interfering or going beyond my promise to Kenisha. I was just eliminating outside possibilities. I know. It sounded pretty lame to me, too, but I did it anyway. "You don't really think Cheryl killed Ramona Forsythe over Ruby, do you?"

He grimaced. "She's definitely milking the disappearance for all it's worth, and while she's at it, she's trying to paint Kristen Summers as some kind of menace to the feline population. That could be for the lawsuit, of course, but *something* is going on there. I'm just not sure what."

"But you'll be looking?"

"Oh, yes. Mrs. Bell has definitely put herself on *my* radar screen. What about you?" He cocked his head toward me. "What are you going to be doing?"

"Looking at things from another angle."

"You know," he said slowly, "one angle worth looking at is that Dr. Forsythe's death might not actually be related to Ruby's disappearance."

I admit I stared at him. My jaw may also have dropped, just a little. "Seriously?"

"It's a possibility," he said. "And it would explain why there's been no ransom demand. Ruby wasn't actually stolen.

She just ran away. Ramona was part of one of our older families, and there are some old feuds that go way back."

Our eyes met. Frank had not inherited the family's magical streak, but he was a witch's nephew, and if he didn't know absolutely everything about his aunt's magic and her coven, he knew a whole lot.

"That's not the first time somebody's said that," I admitted.

"Thought so." Frank nodded. "Well, look, tell Val to try not to worry too much. Probably the killer, and the cat, will be found soon, and this"—he waved toward the windows—"will all be over. But whenever anybody asks, Val and Roger should say they can't comment because they don't want to interfere with the investigation, but like everybody, they want to see Ruby home and safe, so they urge anybody with information to call the police, and not—and I cannot stress this enough— *not* the local paper."

The phones all rang again, emphasizing the point.

"I should get back to work." Frank pushed himself to his feet. "If Val needs someone to help tell her story, I will see she gets a fair hearing."

"Thanks," I told him as I gathered up gloves, purse and nerve. "I told her she could count on you."

He nodded. "All part of the service."

I got up to go, but as I did, a new question formed in my head, driven by the TV talk show I'd watched with Valerie.

"Frank? I don't suppose . . . Have you checked into Pam Abernathy's background at all?"

"Pam Abernathy?" Frank's eyebrows rose. "Her agency's got the Attitude Cat campaign, right? Is there a reason I should look into her background?"

"Um, maybe?"

Frank scrubbed his head, disarranging his dark curls even more. "Heaven preserve me from vague sources."

"Sorry. But—" I began, but I was interrupted by a fresh burst of telephone ringing, accompanied by Maria's exasperated shout.

"Chief! We need you, like, now!"

Frank muttered something under his breath. "Coming!" he shouted. "Let me know if there's anything else I can do to help."

"Thanks."

I said my good-byes and left Frank to the mountain of fast-moving news that had dropped on him and his people. I had other things to do. Maybe Frank was right. Maybe Ruby hadn't been cat-napped and maybe Ramona had been killed because of something else. Before any of us could know that for sure, though, there were possibilities to be eliminated. Some of those possibilities clearly involved Cheryl Bell, who I just happened to know was right this minute having an important brunch meeting over at the Harbor's Rest.

✿ 18 ❧

❦ MARKET SQUARE WAS a zoo.

All kinds of people, tourists and locals alike, were looking between the bushes, into the planters and under the
benches. Hipster kids had their phones out, scanning the
surrounding area like they were looking for rare Pokémon.
Old ladies clustered together waving colored pom-poms and
catnip mice on strings. The lampposts were hung with hand-
lettered posters that said things like ATTITUDE CAT COME
HOME! and PORTSMOUTH STANDS WITH ATTITUDE CAT.

I was beginning to understand Frank's need for so much
extra coffee.

My Jeep was parked nearby, but I didn't get my keys out.
This was probably not smart. What would have been smart
was to go back home and wait for Alistair to bring me some
good news. I had done enough this morning. I could check
in with Valerie and make sure Kristen had arrived okay. I
could work on my coloring book. Work-life balance was
important.

Of course that's not what I did. I headed up Bow Street
for the Harbor's Rest.

Like the Pale Ale, the Harbor's Rest was a Portsmouth landmark. It had been built back in the Gilded Age—a huge white wedding cake of a hotel, with its own marina on the river, and a restaurant that had fed everybody from Babe Ruth to four generations of Roosevelts.

When I got there, the restaurant was smack in the middle of Sunday brunch. Long tables had been set up and filled with pastries and salads, and covered warmers held eggs, bacon and three different kinds of potatoes (I took the ones with cheese). There was an omelet station, a carving station and a dessert table with four different kinds of cheesecake.

I could have set up a cot and lived there happily for a year. Which I didn't. I did, however, help myself to eggs and bacon, fruit salad and an almond croissant in addition to the potatoes—because, hey, you gotta live a little—and carried them over to my table by the window.

I'd barely sat down at one of two open tables by the windows when a cat—a delicate marmalade with expressive gold eyes—hopped up on the chair across from me.

"Meow?" She blinked.

"Hey, Miss Boots!" Miss Boots was the hotel's cat, the latest in a line of Harbor's Rest felines that stretched back seven generations. I happened to know that she wasn't supposed to be in the dining room. But then, I kind of wasn't either, so I figured we could keep each other's secrets safe.

"Merow?" She slid under the table and rubbed up against my ankles.

"No, sorry, Alistair's not here," I told her, and gave her ears a scratch for good measure. Alistair and Miss Boots had recently struck up a . . . well, friendship. I wasn't sure it was a good idea, especially since I knew he'd also been keeping company with Frank Hawthorne's cat, Colonel Kitty. But I also figured they were all adult felines and didn't need a human interfering with their social lives.

Yeah, life with a familiar is more than a little strange some days.

Seeing that her boyfriend wasn't going to suddenly put in an appearance, Miss Boots sauntered off to look for more interesting company, or maybe a dropped bit of bacon. I settled in to enjoy my brunch—at least, as much as I could while keeping one watchful eye on the dining room.

I thought I'd see at least some of the reporters who were so busy following the Attitude Cat story, but I was wrong. The people around me were mostly families, with a scattering of couples grabbing a quick weekend away in the off season. This just made it easier to spot Cheryl Bell when she walked in, and to see that she wasn't alone.

A short, square man with a bristle-brush haircut and bulging arms that strained the seams of his dark blue sports coat walked half a step behind Cheryl, surveying the place like he owned it. Which I'm sure he thought he did.

Cheryl Bell was standing on the restaurant threshold—beaming, in case anyone wanted to take the picture—with Lieutenant Michael Blanchard of the Portsmouth police.

I choked on my potatoes au gratin. I also did something I never would in a million years have believed myself capable of. I ducked down under the table.

Yes, it was ridiculous. Yes, I regretted it immediately. Or at least, within thirty seconds, while I crouched there in the dark, clutching my napkin. I've got only one defense. Lieutenant Blanchard did not like me. He'd accused me of interfering with his cases more than once. I could say he had no reason to, but that wouldn't be quite accurate. If he saw me now, he'd assume I was doing it again. Of course, he'd be wrong this time, but I was never going to be able to convince him of that.

And hiding under the table is going to help, how, exactly? I asked myself. I waited for an answer. I didn't get one.

Okay, Anna. You're going to get up, casually. You dropped your napkin. That's all. Ready? One, two, three . . .

"I suppose I should thank you for agreeing to see me, Lieutenant Blanchard. I still think it would be better to have this conversation in private."

I froze, right where I was.

"You can just cut that out right now, Cheryl," answered Blanchard. There was a pleasant smile in his voice, which just made the words cut that much deeper. "I already know what you want."

From under the hem of the long white tablecloth, I saw two pairs of shoes—a woman's black boots and a man's black dress shoes—maneuver around the chair legs at the next table.

"I'm sorry?" Cheryl answered. She added something else, but I couldn't hear it. Another pair of black shoes, these purely practical lace-ups, stepped into my line of sight. The server asked if they'd like coffee and told them that the drinks special was the House Spicy Bloody Mary.

No, no drinks. Yes, they'd both be having the buffet. The server left. I inched my way forward and banged my head on the table leg. And bit my tongue to keep from exclaiming about it.

". . . You know you are not going to be able to snow me, Cheryl," Lieutenant Blanchard told her, oh so pleasantly. "We've known each other way too long for that. You've got something you want to say, but you don't want it on the record. Okay. I'm here, I'm listening, but nobody is going to get to throw the words 'secret meetings with a potential suspect' around during one of my investigations."

Cheryl said something, but I couldn't hear it. I strained my ears, or at least I tried to. What actually ended up happening was my toes started to curl. I suddenly missed the *Seacoast News*, where the eavesdropping was a lot more comfortable.

There was a long pause. "All right," Cheryl said. "I'm talking to you now because . . . well, because I want to make sure things don't get . . . complicated between us."

"You mean now that there's a murder in the middle of your property dispute?"

"That's exactly what I mean, Michael. I'm already having to defend myself to the media."

"Which is my problem, why?"

"We're old friends, Michael. I just wanted to make sure that we still understand each other."

"In what way?"

"I know how much you want to lock up the *right* person. And with my very public involvement in this case, I might just be able to help you do that, when you need it most."

"Just like old times?" he inquired softly.

"Exactly. But that is if, and only if, no misunderstandings crop up."

There was another pause. I ducked my head to try to peer under the tablecloth hem. I saw a chair scrape back and a pair of men's black shoes move.

"Sorry," said Lieutenant Blanchard. "I've got a lot to do, Mrs. Bell. But I will think about what you said."

"That's all I'm asking, Lieutenant." I could picture the thin, sharp smile and the clenched jaw.

"You have a good day, now." The black shoes walked out of my line of sight.

🐾 19 🐾

🐾 AS SOON AS I got back to my Jeep, I called Kenisha's private number. Which only got me her private voice mail. I left a message. Then I hung up and dialed Frank, which got me the exact same result. So did the calls to all three of Valerie's numbers.

Swell.

I drove home slowly, because I needed time to get my balance back. Finding Cheryl meeting with Lieutenant Blanchard had thrown me for a bit of a loop. Finding out that I was perfectly willing to hide under a table to listen in on their conversation had thrown me for a bigger one.

Finding out that the two of them knew each other, and that Cheryl seemed ready and willing to commit perjury if Blanchard needed it, was making me positively dizzy.

Why would she do that? The answer sure looked obvious. Cheryl knew she was a prime suspect in both the murder and the (theoretical) cat-napping. She wanted somebody else, anybody else, to get the blame.

Still, it was an awfully drastic step to take just because you might come under suspicion. Which must mean that

Cheryl was trying to cover up something worse. Blanchard had to realize that. So was he really listening to her? Was he really willing to use a lie to help arrest the person he wanted to convict, even if that person wasn't the real killer? Or was he just stringing Cheryl along to see what would happen? From what I knew of Lieutenant Blanchard, it might be either.

What do I do? I asked my inner Nancy Drew. *There's got to be something.* But this time, Inner Nancy had no answers.

I stopped at the Market Basket to pick up coffee, cheese and crackers, granola bars and grapes and the very last bag of Best Petz Kitty Kibblez on the shelf. Apparently there'd been a run on Attitude Cat products.

When I carried the bags into the kitchen, though, there was no one around to appreciate my efforts.

"Right," I muttered as I set the bags down in an empty kitchen. "You better be on the case, big guy. I could really use some good news."

Merow.

I froze.

Merow! I turned around in a full circle, but I didn't see Alistair anywhere. Was I imagining that? Or was he, literally, getting into my head?

Maow. This time I was able to identify the wobbling, tinny sound. I put my hand on my heart and heaved a sigh of relief. Alistair was in the basement. The cottage's old vents carried sound through the whole house like a megaphone. There were times when Alistair would, I swear, deliberately sit under the vents and sing me the song of his people. Usually when I'd forgotten to clean the litter box.

A minute later, Alistair came galumphing up the stairs. "Well?" I asked. "Any luck finding Ruby?"

He ignored me and paced up to his food bowl. When he saw the kibble, he sniffed once and turned his back.

"Seriously?" I asked him. He swished his tail back and forth a few times.

"Well, you're not getting tuna," I told him. "Ramona said cat food is better for you, so you're just going to have to get used to it."

Alistair lifted his head. "Maow?" he said, but it wasn't to me. He was looking at the phone on the wall. I didn't even have time to open my mouth before it rang.

"Maow," he announced, satisfied.

"Alistair. You know how I hate it when you do that."

Alistair displayed his concern for my feelings by twitching his ears and jumping up onto the table in the breakfast nook.

I picked up the phone. "Hello?"

"Hi, Anna!" announced my sister-in-law's voice.

"Ginger, hi!" I said back, although not without a twinge of guilt. There'd been so much going on, I'd almost forgotten that Thanksgiving was coming up, fast. "How's everything?"

"Pretty much as usual." There was a crash and a wail in the background, followed fast by some indulgent laughter and the sound of my father's voice saying, "Upsy-daisy!"

"I can tell." I smiled. It had been more or less decided that my father, Robert Sr., would move in permanently with my brother Bob (Jr.) and his wife, Ginger. Their three-year-old son, Bobby III, was delighted.

"You'll never guess who we heard from," Ginger said.

Despite this prediction, I decided to take a stab at it anyway. "Hope?"

Hope was my younger sister and our family wild child. She'd given up on college at about the halfway mark and instead thrown herself into a rotating series of passions, odd jobs and truly odd boyfriends.

"Hope!" agreed Ginger. "She's going to be here for Thanksgiving!"

"Wow. That's great. But I thought she was touring with her band."

"Well, it seems there was a little disagreement about money and . . ."

I felt my eyes start to roll. I tried to stop them and failed. "Where is she?"

"Somewhere around Topeka."

"As in Kansas?"

"Yep." I could picture Ginger nodding vigorously. "She says not to worry."

"Of course she does." I pinched the bridge of my nose. "Well, it's going to be an . . . eventful Turkey Day," I said, and then almost wished I hadn't. I had my own bit of drama planned for the big day.

"You are still coming, aren't you?" asked Ginger anxiously.

"Of course I'm coming! Why wouldn't I?"

"Well . . . I called Grandma B.B., too, and she didn't sound so sure."

"Grandma B.B. told you I might miss Thanksgiving?" What would make her say something like that?

"No, no, sorry. Not you. She said she might not be able to get back in time."

I closed my mouth.

"Yeah," said Ginger into my pause. "That was more or less my reaction. She said she was having some trouble wrapping things up in Arizona. Something about the lease, and the moving company . . ."

"And I bet she also said not to worry, and that she was *sure* everything would be just *fine*, but just in case . . ."

"Um, yes." Ginger sounded like she didn't know whether to be amused or afraid. "Actually, that's exactly what she did say."

I muttered something, which my sister-in-law, who had the unenviable job of being a diplomat in a family full of Brittons, tactfully ignored. "Is everything all right between you two, Anna?" Ginger asked instead. "I mean, when you told us Grandma B.B. was moving back to Portsmouth, we were all so excited . . ." She let the sentence trail off.

It had come as a huge surprise to my family when I announced I was settling down in Portsmouth. Up until then, everybody assumed that, like Hope, I was going to remain a drifter. But my putting down roots in New Hampshire hadn't been as big a shock as Grandma B.B.'s deciding to move back. Grandma had left Portsmouth shortly after she got married and stayed away for more than fifty years.

None of them knew that Grandma had left town because of a feud between the old magical families, because none of them knew about the old families, or that Grandma B.B. was a witch.

Or that I was planning on filling in this little gap in the family history over mashed potatoes and green bean casserole.

"No, nothing's wrong between me and Grandma. Everything's fine," I told Ginger. There was silence, and to my carefully tuned ear, it sounded highly skeptical. "Really, I swear. Everything's fine. I'll call her and see what's up, okay?"

"Would you? It's not like her to be evasive."

No, it really wasn't. Grandma B.B. was famously direct. A sudden sinking feeling started in the pit of my stomach.

"Actually, I was wondering . . ." Ginger paused again. I braced myself. "Has she said anything about a fight with Robert Senior?"

"With Dad? No, she hasn't." Not a recent one, anyway.

"Because when I told him I was worried she might not make it, he said, 'Maybe it's for the best,' only I'm not sure I was supposed to hear that."

Okay. This was not good. This was not good at all. "I'll talk with her, Ginger. I promise. I'm sure it's nothing." Thankfully, Ginger decided to take me at my word.

Ginger and I chatted for a while longer, about how her pregnancy was going (fine, thanks, almost no morning sickness, no, they didn't know the gender yet); about Ted, who was bringing his new fiancée up to meet the family; about Hope; and of course about Bobby III and how he was utterly appalled that Grandpa Bob did not have any stuffed animals or action figures and kept bringing him new ones to keep him company. He'd sit on the bed and carefully explain the personalities and powers of each one, so Grandpa wouldn't get them mixed up. Dad was loving it.

Ginger and I hung up, with me promising again that I'd call Grandma B.B. But what I actually ended up doing was staring at the phone for a very long time.

Grandma B.B. had given up her practice of the true craft (mostly) when she left Portsmouth. She'd even stopped talking to her own mother for years, or at least Great-Grandma Blessingsound had stopped talking to her. Then, when Grandma finally did work up the courage to try to tell her son, my father, about the family heritage, he got angry. Seriously, deeply angry.

If Dad was thinking it might be better for Grandma B.B. to miss Thanksgiving, there had to be a serious reason for it. That old, painful fight was the most serious reason I could think of.

"Merow?"

I lifted my head. Alistair flowed down from the windowsill and snuggled down into my lap, purring.

"I wish it was that easy," I murmured, petting his back. "But you know, maybe I should wait. I mean, Thanksgiving might not be the right time to drop the witchcraft bomb on the family. Especially Dad." I could pick some neutral weekend, maybe in the spring, after Dad had had a chance to really settle in with Bob and Ginger and when Grandma B.B. wasn't around, so she wouldn't have to go through the whole thing again, and . . .

"Mew, mmph." Alistair draped his tail over his eyes.

". . . And if I procrastinate any more, I'll be trying to figure out how to tell the family when Bobby III graduates high school." I rested my chin in my hands and stared out the window at the brown-and-gray garden. My thoughts wandered over the members of my family and how I loved them and was frustrated by them.

I also thought about the fact that magic tended to run in families, especially through the girls.

And Ginger was having a baby.

Who might just possibly turn out to be a girl.

"Well . . . sugar."

"Merow," agreed Alistair.

❧ 20 ❧

❧ MONDAY MORNING DAWNED late, gray and slightly groggy. Okay, it was me who was slightly groggy.

Not one of my friends had called, not Kenisha or Valerie or Frank or Julia. I told myself to be patient. I told myself everybody was really busy right now. I told myself I had plenty of useful real-life things to do, like working on my coloring book or updating my Web site and contacting potential clients.

What I ended up doing was staying up way too late watching cable news reports and surfing Web sites for the latest updates on Attitude Cat and Ramona's murder.

So far, no one seemed to be following up on the connection between Valerie and Kristen Summers. There was also no report of a ransom demand from the presumed but so far still theoretical cat-nappers. The official Best Petz Web site had mostly given itself over to Attitude Cat and the e-mails from well-wishers. But the front page was dominated by the reward notice, offered by Best Petz Worldwide, for any information materially leading to the safe recovery of "our beloved Attitude Cat ™."

That notice had been up since at least Sunday afternoon, and here it was eight o'clock on Monday morning, and nobody had been able to claim it.

Poor Frank, I thought, as I closed down my laptop and sipped my (second of the morning already) coffee. *He can forget about sleep for the next year or so. Those phones are not going to stop ringing.*

"Merow," grumbled Alistair, who was (reluctantly) hunkered down over a bowl of Best Petz gourmet canned food that I'd doctored (lightly) with water from a can of tuna. My cat clearly regarded this as a malicious deception.

"We can't always get everything we want," I told him.

There are times when you really are saved by the bell. In this case, it was the front doorbell. I frowned and left my annoyed cat and my half-finished coffee to go answer it.

"What have you been doing, Britton?"

Kenisha stood on my tiny porch, in her uniform, arms folded.

"Nothing!" I yelped. I also took a step back.

"Then how come I spent a half hour in Blanchard's office yesterday being bawled out for encouraging a bunch of troublemaking Nosey Parkers?" Kenisha marched into my little foyer. Raindrops sparkled on her uniform jacket and cap.

"I don't know! Unless Blanchard's been tracking my cat . . ." *Or has eyes in the backs of his shoes.*

"What's Alistair got to do with this?" Kenisha narrowed her eyes.

"Nothing!" I said again.

"Anna, do you have any idea how much I hate that word?"

I did, as a matter of fact. I couldn't figure out why I kept trying to slip it past her. "Okay, not much. Nothing that's going to cause trouble. I . . ." I swallowed and started again. "I asked Alistair to look for Ruby." I could not believe I was saying this out loud, even to Kenisha. But telling her that was better than telling her I'd spent even a few minutes crouched under a table in the Harbor's Rest dining room, trying to get the nerve to poke my head out after Blanchard

and Cheryl Bell finally left. My calves still hadn't forgiven me.

"You asked *Alistair* to look for . . . ? Of course you did,"
Kenisha snapped. "Because when the district attorney asks
how we found her, he's going to believe it just happened to
be your cat!"

I spread my hands. "Alistair is an outdoor cat. Everybody
knows it. If he goes out and finds another cat, what kind of
explanation is anybody going to need?"

Kenisha pulled back at this, at least a little. "Maybe," she
said. I wanted to tell her she worried too much and that it
would all be fine, but something behind her eyes stopped
me. There are days when the last thing you want from a
friend is a platitude, and Kenisha was very clearly having
one of those.

"Look, do you want to come in and sit down?" I said. "I
was just going to make more coffee." This was true, because
I am pretty much always just about to make more coffee.

"I'm not even supposed to be here. This was supposed
to be just a phone call."

"This?" *What do you mean "this"?*

But before I could find a way to ask that, Kenisha turned
her back and stripped off her flat cap and dark blue jacket
and hung them on the rack beside the door. I watched her
hands shake as she did.

"Kenisha," I said. "What's the matter?"

She didn't turn around. She just folded her arms and
bowed her head. For a minute, I thought she wasn't going
to answer. I bit my lip, uncertain what to do. I liked Kenisha,
a lot, but she held herself farther apart than the most of the
other coveners. I knew she was dedicated to her job and her
craft. I also knew that right now she was struggling hard
with something that might just be too big for her.

I remembered Val telling me about how Kenisha was a
veteran. She was my coven sister and I hadn't even known
that much about her. What kind of friend was I, exactly?

"You said coffee?" she asked the wall.

"Would I say anything else?" I headed for the kitchen,

and Kenisha followed. She settled herself into the breakfast nook while I pulled out my jar of ground beans and started measuring and pouring all the necessary things.

"Anna," she said. "You told Pete that you met Kristen Summers at Ramona's clinic, right?"

"Yes."

"And you said that Kristen said she was going to see her mother?"

"She said her mom was in the hospital, and her sister couldn't get there for a couple of days."

"You're sure that's what she said?"

Friend or no friend, there is something about having a person in uniform ask that question that makes you wish you had a good way to fact-check your own memory. "Yes," I told her. "Of course I'm sure."

Just then, the coffeemaker beeped, signaling that it was finished. I pulled two mugs out of the cupboard.

"So I take it Ramona's death is . . . ?"

"Officially a homicide?" Kenisha finished for me. "Yes. It is."

I let that settle in as I poured. The news had been full of speculation and assumption, but now it was real. A fresh layer of gray laid itself over the already gloomy morning.

I set one mug of coffee in front of Kenisha. She took hers black, and in quantity. She was almost as bad as Frank. "I don't want to ask you anything you can't answer, but—"

She didn't let me get any further. "When we were in Ramona's condo, you didn't happen to notice a laptop any-where, did you?"

"What?" I shook my head just a little, like I thought there was a loose connection that might snap into place. "Um, no. Sorry."

Kenisha curled both her hands around the coffee mug but didn't drink any. "Dr. Forsythe had a laptop computer. Her sister, Wendy, mentioned it specifically when we asked her if anything besides Ruby seemed to be missing from Ramona's possessions." Because of course the cops would be questioning Ramona's family, and her staff and her friends. Which was probably what Kenisha had been doing while I'd been trying to call her yesterday afternoon. "But there's no laptop in the apartment or at the clinic. So I wanted to ask you if you'd seen one."

"Do you think Ramona was killed during a robbery?" I frowned as I sat down across from her. Frank had said something had gone missing from Ramona's apartment. As usual, his information was proving highly accurate.

"Unlikely." Kenisha shook her head. "At least, not a full-blown robbery. Her purse was still there, with her wallet and all the credit cards. She had some antique jewelry in a box on her dresser, but Wendy Forsythe said none of that was touched either."

I was still thinking about this when Alistair trotted up the basement stairs. He twitched his whiskers at us and sauntered over to his food bowl.

"Could Ramona have come home and surprised the burglar?" I asked as I watched my cat sniff at the bowl and realize nothing had changed. "They struggled and the burglar pushed her and ran out without . . . finishing things."

Kenisha dipped her chin and gave me a hard look. "You believe that?"

"No," I admitted. It didn't go with the Vibe I'd sensed in the apartment. I'd felt greed, which would go with a burglary, but there was no panic, like I'd expect if someone was surprised. And there was all that anger.

On the other hand, as Julia was fond of reminding me, my Vibe was not a newspaper. I couldn't expect to read it with one hundred percent accuracy. Besides, even I could work out that if you planned to fake a burglary, you'd at least take a purse, and maybe open a few drawers and scatter stuff around.

Alistair turned his back on the bowl and instead jumped up on the bench beside me. "Merow," he grumbled as he slid onto my lap.

I petted him, but my mind wasn't on the job. I was thinking about my conversation with Frank. "If the computer got stolen, would that mean that Ramona's murder had nothing to do with Ruby? If someone came to steal a cat, why would they also steal a computer?"

"Or vice versa." Kenisha finally took a swallow of coffee, but from the face she made, she might as well have been drinking vinegar. All at once, I saw the real problem.

"You could find that missing computer," I said. "Right away. You could dowse for it."

"Maybe. Don't let what happened the other day give you an exaggerated idea of what I can do." She swallowed more coffee. "The other night, we had your connection with Alistair to call on, and that is extraordinarily powerful. Normally things are not nearly that easy, or that clear. But . . . with Val mixed up in this, and Julia hurting so badly . . ." She stopped and then went on more softly. "I can't help thinking how I could maybe short-circuit this whole mess before it comes falling down on the people who saved my life."

"Except then you'd have to lie to Pete about how you found them both," I said.

"And then lie about the lie. Not to mention risk tampering with all kinds of things like chain of custody, and keeping investigative procedure intact so the defense can't pull it all apart when it comes to trial." She looked out the window at my brown-and-gray garden. "If I give in and break the rules this time, whether or not I'm actually able to find anything, I risk derailing the whole thing."

"But you must have plenty of leads by now," I said optimistically. "I mean . . . you've talked to Pamela Abernathy, right?" I asked. "And Cheryl Bell?"

"Anna, you know better than to ask me about the investigation."

"Yes. Right. I do. So we won't talk about it. I will change the subject." I smiled and said brightly, "Hey, Kenisha, I was having brunch at the Harbor's Rest yesterday, and you'll never believe who I saw!"

Kenisha eyed me suspiciously over the rim of her mug. "Who?"

"Lieutenant Blanchard! And you'll won't believe who he was with. Cheryl Bell! How's that for a coincidence?"

Kenisha said nothing.

"And you know what? The dining room was so full, they got the table right next to mine, and you know, because they were so close, I heard them talking." Kenisha, I reasoned, did not need to know that I was under the table when I heard their conversation. "And, wow, was I surprised, but it turns out they knew each other, back in the day." I didn't say they were friends. Valerie thought Cheryl didn't make real friends. I thought the same about Blanchard. "By the way, how come you and I never do brunch anymore?" I added, and was deeply relieved to see Kenisha smile.

"Because last time you snuck home about six extra pieces of bacon for Alistair."

"That bacon was for me."

"Yeah, right. And you wonder why your cat won't eat his kibble."

"That has nothing to do with it."

"Yeah, right," she said again.

"Me-rr-ow," said Alistair, which sounded way too much like a chuckle for anybody's comfort.

"Anyway. We are not talking about Alistair," I reminded them both. "We are talking about brunch. And how Blanchard and Cheryl Bell are old friends. And how she was offering to do whatever he needed to help make sure the right person got arrested for Ramona's murder."

Kenisha looked at me very steadily for a long time. "Well. You know. Old friends always want to help," she said slowly.

"Yes," I agreed. "They do."

We thought about this in silence while the November wind whistled uneasily beneath the cottage's eaves.

"You're doing it again," said Kenisha suddenly.

"What?" I squeaked. I may have also started. Alistair grumbled again and flowed down to the floor.

"Getting your Nancy Drew face on."

"I do not have a Nancy Drew face."

That actually made her smile. "And I say again, yeah, right."

Whatever face I had, it was starting to blush. Fortunately,

Kenisha's mug was empty, which meant I had to get up and grab the pot.

"But you know," I went on as I carefully topped off her coffee, "after brunch, I was driving home and the *best* idea came to me," I said. "Kristen Summers said that they were thinking about making an Attitude Cat coloring book, and I thought to myself, hey, maybe somebody should go talk to Pam Abernathy about it, since, you know, she's in charge of Attitude Cat publicity?" I did not exactly nudge Kenisha with my toe, but I hoped she picked up the hint anyway. "And she's so involved with Ruby and her owner that she turns up mysteriously at important times and places without any good explanation."

"You are about as subtle as a brick, Britton." Kenisha sighed. "But, since we're just two friends talking about current affairs here, I'll say that it's amazing how few people actually want to talk to the police, and how they seem to have all kinds of reasons for not letting anybody look at their phones to see who has been calling recently. And, since you're so interested in our criminal justice system, I'll also remind you that our local judges have really strict standards of this thing called probable cause before they issue a warrant."

"I did not know that. Gosh. The things you learn when you're just sitting around talking with a friend."

"Yeah, amazing, isn't it?" agreed Kenisha. "And speaking of friends . . . have you heard anything from Julia?"

I shook my head. "I've tried to call, but I keep getting her voice mail." And she hadn't called back yet, a fact that was rapidly moving up the ladder of things I was worried about.

"That's not like her," said Kenisha. "She should be getting us all together so we can work on finding out whether a witch was involved in Ramona's death."

"I know. I was thinking the same thing."

Kenisha watched me, and for once I was very glad for my transparent face. The last thing I wanted right now was for Kenisha to think I had started lying to her.

"Pete's asking questions," she said. "About Julia and the rest of the coven—especially about you."

"Oh."

Kenisha nodded again. "He's being nice about it, really trying to cover my rear, but he's getting worried."

One of the many reasons we all liked Pete was that he was Kenisha's biggest booster on the force. He saw her talent and her dedication and set about teaching her everything he knew. He'd run interference between her and Lieutenant Blanchard at least once that I knew of.

"We should have had this thing cleared up by now. But there are too many pieces, and it's like . . ." Kenisha moved her hands like she was trying to rearrange the air between them. "It's like they're all from different puzzles, so Pete's started looking at how those puzzles line up. And Pete knows about the coven," she added quietly.

"He does?"

"Well, a little. He knows we're all part of a group, anyway."

"A group?" I felt my brows knitting. "What kind of group exactly?"

I don't often get to see Kenisha squirm. "The Portsmouth Area Ladies Book Group and Bonfire Appreciation Society."

I will not smile. I will not smile. I will not . . . "Seriously?"

"Come on, I couldn't tell him the whole truth, and it had to sound like something Julia might join."

"Kenisha, I hate to tell you this, but that does not sound like anything Julia would ever join."

"That's not the point here, Britton. The point is, Pete is starting to wonder if our group has got anything to do with Ramona's death."

"You're serious." It hadn't occurred to me that the police might actually notice how many . . . book readers and bonfire enthusiasts were part of Ramona's life.

"Most murders are committed by somebody the victim knew," said Kenisha. "Which means after family, that community becomes the biggest target for suspicion, and this whole thing started when you and I"—she waved her mug gently to indicate the space between us—"found the body."

And then we lied about why we were even there. I swallowed but couldn't manage to say anything, at least not right away. Under the table, Alistair curled around my ankles and head butted my shins. I picked him up and settled him back on my lap.

"Well, Julia should be glad to hear the news, anyway," I said. "If she really thinks magic was involved."

Kenisha nodded, slowly and reluctantly. "But it means we all might be about to come under a whole lot of scrutiny. I need you to keep an eye on Julia, Anna. Make sure she isn't planning anything stupid."

Stupid? Julia? Inconceivable.

"I know she feels bad about Dorothy's death, but—"

"Julia *blames* herself for Dorothy's death," said Kenisha. "She thinks she didn't do enough back then. What happens if this time she does too much? What if she starts slinging accusations around the community that she can't quite prove?"

My jaw dropped. Literally. I sat there with my mouth open as what Kenisha was actually saying settled into my mind. "You're talking about this thing turning into a witch hunt. A literal witch hunt." With the witches themselves doing the hunting.

"Yes," said Kenisha. "That is exactly what I'm talking about, and I'm asking you to help me make sure that doesn't happen."

I had no answer. None at all.

"Please, Anna," she said. "Everything's riding on this."

"I'll do what I can," I promised, and I hoped that would be enough, because for the life of me, I had no idea how I could possibly stop Julia if she was determined to do something. Even something truly dangerous to herself and others.

Thankfully, Kenisha didn't ask me to elaborate.

"Does Pete really think the coven is getting in the way of the investigation?" I asked Kenisha softly.

"Not yet, but he will. Especially once Val's name gets roped into this."

Because Pete was a thorough, methodical detective. He

wasn't going to miss the fact that there were a whole lot of Kenisha's . . . book group . . . clustered around this mess. He was going to be wondering if we were trying to protect one another from . . . well, from him and the rest of the cops, and how far we might go to do that.

Then I remembered something else, and when I put it next to the fact that Kenisha had come here asking specifically about Kristen Summers, it did not look good.

"Kenisha, I was over at Val's on Saturday. She was talking to Kristen, and she invited her to stay over until things get sorted out."

"I know," Kenisha said. "Pete's there now."

❧ 21 ❧

🐾 *WHAT?* I JERKED back, splashing coffee onto the table. Alistair meowed in protest at this abrupt motion and vanished.

"Pete is over at the B and B talking with Kris Summers and Val," said Kenisha. "And I'm over here, talking with you."

"But . . . you can't possibly suspect *Valerie* of anything," I said. Except she'd just been sitting here telling me Pete suspected all of us now.

And as I thought that, a memory bubbled to the surface. I saw again how nervous Ramona had been during Cheryl and Kristen's argument, and how certain I'd been at the time that there was something going on. And then I had to go and remember how I'd wondered whether Kristen had really left town for Minnesota like she said she did.

"I don't like it either," Kenisha said. "But until we've got some real answers that we can take to Blanchard, we have to keep everybody in this mess under suspicion, especially the part of everybody who already has a record." She stood up. "I've got to get going, Anna."

"Sure. Okay."

I walked her to the door. Alistair padded after the both of us, but only as far as the stairs. He sat at the bottom, watching Kenisha put on her jacket. I got the weird feeling that he wanted to make sure she was really going to leave.

It was not a feeling I enjoyed. At all.

But Kenisha did leave, and I did lean my forehead against the surface of the door and wonder what on earth I'd gotten myself into this time.

"Merow?" said my familiar from his post by the stairs. "Merp?"

"Yeah." I sat on the bottom step. Alistair climbed up into my lap and settled down.

"Merp?" he said again.

"I don't know either," I told him. "I mean, what am I supposed to think? Julia's worried because a witch might have had something to do with Ramona's death. Pete is thinking the same thing, and he might be looking at Val. Val is worried because Kristen might get accused of murder and robbery. Cheryl Bell is ready to lie for Blanchard to *keep* from getting accused of it."

I lifted my cat up so I could look him in the eye.

"Alistair, you *have* to find Ruby," I told him. "Please, big guy. This is all getting out of hand, fast."

I put him back down on the floor. Alistair licked his tail vigorously for a minute, blinked up at me, and vanished.

I folded my hands on my knees and settled my chin on top of them. I also tried to set aside the idea that for a split second, Alistair actually looked guilty.

I SAT ON the steps for a long time after that, trying to sort out what all the things Kenisha said might possibly mean, and what I should or shouldn't do about any of it. I would have kept on sitting like that, with my head resting on the backs of my hands, but the kitchen phone rang.

"Let it go," I counseled myself. "It cannot possibly be anything good. Let it go."

But I didn't. I got up with a groan and went to answer it.

"Hello?" I said with the level of enthusiasm I normally reserve for political pollsters and sales calls.

"Anna! Is that *any* way to answer the phone?"

"Grandma B.B.!" I exclaimed. "How's Arizona?"

"Oh, just lovely. Hot, and goodness, I'd no idea how much *stuff* I'd managed to get into this house."

I could picture my plump, cheerful grandmother clearly. She'd be standing in the middle of her overflowing living room wearing a brightly colored print top, with her bobbed hair swept back from her forehead and tied in a matching chiffon scarf so she could stare at her surroundings, all but willing them to get in line.

I laughed. "I say that every time I move."

"Yes, well, you have *many* talents, Anna, but traveling light has never been one of them. I, on the other hand . . . But that's not why I called, dear. I've been hearing about this horrible situation with Ramona Forsythe, and a little bird told me you might just be involved . . ."

A little bird. Right. When it came to her grandchildren, Grandma B.B. had a finely tuned radar. I wondered if she had some kind of spell set out on us, but I'd never quite gotten around to asking.

"Yeah," I admitted, because trying to put one over on Grandma B.B., even long-distance, was a pointless exercise. "I'm involved."

"And is . . . is Ramona Forsythe related to the old Forsythes?"

"Yeah. She is." I rubbed my forehead. Of course Grandma B.B. would know the Forsythes. She hadn't lived in town for a long time, but she still knew all the old families in Portsmouth.

"Oh, dear," she murmured. "Julia must be very upset."

"She is, Grandma." Upset enough that nobody had heard from her in a couple of days.

"Tell me everything."

So I did, and while I did, I looked out the window at my wilted garden. As I did, I saw some of the stems I really should have trimmed back rustle. Alistair picked his way delicately out of the flower bed. From this distance, it looked like he had something in his mouth. I hoped it wasn't the rabbit. I'd developed a strange admiration for the elusive little parsley chomper.

Alistair looked in the window, and he vanished. Not, I swear, before that same guilty look I'd seen before crossed his furry face. Which was ridiculous, but there it was.

"Anna?" prompted Grandma B.B.

"Yeah. I'm here. Sorry. Distracted there for a second."

"I knew something was wrong. I can tell from your voice." Oh, great. As if That Face wasn't bad enough, I apparently had That Voice to go with it. "Now, what is it that's *really* bothering you?"

"What's really bothering me?" I repeated. "Grandma, what's really bothering me is I can't figure out which of six or eight possible messes got Ramona Forsythe killed. I mean, is it the mess with Val and Kristen Summers, or the one between Julia and the Forsythes, or the one between Kristen Summers and Cheryl Bell? Or is there another one entirely that we haven't even heard about yet?"

"Now, *Anna*, calm down, dear. You'll work it out. I know you. You just have to put your mind to it."

"Maybe I don't want to put my mind to it," I muttered. "Maybe I'm tired of putting my mind to it."

"I understand how you feel, dear, but this is *family*. We can't just give up."

Which reminds me. "Speaking of family, Grandma, you are coming back to Portsmouth, aren't you?"

"Anna! Such a question." She paused. "Did Ginger call you?"

"Yes, she did."

"Well. She's so sweet, but she's got so much going on right now. I should have realized she might misinterpret a tiny delay."

"Oh, no. You do not get to put this on Ginger," I told her. "This is about you." *And just maybe about Dad.*

"I *never* said I wouldn't be there." I could hear her getting her back up, but it wasn't going to work this time.

"Grandma, this isn't like you." I said. "Have you been fighting with Dad?"

"No, of course not! Well, not recently." There was silence, which also wasn't like her. "Well. I suppose there's no getting around it. Anna, I want you to reconsider your decision to tell your father about your magic."

I swallowed. "It means that much to you, Grandma?"

"I know it seems like I'm just being a coward, but, dear, sometimes it's, well, it's kinder not to tell everything you know."

"I don't want to keep secrets from my family."

"I *understand* that, dear, but sometimes it's necessary, for your own sake, not just those you love . . ."

"Secrets come out, Grandma, in bad ways, and when they do . . ."

"I couldn't save your mother, Anna."

Everything froze solid—my thoughts, my breath, my heart, everything.

"When we found out that the chemotherapy wasn't working, Robert came to me, and he asked . . . he said he was sorry about how he'd acted when I told him I was a witch. He begged me to find a spell, something, anything that would save her. I had to tell him . . . I had to tell him it was beyond my power."

"Oh, Grandma . . . ," I breathed.

"I will never forget how he looked at me. Never." She was crying. I knew it. I wished I could reach through the phone and hug her and not let go.

"I don't want you to ever be in that position. If someone gets sick or hurt again. If Ginger, or Ted, or . . . or . . ."

Bobby III. Or Ginger's new baby. "It's okay, Grandma. You don't have to say it."

"But you do understand, dear? You see what I mean."

"Yeah," I said quietly. "Yeah, I do see."

"So you'll at least think about it?"

"Yeah, I will," I said. "I promise."

"Thank you, Anna." She sniffed.

We couldn't hug, but we could talk, and we did, about the family and about moving, and all those tiny little things that help you ease your way back from the hard, cold places inside. When we both knew the danger of either one of us breaking down had passed, we said the kind of extended good-byes you do when talking with someone you've known and loved your whole life. But these did wind down eventually, and I hung up and collapsed back on the bench in the breakfast nook with a sigh.

"Well, gang," I said to the house and the garden outside and my missing cat. "Looks like we're staying in the broom closet. So, now what?"

There was no answer from any of them.

Surprise.

❦ 22 ❧

🐾 MY CONVERSATION WITH Kenisha had left one thing abundantly clear. The only way my family and my coven were staying out of trouble was if Ramona's murder got solved as quickly as possible. Every day the questions dragged on, people I cared about were left open to suspicion, which meant they'd be tempted to make decisions we'd all regret.

So, ten o'clock Tuesday morning found me downtown again, in my dark pencil skirt and sensible black boots, following the directions I'd scribbled on a page from my notebook to the offices of Abernathy & Walsh.

It turned out those offices waited on the third floor of a square, uninspiring box of building that had been sandwiched into its space sometime during the seventies. It would be easy to tell I'd found the right place even without the company name painted in gold on the glass door. The walls were covered with posters of various professional cats. Of course Attitude Cat was well represented in various settings, rejecting various unsatisfactory items in favor of the Best Petz brands.

The two desks in the front office were occupied by a pair of young men who looked like they were straight out of college. The one on the right had light brown skin and dark black hair. The one on the left was trim and tan with blond hair that might have been highlighted. Both wore brightly colored button-down shirts (purple on the left, electric blue on the right) and khakis. Both had headsets attached to their ears and were typing away at lightning speed on their laptops.

Neither one of them so much as noticed me as I stepped onto the thick new carpet.

". . . No, Dave, seriously, you'd be doing me a solid . . . you're the man! Thanks, bro! I totally owe you."

". . . Judy, there's nothing to worry about. We will make the deadline. Yes, yes. You will be getting it today . . . yes . . . great . . ."

Eenie, meenie, miny, moe . . . I turned toward the right-hand guy in the blue shirt, just as the interior door flew open and Pam Abernathy, a pair of reading glasses perched on her nose, leaned out.

"Zach! You were supposed to have Oliver Campbell on the phone ten minutes ago! What in the h—" She saw me, and she froze. "Can I *help* you?"

Zach, who was the left-hand guy in the purple shirt, and his counterpart in blue both froze, but there was no covering the fact that they were both noticing me for the first time. Or that Pam noticed them noticing and did not like what she noticed, at all.

Zach started to his feet, smoothing down his blond highlights, and then his bright purple shirt. "Um, sorry, Ms., um . . ." I couldn't tell if he was apologizing to me or to Pamela.

"Sit down, Zach," Pam snapped. "Damon, you find out what is going on with Oliver. And, Ms. . . . ?"

"Anna Britton."

"Ms. Britton. *Please* do come in." Pam stood back to let me walk past her into her private office. "Damon . . ."

"Oliver Campbell. On it."

Pam Abernathy's office was small, but it gleamed with glass and chrome. In addition to the desk and the pair of visitors' chairs, there was a long table covered with what I recognized as mock-ups of posters and magazine ads, and even some real sample bags filled with kibble. All of them featured Attitude Cat and the name BEST PETZ ULTRAPREMIUM BRANDS, followed by some variant of the phrase "For the cat who accepts only the very best."

Best Petz was clearly rolling out a new line of feline goodies.

Pam closed the door. She walked around her gleaming desk and paused to scribble a quick memo on the paper blotter, which was already densely covered with notes and numbers. Then she dropped into the red leather chair, tossed her reading glasses down beside her open laptop and sighed deeply.

"What I would not give for five minutes' peace and quiet," she said to me and the ceiling.

"I'm sorry. I can see this isn't a good time . . ."

"No, no, no." She waved wearily in my direction. "There isn't going to be a good time, at least not until we've found Ruby again." She gestured toward the posters and bags and other ad material on the table. "Besides, I recognize you. You were there, that night." There was no need to ask which night she was talking about, or where "there" was. "Are you . . . with the police?"

"Um, no," I confessed, but probably a little more slowly than I should have. Yes, I did briefly entertain the thought of pretending I was with the cops. But I remembered in time that this would be a bad idea, if for no other reason that when Kenisha found out, she'd skin me alive.

I watched relief settle in behind Pamela's gray eyes. "Well, thank goodness for that," she said. "I'm sorry, no offense, I know everybody's got a job to do, but I spent most of yesterday afternoon being talked at by this *person* . . . Lieutenant Blanchard. I don't know when I've been so exhausted and confused, and with everything piling up . . . I didn't even have a chance to get breakfast this morning."

I winced in sympathy.

"But I'm sure I saw you talking with one of the officers." She narrowed her eyes at me. "An African American woman, I think?"

"Officer Freeman," I agreed. "She's an . . . acquaintance of mine."

"Well, then maybe you can tell me, have the police said anything about what they suspect? I've tried to get someone to talk to me, but I've had absolutely no luck."

"As far as I know, they haven't reached any definite conclusions yet." Now, there was a nonanswer even Pete Simmons would have been proud of.

"And Ramona?" Pam leaned across the desk, her hands clasped so tightly I could see her knuckles start to turn white. "Do they know she was pushed? I mean, do they *really* know?"

What happened with the vet? The voice from the phone call echoed in my mind. "They think it must have been something like that, yes."

A knock sounded on the door, and a split second later Damon leaned inside. "Sorry to interrupt, Pam. I got through to Oliver. He says he's in an emergency meeting and can he call you back?"

Pam's perfectly made-up face crumpled, but she rallied quickly. "Of course, but tell him I'll expect to hear from him by tonight, or we're going to have to consider a different strategy. Do it *nicely*."

"Yes, boss." Damon gave her a quick salute and ducked back out.

As soon as the door shut, Pam dropped her head into her hands. "Sorry. Sorry," she mumbled. "I . . . just wasn't expecting that. When people stop taking your calls . . . well." She shook herself. "Never mind. Not your problem. What can I do for you? And would you be willing to do a walk-and-talk? If I don't get something to eat, I'm going to fall apart, and that is *not* going to do anything for my image." She smiled faintly.

"Sure," I said. "Do you like Popovers on the Square? It's not too far."

"Everywhere's too far in this weather. I'm a Virginia native. I've never gotten used to your Yankee climate."

Actually, to be a true Yankee you have to be from Connecticut, or a member of that baseball team in the Bronx, but I didn't point this out.

"Let me get my coat," Pam said.

FIVE MINUTES LATER we were sitting in the back of Popovers with veggie scrambles and hot coffee, and a Danish for Pam, who really didn't look like she had any more than a passing acquaintance with any kind of pastry. I tried to ignore the news vans cruising the square. Pam, however, stared at them as if fascinated.

"No such thing as bad publicity," she murmured.

"Is that really true?" I asked as I tore my popover in half and scooped up a little veggie scramble.

"Most of the time." She smiled. "But there are exceptions. We would all be much better off without everyone jumping to the conclusion that Ramona Forsythe had been murdered." She scowled, and then she saw my face. "Sorry," she said. "I seem to be saying 'sorry' to you a lot, don't I?" she added ruefully. "But I know how I must sound."

I gave her a weak smile because I really didn't know how to answer.

"So, Anna." Pam leaned forward and her smile broadened, but it did not reach her sharp gray eyes. "I hope you don't mind my asking, if you aren't with the police, what were you doing at Riverview Condominiums that night?"

"Ramona Forsythe was my cat's vet," I said. "Which is how I met Kris Summers."

"Really?" Pam arched an eyebrow. "I didn't realize you knew Kristen."

"A little. We've got a mutual friend as well as a mutual veterinarian. Valerie McDermott."

If I expected a reaction, I was disappointed. "Which just shows what a small town Portsmouth really is." Pam tore off a piece of Danish and munched it thoughtfully.

"You're not local? I think you said you were from Virginia?"

"And y'all are just *charming* up hey-ah," she said, pouring on an accent as thick as butter. "Yes. I always wanted my own agency, so I decided to start somewhere small and work my way up."

"It must have been a real coup to get the Best Petz business."

"That was all Ruby's doing." She pushed some scramble around on her plate.

"Really? Were you and Kris friends?"

"Oh, no, I'd never met her. But she wasn't the only one who went to that audition on a whim. Or perhaps I should say out of sheer desperation." Pam paused and watched another news truck maneuver its way carefully through the square's pedestrian traffic. "I had just started up Abernathy & Walsh, and at the time, it looked like we weren't going to last out the year. We were literally looking under the cushions for spare change to pay for office supplies."

"Ouch."

"You can say that again. I was chasing after anything that might get us taken seriously, and, well, everybody loves cats, right? And when Kristen put Ruby through her paces at that audition, people were utterly charmed by her, her look, her presence, well, her attitude. They even had the camera crew in stitches. When she was done, I walked right up to Kristen and told her not to sign anything and not to take the money. I told her that she had the chance at something much, much bigger than a little penny-ante publicity-stunt prize."

"And Attitude Cat was born?"

Pam nodded. "And Abernathy & Walsh found its niche in the world of animal publicity." She stopped and set down the last bit of Danish. "But enough about me. You never told me what brings Anna Britton to Abernathy & Walsh this morning."

I took a deep breath and screwed on my best professional smile. "I understand, Ms. Abernathy—"

"Pam."

"I understand, Pam, that you are expanding the line of Attitude Cat branded products. I'm wondering if you have considered a coloring book." Adult coloring books were an undeniable phenomenon, and these days it seemed like everybody and everything had one. Suggesting one for Attitude Cat would not be that much of a stretch, even if I hadn't heard Kris mention that they were thinking about one.

Pam listened to my pitch about the reach and scope of the books, and about my personal experience, all with her head cocked to one side and a gleam in her eye that was close to a look of interest, but not quite there.

When I finished, Pam's smile thinned.

"Well, Anna. That sounds very interesting," she said. "However, the secret of the Attitude Cat brand is consistency and character development. With the rise of the Internet and social media, people expect a developing story and opportunities for interaction with their placed characters. Every aspect of Attitude Cat has to be synchronized, from the commercials to the T-shirts to the social media feeds and even any potential coloring book. Attitude Cat has to be current and move smoothly through her world." Pam stabbed her fork toward the window to emphasize the point.

"That must be a lot to keep track of," I said, thinking of all the samples and mock-ups I'd seen in her office for the new "ultrapremium" products. "I imagine a whole lot of things have been put on hold until Ruby is found."

"Actually, our timelines have all been accelerated." There was an edge of satisfaction under those words that sent an uncomfortable shiver down my spine. "Attitude Cat's brand recognition is through the roof. People are clamoring for her products as a way to show their support."

"Really?" I pushed the last bit of my popover away.

"Really," she said. "I know, it seems ghoulish, but, well, that's the way of the world."

"Still, it must have been a real shock when you heard Ruby disappeared," I tried.

"Otherwise I wouldn't have fainted on the spot like that,

you mean? Oh, yes, it was a shock." Pam folded her napkin and blotted her mouth carefully so as not to smudge her lipstick. "I'd come expecting trouble, but . . . nothing like that."

"Oh, that's right," I said, trying to sound casual. "You said you got a phone call from Ramona saying something might be wrong."

"Actually, I don't think I said it was from Ramona," she corrected me. "I'm pretty sure I told you what I told the police. I didn't recognize the number or the voice."

"Did you know Kristen was boarding Ruby with Ramona?"

"I did, because it was my idea."

I must have looked startled, because Pam's smile spread out even thinner. "Ramona is—or rather she was—our in-house vet. We kept her on retainer to help make sure that all our stars were healthy and happy and to ensure we're following *all* the safety rules on the set.

"Now, Anna," Pam said in a way that managed to be both smooth and pointed. "I've been straight with you. I need you to be straight with me, especially if we're going to have any possibility of entering into a business agreement." She leaned in close. "That night, in front of Ramona's building, did you just happen to pick up my phone?"

❧ 23 ❧

🐾 *UH-OH.*

I looked at Pam. Pam looked at me. Her gray eyes glittered with a cold, hard light. She didn't actually say *Gotcha*, but then, she didn't have to.

For a split second, I considered lying. But just in time I heard the echo of all my friends telling me how I should never play poker. Besides, Pam Abernathy was a seasoned PR executive. She dealt in artfully decorated lies for a living.

"Ummm . . . yes," I said. "It was ringing, and I picked it up." I thought about adding something about force of habit or instinct but decided to quit while I was ahead.

Pam nodded as if she meant to be encouraging. "And exactly what did you hear?"

"A very upset person asking if everything was good with the vet."

Pam frowned, hard. "A man or a woman?"

"I couldn't tell for sure. We had a bad connection."

"And they didn't give you a name?

"No."

"But you're sure that's what they said? They just asked

about the vet; they didn't drop any names or make any accusations, nothing like that?"

"No. Another call was coming in."

To my surprise, Pam Abernathy started to laugh. It was so loud and so unexpected that I jerked backward in surprise. The laughter went on, long enough and hard enough that the people at the nearest tables turned their heads to stare. I shifted uncomfortably. I didn't think I'd said anything *that* funny.

"So you . . . Oh my word! Don't tell me you assumed . . . !" She stared at me. I don't know for sure what she saw but it brought on a fresh bout of laughter. "Oh, you did! You imagined me running into the apartment, pushing Ramona off her balcony, running away, and running back so I could act all shocked and faint in front of the cops! That's why you came snooping around this morning!" She gasped. "A few overheard words and you come snooping around . . . so I thought . . . oh, oh, I thought you'd actually . . ."

"I'd actually what?" I tried to force some steel into the question. It didn't work. Pam just dabbed at the corners of her eyes with her knuckle.

"Oh, Anna. I'm sorry. It's stress; that's all." She paused a minute and swallowed several deep breaths. When she was calm, she went on. "Oh, bless your heart. That call was from my partner, Milo Walsh. I tried to get hold of him immediately after I got the initial call about Ruby. The one I told the police about," she added, in case I'd forgotten. "He was calling back to find out what happened. That's all."

"Oh."

She smiled again, and it was not an entirely nice smile. "I'm sorry if you expected to have something more to tell your friend Officer Freeman. And in case you were working your way around to it, when poor Ramona died, I was at my office, cruelly keeping both Damon and Zach late working on the Ultrapremium campaign. A fact that they were both happy to confirm when Detective Simmons asked."

I felt a flush creep across my cheeks. Not because I had in fact planned on telling Kenisha about what I learned today, if I learned anything, but because Pam Abernathy had clearly suspected that was why I'd shown up at her office from the beginning.

Somewhere, Nancy Drew was shaking her head at me.

"Never try to kid a kidder, Anna." Pam's smile remained plastered on her face, but any actual feeling behind it had long since evaporated. "But don't worry. I won't hold it against you." Except I got the very strong feeling she already did. "Actually, I admire you for trying to seize the moment. It shows initiative."

"Well, Pam . . ." I tried to muster my professional manners to make some kind of semigraceful exit, but Pam wasn't looking at me anymore. She started to her feet and ducked around the corner of our table. I twisted in my seat and saw Kristen Summers threading her way toward us.

"Kristen!" Pam put her arms around the other woman and hugged her. Kris returned the embrace, stiffly and reluctantly. "What are you doing here!"

"I . . . Zach told me you were here." Kris reached up and tucked back one lock of brown hair that had come loose under her braid.

"He sent you . . . ?" cried Pam. "I'll be having a talk with him about that. He should have come to get me."

"No, it was my idea."

"Well, come and sit down anyway." Pam sank back into her chair and patted the seat next to her.

Kris did sit down, but she didn't take off her hat or her coat. "Hi, Anna," she said, like she had just noticed I was there.

"Hi, Kristen," I said. "I'm so sorry about what's happened."

"Yeah, me too." She dug her hands into the pockets of her coat. "I keep telling myself we'll get through it . . ."

"Of course we will!" announced Pam.

Kristen ignored her. "And I'm fine, in case you're about to ask," she said to me. "Just a little sleep deprived."

"And of course you must be so worried about poor Ruby!" prompted Pam. "Honey, have you heard *anything*?"

Kristen shook her head and rubbed her eyes with the back of one mittened hand.

"Do you want some coffee or something?" I asked. "I'd ask if you want breakfast, but since you're staying with Val and Roger, you've probably eaten enough for a week by now."

Kristen's mouth twitched into a small smile. "They're so great."

Pam seemed less sure about that. "I really don't like you staying with them, Kristen. It looks like you're hiding."

Kristen just looked at her, and there was something well beyond a sleepless night in her face. The skin on the back of my neck bunched up. Something was wrong. There was something Kris wasn't saying yet, but it sat behind her eyes like a wall of ice.

"Pam, we need to talk. I mean now."

"Of course. We're done here, right, Anna?"

Kristen didn't give me a chance to answer. "The police are questioning me," she told Pam.

Pam went white. For a second, I thought she might faint again.

"Oh, Kris," she croaked. "Please, please, *please* tell me you didn't talk to them without our lawyer."

"I . . . yeah," murmured Kristen to the tabletop. "I did. Yesterday."

"What! You . . ." Pam's jaw clamped down hard around whatever she was going to say. I watched her silently count to three. When she spoke again, her words were very even, and very strained. "That was not the best decision. We *talked* about this. You should not be meeting anyone alone, not the press and certainly not the police." She unsnapped the pocket on the side of her shiny black purse and pulled out her phone. "I'm calling James, right now." She worked her smartphone with one hand while gripping Kristen's wrist with the other as she pulled her to her feet. "You'll excuse us, Anna?" she said over her shoulder.

"Of course," I murmured, but the pair of them were already out of earshot.

❦ 24 ❧

❖ I SAT WHERE I was, with the remains of two break-
fasts in front of me and the rest of the world going about its
normal Tuesday morning routine.

Or seminormal anyway. Out on the square, a news crew
was setting up and a blond man in a greatcoat was talking
with a cluster of old women in black-and-white hats carrying
a banner that read RUBY COME HOME.

I pulled my phone out and hit Val's number and waited
while it rang.

"Hi, you have reached the private voice mail of Valerie
McDermott. To reach McDermott's B and B . . ." I bit my
lip while the message unspooled. ". . . But if you actually
want to talk to me, leave a message."

"Val, it's me," I said. "I was talking to Pam Abernathy
and Kristen showed up. Val, what happened yesterday? I
know Pete was over there. Are you guys okay?" I paused,
like I thought I was going to get an answer. "Call me, will
you?" I added, and I hung up.

I stuffed my phone back into my purse and drummed my

fingers on the tabletop. This morning was not off to a good start, especially where my resolution to help sort out what had happened to Ramona Forsythe was concerned. The only thing I'd learned from Pam Abernathy was that I wasn't as smart as I thought.

No. I flattened my hand against the tabletop. That wasn't quite true. I had learned something. When she'd had that laugh attack, she hadn't been laughing at me from surprise, or even contempt.

That was relief—sheer, shocked relief. Pam had been worried about what I found, or heard, on her phone. Worried enough that she was willing to sit through my not-very-good charade of a pitch session.

That must mean something. I just wished I knew what it was. There was something in the way she talked, about Ramona, about what had happened, that bothered me. I just couldn't put my finger on what.

I thought about ad campaigns and ideas and characters. I thought about all those new samples and mock-ups I'd just seen in Pam's office. I thought about how many people seemed to depend on Ruby, or at least the image of Ruby, for their livelihood. I thought about how two of those people were Pam and Kristen, and how angry Kristen had looked just now.

I thought about Cheryl sitting across from Lieutenant Blanchard and calmly offering to lie if Blanchard needed it.

I thought about Alistair, and how he hadn't been home, hadn't been eating, hadn't been . . . *there* since I set him the job of finding Ruby. I thought about how the one thing that could keep Alistair from going where he chose was magic. I thought about Julia and her contention that a witch was involved in Ramona's murder. I thought about Kenisha and how worried she was that Julia might do something drastic if that turned out to be true.

Julia, who still hadn't called me back, or come around to the cottage, or anything else since that emergency coven meeting at the Pale Ale.

I bit my lip and made up my mind. Questions about Pam

Abernathy, Cheryl Bell and even Ruby could wait. I needed to sort out what was happening closer to home.

"SORRY, ANNA," SAID Gabrielle when I got to Midnight Reads. "Julia's not here."

"But . . . Julia's always here." Midnight Reads was Julia's pride and joy. It was open six days a week, and every single one of those days found Julia in her office or behind the counter or somewhere in between.

"Yeah, I know, surprised me, too." Gabrielle straightened the copies of Lee Childs's latest on the NEW ARRIVALS table. "But she said she's feeling a little under the weather and—"

"Under the weather?" I cut her off. "She's sick? Has anybody checked on her?"

"She says she's fine—"

"Julia always says she's fine. Is she upstairs?"

"She should be."

I didn't wait to hear anything else. I just left the shop and took the side alley shortcut to the stairs and Julia's apartment. I got to her door and took a second to catch my breath, because I'd kind of run up the stairs. I raised my hand to the plain brass knocker on the door. Before I could do anything, though, the door flew open.

But the woman standing there was not Julia.

She was younger, for one thing, which in this case meant she looked around sixty. She was about my height, with that round, comfortable build that makes you think of hugs and cookies and knitted sweaters.

The look in her eyes, though, made me fall back two full steps so she'd have plenty of room to get past.

"Oh, Julia," the woman said crisply. "You seem to have another visitor."

Now Julia did come to the door, and it was instantly evident that Kristen Summers wasn't the only one who'd had a rough night. I'd never seen my mentor like this. She was pale and bleary-eyed. Her white hair fell loose around her shoulders with just a headband holding it back from her forehead. Max and Leo peeked anxiously around the edges of her plain black skirt. She was slumping. Something close to panic bubbled up in me. Julia never slumped.

"Anna!" Julia exclaimed. "Is everything all right?"

"Well," said the other woman. "So this is the famous Anna Britton." She did not wait for either of us to confirm or deny the fact, or the adjective. "I had a feeling you might be showing up sooner rather than later."

"I'm sorry," I said. "But you are . . . ?"

"Wendy Forsythe. I'm Ramona's sister."

Now that she said it, I could see the resemblance to Ramona, especially in her build and around her eyes.

"I'm sorry for your loss," I told her.

"How kind," she replied, but the words all had ragged edges that grated hard against my mind. I remembered how Allie had asked if the Forsythes would be all right with the guardian coven looking into Ramona's murder. Right now, the answer did not look positive.

"Thank you for stopping by, Wendy," Julia said. Her voice was hoarse, as if she'd been shouting. "I'll call you later."

Wendy did not answer, or even look back. She just lifted her chin and marched straight down the stairs.

Julia sighed and waved me inside.

"Has something happened, Anna?"

"That's what I wanted to ask you." As soon as I crossed the threshold, Max and Leo began their usual investigation of my toes and ankles. The whole business seemed far more serious than usual, though. Instead of wagging and yipping, they were quiet, and their tails hung low.

Julia didn't answer. She just turned and, leaning heavily on her walking stick, led the dogs and me into her living room.

Julia's apartment was a little fussy and a little grand, with its Victorian gold plush and mahogany furniture. It was here, safe within the confines of her home, that her hidden love of knickknacks, mostly featuring dachshunds, was revealed. They filled every surface that wasn't covered by books or her impressive collection of crystal balls of assorted sizes and colors.

Julia had set up her altar against the apartment's eastern wall. The candles were lit, and the scents of warm wax and incense filled the air. A blue velvet cloth with a silver pentacle had been laid down. Five crystal spheres were arranged on the points—a rose quartz, a tigereye, a jade, a smoky quartz and one that was pure, clear glass. Whatever Julia had been doing, it had involved some pretty serious magic. The remains of it crackled through the air and crawled up my arms.

But why was she working alone instead of gathering the coven?

"Did Wendy . . . what did she . . ." I stopped, because technically, what Wendy Forsythe wanted with Julia was none of my business.

Julia moved over to her coffee table. Three handwritten journals, the kind practicing witches call "books of shadow," had been spread out between the crystals and the china dachshunds. Julia stooped to close them. I saw her hand shake. That was the last straw.

"Julia, are you okay?"

"I am fine. There was no need for you to come."

"Um, yes. There kind of was," I told her. "And you are not fine. You need to sit down."

"I am perfectly capable of taking care of myself, thank you."

I ignored this. "Have you eaten anything this morning?"

Julia lifted her chin, but I didn't see any point in waiting for the answer. Instead, I marched into the kitchen with a determination that would have done Roger proud. A quick tour of the fridge and the cupboards revealed the makings of a turkey sandwich with tomato and cheese. I put that on a plate with a bunch of grapes and poured a big glass of orange juice to go with it. Leo scampered around my feet, supervising and yapping. Max stayed at Julia's side, but now his tail was wagging. Good. The dachshunds agreed with me.

"Here. Eat." I handed Julia the plate. *Maybe I should call Roger and get him over here.* She needed somebody to make a proper meal for her.

"Anna . . . ," began Julia wearily.

"No buts, young lady." I folded my arms and glowered at her in my best imitation of Kenisha on duty. "You eat or I'll call Grandma B.B. and tell her you're neglecting your health."

The threat worked. Julia ate half of her sandwich, accompanied by long swallows of orange juice. I settled myself onto the sofa. While Max stayed at Julia's side, Leo trotted over and plumped himself down at my feet, wagging and looking up at me, I think gratefully.

"So, what's the matter, Julia?" I asked her finally. "And please don't tell me 'nothing.'"

Julia sighed and set the sandwich plate aside.

"Max and Leo, and I . . . have been unable to find Ruby."

"We haven't been looking for that long," I tried.

Julia's mouth tightened up. "Forgive me, Anna, but if my familiars cannot find something, it is not because they are not trying hard enough. Something is preventing them."

"Alistair hasn't been able to find anything either."

"What?" she snapped.

"I've been trying to get Alistair to help find Ruby, but . . . he's been acting strange, Julia. He's been gone way more than usual, but I can't tell what he's doing or where he's going, or anything." I stopped because I was choking up. "You don't think . . . Ruby could be dead, do you?" It would explain why she hadn't come home and why there hadn't been a ransom demand yet.

Julia shook her head. "That would not keep Max and Leo from finding her. No. What you've said about Alistair confirms what I suspected. Ruby is being magically hidden."

Which didn't answer the question about whether she was still alive. I rubbed my hands together.

"Why would anyone bother to keep her hidden?" I asked slowly. "I mean, cat-napping for ransom makes sense, but there's been no call or note or anything. And if whoever has her wants the reward, Best Petz has already set up the hotline. They can call anytime. Other than that, what would be the point of holding her? I mean, it's not like a cat is going to be able to say who killed Ramona. Right?"

Julia leveled a long, steady look at me. I felt my shoulders and my eyebrows bunch up.

"Seriously?"

Julia sighed. "No, probably not. However, those of us with familiars may be able to . . . glean some information from the presence of an intelligent animal. Something you are surely aware of by now."

"Um . . ."

"Anna," said Julia sternly. "This habit of yours of trying to pick and choose what you are comfortable believing in is a luxury you can no longer afford."

Was that what I was doing? Maybe. It was certainly close enough to make me want to change the subject.

"It also may be, of course, that there is something about Ruby, whatever her condition or location, that would offer a clue to the identity of Ramona's murderer." Julia frowned again. Max pawed at her skirt. She lifted him into her lap and petted his back restlessly, her gaze distant and troubled. Leo trotted over and plumped himself down at her feet, wagging his tail until his entire doggy bottom shook. Julia sighed with exaggerated patience and picked him up to settle on her lap beside his brother.

"There is magic in this," she said to me. Well, to us, really. "There is magic around Ramona's death and there is magic around Ruby's disappearance. It has no clear shape, no intention I can put a name or face to." She reached up, as if trying to wipe something out of her eyes. "As difficult as it is for me to admit it, I cannot make the pieces fit into any kind of coherent whole."

"Kenisha said almost the same thing."

Julia's focus snapped back to the apartment and to me. "Did she? What else has she said?"

"That she's worried about you, Julia, and so am I."

Instead of answering, Julia got to her feet. She crossed

the room to one of the bookshelves, Max and Leo trotting dutifully behind. She picked up another of her crystals—a smoke gray quartz sphere about the size of one of baby Melissa's fists—and carried it to her altar. She set it down in the exact center of the pentacle and stared at the arrangement for a long time.

When she turned to face me again, Julia's gaze was calm and clear. "Anna, if you will permit it, it is possible to use the craft to render you some assistance in your inquiries."

"Ummm . . . what kind of assistance?"

"It would be a form of attraction . . . a kind of summoning. Those with the answers you seek will be drawn to you, or you to them."

"You can do that?"

"I can, but only with your permission. It would not be permanent," she said. "The influence will only last a handful of days."

I hesitated. I trusted Julia absolutely, but this still felt like jumping off the deep end. At the same time, I was the one who'd lain awake all night wishing there was some way to sort this mess out before my friends got hurt. And here it was. But something in me just plain did not like the sound of it. I was seeing Kenisha's face in my mind and hearing her lectures about mixing magic and law enforcement.

On the other hand, this sounded like something that would require a serious ritual. That meant we'd need to summon the coven. Hope bobbed up inside me. With the others to help, maybe, just maybe, we could get Julia to open up about what she was feeling and what she was doing.

"Okay," I said. "I'm in."

❧ 25 ❧

🐾 MY AGREEMENT SEEMED to hang in the air between us for a very long time.

"So mote it be," murmured Julia finally. She also let out
a long breath. She'd been afraid I'd say no. That idea left me
unexpectedly uncomfortable.

"I'll need your wand, please, Anna."

I frowned. "But . . . wait . . . don't we . . . I mean . . .
shouldn't we get the others?" I'd had it drilled into me that
any serious ritual work should be done using the buddy
system. Someone had to be on watch, to help keep the space
clear of harmful influences, or in case the spell went wrong,
or the practitioner needed help staying calm and focused.

"There is no need to trouble them," said Julia. "This is
perfectly within the realm of my capabilities. Your wand,
please."

Of course I had it with me. I'd had no idea what I'd be
facing when I left the house this morning, so I'd decided I
should be prepared. I just wished I didn't feel so reluctant
to hand it across to her.

Julia thanked me as she took the wand, and she set it

down on her altar, next to the gray quartz sphere. She lifted her walking stick and laid it lengthwise across the edge of the altar.

Trust Julia to have something a little grander than the usual witch's wand for her spell work.

Max and Leo settled themselves down, one on either side of the altar, heads up, tails still.

Julia raised her arms so that her hands were palm down over the pentacle and the crystals. She closed her eyes.

The air around us settled into stillness. The candle flames did not so much as flicker, and their white smoke rose in straight lines.

My fingers prickled, and my palms, and my wrists.

Julia's hands hovered over the central crystal—the one that was clear glass—and then drifted to the rose quartz sphere and then to the tigereye, then to my wand and back to the center. I swear I felt the walls shift. The world around us was coming to life, or maybe just realizing how much life it had.

Something heavy draped over me, like an invisible blanket. The hairs on the back of my neck stood up straight, and my heart banged out of control like I had tried to run a four-minute mile. The sensation, the magic, settled against my skin and slowly dissolved into me.

"So mote it be," murmured Julia. "So mote it be."

"Yip!" agreed Max.

"Yap!" added Leo.

And just like that, the atmosphere lifted and my heart slowed down. The room was just like a normal room again, and the magic, because that's what had been weighing us all down, evaporated.

Julia took a brass candle snuffer off the nearest shelf and used it to extinguish the candles. Only when that was done did she turn to face me.

"I believe I'll have the rest of that sandwich now, Anna," she said. "You should probably eat something as well."

I wasn't going to argue. My insides were a riot, as if my body couldn't make up its mind whether to be frightened or elated. I helped Julia back to her chair and handed her the plate with the uneaten half sandwich on it. I made myself my own turkey and cheese and carried it to the living room. I stared at it. I was hungry—starving, in fact—but at the same time I was a little afraid to try to eat, because my stomach wouldn't stop doing flip-flops.

"Umm . . . so what do we do now?" I asked instead. "I mean, do I go home and wait for the phone to ring?"

Julia smiled at me, just a little. "Unfortunately, it will not be that easy. You will need to continue with what you have been doing—asking questions, seeking solutions. Going about your daily life. Only now circumstances . . . you could call it luck . . . will be more likely to be in your favor."

I looked down at my sandwich, and my stomach turned over again. I was familiar with summonings. Dorothy Hawthorne had done something similar to bring to me to Portsmouth in the first place. But if I was honest with myself, I hadn't liked the idea much then, and I didn't like it much now either.

"I don't believe I told you, Anna, but before you arrived just now, I had a call from Rachael Forsythe." Julia started picking the grapes off their stems but was setting them down on the plate instead of eating them.

"Rachael? She's Ramona's daughter?"

"Yes. She's been away finishing up her veterinary degree, but she arrived home this morning."

Julia added another grape to her line. Both Max and Leo flopped down on their doggy tummies and watched, curious to know how it would all end. "Rachael wanted to be sure I knew that Ramona's funeral will be held tomorrow. Did you want to be there?"

"Yes, I did. I do." I finally managed to pick up my sandwich and take a bite. It tasted fabulous, and now I was having to try not to wolf the whole thing. Magic seemed to have one universal side effect. No matter which side of the spell you were on, it left you hungry. "That is, if it won't upset Wendy," I added carefully. "She didn't sound happy when she left."

"Wendy seldom sounds happy," said Julia. "Especially when she cannot get her own way."

I wanted to ask what she meant by that, but her expression did not invite extra questions.

"Do you want me to let Val know about the funeral?" I asked instead.

"If you would." Julia got to her feet. "Now, I really should get myself back downstairs. I have left Gabrielle to carry the day long enough."

I swallowed my last bit of sandwich and got up too. I also stashed my wand back in my purse. If I was handling it a little more gingerly than usual, I suppose that wasn't too surprising.

Julia laid her hand briefly on my shoulder. "Continue to ask your questions, Anna. Continue to use your gifts, all of them. The answers *will* come to us."

Julia's eyes sparkled. It seemed to me that magic she had worked had restored her strength to her. Even the dachshunds looked happier. So why was a cold shiver running right up my spine? And why was I wondering even a little bit if there was something my friend and mentor hadn't told me?

"I'll try," I told her. It was the only truly honest answer I had.

"And you will call me if anything significant occurs?"

"Right away," I said, and I hoped she didn't notice I was hurrying just a little as I pulled on my coat and hat and paused to give Max's and Leo's ears a farewell ruffle. I suddenly felt like I wanted some space, so I could settle down and think. I was moving into new magical territory here. Julia usually advised extreme caution with my training, but this time she was the one behind me and pushing hard.

But only because it's really important, I told myself. *Only because I agreed. I could have said no, but I was trying to be clever.* Guilt and worry surged inside me.

Julia touched my arm. "You know that I agree with Kenisha," she said. "The true craft should not interfere with law enforcement. And we are *not* interfering. We are unraveling the thread of magic that binds this wrong, so that

Kenisha and the police will be able to do their job. That is what I promised, and this is how we will fulfill that promise."

I made myself stop fussing with my purse and my gloves and my hat and meet Julia's gaze. We stood there like that for a long time, until I decided I believed her.

At least, I decided that I wanted to.

I WALKED DOWN the stairs and out onto the square and took a deep breath of bitter November air.

So, what do I do now? I mean, it was one thing for Julia to say I should just go about my business. How had she put it? Ask my questions and use my gifts. It was another to actually try to do that. Especially when I was standing here feeling something that I could only label as witch's remorse.

I put my hand over my purse as if I thought I'd be able to feel my wand through the thickness of my winter glove. I kept waiting for the tug of a kind of invisible string, or maybe a voice in the back of my head, saying, *Hey, Britton! This way!*

Of course nothing happened.

I sighed. Okay. One thing I knew for certain. Whatever else I was supposed to be doing, I had a job waiting on me. I would go home and hole up in my studio for a while. I could stay quiet and work on my coloring book until I got a little more comfortable with what had just happened. Maybe Alistair had found Ruby by now. Maybe I'd get an answer from Val when I called again. Or maybe I could go over and talk to her and maybe find out what Kristen had been saying to Pam Abernathy.

I turned right and plowed straight into a lawyer.

❧ 26 ❧

🐾 "MS. BRITTON!" CRIED Enoch Gravesend as he caught my elbow. "A thousand apologies! My mind was unforgivably distracted. Are you quite all right?"

"I'm fine, really." I laughed. "Are your baked goods okay?"

"Ah!" Enoch smiled fondly at the bakery bag he clutched in one black-gloved hand. "You have caught me indulging in one of my many vices. French crullers."

Enoch Gravesend, Esq., is not just any lawyer, or even just a fellow member of the over-the-top-old-family-name club that so many of us New Englanders belong to. He was a fully fledged Character. Yes, the capital *C* there is on purpose. Enoch deserves it. But his flamboyance was built on a world of experience. That and the fact that his family had been in New Hampshire long enough that they'd been on visiting terms with this mouthy young upstart named Daniel Webster. That sort of thing meant a lot in these parts.

Enoch was a big, broad, white-haired man who tended to dress like he'd just stepped out of a courtroom drama from a hundred years ago. Today he wore solid black, from his boots to his creased trousers to his overcoat with its velour collar turned up against the wind to his bowler hat. To tell you the truth, he looked like he was on his way to audition for the role of a banker in *Mary Poppins*.

I remembered the spell Julia had laid on me. My mouth went a little dry and I tried not to think about it too much.

"Actually, Enoch, I was hoping to talk to you, if you've got time?"

Enoch glanced up at the clock in the North Church tower. "We are both in luck. I can give you an entire twenty minutes of my undivided attention. If you will be so good as to walk to my offices so we can get out of this truly foul weather?"

Of course I agreed, and I fell into step beside him. I also tried to ignore the feeling of being watched that was creeping into the back of my head.

ENOCH'S OFFICES TOOK up half of a Federal-style house in the historic district. The furniture, the paneling and the shelves filled with law books were dark, polished wood. Everything conveyed an air of steadiness and patient solidity. Enoch took my coat and hat and hung them on the bentwood rack by the door. He also pulled out a chair for me before settling himself behind his desk.

"Recognizing that doughnuts are more traditionally associated with law enforcement than the precincts of the courts, can I tempt you to a cruller?" He held out the bag to me. I smelled sugar and vanilla. I folded my hands across my purse.

"No, thanks," I told him. "I just ate." Twice, actually.

"Very well, then." Enoch set the bag aside. "What can I do for you today, Ms. Britton?" Enoch spread both hands, indicating that he, his office and his library were entirely at my service.

Cheryl Bell's voice as she talked to Lieutenant Blanchard rang through the back of my mind. "I need to find out about the Attitude Cat lawsuit," I said. If Cheryl Bell really could profit from Ruby's disappearance, then I needed to know how and why. Cheryl wasn't a witch, but it was possible she was getting some magical help. There was a lot of that going around just now.

Enoch steepled his fingers at me. There was also a certain amount of looking down his nose. "What specifically do you want to know?"

"Whether or not there'd be any reason for somebody . . . involved in the suit . . . on either side . . . to have Ruby be . . . well . . . not around anymore."

Enoch arched his bushy white eyebrows. "Do you mean would it give them an advantage in court?"

"Something like that, yeah," I said. "Or maybe if there's no cat, there's no reason to fight about her?"

He smiled, and I got the distinct feeling it was at my naïveté. "When it comes to the motivations behind the particular suit filed by Mrs. Bell, the ownership of the cat in question is fairly symbolic. The actual item value here is the intellectual property, the invented character of Attitude Cat, if you will. Ms. Summers and Ms. Abernathy were fairly intelligent and careful about how they approached matters. No matter who has possession of the living cat, Ms. Summers would continue to own all the character and branding rights."

At this point, Enoch launched into a long speech about trademarks and intellectual property and incorporation. I tried to keep from nodding off or reaching for a cruller. I did absorb enough of it all to realize that what Enoch was telling me was that the Attitude Cat brand, and the money and the cottage industry built up around it, wasn't about the real cat. It was about the *idea* of the cat.

Enoch paused for breath, and I saw my moment. "So, Cheryl Bell isn't really trying to get hold of Ruby. She's just after a payment from the Attitude Cat bank account?" I asked.

"Exactly," he said. "Large retail corporations such as Best Petz are notoriously skittish about controversy. If she can cast doubt on the wholesome nature of Attitude Cat, she can damage the brand's earning potential for all concerned."

"In other words, if Cheryl can drag Kristen through the mud, that mud might start sticking to the idea of Attitude Cat, and people decide they don't like the brand quite so much, and everybody stops making so much money." Including Kristen. Including Abernathy & Walsh.

Enoch watched me without blinking. "Of course, I would not ever comment on an ongoing lawsuit, even one that was not mine. I can say, however, it is not unheard-of for people to file nuisance suits in the hope that they will be paid to go away quietly."

"What if it does go to trial?" I asked. "What are Cheryl's chances?"

"That, at the moment, is an open question. We here in New Hampshire are a fairly staid group. Despite the occasional flirtation with flamboyance," he added with a reasonable attempt at modesty. "We do not like drama or interference, especially from outsiders. Our judges are no different. Mrs. Bell's attorneys have been fairly aggressive in their approach and have wrangled a number of court orders and filed all sorts of motions. Mrs. Bell herself has been public and indiscriminate in her accusations. The media"—he pointed toward the window—"is lapping it up, but the judge on the case is believed to take a dimmer view. Like some other honorable members of the bench, she is less than amused at all this trouble over a house cat."

"That doesn't sound exactly impartial."

He smiled. "No. I'm afraid it doesn't. We don't often admit this, Ms. Britton, but in court, matters frequently come down to which side can tell the best story, and when judges are mulling over that story, they can take into account behavior outside the court, whether they are supposed to or not. If I were a betting man, I'd put Mrs. Bell's chance of claiming ownership of the feline in question at roughly three to one against. That is if"—he held up his index finger to cut off my comment—"Ms. Summers, or Best Petz, continues to choose not to settle."

Well. That certainly sounded like enough motive for Cheryl to take drastic measures to keep from having to go to trial. But would those measures really include making Ruby vanish? How could that possibly help her case?

Whatever was showing on my face, Enoch clearly didn't like it.

"I suppose, Ms. Britton, that it's too late to advise you to stay away from what appears to be a colossal mess?"

"Sorry."

He waved his hand. "I suggest you keep my number on speed dial."

Unfortunately, that felt like a really good idea. "Thanks, Enoch."

"At your service, Ms. Britton," he answered. We both stood, we shook hands and I put on my coat and pulled my hat down over my ears, and, because I was standing in a lawyer's office, I thought of something else. I'd been wondering if Ramona's death had really had anything to do with Ruby's disappearance, or if maybe we were all being distracted by the glamour of Attitude Cat.

Here was a chance to find out.

"Enoch?" I turned around. Enoch was busy flipping through the papers in an open manila folder.

"Yes, Ms. Britton?" he said, but he did not take his attention away from the papers.

"Have you heard any rumors about Ramona Forsythe being in any kind of trouble before she died?" I paused.

Enoch closed the manila folder before he spoke. "That, Ms. Britton, I'm afraid I cannot tell you," he said. "To mention whether Dr. Forsythe or anyone else in this case, like, say, Ms. Abernathy, was having financial difficulties would be a breach of client confidentiality."

I looked at my lawyer and my lawyer looked at me, and we both decided to pretend he had not just answered my question.

❧ 27 ❧

🐾 RAMONA FORSYTHE'S FUNERAL was packed to the rafters, or it would have been if we had been inside.

As it was, the service was held in Prescott Park. A white pavilion had been set up over the rows of folding chairs, with standing heaters all around. While it was brisk, it wasn't bitter. There wasn't any rain, and the sun even put in a brief showing. I suspected that some of the mourners might have helped ensure that particular bit of good luck. Ramona Forsythe might not have had a coven, but she had a lot of friends. According to what Julia and Val told me later, pretty much every practitioner of the true craft in three states was there.

The air practically crackled with suppressed power.

Of course it wasn't just witches who attended. The reason to hold the service outside was so that anyone who wanted to could bring their pets, and plenty of people had wanted to. There were dogs of all sizes and breeds. Cats crouched in carriers and on leashes. There were birds, on arms and gloved hands or in cages. I saw a chameleon in a small terrarium, a hamster in a plastic ball, and a pair of fish in a bowl. Even Alistair put in an appearance, a discreet one, crouched under my folding chair next to Max and Leo, who sat on the grass at Julia's feet wrapped in their doggy sweaters.

Then there were the colleagues from the veterinary community, and those who were just friends. Roger was there with Val and baby Melissa. Martine had not been able to come, but Sean McNally was there, along with his father, Sean Senior, aka Old Sean.

I sat with the other members of the guardian coven in a row toward the back. Faye and Shannon, Allie and Trish passed Kleenexes around. Val and Roger held hands. Even baby Melissa seemed to sense this was a serious occasion and remained quiet in her sling under her father's coat.

Kenisha was there too. She wore a black overcoat and flared black maxiskirt, which might have meant she was just there as a mourner or that she'd been asked to go lightly undercover to keep an eye on things. She certainly wasn't talking about which it was, or about anything else for that matter.

Julia sat ramrod straight, silent and dry-eyed, watching the Forsythe family, who sat in their own rows beside the lectern that had been put in place for the speakers.

I think I would have been able to spot Ramona's daughter, Rachael, among the family, even if Val hadn't pointed her out to me. She sat next to her formidable aunt Wendy looking very small and very young in her long charcoal gray coat and broad-brimmed hat. Her mind was clearly not on the people who stood at the lectern to offer their condolences or remembrances, though. Her gaze kept drifting from the speakers to the assembled mourners.

Who are you looking for? I wondered. *Is somebody missing?*

I made myself sit still and keep my eyes straight ahead. But that didn't stop me from running over all the faces I'd seen so far, and the ones I hadn't. Only one stood out, though.

"Is Kristen coming?" I murmured to Val.

"No," she answered as she leaned over to adjust the fold

of Roger's coat around little Melissa's shoulder. "She said she didn't want to cause problems."

"What kind of problems?"

But Val just shook her head.

The reception was held immediately after the service. People stood around the space heaters holding plates of food in gloved hands, or milled through the park with their pets to talk and share their memories of Ramona. The Forsythe family filtered through the crowd, shaking hands, saying thanks, offering comfort and being comforted. My coven sisters were pulled off in different directions to talk with friends and acquaintances. Me, I was approached by a tall, good-looking Irishman in a vintage black suit that really looked quite fetching on him.

"Hi, Anna." Sean bent down and gave me a peck on the cheek. He smelled of soap and the clean outdoors. "How are you doing?"

"I don't think I even know where to start." I looked up at his concerned eyes and tried not to imagine how very much I'd welcome a hug right now. If Val saw, I'd never hear the end of it.

He smiled. "You'll figure it out. I have confidence."

"Failing that, you have alcohol."

He chuckled. "One of the many advantages of dating a bartender."

Dating. Yes. Right. That was what we were doing, wasn't it? Except everything around me had been turned on its head, yet again, and I barely had time to handle my own life let alone explore any social possibilities. I should tell him I needed a break. I should tell him . . . Well, there were a lot of things I should tell him, but I couldn't make myself say any of them. The part of me that was not sensible, and didn't seem to understand that Sean would be better off if whatever it was between us never went any further, also seemed to be the part currently in charge of my vocal cords.

"Sean . . . ," I began.

He cocked his head toward me. His eyes were twinkling.

I swear, he could make that happen on command. It wasn't fair. "You're not standing me up, are you?"

Panic hit. "Did I forget something? Did we . . . ?"

"Easy, Anna." He laid his warm hand on my shoulder. How did he manage to have warm hands in this weather? "I was joking."

"Sorry," I mumbled. "I've just . . . it's been a crazy couple of days."

"I know," he said softly. He stuck both hands in his suit pockets. "I've been . . . I keep thinking I should call, and then I keep thinking I should give you space and . . ." He sighed. "What can I do to help?"

"Maybe you should help yourself and stay away." I'd meant to be firm. Someone around here should be strong and sensible about this. But the words came out as only a whisper.

"No," said Sean. "That is definitely not the answer. Would you like to use one of your lifelines?"

"You have no idea how much."

Sean scratched his chin and gave every appearance of considering this carefully. "Well, I hate to throw you into the arms of another man, but, you know, that looks like Frank Hawthorne over there."

I followed his gaze. "You mean the guy standing on the fringes casually taking notes? Yes. I do believe that is Frank."

"Go get 'em, tiger," he said. "And call me tonight?"

"Okay. I will," I said, but I seemed to be having trouble turning away. There was something I wanted to ask, but I had no idea how.

Sean grinned. "And just in case you were wondering, Anna, you are not going to scare me off."

"No," I answered. "I guess I'm not."

And he smiled and I smiled and his eyes twinkled, and I think, for just a minute there, my eyes might have twinkled back.

I PAUSED BY the buffet table for a plate of carrot sticks and miniquiches. This was mostly protective coloration. It allowed me to look semicasual as I strolled toward Frank Hawthorne, who stood at the edge of the gathering in a dark blue suit and overcoat I had no idea he owned.

He still had his notebook out and was still scribbling. I suspect he'd started when the service did and hadn't stopped since.

"Hi, Frank." I held out the plate of snacks.

He waved the end of his pencil at me in greeting but shook his head at my offered plate of carrots and quiche.

"Notes on the service?"

"Head count," he answered, without hesitation or any trace of shame. But that's Frank, an unabashed professional, even at a funeral.

"Anybody in particular missing?" I asked him, thinking about how Rachael Forsythe kept watching the crowd.

"Actually, there is," said Frank. "Cheryl Bell."

I could not believe I hadn't noticed that. But he was right.

"Well, she wouldn't exactly be welcome, would she?"

"She doesn't have to be welcome. There's a camera truck up the street. I can't believe she's missing the chance to be in front of it." He paused. "I don't suppose you saw Kristen Summers, did you?"

"She didn't come," I told him. "She said she didn't want to cause problems."

"Can I ask who told you that?"

I smiled. Frank shrugged and made a few more notes.

I took a deep breath. I hated using a funeral to ask awkward questions. It felt disrespectful, but I didn't know when I'd get another chance to bring this particular subject up with Frank. "Frank . . . have you heard anything about Ramona Forsythe having any kind of legal trouble?"

Frank's pencil went still. "Why do I get the feeling I could ask you that same question?"

I bit into a carrot stick. Frank frowned. "Anna, are you going to try to tell *me* you are protecting a source?"

"No, not really. But . . . I was talking to Enoch Gravesend yesterday, and something he said, or, rather, something he didn't say, got me wondering."

"Uh-huh." Frank scribbled down another note. "Well, there's certainly nothing on the surface. I've been looking. When I haven't been fielding phone calls about the cat." He grimaced. "I don't suppose you've heard anything about her, have you?"

I shook my head. Last night had been another long one, with Alistair not home, and his kibble bowl was full in the morning. I was starting to think Julia must be right. It had to be magic that was keeping Ruby so thoroughly hidden. I wondered again if she was even still alive.

"Did Enoch not say anything else helpful?" prompted Frank.

"Well . . . he didn't talk about Pam Abernathy."

Frank considered this. "Did he talk about Cheryl Bell?"

"Her he talked about. At least, he talked about the lawsuit."

"Hmm. Interesting." Frank made another note. "Thanks. I'll do some digging. See what turns up."

I wondered if Frank knew that Kristen was staying with Val. I wondered if he and Kristen had talked yet, with or without Pam there, and what they'd said.

I glanced over at the little knot my coven sisters had formed around Julia. Kenisha was not standing with the others. She was on her own, standing by the far edge of the pavilion, sipping something from a paper cup, and watching me and Frank.

I grimaced and turned away before Frank could see whom I was staring at. Too late. He made another note.

"Um . . . Frank . . . ," I began, but I was too slow.

"Sorry, Anna, gotta go work the crowd." He smiled. "But I will call you if I find anything, okay? Okay."

Before I could answer, Frank had slipped away into the gathering, stopping to talk with people here and there and to pet the dogs and admire the birds and the hamster. Frank was a people person; that was part of what made him such a good journalist. Everybody liked him, and they liked talking to him.

I sighed and tried not to feel guilty about us both.

So, Anna, what do you do now? I asked myself as I popped a now-cold miniquiche into my mouth. Myself had very few useful ideas. I didn't like the glances the Forsythes, particularly Wendy, were casting at my coven sisters. I didn't like how the coven was on one side of the pavilion, while Kenisha was alone on the other. I didn't like both Kristen and Cheryl not being there.

I didn't like the feeling I'd come here just to fish for gossip. I really didn't like the feeling that if I stayed, I was going to ask one question too many.

For once, I decided, I would listen to the better angels of my nature. I tossed my empty plate into the recycling bin. It was time for me to give my condolences to the family and go. No. Really. This time I meant it.

As usual, however, it turned out my better angels had shown up a little late.

"Excuse me, Anna Britton?"

I turned and found Rachael Forsythe standing right behind me.

❧ 28 ❧

🐾 "HELLO, RACHAEL. I'M very sorry for your loss."
It is, of course, the standard phrase, but I did mean it.

"Thank you."

Rachael Forsythe had her mother's round, open face and
her same brown hair, although she wore hers cut in a
pageboy.

"I'm sorry I didn't get the chance to know your mother
better," I went on, mostly to stave off any kind of awkward
silence, which would be very awkward indeed.

"You made an impression, though," said Rachael. "She
talked about you."

"She did?" I drew back, just a little.

Rachael shrugged. "We talk a lot. That is, we did.
We . . ." She shook her head, hard. "Sorry."

"Don't be. When my mother died, we were so busy for
a couple of weeks, with all the arrangements and the thank-
yous, it was like I could put what happened out of my mind,
but then I'd sit still for five minutes and it would hit me that
she was really gone."

"What did you do?"

"I cried. A lot. And I had my family, and my dad . . ." I stopped and bit my tongue. No one had talked about Rachael's father yet. There was usually a reason for that.

The corner of Rachael's mouth twitched. "Mom and Dad split up when I was in high school. He died bungee-jumping with his twenty-year-old third wife." She looked at my face. "Don't worry, no one knows what to say about that."

I felt myself smile, just a little. "Sometimes there's just nothing good to say."

"Like how right now there's no good way to ask what Mom said about you?" suggested Rachael.

Busted. Again. I really was going to have to do something about this complete lack of a poker face. "Yes, like that," I agreed.

Rachael's smile was sad but genuine. "Mom told me you were a member of Julia's coven." She nodded toward my mentor where she stood with a group of women and their dogs. "Which put you on the wrong side of some old family arguments. She said that you were Alistair's partner and Annabelle Blessingsound's granddaughter, and that you sometimes . . . you had a knack for finding things out."

She looked across the crowd, but the distance in her gaze told me she was seeing something much farther away. "My mother really was murdered, wasn't she?"

What should I say? What would be kinder? But there was no kind way to talk about a mother's death. The only question was whether I'd lie or tell the truth. And I was not going to lie.

"I think she was, yes," I said. "So do the police."

"Because of something to do with Ruby?" There were equal parts fear and hope mixed into that question, and something else as well: anger.

"Nobody's sure yet. But the police have their best people on this. Including Kenisha Freeman." I nodded to where Kenisha stood with Pete Simmons. Trish had come up to them both, and they were talking while she restlessly thumbed her phone. "She's a coven sister and she knows what she's doing."

"I'm sure she does." Rachael rubbed her gloved hands together, hard, like she was trying to get rid of something nasty. "Aunt Wendy says you've already been . . . well, Aunt Wendy calls it sticking your nose in."

Aunt Wendy right now was standing with a cluster of other Forsythe family members near the lectern and staring daggers at her niece and me.

Rachael grabbed my hand and held on.

"I just wanted to say, please keep going," she said. "Whatever happens, whatever Aunt Wendy says, promise me you won't give up. I want whoever did this found. I want them locked up. I want . . ."

Whatever Rachael wanted, she couldn't finish telling me. I looked into her eyes and saw the echo of a kind of pain and anger I remembered all too well. Even though I understood it, Rachael's intensity made me uneasy. "Rachael, can you answer a question?"

She glanced sharply over her shoulder, looking for her aunt Wendy, I was certain. Aunt Wendy was gesturing the Forsythes she was standing with toward the line of cars parked on the street.

"Anything," Rachael said.

"Did your mother own a computer?"

"Of course she did. In fact, I just helped her set up her new laptop when I was home on break. Why?"

"The police can't find it. Did your mom say anything about losing it? Or if it got stolen? Or . . . ?"

Rachael picked up on that hanging "or" right away. A light sparked in the back of her eyes, and she fished in her small black purse.

"Do you know, I'm going to have to clean out Mom's rooms, but I'm not . . . not ready yet. Maybe you can go in . . . and take a look for me?" She held out the keys.

The hairs on the back of my neck prickled, and I glanced around. There was Julia, and yes, she was watching me and Rachael. I thought about the spell of attraction she worked on me and for me, and my stomach turned over uncomfortably.

"I . . . um . . . Are you sure, Rachael?"

"Please," said Rachael softly. "It would really help. I need to know there's somebody who's on my side."

I heard what she was saying at the same time I looked into her eyes. There was something else there, beyond the grief and the anger: a cold determination that I recognized and understood. That didn't stop it from sending a cold thread of fear through me.

I told myself I was already up to my neck in this. I was already asking questions and digging dirt for Val and Kristen, and Kenisha and Julia, and myself. Adding one more person to that list wasn't going to make any real difference.

I closed my hand around the keys and nodded. I just couldn't turn away from someone else who had just lost her mother.

Rachael did not smile. Grim lines settled into place around her eyes, and for a moment, she looked a lot like her aunt Wendy, who just happened to be sailing right up to her side.

"Rachael, there you are." Wendy's smile was thin and small as she took her niece's arm. "I've been looking all over for you. It's time to leave for the cemetery, dear."

"Yes, of course," said Rachael, but her eyes did not leave mine. My fingers prickled. *It's the cold,* I told myself. *Really. Just the cold.*

Aunt Wendy's gaze flickered between us. "Could you go find Angela for me?" she asked Rachael.

Rachael blinked, and the prickling vanished. "Right. Yes. It was good talking to you, Anna. Be sure to bring Alistair by the clinic soon. I'm helping Jeannie and everybody out with the *special* patients, and I'll be glad to have a look at him."

This last remark came out of the blue, but I knew what it was. It was Rachael's way of providing cover for this conversation, and the next one—the one we were going to have after I'd searched her mother's apartment.

Whatever Rachael thought I might or might not find, she did not want Aunt Wendy to know I was looking.

Rachael nodded once, as if confirming my thought, and moved away into the crowd, leaving me to face the formidable, and quietly seething, Aunt Wendy.

At least I thought she was seething until I took a second look. Those were tears shining in her eyes.

"Now, Anna Britton." She faced me without any other greeting. "I don't know what you think you're up to, but you need to stay out of this. Whatever she said to you, you should realize that she is furious and she is not thinking straight."

I found myself wondering which "she" Wendy was talking about. Was it Rachael or Julia? I opened my mouth to ask, but Wendy had already turned away and stalked back to the cluster of her family who were gathering to go say their last farewells to the mourners.

Well. What now? I bit my lip and glanced toward my coven sisters where they were gathered around Julia, all of them talking together. Almost all of them. Kenisha was still on her own at the far edge of the gathering, sipping her drink and watching us. I was sure she'd seen me with Rachael and Aunt Wendy, and probably Frank as well.

I didn't like the fact that she was not over with the others. I really did not like the fact that I was standing here with Rachael's keys in my pocket.

But I realized all at once that those keys gave me a perfect way to square at least one of the particular circles that surrounded me.

I headed through the thinning crowd toward Kenisha.

"Hey, Britton," she said softly.

"Hi," I said back. "Not feeling much like socializing?" I nodded toward the others.

"Nope."

"Nothing new wrong?"

"Not yet. I just don't want to accidentally start something." I wished she wasn't looking at Julia right then.

"You know, if you're really worried about Julia, you could just talk to her."

"I know. It's going to have to happen, but . . ." She didn't finish that sentence, and she clearly did not like the fact that she couldn't finish it.

I decided now would be a good time to change the subject. "I was talking to Rachael Forsythe."

"I noticed."

"She's really upset."

"Noticed that too."

"She gave me the keys to her mother's apartment."

Kenisha's head snapped around. "She *what*?"

"She gave me the keys to her mother's apartment. She asked me if I would look for that missing laptop, because she's not ready to go in and face it yet." I paused and made sure I had her full attention.

"She asked you to go look in her mother's apartment?"

"Yes."

"And she gave you the keys? All on her own? Without any prompting?"

"Yep." I held the ring up for her to see.

"That's . . . unexpected." Kenisha did not like this turn of events, I could tell. But I couldn't tell exactly why.

"Do you think I shouldn't go?"

"That depends," said Kenisha slowly. "Do you think there's something there Rachael Forsythe really wants found?"

I lowered the keys. I also thought about the anger in Rachael's eyes. It was the kind of anger that could lead you to do something foolish.

"Yes," I said slowly. "I think it's possible."

"Then I think you should go," Kenisha told me. "And I think you should take me with you."

❧ 29 ❧

❧ THE FIRST THING I noticed when I pulled into the parking lot of the Riverview Condominiums was that all indications that the place had recently been a crime scene were gone. The second was that Kenisha, despite the fact that I knew she hadn't gone a mile over the posted speed limit, had somehow beaten me there.

This time there was no helpful neighbor to hold the door, so we used the keys to get inside. As we headed down the hallway, I dug my hand into my purse and curled my fingers around my wand.

"Anna?" Kenisha stopped in front of the door of 2B.

"Yes?" I blinked at her. The air was still heavy with anger and greed. I should have taken the time to get my shields in place before we came in, but I'd been too distracted with my thoughts about the funeral and how Rachael had been so ready to let me into her mother's apartment. And then there was Aunt Wendy, who was guarding her family as if there might be something to hide. And what about Kristen, who hadn't been there? And Pam Abernathy? And Cheryl Bell?

"Yo, Anna!"

"Sorry." I blinked again.

"Your Vibe still there?"

I nodded. "I'm going to need a second."

Kenisha gestured for me to give her the key. I did. I also brought my wand out of my purse and closed my eyes, deepening my focus and raising my defenses.

When my shields were as solid as I could make them, I nodded to Kenisha. She knocked and waited. When there was no answer, she opened the door.

Ramona's apartment was a lot warmer this time. Someone at some point had closed the doors, but not the curtains. Watery gray daylight filled the silent living room. The angry, greedy Vibe beat against my shields, demanding to be noticed.

"Now, Anna, if you find anything that you think maybe could be related to the case, including that laptop, you look but you do not touch. You call me, okay?"

"Okay," I agreed.

"Okay," she said again.

There was nothing else to say after that. I turned my back on Kenisha and faced the empty apartment.

Where do I even start?

Evidently, I started by wandering and trying to get to know something about the woman I'd met only once before she died.

Ramona Forsythe had liked to read. That much was easy to see. Her bookcases were full of an eclectic combination of paperbacks and fat textbooks about veterinary medicine. And she'd loved her family. One whole wall of the dining room was covered with family photos. There were faded shots from the seventies and eighties of little girls in shorts and pigtails. I assumed these were Ramona and her sisters. I thought I recognized Wendy's broad forehead and stubborn chin on one of those smiling kids. There were photos of people who might be parents and grandparents, and great big groups of young adults who must be cousins. I recognized some of them from the funeral.

Most of the photos, though, were of Ramona and Rachael. Ramona had displayed the whole timeline of her daughter's life, from a wrinkled, red infant at the hospital to a confused-looking baby in a party hat to a grinning young woman in her graduation robes waving her diploma over her head.

There was an antique sideboard under the photos. I pulled open the drawers and found napkins and tablecloths, as well as some clothes and books that could have been birthday or Christmas presents tucked away for later.

I closed that drawer and tried to ignore the fact that my eyes were stinging. My shields wavered, and I had to take several deep breaths and realign my focus. As I did, I felt something familiar, and unwelcome. It was the slow prickling in my fingertips that signaled the presence of magic, and somewhere close.

"Kenisha?"

"Yeah?"

"Is something going on?"

"Depends what you mean." Kenisha did not turn to look at me. She kept her gaze on the balcony and the rocky strip of riverbank below. "Something definitely happened, though. Julia was right. Somebody did break Ramona's wards."

"You can tell."

"Yes. Kind of. I can feel the echo, but it's not steady, like it would be if they were lifted naturally."

"So Julia was right. A witch broke the wards to be able to get in here."

"A witch broke them." Kenisha turned away from the doors. She frowned at the apartment, and I hoped she never looked at me like that. "The question is *when* did they do it? Before or after Ramona was killed?"

"I thought wards were, like, you know, a fence, or an alarm system, to keep people out. Why would anyone bother to shatter the wards after she was killed?"

"To make it look like a witch was involved in the murder when maybe she wasn't."

She was talking about a magical frame-up. I really did not want to think about that.

"I'm going to have a look upstairs."

"Good idea."

RAMONA'S BEDROOM UP in the half loft was as tidy as the rest of her apartment. Her socks were all in the wicker hamper and her laundry basket was empty. She had more photos of friends and family on the walls, along with lots and lots of pictures of animals. Probably patients. I was pretty sure I recognized several of the dogs, and that chameleon.

The space was lightly furnished with a low futon-framed bed, a plain dresser and not much else, except for a beautiful Shaker-style cedar chest pushed up against the footboard. I glanced over my shoulder on reflex before I lifted the lid. Inside, carefully stowed, were the regalia for Ramona's altar—candles and candleholders, a plain white cloth, a heavy brass cup, a crystal box filled with salt. I knelt down, lifted out each item and set them all on the carpet, until the chest was empty.

"Well, sh . . . sugar," I murmured. Because now I could see that Ramona's computer wasn't the only thing that was missing.

"Kenisha?" I called without getting up from in front of the chest.

"Yeah?"

"Have you spotted Ramona's book of shadows anywhere?"

Most witches kept a book of shadows. Each one was different, but they were all some kind of record of the magical workings and philosophy of the witch who wrote them. Julia had been working from hers when I visited her. I had inherited a small bookshelf full of my predecessor Dorothy Hawthorne's writings, and of course, the first thing Julia had me do when I took my apprenticeship vows was to start my own.

"Not yet." Kenisha came trotting up the stairs. "Why?"

I gestured toward the contents of the chest laid out on the carpet. Kenisha puffed out her cheeks.

"Okay, something else to look for."

"But—"

"We are not going to jump to conclusions," she told me. "Not everybody is out of the broom closet. Ramona was at least being discreet; otherwise, she would have had the altar permanently set up somewhere. Some people hide their books."

"Yeah, but . . ."

"But what?"

"Well, the books I inherited from Dorothy . . . they aren't just a record of spells and ceremonies. They're diaries. What if Ramona kept the same kind of books? What if . . ."

"There was something in there the murderer didn't want known?" said Kenisha slowly. "So they took the books when they took the laptop?"

"Which would mean they'd have to know they were important."

We looked at each other. A witch's book of shadows was deeply private. If you shared it at all, it was only with those closest to you. Ramona didn't have a witch's coven, but she did have a witch's family.

I thought about Aunt Wendy, with her hard eyes and her determination to keep me from doing exactly what I was doing. I thought about how haggard Julia had looked after Wendy left her apartment, and how she hadn't said a word about what she and Wendy had talked about, but she had laid this spell on me to help me find the answers we needed.

"Julia suspects Wendy Forsythe." The words popped out, but as soon as I said them, I knew it was true. "They had an argument the other day."

"I was afraid of this," muttered Kenisha. "All the coven history is getting in the way and people are going to screw everything up trying to keep their own secrets." She added a few other things under her breath. "All right, keep looking up here. I'll go downstairs and check the bookcases."

I put the regalia back in the chest and closed the lid. There weren't a lot of other places to look, or a lot else to find. No convenient diary or appointment book waited under the neatly folded scrubs and jeans in Ramona's dresser. No laptop computer or tablet or cell phone or notebook had been shoved behind the sensible shoes in the built-in closet or left on the top shelf with the sweaters.

I was clenching my teeth down around my frustration when I heard a new sound.

"Merow?"

Alistair! I jumped and stared around frantically.

"Merp?"

This time I realized where the sound was coming from. I got down on my knees and peered under the bed. In addition to the usual dust bunnies and unidentified lumps and bumps, Alistair crouched under Ramona's bed.

"Merow?" He blinked his big blue eyes at me.

I glanced toward the stairs. I couldn't see Kenisha. I thought I heard rummaging sounds coming from the other room.

"*Now* you show up?" I whispered furiously to my cat. "Where have you *been*?"

Alistair lifted his chin in a gesture that would have done Attitude Cat proud.

"Okay, okay." I sighed. "But what . . ."

Alistair reached out one paw and batted at a piece of . . . something. It was round and about the size of my little fingernail. On reflex, I reached for it, but at the last minute I curled my fingers up.

"Okay," I whispered again. Alistair blinked at me one more time and vanished.

"Uhhh . . . Kenisha?" I called. "I think I found something."

"*Don't touch it!*" she shouted. This time, she grabbed her maxiskirt hem and sprinted up the stairs. I scooted sideways and held up both virtuously empty hands.

Kenisha pulled a little flashlight out of her purse. Of course she had a flashlight. Kenisha was always prepared.

She knelt, and shone the light on the dust bunnies, cardboard boxes and two gleaming silver baubles.

I recognized them, or at least their type. I'd seen something like them very recently.

Kenisha took her cell phone out of her jacket pocket and lay down so her cheek was pressed against the carpet to snap a picture.

"We do not touch them," she told me when she straightened up. "I'm calling Pete right now and we're getting him down here because . . ."

"Find something interesting?"

We both cringed and we both turned to look over the loft's half wall. Pete Simmons stood in the doorway, hands deep in his coat pockets, furry hat pushed back on his head.

And Lieutenant Blanchard stood right beside him.

❧ 30 ❧

❧ "WELL, HELLO, MS. Britton. How nice to see you again."

Lieutenant Michael Blanchard (Jr.) had a thousand-watt smile and Hollywood-white teeth. When he flashed them all, like he was doing now, he bore a really uncanny resemblance to a great white shark who'd just spotted his next meal.

"Hello, Lieutenant Blanchard," I said. "Hi, Pete."

"Hi, Anna," Pete said, but he wasn't looking at me. His attention was all on Kenisha.

"Rachael Forsythe gave Anna the keys to her mother's apartment," Kenisha told them both. "She asked if Anna would have a look for the missing laptop."

"So we heard," said the lieutenant.

Heard? From whom? Aunt Wendy? Rachael? Julia? Then I looked at Lieutenant Blanchard again.

Cheryl Bell? Not possible. She wasn't even there.

I looked at Pete, but Pete just gave me the tiniest shake of his head. He didn't know where the tip had come from either.

"I am going to assume you two won't mind if we come

on up and see what you've found," said Blanchard with his usual sneering, exaggerated courtesy.

Of course we didn't mind. In fact, we both backed away as far as the loft would let us while the lieutenant snapped on a pair of disposable blue gloves and reached under the bed.

"Sir . . . ," began Kenisha.

"And that delicate sound is Officer Freeman belatedly wondering if we have permission to conduct a new search, now that the apartment is no longer a crime scene," said Blanchard. Blanchard close-up wasn't any more pleasant than Blanchard at a distance. I could feel a smug kind of self-satisfied greed rolling off him, an uncomfortable echo of the Vibe that thrummed on the other side of my shields.

"We do," said Pete.

I bit my lip. Hard. Somebody had called the cops. One glance at Kenisha's stony face told me I wasn't just being paranoid. Somebody had called the cops, and they might have done it because they knew we were here.

That meant it had to be Wendy.

Or Rachael.

When Lieutenant Blanchard straightened up, he cupped the Aldina beads in his gloved palm. Pete already had an evidence baggie out and ready.

"Those weren't there when we searched the first time," said Kenisha.

"We'll need to check the photos," said Pete. "But I'm pretty sure she's right, sir."

"Any idea what these even are?" Blanchard asked Pete.

"They're beads off an Aldina bracelet," I said, before I remembered I was not anybody the lieutenant wanted to hear from.

Blanchard gave me a look that said he doubted I could have identified my own grandmother from a photo lineup. Pete, however, just held the bag up to the light.

"Looks like it," he agreed. "My wife has been angling for one for Christmas. I had to order it back in June. Those things are impossible to find."

"How nice," Blanchard drawled. "And I don't suppose

any of you happen to know if any of our suspects wear . . . what the hell did you call it?"

"Aldina," supplied Pete. I clamped my mouth shut, but not fast enough. "Any ideas, Ms. Britton?"

If it was just Pete, I wouldn't have had any problem saying what I knew, but standing next to Lieutenant Blanchard made me want to exercise my right to remain silent. Remembering that conversation I'd overheard at the Harbor's Rest did not make spilling the beans any easier.

Blanchard sighed with exaggerated patience. "Maybe *you* know, Freeman?"

Kenisha was staring at me. I could all but feel her trying to work out why I was hesitating.

"There is someone involved who wears this type of jewelry," she said slowly, giving me time.

"And that mysterious person is . . . ?" Blanchard made a hurry-up gesture.

"Cheryl Bell," she said.

Blanchard did not blink. He did not turn a hair, let alone flush or blanch or any of those other things people are supposed to do when they're shocked.

What he did do was glance at his watch.

"I've got a press briefing. I'm taking charge of this evidence. Freeman, I want a report on my desk before noon. I don't suppose any of you has done something really useful, like found that damn cat?"

We shook our heads, me included. Blanchard said one short word that would probably not be repeated at that press conference.

"You." He turned to me. "I do not want to see any of you or your Nosey Parkers around here anymore. This investigation is ongoing and you are not messing it up. Do I make myself clear?"

"Yes, sir," I said, because Blanchard was looming, and his looming always encouraged that kind of response.

"Smart woman." He flashed his shark's grin at me. "Simmons, Freeman, you make sure she gets out of here without causing any trouble."

"Yes, Lieutenant," Pete answered. "Will do. For sure."

Blanchard shot him one of the dirtiest looks I have ever seen and marched out the door. As soon as it swung shut, Pete gave a long whistle. He also started jingling the keys in his pocket in a slow, thoughtful rhythm.

"Okay, Kenisha," Pete said. "Just us here now. Is there anything else I should know?"

"No," she said immediately. "Rachael Forsythe asked Anna to look for her mom's computer. Anna asked me to come along in case she found it, or anything else important."

"And you two found those beads or bangles or whatever you call 'em?"

"Affirmative," said Kenisha. I nodded in firm and enthusiastic agreement.

Pete jingled his keys a few more times.

"Um . . . ," I began. Both cops turned, eyebrows raised in surprisingly identical expressions. "Did Kenisha have a chance to tell you that Blanchard and Cheryl Bell know each other?"

"Yes, as a matter of fact, she did mention it," said Pete. "And that makes this whole scenario very interesting, don't you think?"

Kenisha watched Pete without answering. A whole world of calculations flashed behind her amber eyes. I felt that jolt of near-telepathic communication pass between the two cops again.

And I knew what the problem was.

"The beads . . . they really weren't there when the crime scene people went over the place before, were they?"

"Maybe the guys missed them." Pete didn't take his eyes of Kenisha. "Like I said, we'll have to check the crime scene photos. Staff's been stretched thin lately, and that new guy couldn't find his own . . . elbow with a map and a flashlight."

"But maybe they were planted," I said.

Kenisha's jaw tightened, and all at once I felt like I'd just sworn in church.

"But maybe they were planted," agreed Pete, slowly and thoughtfully. "And we found them, just like we were sup-

posed to." The detective turned his permanently droopy eyes
toward me. "Anna, I don't suppose Rachael Forsythe said
anything about who else has access to this apartment?"

"Dr. Forsythe has a lot of family in the area," Kenisha
reminded him. "Several of them have keys to the place. Tony
got the full list when he was doing the interviews."

"But who . . . ?" I stammered.

"Who has access to the apartment and might want to
frame Mrs. Bell?" Pete calmly finished my question for me.

I tried to picture the formidable Aunt Wendy shoving
two little beads under a bed with the crumbs and dust bunnies, and failed. But there was somebody else who would
be very glad to have Cheryl Bell not be around and making
trouble anymore.

Kristen Summers.

As soon as I thought that, though, I realized it was impossible. Kristen didn't have a key to Ramona's apartment. And
even if she did, she'd been in Minnesota when Ramona died.

Hadn't she?

I turned toward Kenisha, trying to find some innocuous
way to frame the question. But Kenisha wasn't paying attention to me anymore. She'd had an idea. I could practically
see the lightbulb shining over her head.

"Do we know for sure whoever is trying to set up the
frame used a key?" she asked Pete.

As soon as she said it, both cops headed for separate
doors: Pete took the front, and Kenisha took the balcony. I
stood in the middle, forgotten.

It took maybe ten seconds for Kenisha to call, "Pete!"

"You got something?"

He was across the room before she could answer. I'd had
no idea that Pete could move that fast. They were bent over
the latch for the balcony doors. By carefully and quietly
stepping forward and kind of sideways I could see over
Pete's shoulders that the shiny silver finish on the doors'
aluminum trim was scratched and nicked.

"Was that there before?" asked Pete.

"It wasn't on the report," said Kenisha.

Pete sucked in a breath. "We really need to go back and check the crime scene photos."

Kenisha's jaw hardened. "Right. Okay. I'll get back and write that report and then . . ." Both of them were now looking at me. "Right," she said again.

"I'll meet you there," said Pete. "Ms. Britton? Do you need a lift anywhere?"

"No, thanks, I've got my Jeep."

"Then you have a good day."

I was being dismissed. I looked past Pete to Kenisha, but she shook her head. There was nothing more to say here, at least not while I was listening. So I pulled on my parka and my knitted cap and headed back out into the cold.

The first thing I did when I climbed into my Jeep was to start the engine warming up. The second thing I did was close my eyes and breathe deeply and release the shields I'd been holding clenched so tightly around me.

The third thing I did was pull my phone out of my purse and hit Val's number.

"Anna," said Val as soon as she answered. "What's going on?"

"Is Kristen there?"

"Yes. Anna—"

"I have to talk to both of you."

"Sure, of course." I did not bring up her recent stretch of not answering my phone calls after that "of course." "Are you on your way?" she asked.

"Yes, and Val . . . it's not good."

Val was silent. Then she said, "Okay."

We said good-bye, and I hung up. I also stared out the windshield for a long time, thinking about all the things we knew that Kenisha could not tell Pete.

The wards on Ramona's apartment had been broken. Ruby was being hidden beyond the reach of Julia's magic and her familiars. Ramona's books of shadow were missing, along with her laptop.

Kenisha said that she felt like she was looking at two different puzzles. But maybe it was just one big puzzle, with two different perpetrators, only one of whom needed to be a witch.

It had to be a witch who broke those wards. You also didn't need to be a witch to steal the books of shadow once the wards were broken. You just needed a witch to tell you they might be important.

And you didn't need magic to jimmy the door on a second-floor balcony or plant a couple of Aldina beads under a bed. All you needed was some skill, some motivation and some time.

Skill you might have picked up during a juvenile career as a thief and pickpocket. Motivation that might include trying to stay out of jail, and time could be chosen. Like during a funeral that would conveniently occupy pretty much everybody who might otherwise turn up at this empty apartment.

That witch might be an old friend who knew about your record and who could be convinced to help you to try to keep herself, and her family, out of trouble.

Julia said I didn't have the luxury of disbelief. But I couldn't possibly believe any of this about Kristen or Rachael Forsythe. I was so sure they were good people. I'd liked them both instantly.

I especially couldn't believe it was about Valerie.

Could I?

Unfortunately, it wasn't my belief that mattered. It was Kenisha's—and Pete's.

And Lieutenant Blanchard's.

❧ 31 ❧

🐾 I'D JUST PUT the Jeep in reverse when my phone rang.

I didn't plan on answering, but I did check the number. I couldn't help it. When I saw it was Frank calling, I cursed the man for his lousy timing. I also put the Jeep back in neutral and hit the Accept button.

"What's up?" I asked after we'd said hello.

"Do you remember that little chat we had at Ramona's funeral?" Of course I did. It had only been a couple of hours before. A couple of very long hours I would give anything to have back now.

"Turns out you were right."

That was fast. But then, this was Frank. He could chase down a news lead faster than Alistair would chase rabbits out of the garden.

"What was I right about?"

"A lot. Where are you?"

I looked up at the Riverside Condominiums sign and decided Frank probably didn't need to know all the details. "Heading for downtown," I told him. "Should I meet you somewhere?"

"I'm at home. Can you come here?"

"Give me five minutes."

"You got 'em."

We hung up.

Okay, okay. I took a deep breath. *This is good. This is answers.*

I'd hear what Frank had to say. Then I'd go talk with Val and Kris. Just to get a couple of things clarified. Not because there was any reason at all to suspect either of them of anything. Kris was angry at Cheryl for all the trouble she'd caused, but Kris was not a witch. She couldn't break Ramona's wards or hide Ruby out of reach of Julia's magic or her familiars. She wouldn't have known the books of shadow were important.

Valerie, of course, was a witch. But Val was sensible and levelheaded. She was loyal too, but there were limits to how far she'd go to help a friend. She would not have used her magic to let Kris into Ramona's apartment or to help hide Ruby. She would not have gone in herself to steal the books of shadow on the off chance there was something in there that could hurt her or her family. That was not at all what she'd been doing during that time when she wasn't answering her phone. No way. Uh-uh. Not possible.

But once I'd cleared things up with them, then I'd be able to go talk with Rachael Forsythe. I mean, Rachael had given me, a virtual stranger, the keys to her mother's apartment. She knew me and my complicated, and active, Portsmouth history. And she was Ramona's daughter, and, of course, she was a witch. Just like her aunt Wendy, who was already very suspicious of Julia and of me. And who just might have called the cops on the off chance we were up to no good.

I was absolutely, entirely positive that when I talked to Rachael, I'd discover that it must have been Aunt Wendy who broke the wards. She must have thought there was something in Ramona's books that might embarrass the family and she took them for safekeeping. That was all. It was nothing to do with Ramona's murder. Not really.

And once I'd gotten all *that* cleared up, I could tell

Kenisha everything I'd learned. Kenisha could find a way to point Pete in the right direction, which would prove to be away from my friends and away from Ramona's grieving daughter.

And that would be the end of it. We would know exactly what part magic played in this mystery, and Julia could stop worrying about it and Kenisha could stop worrying about it, and we could all get back to our normal lives.

This was good. I had a plan. I liked plans. Now that I had one, I would start feeling better. Any second now.

FRANK LIVED IN the historic district. His house had been standing when Portsmouth's men marched away to fight in the Civil War, and it had been divided into apartments around the time Portsmouth's women went to work in the factories and fisheries during World War II.

His apartment was at the top of the house, toward the back, and he yanked the door open before I had a chance to knock more than twice.

"Come on in."

Frank had swapped out the blue suit he'd worn to the funeral for plaid flannel and jeans, what my brother Ted called "lumberjack chic." His wavy black hair was sticking out in all directions, which meant he'd been running his hand through it. Which meant he'd been thinking. A lot.

"Am I going to need to sit down for this?" I asked as I followed him into the living room. Frank's apartment was the direct opposite of Ramona's. Ramona's had been neat, spare and very modern. Frank's was battered and crowded. The furniture was all secondhand and the primary decoration was floor-to-ceiling bookshelves. Every flat surface was covered with stacks of manila folders, magazines and newspapers and yet more books. A pinholed map of Portsmouth was taped to the wall over his desk.

It was also hotter than blazes.

"Sorry about the heat." Frank gestured me toward his sagging couch and made a detour into the kitchen to wrestle the double-hung window open. "Can't get the radiator to turn off. Super's supposed to be on it."

"Ah, the joys of a vintage apartment." I moved a stack of dog-eared science fiction paperbacks from the 1940s and sat down.

"Tell me about it." Frank dropped into a worn leather armchair and started rearranging the piles of folders and books that covered the coffee table. A midnight black cat emerged from under the chair and jumped up to help.

"Off, cat." Frank lifted her away and set her back on the floor. Affronted, she meowed and leapt onto the back of the chair so easily, you'd be forgiven if you didn't realize she was missing one back leg.

The cat's full name and rank was Colonel Nick Kitty. When she first showed up, Frank had mistakenly thought she was a male and decided to name her after the comic book character Nick Fury.

"What did you find?" I asked. Colonel Kitty was interested as well. She stepped delicately onto Frank's shoulders and draped herself around the back of his neck.

"You're probably not going to like it," Frank told me as he flipped open one of the folders. Colonel Kitty batted at his ear.

"I already don't like it, but I need to know, whatever it is."

"Ramona Forsythe was in trouble." Frank leaned back, which annoyed Kitty. She mewed and flowed down from his shoulders to his lap. "Money trouble."

"But . . . ," I stammered. "Ramona was a veterinarian. They make really good money."

"They do, unless they spend more than half their time on pro bono work, which Ramona did." Frank scratched Colonel Kitty's ears absently, and I suddenly, strongly wished Alistair was here. I really needed something besides the couch arm to hold on to.

"How'd you find this out?" I asked.

"Ramona used an accounting firm, and I happen to know somebody there who owed me a favor." I suspected a certain editing of events but didn't say anything. I mean, it wasn't as if I could throw stones.

"According to my source, Dr. Forsythe was juggling six or eight different credit cards," Frank went on. "Some had truly awful interest rates. That was on top of regular payments on assorted loans."

"What kind?"

"Student loans, mostly. Hers and her daughter's."

I pictured Rachael standing in front of me, afraid and angry and trying to find some kind of reassurance that Ramona's death was a murder. She'd also wanted to be sure it was connected to Ruby and not anything else.

Before I'd walked into Frank's apartment, I'd been worried that Rachael had wanted us to find those planted Aldina beads. Now I wondered if Rachael was so anxious to hear Ramona had been murdered because the alternative was that her mother might have done something terrible because she couldn't pay the bills.

I bit my lip. Frank, of course, noticed.

"Anna . . . where were you when I called?"

I shook my head. "It's not important."

"And I'm supposed to believe that?"

I looked at him. It wasn't that I didn't trust Frank, but he was who he was. He couldn't stop putting together a story any more than I could see a blank piece of paper without doodling on it.

So, I did the obvious thing. I changed the subject.

"Frank, what have you found out about Cheryl Bell?" Because there was no way on this good green earth that Frank had neglected to check out Mrs. Bell's background.

Frank grimaced. "She lived in Portsmouth until she was nineteen. She was friends with Kristen and Valerie. She left suddenly and vanished off the map for about five years. When she resurfaced, it was in New York City as the wife of a prominent plastic surgeon named Milton Bell. After that, she became a feature of the society pages and gossip columns until her fast and acrimonious divorce."

I blinked. "There are still society pages?"

"Who'd've thought, right?" Frank shrugged. "Anyway, the high life can be addictive—and expensive. I don't know exactly what the divorce settlement was, but Cheryl strikes me as the kind of person who would run through it pretty quick. Now, call me cynical, but since Mrs. Bell hasn't yet remarried, she might need to find herself another source of income."

"Don't be a Neanderthal," I said primly. "Why couldn't she get a job?"

"Cheryl does not seem to be the working kind. Her idea of establishing an income stream tends to involve taking money away from other people."

Unfortunately, I couldn't disagree. It fit too well with everything I'd seen of her so far.

"Is there a reason she needs the money? I mean some reason other than that she's got expensive tastes?"

"I've been trying to find that out. Unfortunately, Mrs. Bell is not eager to talk about herself, or her past, except for how she was a good friend and doting cat owner who has been so cruelly wronged."

While the humans were engaged in this boring and unimportant conversation, Colonel Kitty bounded into the kitchen.

"Meow!" she announced, skidding to a halt by the dining table.

"Merow," answered a second voice.

"Alistair?" I twisted around in my seat.

A huge chestnut tree spread its branches outside Frank's kitchen window. In summer, the green light made the place feel like a gigantic tree house. Now that it was November, the branches created stark black lines on the other side of the glass. One of those branches was currently occupied by my big, gray, highly truant cat.

"Merow!" Without waiting for an invitation, Alistair jumped through the open window and landed on the kitchen table.

"What the heck?" said Frank. "What's he doing here?"

"I don't know," I said. "He's been . . . mostly gone since

Ramona died." Because he was Dorothy's nephew, Frank had pretty much grown up with Alistair, and he knew as much about his magic as anybody who wasn't an actual witch.

Alistair jumped off the table and down onto the floor beside Colonel Kitty, extending his neck to nuzzle her. Kitty sniffed.

"Merow!" The black cat retreated, back hunched, hackles raised. Alistair scrunched backward. Colonel Kitty made a rude noise.

"What's that about?" I demanded. "I thought you guys were friends."

In fact, before he'd taken up with Miss Boots over at the Harbor's Rest, Alistair had been . . . seeing . . . Colonel Kitty. Now, though, Kitty pawed the air in front of him and Alistair streaked into the living room like greased lightning and darted under the sofa.

I stared. Several ideas dropped like bricks into the middle of my mind, and they made a very big splash.

"Anna?" Frank waved his hand in front of my face. "You still in there?"

"Uh . . . yeah," I croaked. "Yeah. Still here. Sorry." I shook myself, trying to clear the ripples in my mind. I could sort out the cats later.

"Frank . . ." I paused and started again. "Frank, there's something I have to tell you, but you have to promise me you won't write about it."

Frank looked at me for a long time, and nodded.

I swallowed. Kenisha was going to kill me. Pete was going to kill me. I was going to have to leave town. I was doing it anyway, because I needed help, and I didn't know where else to go. "Before I came here, I was in Ramona's apartment. We found some bangles under her bed that could have come from one of Cheryl Bell's bracelets."

Frank's fingers twitched.

"The thing is, Kenisha and Pete are both certain that they weren't there when the apartment was searched."

"So the question is how did they get there? And when?"

I nodded. "Lieutenant Blanchard took charge of them."

Frank looked at me and I looked back. "You are not suggesting that Lieutenant Blanchard might make that evidence . . . go away, because Cheryl Bell is an old friend of his?"

"I think I don't know. Kenisha and Pete seemed to think there were signs of a break-in, but . . . but there's no way to tell when it happened, at least until they check the crime scene photos. Kenisha thought maybe things had changed since the night of the murder, but she wasn't sure."

Frank blew out a long, hard sigh. Colonel Kitty jumped up on his lap and head butted his chin. He grumbled a little but started scratching her ears. Alistair looked out from under the sofa, forlorn and innocent. Colonel Kitty did not look back.

Alistair sagged, slunk backward and vanished.

"There's something else," said Frank. "It's just a rumor so far, and it might turn out to be nothing, but . . ."

Which was when my phone rang. Again.

"Oh, of *course*." I dug the noisy appliance out of my purse. I meant to shut the ringer off, except the screen said it was Val calling.

"One sec," I told Frank instead and hit the Accept button.

Val didn't even wait for me to say hello. "Anna, where are you?" she shouted in my ear. "Are you at the police station?"

"What? No! Why? What's happened?"

I heard Val gulp air. "Pete and Lieutenant Blanchard just left. Anna . . . they've arrested Kristen for Ramona's murder."

❧ 32 ❧

🐾 "KRISTEN!" I SHOUTED. "Why Kristen?"

"Kristen?" echoed Frank, sitting up very straight. Colonel Kitty merowed sharply, stuck her nose in the air and stalked away into the bedroom. "What's happened to Kristen?"

"I'm trying to find out!" I told him.

"Where are you?" demanded Val. "Who are you talking to?" At the same time, Frank got to his feet and came to stand right behind me.

"Who is that?"

"Frank. Val," I said to them both. "What . . ."

"What are you . . ."

"Why is she . . ."

I yanked the phone away from my ear.

"Be quiet, both of you!" I requested.

Frank shut his mouth. From the silence on the other end, I assumed Val had done the same.

Now that we were all behaving reasonably, I was able to put the phone to my ear again.

"Valerie," I said. "Let me be clear about what you said before *Frank* interrupted. Are you telling me that Kristen Summers has been arrested for the murder of Ramona Forsythe?"

Frank's eyebrows shot up. He opened his mouth. I glowered at him. For once it worked, and he sank back into his chair.

"Yes," Val answered. "Are you telling me Frank is sitting there with his notebook open?"

"Yes," I said. Okay, the notebook was not literally open, but that was beside the point.

"Why did they arrest Kristen?" demanded Frank. "She wasn't even in town when Ramona died!"

"Say again, Val?" I pinched my free ear shut.

"I don't know why they did it!" wailed Val. "I couldn't get Pete to tell me anything, and Kenisha isn't answering her phone."

That meant Val had no idea that someone might have tried to frame Cheryl, or that Kristen might have had the time to set up the frame, because like Cheryl, Kristen hadn't been at the funeral. Unfortunately, this was the kind of thing that might lead even reasonable cops like Pete and Kenisha to believe that Kristen might be the one who'd committed the murder.

Frank was flipping notebook pages again. Colonel Kitty jumped back up on the chair arm and meowed and head butted his elbow.

"But . . . Kristen was in Minnesota when Ramona got killed," I said to Val, and Frank, and myself.

Frank yanked a folder open and skimmed the pages inside. And promptly turned as white as a sheet.

"Well, that's the problem," Val said softly. "Kristen didn't go to Minnesota."

"What?"

Frank was looking right at me now, and his color was not getting any better. In fact, he'd turned a little green around the gills.

"Kristen didn't go to Minnesota. She got on the plane, and she was supposed to catch a connecting flight at O'Hare. But she didn't. She took a train to New York instead."

"New York!" I repeated.

Frank held up his notes to me, tracing a big circle with his finger around a set of words. I grabbed the paper out of his hand and squinted at it. There were a bunch of lines of his usual illegible shorthand, but one question had been written very clearly:

PROBLEMS WITH NEW BEST PETZ ULTRA-PREMIUM LINE??

"This is what I was trying to tell you." He stabbed his finger at the paper.

"Oh, you are *kidding* me!"

"It's just a rumor. I haven't been able to confirm anything."

"Anna?" said Val. "Anna, what's going on?"

"I don't know," I was talking to her, but I was looking at Frank. Frank wasn't returning the favor. He'd pulled his phone out of his pocket and thumbed the screen as he headed into the bedroom and closed the door.

"Anna!" Val demanded.

"Sorry. Sorry," I said. "Why did Kristen go to New York?" *And why did she lie about it? And even if that's where she went, do we know for sure she wasn't in town when the murder happened?* I closed my eyes briefly. That was a question I really wished I hadn't thought to ask myself. "Was her mother ever in the hospital at all?"

"Yes," said Val in a whisper. "But her sister got there last week."

"So what was Kristen doing?"

"She wouldn't tell me!" Misery and anger bunched up together in Val's voice. "And I would have told you before, but she asked me not to talk to you about any of it. I'm sorry, Anna," she added. "I really am. I needed to help Kristen. She was so upset and . . . I never thought . . . I can't believe . . ."

"Okay, okay," I said, trying to calm us both down. It wasn't easy, though. This was very bad. Not only had Kristen lied about where she was going and what she was doing, but she'd tried to conceal her movements, which meant she thought someone would be watching her. Which all meant that as soon as somebody *was* watching her, she looked guilty of . . . something.

"We don't know anything for sure," I said. "Is Kris okay? What's going on with her now?"

"I don't know. They wouldn't let me go with her. I called her lawyer, though."

"That's good. Where are you?"

"Home," she told me.

"Is Roger there?"

She said he was.

"Okay. I'll be there as soon as I can . . . but there's something I've got to do first."

"What?"

I looked across the apartment to the kitchen table, where Colonel Kitty was still on patrol. Should I tell Valerie about Frank's rumor? I bit my lip. No, I decided. Not yet. Not until I knew more about it.

"I think I know how to find Ruby," I told her instead.

"Oh, Anna, do you? That could solve everything!"

Well, not everything, but it would help a whole lot. "It's a maybe," I told her. "A very big maybe."

"Is there anything I can do?"

"No. But I swear, I'll be there as soon as I've found out anything."

"Please hurry."

"I will."

We said good-bye and I slid my phone back into my purse. I also curled my fingers around my wand and stood there. I wasn't praying exactly, or even wishing. I was just hoping as hard as I could.

It didn't work.

"I'm sorry, Anna," said Frank behind me. "It's not looking good."

Tell me something I don't know. I gathered my shredded nerve and faced him. "What did you find out?"

"Just what Val was telling you. Kristen Summers has been arrested. She lied, she concealed her movements and she had a motive."

"What motive could Kristen possibly have for killing Ramona?"

Frank laced his fingers into his hair like he was trying to keep the top of his head from flying off. "There's a possibility, but, like I said, it's just a rumor. I can't confirm anything yet."

"You say that one more time, Frank Hawthorne . . ."

"Okay! Okay!" He took a deep breath. "Ramona Forsythe was on retainer to provide veterinary services to Abernathy & Walsh, right?"

"Right,"

"Which means she went along on a lot of the Best Petz photo shoots and publicity events to help make sure everything was up to ASPCA standards where Ruby and her stand-ins were concerned."

"And . . . ?"

"And . . . she might have heard this rumor, and I stress—"

"Frank!"

"—that Best Petz new ultrapremium line of cat food was actually just a cheap brand from China that they snuck in under the radar and slapped a new label on."

My jaw dropped, something Frank tactfully ignored.

"You see the problem?" he asked. "If this is true, and word gets out, it could sink Attitude Cat."

Because Best Petz's reputation would take a massive hit. Companies went under for stuff like this. And if Best Petz went under, they would take Attitude Cat down with them.

❧ 33 ❦

🐾 "I DON'T BELIEVE it," I said, trying not to hear how my voice shook. "Kristen Summers is not a murderer!" Unfortunately, I knew I had to convince myself as much as Frank, and it kept getting harder.

"She also wasn't in Minnesota, or at the funeral," said Frank quietly.

"Cheryl wasn't at the funeral either!"

"Because she was doing an interview with *Cat Channel News*. That's one of the things I was confirming in the other room."

I felt myself staring again. "There's a cat channel?"

"Twelve forty-seven on your cable listings. All cats all the time. They sponsored a film festival last year," he added.

Right. Okay. I pressed my hand against my mouth and tried to pull my thoughts back to what was actually important. I thought about those beads I'd found under Ramona's bed. I thought about how Kenisha and Pete thought they might have been put there deliberately. And even though I really didn't want to, I thought about how if I wanted to frame somebody for murder and cat-napping, Cheryl was the person I'd pick.

I thought about how Enoch had said that when it came to the money being made by Attitude Cat, it wasn't the actual cat that was important. It was the idea of the cat. Here, for the first time, was something that might jeopardize the idea of Attitude Cat. Nobody loved a spokesfeline that was caught advertising cheap junk under false pretenses.

"Okay, okay." I pinched the bridge of my nose and tried to keep breathing. "I've got to get over to Val's." And there were a few things that needed to happen before I could. They were not, however, the kinds of things I was ready to tell Frank about. "I'm assuming you're about to call in every favor you've got trying to confirm this Best Petz rumor?"

"You better believe it."

"Will you tell me if you find out anything?"

"If you'll tell me if you find out anything."

"Okay," I agreed, and I was fairly sure I meant it.

Frank decided to believe me, and I gathered up my stuff and ran down the creaking stairs out to my Jeep.

We had to find out what had happened to Ruby. We had to know if she really was stolen or if she just ran away. Because we had to know if Ramona's murder really had anything to do with Attitude Cat and Best Petz or if it was caused by a separate set of troubles. Either way, Ruby was the key.

And I knew who was holding that key. I just had to hope I could finally get him to talk.

Or at least meow.

AS SOON AS I got home, I yanked off my coat and hat, went into the kitchen and pulled a fresh can of tuna out of the cupboard and popped the top. The smell reminded me I hadn't eaten since that miniquiche at Ramona's funeral. *Later,* I told my grumbling stomach.

I dumped the tuna into the bowl on the floor and waited. Nothing happened.

"Alistair?" I said to the empty kitchen.

Still nothing. I muttered a few things nobody else needed to know about as I dug in my purse and pulled out my wand.

I was never going to hear the end of this, but we were way past nibbles, treats, and begging.

"Come on, cat." I lifted my wand and tightened my focus, or at the very least my frustration. "There's tuna and I'm calling you and you *have* to be here."

This was not an invocation Julia would have approved of, but it did work.

"Merow."

Between one eyeblink and the next, Alistair was sitting beside the food bowl, lapping up tuna juice and for once not looking very happy about it.

That made two of us. I folded my arms at him like I actually thought that was going to make a difference.

"All right, Alistair, what is going on?"

Alistair scooted around so his back was toward me.

"Uh-uh, not this time, mister." I put down my wand and picked up my cat so I could look him in the baby blues. He meowed, outraged. I ignored this. "You've been acting strange all week, and you've barely been home and you've got Colonel Kitty ticked off, and Miss Boots is missing you. That can mean only one thing."

His tail twitched and he wriggled in my hands, but I held on.

"Who's the new girlfriend, Alistair? Where is she? You *have* to show me."

I put him down on the counter.

Alistair immediately jumped down to the floor and slunk around the counter. Not popped, not galumphed. Slunk. Head and tail down.

"Alistair?"

"Merow." Now I could see he was headed for the basement. That was when I noticed the cellar door was open. "Merow."

"What the . . . ?" I didn't even remember leaving the door open. I shivered, and this time it was from something other than a draft.

"Merow," said Alistair again, and started picking his way carefully down the stairs.

Well, what's a witch supposed to do? I sucked in a breath, snapped on the light in the stairwell and followed my cat.

The cottage basement was old and unfinished. There was an ancient but adequate washer and dryer down here and some splintery wooden shelves from back when it was an active root cellar. I suspected I was letting down generations of thrifty New Hampshire housewives by not canning tons of peaches and blueberry jam. But since I could barely scramble an egg, attempting to preserve things had never seemed like a good idea. The oil heater was down here too—a feature of small-town life I was still getting the hang of—along with some old furniture left behind when I rented the place. There were some cardboard boxes I was accumulating as well, because when you've got a basement, boxes just happen to you.

I pulled the chain on the old lightbulb and blinked as it flashed on. Alistair was sitting in a corner near one of the sets of shelves. In the shadows, something moved. Something big.

I admit it, I took a step back.

"Merow," said my cat, and I swear he rolled his eyes.

Before I could answer this bit of feline disdain, a sleek black-and-white shape emerged from the darkness.

"Oh, you have got to be kidding me!"

But there she was. Ruby. Attitude Cat. She was in my basement, crouched next to my familiar, who immediately began nuzzling her ear.

Julia had been right. Ruby was being hidden by a witch. Or at least, by my warded house, and my stupid, fickle, magical tomcat.

"Meep?" Ruby pressed against his side and Alistair licked the top of her head.

"Merp," agreed Alistair.

Of course Alistair had found Ruby. He might even have started looking before I had to ask. After all, he'd been the one who pointed out she was missing the night we first found Ramona. Once he did find her, of course he couldn't just *leave* her. He had to bring her someplace safe. Maybe she'd been in danger; maybe he was just being chivalrous. Maybe she'd followed him, because after all Ruby was a cat too, and therefore one of nature's escape artists. Or maybe it was because Alistair was a big gray softie, not to mention willing and able to fall in love with every single lady cat who crossed his path.

"And you acted all surprised when Colonel Kitty got mad," I muttered.

Alistair, Mr. Innocent, shrugged, a long ripple of silver fur, and nuzzled Ruby again.

I stared at them both as the full magnitude of the mess I was in sank through my skin and down to my bones.

My gallant, magical, too-clever-for-my-own-good cat had ruined any chance of us finding out anything about the murderer, or even the cat-napper. If Alistair had led me to wherever Ruby was being kept, I might just possibly have gotten Pete or Kenisha to believe that I'd gone out looking for Alistair and found Ruby instead. Or we could have said Julia's dachshunds had gotten away from her (never mind that this had not happened in living memory) and wriggled their way into wherever Ruby was hidden.

But now . . . now we had no chance of even figuring out whether Ruby had actually been kidnapped or if she'd just run away.

My knees buckled until I was sitting on the basement stairs.

Maybe I could get the coven together and work a spell. I was a seer. I could try to see through this. We'd done something like it before. But what good would it do? Even if I could conjure a vision, I couldn't take it to court, or even to Kenisha.

"What about DNA?" I whispered to myself and the cats. "Wherever she was, there'd be DNA evidence, cat hairs and . . . stuff . . . and . . ."

And so what? So what if somewhere in Portsmouth there was a room full of cat hair and shredded furniture? Even if

I could find it, how could I convince anyone I'd just happened across the right place and recognized it for what it was? To get that to be at all plausible, not only would I have to find the hypothetical cat room; I'd have to put Ruby back in it.

And then I'd have to figure out how I'd explain why she'd been in my basement, just in case anybody thought to check for similar evidence down here. And given the way the rest of this mess had gone, somebody just might.

This was why Kenisha didn't mix magic and law enforcement. This, right here. Our best and biggest chance at helping Kristen, and Rachael, and Julia and Kenisha, was gone, because my familiar had taken matters into his own hands. Um, paws.

Alistair finally seemed to twig to the fact that I was really upset. He came over and circled around my ankles.

"Merow?" he rubbed his hard, brave, chivalrous, frustrating head against my shins. "Merow?"

I lifted my own head and took several deep breaths to try to steady myself. It almost worked.

"Meep?" added Ruby.

She was shivering again. That jolted me into action. There comes a time when, no matter how smart or magical your familiar is, you have to remember who is the human around here.

"Okay. Come on, Ruby, there's a good girl." I scooped Ruby up and she snuggled into my arms as I carried her up the stairs to the warmer (and cleaner) kitchen. I got out a second bowl and poured in some kibble, which, unlike some cats, Ruby did not turn up her nose at. Alistair stood sentry beside her while she ate.

I sank onto the bench in the breakfast nook and watched them both.

I am not a cat expert. Alistair is the first animal I've ever owned personally, and he's not exactly your typical domestic shorthair. But I had lived with my roommates' pets, and my family ran through the usual series of furry mammals of various sizes and species when I was growing up. Ruby was hungry, and she was cold, but she looked pretty clean and she was eating, so I guessed she must be basically all right.

I was grateful for it. There was no way I was going to be able to get her properly checked out by Rachael, or anybody else, until I figured out how to let people know she was here and okay, preferably without getting myself arrested.

❧ 34 ❧

🐾 "ANNA! OH, THANK goodness!"

Val wrapped me in a hard hug the second I stepped in through the B and B's kitchen door. "I was worried something happened!"

"Something did." I looked over her shoulder at the uncharacteristically dim and silent kitchen. "Uh, where's Roger?"

"He took Melissa over to his sister's so I could . . . concentrate on other things." Val twisted her hands. She looked pale, and her curly hair hung loose around her shoulders. She kept pushing it back out of her face. "What happened? Please, please, tell me it's something good!" she demanded.

"I don't know yet," I admitted. "But I found Ruby."

"What?!" Val grabbed me by both shoulders. "Anna, that's fantastic! Is she all right? Where is she?"

"My house."

"*What?* How is that even possible?"

"Alistair," I reminded her. "I'm guessing he found her soon after she went missing. I don't know how, but he got her to the cottage, and he's been hiding her there ever since."

Valerie put out a hand to steady herself against the counter. "But . . . why?"

"I don't know."

"But he's your familiar."

"He's still a cat. Clear communication is not exactly his thing."

Val frowned but conceded the point. She knew Alistair almost as well as I did. "But she is okay?"

"As far as I can tell."

"Oh, jeez, Anna," she breathed. "You've got to tell somebody, right away. If you're caught with Ruby, they'll arrest you for holding stolen goods."

Or for grand theft or burglary or murder, or all of the above.

"How am I going to explain her, though?" I spread my hands, like I thought I might be able to grab hold of an answer. "Nobody is going to believe Attitude Cat just happened to pick my basement to hide in."

Val closed her mouth so sharply, her teeth clicked. "This is why Kenisha always tells us to keep magic out of law enforcement."

"Yeah. I was thinking the same thing."

Val perched herself on one of the tall stools next to the brushed-steel counters. She nudged another toward me with her slippered toe, and I climbed up.

"At least we can let Julia know that there wasn't a witch involved with Ramona's death," Valerie said, clearly trying to find a silver lining somewhere on the cloud hanging over us. "The only reason she couldn't find Ruby was the wards on your house."

"Um . . ."

"I don't like that 'um,' Anna," Val told me sternly. "Or that look."

I didn't either, but there was no backing away from it. "Val, there's something I have to say. I don't want to, but I have to."

"What is it?"

"When we were in Ramona's apartment, we found her tools for the craft, but . . ."

"But what?"

"Her books of shadow are missing." I said. Val looked at me blankly. "If somebody was looking for information or evidence, or if they wanted to cover something up, they would think to take a laptop, but . . ."

"But only another witch would know that there might be something useful in the books of shadow," Val finished for me.

"And then there's the fact that her wards were broken."

"Oh," she said. "Right. I'd forgotten about the wards."

I looked at her and I didn't say anything else. I couldn't. Slowly, Val realized what was keeping me so quiet.

"Anna, you cannot possibly think *I* broke Ramona's wards or stole her books."

"I don't. Really. I just . . ."

"You just found out I used to be a thief and thought maybe I'd started up again!"

"No! I promise, Val, I never!" Except I did and I had, and I really kind of hated myself for it. "I just . . . You and Kristen are friends. You watched each other's backs for a long time. I know what that means to you . . ."

Even in the kitchen's half-light I could see how Val's freckled face flushed pink. "I don't *believe* we are actually talking about this!"

Neither did I. "Val, Kenisha knows the books are missing."

She froze. "Kenisha was there? I mean, I saw you two talking at the funeral . . ."

"I couldn't go to Ramona's apartment alone."

"Wait, wait." Val shook her head, like she was trying to knock something loose. "What were you even doing in Ramona's apartment? You can't tell me it was Kenisha's idea."

"It wasn't. It was Rachael Forsythe's. She said she wanted my help to find out what happened to her mother and gave me the keys to Ramona's condo so I could go try to find the laptop."

"Just like that?" Val's forehead wrinkled.

"Well, almost. I'm not sure." Val glared at me. That look was going to give Melissa trouble when she got older. I mean, I was a grown woman, and I still couldn't stop myself from confessing about my conversation with Julia and the spell she'd worked for me and on me.

Val pressed her hand over her mouth. "Oh, no. No. This is not good. There's no telling where a spell like that will take you."

"I'm starting to get that idea," I said. "I shouldn't have agreed to it."

"You shouldn't have agreed! Julia should never have suggested it! What was she thinking!"

"Probably the same thing I was. That we need to figure this out fast, before anybody else gets hurt."

"Except that's not what's happened."

"No," I agreed. "It really isn't. And it gets worse." I told her about the beads and the scrapes on the doors.

When I finished, it was Val's turn to be quiet and visibly miserable.

"Val." I took her by the shoulder. "I swear, I don't think you had anything to do with this, and I know Kenisha's not going to say anything . . ."

"Until she has to," Valerie breathed. "And she's going to have to because Kris has been lying about what she's doing, and because she's been staying here, and because everybody knows that she . . . that we . . ." She stopped. "What am I going to do, Anna?"

"We," I said firmly, "are going to finish what we've started and figure this out. And just in case that takes a little while, we are going to call Enoch Gravesend. He is going to go with us to talk to Kenisha on the record, before she or anybody else has come to talk to you."

"You're right. You're right. I just . . . You get so used to keeping some things a secret, it's hard to know when it's time to tell the truth."

"I know, Val, believe me."

Val was about to say something in answer, but she never

got the chance. A staccato banging cut through the quiet kitchen. We both jumped.

"What the heck . . . ?" Val hopped off the stool while I was still dealing with the fact that my heart was racing out of control, and I was telling myself it was just someone knocking—no, pounding like there was no tomorrow—on the front door.

"A guest forgot a key?" I asked.

"We're closed," she reminded me, snapping on the lights in the foyer.

The B and B's grand front door was flanked by two stained-glass sidelights. A face pressed up against the gold pane. When the face's owner saw us, she started pounding again, like her life depended on it.

Maybe it did, because that person on the porch was Pam Abernathy.

❧ 35 ❧

❧ "MRS. MCDERMOTT?" PAM all but fell into the foyer when Valerie opened the door. "I'm . . ."

"Pam Abernathy," Val said. "I recognize you. Please come in."

Except Pam already was in. Clearly, she'd rushed to get here. Her hat was crooked and her coat misbuttoned. She clutched one glove in her hand. I guessed she'd taken it off so she could pound the door louder.

"Thank you." Pam gasped and straightened up, visibly trying to get her breath and composure back. "I . . ." But she stopped, and she looked at me, probably noticing for the first time that I was even there. "Oh. Ah. Hello, um, Anna." She did not wait for an answer before turning back to Valerie. "I'm so sorry to intrude like this, Mrs. McDermott, but I need your help."

"It's Valerie," said Val. "And how can I help?"

"You have to tell me what Kris has been saying to you." Ah.

"You know about the arrest, then?" said Val slowly.

"I know it happened, but I can't get in to see her. And I

can't wait. The story is out. By tomorrow, it will be all over the news that Attitude Cat's owner killed Ramona Forsythe."

"But she didn't do it!" snapped Valerie.

"Yes, I know that." Pam's voice trembled. "But when people hear about an arrest, especially when it's someone connected with a celebrity or a famous brand, they assume the worst." She gripped the glove like she meant to strangle it. "We—I have to get out in front of this story. It's the only way we can help Kristen." Pam grabbed Val's shoulder hard enough that my friend winced. "If she's said *anything* to you, anything that the police might be able to use against her, twisting it, of course, because we know . . ."

"She didn't do it," Val finished. She also pried Pam's fingers off her shoulder.

Pam, realizing what she was doing, lifted her hand away and smoothed down her rumpled, crooked coat.

"I'm sorry," she said. "But this is awful. It's awful for me—us—and for Kristen. I know what I sound like, but really, I don't want anything to happen to her. Please," she said again. Her whole body was shaking now.

"Look, why don't you come into the living room," Val said. "We can all talk, okay?"

Pam looked at me, not at all thrilled to have me included in the conversation. But in the end, she just shrugged and followed Valerie.

Val took us both into the B and B's normally sunny great room. She flipped on the switch for the chandelier and pulled the drapes shut across the French doors that led to the terrace.

Pam sat down on the gracefully curved sofa but did not take off her coat or her hat or let go of that poor, abused glove.

"Pam . . ." I sat down across from her on one of the tapestry chairs. I also hesitated. I did not want to have to ask this, but Pam was the one person besides Kristen who would know about the business around Attitude Cat. "Was there any reason you know of that Kristen would need to go to New York on short notice?"

"New York?" Pam's eyes darted from me to Valerie, who was standing by the fireplace and looked like she wished she didn't have to be in the room at all. "No. Why?"

"It's just that, I was wondering . . ." I watched Pam twist her glove. The thing was going to start begging for mercy any second now. "There's a rumor going around that there might be a problem with the new Best Petz line."

"What!" Pam started to her feet. "That's ridiculous! What rumor?"

"A rumor that the new premium food is, well, it might be a case of false advertising. Maybe Kristen was trying to find out more—"

"Then she would have come to me! She wouldn't have gone gallivanting off on her own! She knows I have always looked out for her and Ruby!"

"She did go to New York, though," said Val.

"And she didn't tell anybody," I said. "Not even you or Ramona."

"Oh my G—" Pam swallowed, her face deathly white. I started out of my seat, just in case she was going to pass out again, but she waved me back. "I'm fine, I'm fine. I just . . . Oh, Lord." She dropped back down onto the sofa and dragged in a deep, rasping breath. "Thank you for telling me this. I'm sorry. I . . . I have no right to ask this, but please, please keep this to yourselves."

Val and I exchanged uneasy glances. "Pam, if you know anything about Best Petz or Ramona, you have to tell the police."

"But I don't!" she cried. "I don't know anything! All I ever did was work to make sure everyone could get what they wanted. That's all!" A tear trickled down from the corner of her eye. "This is not my fault. They . . . She should have trusted me. She should have known I'd be looking out for all of us." These last words came out in a harsh whisper.

"But—" I began.

Pam wasn't ready to hear any more, though. "No. This is *not* my fault. If Kristen Summers can't trust me after all I've done . . . she can face the consequences on her own."

She hurried out of the room, heading for the front door.

Val and I stared at each other. I was the one who jumped to my feet first.

"Pam, wait," I tried, running down the narrow hall after her.

"Please, Pam . . . ," said Val, half a step behind me.

But the door slammed behind her and by the time we got it open and had both reached the bottom of the curved front stairs, Pam Abernathy was already in her car. She didn't even look at us as she gunned the engine, backed out of the driveway and tore down the street.

Val and I stared until her taillights vanished around the corner.

"Well," said Valerie.

"Gosh," I said.

"You think she's worried about something?" Val remarked.

"Could be, yeah."

There didn't seem to be much else to say, especially not with the November cold digging its way under my inadequate shirt. We went back inside. Val closed the door and locked it.

By silent agreement, we both returned to the kitchen. Val turned all the lights on, for which I was grateful. I already felt like I was stumbling through the dark.

"Coffee?" Val asked me.

"Oh, yes. Please."

Valerie moved around the big, quiet kitchen, measuring beans, filling the electric kettle and getting down the French press from the cupboard. I watched her, my mind roving restlessly over everything I'd learned over the past few days and everything I still didn't know.

"So," said Val as she poured the hot water into the pot, releasing the blessed scent of hot coffee into the room. "Are you going to tell me about this cat-food rumor?"

I did. Including the number of times that Frank had stressed that it was just a rumor.

Val settled the lid on the pot. "It doesn't make sense."

"Actually, it kind of does. I mean, if Ramona found out Best Petz was committing fraud and threatened to expose them, she'd cost a lot of people a lot of money."

"Well, that would explain why somebody stole her laptop." Valerie opened the fridge and pulled out a big bowl of pasta salad covered in plastic wrap. "I mean, if Ramona was not only hearing about a fraud, but trying to gather evidence of one, the proof would all be on her laptop, right? If the evidence goes away, the problem's solved. But it doesn't explain the murder or Ruby vanishing." She started scooping pasta into a couple of bowls.

"Well, it could mean that whoever killed Ramona might not have been after Ruby. Maybe they were just after Ramona's laptop and whatever she'd found out about the Best Petz fraud, and she came home unexpectedly and surprised the burglar—"

"But that makes it even less likely to have been Kris. She and Ramona were friends. She could have gotten in to see her anytime." Val pushed the coffee and one bowl of pasta salad toward me.

"Right," I said, and I really wished I could make myself shut up, because Val was one of my best friends, and nothing I had to say was going to make either one of us feel any better. "Because you and I are friends too, and if I needed to take your computer, I could just walk up to you and ask for it."

The salad was a caprese, with chunks of tomato and mozzarella mixed in with the penne pasta. Roger had been determined that no one would go hungry while he was out of the house, and I silently thanked him for it.

Valerie drummed her fingers on the side of the pasta bowl. "Something's not right here. You're saying somebody killed Ramona because she found out there might be a problem with this . . . what did you call it? Megapremium cat-food line?"

"Ultrapremium."

"Ultra. Right. But this is a new line, right? It hasn't even really been advertised yet?"

"From what I saw when I went to Pam's office, it's all still in the planning stages. Although she did say the timeline got moved because of all the interest after Ruby disappeared."

"But even then, the solution ought to be simple." Val waved her fork. "They just don't go through with it. Best Petz puts out a statement saying they found out about inferior food, they change suppliers, and they look like responsible corporate citizens. End of problem. Nothing worth killing over."

I nibbled a piece of mozzarella. "It'd still be really expensive."

"Best Petz is a big company. They should be able handle the cost." Val paused in the act of spearing a fresh bit of penne. "You know who couldn't handle it?"

"Pam Abernathy?" I said immediately. Abernathy & Walsh was a small agency, tightly tied to one particular star and one particular company. If the rumor about Best Petz slapping premium prices on inferior products spread, it wasn't just Kristen and her cat who risked being left out in the cold. It was Abernathy & Walsh.

I thought about that broken-up phone call. Then I thought about my conversation with Pam at Popovers. There was still something I didn't like about it. Something she'd said or something she'd done, but I couldn't figure out what.

Despite that, I shook my head. "It can't be Pam."

"Why not?"

"Because she's got an alibi," I said. "She was in her office, working on the Ultrapremium campaign, with both her assistants. She told the police."

"And they confirmed it?" asked Val.

I eyed her. "Are you seriously asking if Kenisha and Pete forgot to check out somebody's alibi?"

"No, of course not." Val sighed again. "I guess I should have known it couldn't have been that easy. Although," she added, "Pam was upset enough. You heard her. She said Kris deserved whatever happened to her . . ." Val's voice faltered.

"She just found out her biggest client not only got arrested, but she'd been lying," I reminded Val. "You'd be upset too. Maybe she'll change her mind when she's had a chance to calm down."

Val took a swallow of coffee. "We're forgetting about someone," she said slowly. "Cheryl."

"What about her?"

"If anybody has reason to be upset because Ruby's career might be over, it's Cheryl. She's counting on being able to make a whopping great load of money off her lawsuit. If the Attitude Cat brand suddenly becomes worthless, she loses her goose and all its golden eggs."

She had a point. I turned the thought over in my head as I turned over a few more mozzarella chunks.

"I don't suppose there's any connection between Cheryl and Pam?"

"Not that I know of. Why?"

"Because if there was, then Cheryl might have found out from Pam that Ramona was planning to blow the whistle. That would give Cheryl a reason to kill Ramona and steal the laptop."

And maybe drop a couple of her beads in the apartment in the process. "But that still wouldn't explain why Kristen made a secret trip to New York City."

"If we can prove Cheryl killed Ramona, we wouldn't need to know why Kris went to New York!"

"Val," I said slowly. "I want to find out who killed Ramona too, but the clock is ticking for Kristen right now. If Pam's really not going to come forward, we've got to find some way to prove that Kris's trip to New York didn't have anything to do with the murder."

"Why would it?" Val shot back. "Even if she did know about the fraud rumors, Best Petz headquarters are in Boston."

I sighed. "Val, I know she's your friend, but you've got to look at this from the outside. Kris lied. She lied to Ramona and she lied to the police. Why? What's so important? What's in New York?"

Valerie nibbled a piece of penne and considered the question. "Statue of Liberty," she said. "Empire State Building, cronuts . . ."

And something else. Something important enough to make me set my fork down.

"Madison Avenue," I said.

"What are you talking about?"

"Madison Avenue." I gripped the edge of the counter. "New York is the center of the public relations world. Abernathy & Walsh is just a Portsmouth agency. They're small. Maybe a bigger agency has approached Kris and made her an offer for the Attitude Cat account."

Val shook her head. "She's never really shared the business details. I always got the impression she left most of it to Pam."

Which reminded me of something else, something from that very first meeting. "Did Kris ever say anything to you about wanting to get out of the Attitude Cat business?"

"Huh? No. Why would you say that?"

I shook my head. "When I talked to her, the day I met her at Ramona's clinic, it sounded like she was tired of the business and was planning to pull out."

"But now you think maybe she was just tired of Abernathy & Walsh?"

"Maybe. Maybe Kris found out something about Abernathy & Walsh that made her change her mind about who should to represent Attitude Cat."

"Like maybe that Pam knew about the fraud but wasn't going to tell anybody?"

"And how would she have found that out?" I mumbled around my mouthful of pasta.

"Ramona!" we said together.

"Jinx!" added Val. I ignored her.

"Suppose Ramona told Kris there was a problem at Best Petz. Ramona decides she's going to blow the whistle, but since she's friends with Kris, she wants to give Kris a chance to get out before that happens. Kris decides she's going to see if she can find alternate representation and a fresh gig for Ruby. But she doesn't want to let Pam know she knows, so she goes to New York without telling anybody." And takes the train, because the train station doesn't have the number of cameras and scans and checks that an airport does.

"That would mean Kris had nothing to do with Ramona's murder! All she has to do is tell the police the truth!"

"All she has to do is get them to *believe* the truth." I frowned at the pasta on my fork. "After everything she's done, and when we don't even have any real evidence that there is a fraud, let alone that Kristen *or* Ramona knew about it." I nibbled restlessly. "So, either we find the missing laptop . . ."

"Which might be at the bottom of the Piscataqua," Val pointed out. "That's what I'd do with it."

"Or we wait for Frank to see what he can uncover."

Val shook her head. "Kris might not have that kind of time."

"Or we take the direct route." I shoved my bowl away.

"Anna," said Val. "You're making that face again."

"I am not," I told her. "But I am going to talk to Rachael Forsythe. If Ramona told anyone about what she knew, it would be her daughter."

"Who happens to be a witch, as well as a vet," said Val thoughtfully.

"And who might know where her mother kept her books of shadow," I added.

"And her laptop?"

"And her laptop," I agreed, even though it did not make me happy. At all. "Although that'd be weird, wouldn't it? Considering she didn't mention that at all when she sent me into her mother's apartment."

36

WHEN I PULLED into the parking lot of the Piscataqua Small Animal Clinic the next morning, mine was pretty much the only car in evidence.

I didn't really want to be here. I'd wanted to go with Val to the police station to talk with Pete and Kenisha, but Roger—and Enoch—insisted it would be better if I stayed away until I was asked for.

"It is possible for the police to have too much information," said Enoch portentously. "It can lead some of them to make the occasional error in judgment."

I did not ask which "some of them" he was referring to, and Enoch did not tell.

After I'd gotten home from Val's, I tried calling Sean because I'd promised I would. I got his voice mail and left a message saying I'd try again later. I'd hung up and tried not to feel disappointed. Instead, I'd gotten ready for bed and burrowed under the covers and the two purring cats.

I fell asleep with not one, but two cats curled up beside me. My last waking thought was that I was going to have to decide what to do about Ruby. Real soon.

But for now, I had to talk to Rachael.

A large, neatly written sign had been taped to the clinic door:

**DUE TO THE LOSS OF DR. RAMONA FORSYTHE,
THE PISCATAQUA SMALL ANIMAL CLINIC IS
CLOSED. WE WILL BE REOPENING AS SOON AS
POSSIBLE. IF THIS IS A VETERINARY
EMERGENCY . . .**

There was a phone number after that.

I ignored the sign and the phone number. Instead, I made sure my shields were firmly in place, touched my wand for luck, and pressed the button beside the clinic door. I also tried to gather my nerve. I had all kinds of reasons to be here, and I didn't like any of them. Everything that had happened the day before had shed new light on this very tangled situation. Unfortunately, that light meant that I was about to have to ask some very uncomfortable questions of a young woman who'd just lost her mother.

Just as I was starting to wonder if I ought to call the emergency number after all, Jeannie popped out of the back. Her eyes widened when she saw me, but she hurried forward anyway.

"Hi, Anna." She unlocked the door to let me in. "I'm sorry, but we are closed."

"Hi, Jeannie. I know. I was just coming by to . . . check in on Rachael. How are you holding up?"

"It's been pretty rough." The ragged edge to her voice told me this was a serious understatement. "It's hard enough losing Ramona, but . . . the police . . . they've been asking all kinds of questions."

"It's their job."

"I know, I know, and I really want them to find out who did this. Who would hurt Dr. Forsythe?" She spread her blue-gloved hands. "She was the best. She hired me as soon as she found out I wanted to be a vet, and was tutoring me and . . ." She sniffed and dabbed at the corner of her eye with her wrist. "She was just the best, you know?"

"I know." I squeezed her shoulder sympathetically, and she smiled.

"I don't suppose anybody's heard anything about Ruby?" she asked

"Everybody's looking," I said, because it was true. "She can't stay lost forever."

"Let's hope not. Anyway, Rachael's in the back." She jerked her chin behind her. "You can find it? We've still got some cats we're boarding, and I have to . . . take care of things." She held up her gloved hands.

I assured Jeannie I could find my way, and let her get back to the cats and their much simpler problems.

THE DOOR TO the clinic's business office was open. A strong smell of fresh paint wafted out to meet me. Rachael sat behind a desk stacked with clipboards and folders. She wasn't paying attention to them, though. She just sat in the swivel chair, staring at the wall. There'd been a poster taped there recently. I could see the torn bit of paper stuck to the wall under the strip of Scotch tape.

I knocked on the doorframe, and Rachael jumped.

"Anna! I'm sorry, I didn't . . ." She started to her feet, but I gestured for her to sit back down.

"Are you okay?" I asked. "I can come back . . ."

"No, no. I'm fine. Come on in. I was just . . ." She swallowed and gestured me to the orange plastic visitors' chair. "I wanted to try to start getting a handle on things, but it's hard. There's just so much . . . *Mom* everywhere." She spread her hands to take in the whole office.

"You should give yourself time."

"I probably should, but we've got patients that need to be taken care of now, and, well, frankly, we're going to need the money. Mom was a great vet but lousy at business." She grimaced. "That sounds so . . . so . . ."

"Human and normal," I assured her. "We wish the world would stop, but it doesn't."

She shot me a grateful look. "No. It doesn't. And I don't want you to think . . . I mean . . . The problem was that Mom cared so much. She wouldn't turn anybody away, whether they could pay or not. It was all about the animals and the people for her." There was a ring of pride in Rachael's words, but regret as well. I remembered Frank talking about the student loans for Rachael as well as for Ramona. I wondered if Ramona and her daughter had butted heads over money. I wondered if Ramona and her formidable sister had.

"You really should take it easy, at least for a while," I said. "I know—"

But Rachael cut me off with one shake of her head. "I'd rather keep busy. Speaking of busy . . ." She leaned across the desk. "Did you find anything in Mom's apartment?"

"Well, yes, actually." I laid my hand over my purse, trying to draw some steadiness from my wand. I did not like that eager glint in Rachael's eyes. "We found a couple of beads that look like they might have come from one of Cheryl Bell's bracelets."

"I knew it!" shouted Rachael. "She's been after Mom to take her side about Attitude Cat for the past couple of years!" Then she stopped. "Wait. You said 'we.' Who else was there?"

"Kenisha Freeman."

"I didn't say you could do that!" Rachael was staring at me, shocked and outraged. A sick sensation that had nothing to do with the paint fumes settled in my stomach.

"I know," I said. "But she's with the police, and I needed her there in case I found anything important. Otherwise, it might not stand up in court as evidence."

"Oh." Rachael slumped back in her chair. "Okay. I guess that makes sense. So." Rachael took a deep breath. "Have they arrested Cheryl yet? I've been so busy here, I haven't heard anything . . ."

"Actually, they arrested Kristen Summers."

Rachael froze. *"What?"*

I felt a little piece of my heart crumble. "They think the

beads might have been planted by someone who wanted to frame Cheryl. They found that the balcony door was jimmied as well," I added, but Rachael wasn't listening.

"But . . . how can they even tell?" shouted Rachael. "I mean, Cheryl's . . . she's such a raging . . . she would stop at nothing to get her hands on Ruby and the money! She must be the one who killed Mom!"

"I understand how you feel, believe me," I said. "I don't like Cheryl either. But—"

"And they're her beads! You saw them, right? You said so! Why would they think Kristen had anything to do with them being there?"

"The police take pictures when they search a crime scene. The beads don't show up anywhere."

"They could have missed them the first time! It happens!"

It did. And Pete had his doubts about one of the new photographers. But there was the other thing. The thing that wasn't going to show up on any crime scene photo, no matter how good. "Rachael, the wards on your mother's apartment were broken. Did you know that?"

"Of course I knew!"

"But then why haven't you . . . I mean—"

"Is that what this is about? Ugh!" She threw up her hands. "Aunt Wendy tried to warn me! She said Julia's people jump to conclusions! She said they don't trust anybody outside their own circle!"

"It's not that, it's just—"

"It's just that I broke the wards when I came back to town," she snapped. "It's my job as her closest relative! I have to break any wards or other spells that might be active to ensure there's nothing left to hold her spirit back from crossing over!" Which certainly explained all the fresh paint. Rachael was undoing her mother's wards here. "That's how we do things in our family," Rachael went on. "Which you'd know if you'd bothered to ask!"

"That's what I'm doing now," I said, trying to keep calm. "And now you've told me. I'm sorry, I didn't mean to upset you."

What I didn't say was that this was the kind of thing Julia should have known. And probably should have told me.

Rachael was glaring at me. "Something tells me you've got another question lurking under there someplace."

Because she could read my transparent, and awkward, expression. Just like everybody else. "Rachael, did your mom ever say anything to you about Best Petz? Maybe about their new Ultrapremium cat food?"

Rachael frowned. "Where is *this* coming from?"

"There are rumors that Best Petz was importing cheap cat food from China and slapping the exclusive label on it. I was wondering if your mom had heard anything about it."

"So, first you think a witch broke Mom's wards to murder her or plant fake evidence," snapped Rachael. "Now you think Mom got killed because of some rumor about cat food?"

"I don't know," I told her honestly. "That's why I'm asking you if she knew anything. I know Abernathy & Walsh were paying her a lot of money for her consulting work with them and Best Petz—"

Rachael shook her head, hard. "Best Petz has nothing to do with Mom's murder. Nothing. This is about Cheryl Bell and how badly she wants Ruby and the money."

"But how can you be so sure?"

"I told you! Cheryl's been nagging Mom for years now to say that Ruby was her cat. I told you and I told the police. Not that they listened to me either," she added bitterly.

"Do you have anything to prove what you're saying about Cheryl and your mother? Recorded phone calls, e-mails, anything?"

Rachael glared at me. "How could I? Her laptop is gone, remember?" She stressed the last word. "I bet that's why Cheryl took it. So no one could find all the e-mails she sent."

"So, you think Cheryl stole the laptop and Ruby?"

"I know she did," said Rachael again.

"But how do you know?"

"I just do! I thought you would understand."

"I do, Rachael." I understood that she was grieving and

angry. I also understood that she was very frightened by something. So frightened in fact that she might just be trying to throw suspicion onto Cheryl Bell. "But the police are going to need proof."

"They have proof now! They have those beads!"

"That's not enough. In fact, those beads are helping convict Kristen."

"But I don't see how!"

"She wasn't at the funeral. They think that's because she was breaking into your mother's apartment to plant the beads and frame Cheryl."

"That's crazy! I know Kristen. She and Mom were friends. She loved Ruby! She couldn't . . . she wouldn't . . . I know it!"

"I know that's what you want to believe, but unless you can find your mom's laptop or her phone, or something else definite, you knowing isn't enough."

Rachael leaned forward and grabbed my wrist. "But, Anna, you know it was Cheryl, too, don't you?"

My fingers prickled. Something warm slipped around the outside of the shields I'd raised before I walked in.

Oh, no.

Slowly, I pulled my hand out of Rachael's grip. Our eyes met. *Please, no. You did not just try to use your magic on me.*

But the color had drained from Rachael's cheeks, and I knew that was exactly what she'd done. If I hadn't had my shields in place, it might have worked, too.

Maybe she meant to say something. Maybe I did. We'll never know which one of us would have broken the stunned silence first, because right then a loud buzzing cut through the room. Someone wasn't just ringing the clinic bell; they were leaning on it.

In a heartbeat, Rachael was on her feet and darting out the door. I followed behind as fast as I could, my hand diving reflexively into my purse to reach for my wand.

Jeannie had beaten us both to the lobby. She had the front

door cracked open and was talking to a wild-eyed woman who was clutching what looked like an empty towel in her hands.

"I'm so sorry," Jeannie began. "You'll have to—"

"No!" shouted the woman. "Please! You have to help me! She's dying!"

❧ 37 ❧

🐾 "IT'S ALL RIGHT, Jeannie." Rachael moved forward and took the towel from the woman's arms. Inside the folds, a sweet little tuxedo kitten blinked blearily up at us. The rims of her eyes were red, and even I could see her breathing wasn't right. The fur around her jaw was matted and tangled.

"Please! Can you help? My little Mittens . . . ," the woman sobbed.

"Of course. Bring her into Room 3," said Rachael.

Jeannie shot her a look. I remembered that Rachael hadn't actually gotten her license yet, and I wondered if Jeannie was going to call her out.

But all Jeannie did was take the woman by the shoulders. "This way," she said as she steered the distressed cat owner toward the room.

"Anna?" said Rachael softly. "I have no right to ask, but would you wait here? I might . . . that is, Mittens might . . . need your help."

There was no way I could refuse a request like that. So, when Rachael disappeared into the exam room, I sat on the bench in the empty lobby. I flipped through a cat magazine, until I got to the fourth ad with Attitude Cat sitting beside a scratching post, or a bag of kibble. I dropped the magazine and started pacing from the bench to the door and back again.

"Merow?"

I looked down. It was Alistair. He curled around my ankles. I stared for a second, surprised; then I remembered that Rachael had been undoing her mother's wards. The clinic was officially open for familiars, even when the exam room door was closed.

"Oh, big guy." I scooped him up at once and hugged him close. I needed to get my head together. The tangle around Ramona's death was getting to me.

Rachael's explanation for the broken wards made a lot of sense, especially since I could see for myself that she'd been busy painting over all the circles her mother had woven around the clinic. But there was still her vehement insistence that it was Cheryl who must have committed the murder. Her suspicion was understandable. It might even be right. But now I had suspicions of my own. Like that she might be setting me up to help make sure Cheryl got arrested, whether she was actually guilty or not.

"What do we do, big guy?" I whispered to Alistair. "If Rachael's the one who planted those beads, and maybe took her mother's books, she's covering up for someone. But who? Kristen? Aunt Wendy? Pam? No, not Pam. Pam's the only one with an alibi." That I knew about, anyway.

The door to Exam Room 3 opened. Alistair's ears twitched, and he vanished a split second before Mittens's owner walked out with Rachael and Jeannie following close behind her.

"I don't understand . . . ," the woman cried. "I don't. She never goes outside. I told Dr. Forsythe that—the other Dr. Forsythe, I mean. I've been so careful . . ."

"I know," said Rachael soothingly. "This is not in any way your fault, Ms. Lewis. You have to believe me about that. Mittens is going to be fine. We're just going to keep her for a couple of days until we're sure the crisis is over. You're welcome to call at any time to check in on how she's doing."

"Yes, yes, of course." Ms. Lewis sniffed and rubbed her eyes. "I . . . I'm sorry. I'm such a mess."

"It's all right." Rachael had put a lab coat on in the exam room, and now she pulled a Kleenex out of the pocket and handed it to Ms. Lewis. "She's part of your family. It's natural that you're upset. Is there maybe somebody you can call to help you get home okay?"

"I, um, no, I'm fine." I could feel the effort Ms. Lewis was making to rally herself. I kept my breathing as steady as I could and tried to muster some healing energies. I could just imagine how upset I'd be if that was Alistair in there.

"Go with Jeannie," Rachael told Ms. Lewis kindly. "She'll make sure you've got all the information you need." Rachael smiled encouragingly. She also shot me a glance and jerked her chin toward the exam room.

Jeannie led Ms. Lewis to the reception desk. I waited until they were both turned away before I ducked into Room 3.

"Anna, listen to me," Rachael said urgently as she closed the door. "I've got no idea what you must be thinking about me right now, but I need your help."

I had no idea what I thought about Rachael either, but the urgency in her voice was real. "What's the matter?"

"We need to do a healing ritual." Anger tightened Rachael's face. "That kitten . . . She's been poisoned."

"Poisoned!"

"Cyanide."

A shudder shot through me.

"The good news is Lisa got her to us in time. There is effective medical treatment, so we've got a decent chance, but Mittens is so small . . . I want to do everything possible." The exam room had a back door with a big square window. Through it, we could see into the main treatment area. Jeannie was there, carefully adjusting little Mittens's position in a padded box and checking the IV bag on its stand. I gulped.

"Right," I said, trying to steady my voice—and my nerves. "What do you need?"

"You, and Alistair if you can get him here . . ."

"Merow."

Just like that, Alistair was sitting bolt upright on the examination table. Rachael didn't even seem startled. She just pulled the shade on the back door down.

"Do you have your wand?"

"Of course."

This was evidently not the first time Rachael or her mother had done ritual work on the premises. Rachael unlocked a drawer under the exam room's sink and pulled out a black velvet cloth decorated with an elaborate circle of blossoms, moons and Celtic knot work woven in blue, green and gold. She spread this across the sterile examining table, then brought out a cup, which I filled with water from a bottle in the room's minifridge. She also got out a lacquered box of salt, a green candle, a dish of dried apple and rose blossom incense and an amethyst geode.

Alistair sat on the edge of the table, his eyes wide and unblinking. Rachael dimmed the lights and pulled a pack of matches out of the drawer, and then a wand. It was simpler than mine, just a length of dark wood polished so smooth it gleamed in the candlelight. A silver thread spiraled around it.

She lit the green candle and the cone of incense in its dish. We breathed the mingled smells of smoke and blossoms. Alistair started to purr, a steady, hypnotic thrum. I felt my thoughts focus. My hands and arms began to prickle as the energies inside us rose and spread.

"In need I call, in hope I ask . . . an' it harm none, an' it harm none . . . ," Rachael intoned.

I raised my wand. Alistair's purr deepened.

"I call upon the spirits of the north, the spirits of the earth from which all life comes." Rachael touched her wand to the amethyst geode. "I ask that you lend us your deep and steady strength for the healing that we seek."

Moving clockwise around the circle, Rachael touched each of the symbols in turn, invoking the spirits. The prickling in my hands and arms intensified. As Julia had taught me, I pictured curtains of colored light rising from our circle: shimmering black, gold, rich red, a deep blue like the color of the morning sky. I pictured them swirling together, warm with life and clean energy.

I lost all sense of time. I couldn't even feel the wand in my hand or the floor under my feet. The light, Rachael's chant and the underlying thrum from Alistair all wound together—bright, vibrant, powerful, calming and exciting all at once.

Then, as slowly as it had built, the magic began to ebb. I began to settle back into my own blood and bones. I could distinguish individual sensations again, including Rachael intoning the words that would close the spell.

"So mote it be," I said with her. "An' it harm none, so mote it be."

It was over. Despite everything that frightened and worried me about Rachael, we still grinned at each other. She held up her hand, and I slapped it in a witches' high five. The gesture was only slightly marred by the fact that I really, really needed to sit down now.

"I'm just going to check . . ." Rachael didn't need to finish. She just slipped back into the treatment area. I sat on the bench, trying to recover my breath and not shake, or wolf the battered granola bar I dug out of the bottom of my purse.

"Merowp." Alistair jumped into my lap and head butted my chin.

"I'm fine. I'm good," I told him. I also stroked his back so he'd settle down, because having his head pressed right up under my chin made it difficult to eat the granola bar, which at the moment was tasting better than it had a right to.

"Merow?" He pawed my purse and jumped down to nose at the granola crumbs. "Merp?"

"Sorry," I said around my mouthful. "I don't have any nibbles."

"Merow!" he announced, making it perfectly plain what he thought of this gross negligence on my part.

Fortunately, just then Rachael came through the room's back door, a huge, relieved grin on her face.

"We did it! Mittens is breathing better and she's sleeping peacefully. She's going to be fine."

We hugged, a spontaneous expression of delight and triumph. Rachael passed me a fresh bottle of water from the fridge and cracked open one of her own. We toasted each other and both took long swallows. It was almost enough to make me forget what had happened before. Almost.

I lowered my bottle. "Rachael . . . ?"

Rachael, however, was not in the mood to talk. "You should probably go get some rest. That ritual was pretty intense."

"Right. Sure. But. It's just . . ." I was hesitating. There was something I hadn't asked yet, but I couldn't put my finger on what it was. Then I did.

"Did you take her books of shadow, too?"

"What?" Rachael pulled back, startled.

"Your mother's books of shadow," I said. "They're not in her apartment. Did you take them, too? When you broke the wards?"

"Oh. Yes," she said slowly. "Of course I did. I have them at home."

She looked at me, straight and steady and not blinking at all. "I'm sorry, Anna. I'm going to have to ask you to go." She held open the door. "I'll call you later, but right now I've got to help Jeannie take care of things, and then I really should call Aunt Wendy and . . . well, there's a lot to do still. You understand?"

I understood, maybe a little better than I wanted to. I gathered up my things. I also held out the apartment keys for her to take. Our eyes met one more time. Oh, I understood all right. Rachael wanted me gone. She didn't want to hear the other questions I had.

At least not until she had a chance to plan how she could answer them. Because every instinct I had told me that

Rachael had just lied about the books of shadow. She didn't take them. And if I had to bet on it, I would lay money on the fact that until I told her, she hadn't even realized they were missing.

❧ 38 ❧

🐾 WORKING MAGIC TAKES energy. The stronger the spell, the more effort it requires. This is why every witch I know keeps some kind of snack handy.

But despite the granola bar, I was still starving. I was also seriously uneasy. Rachael Forsythe was not telling me everything she knew about the mystery surrounding her mother's death. She'd been so desperate for me to believe that Cheryl Bell must have been the one who killed her mother that she'd actually tried to use her magic to influence me. Did that mean she was the one who'd planted those beads under Ramona's bed? Or just that she knew who did?

How on earth was I going to find out which it was?

Thinking on an empty (and grumbling) stomach was never something I was much good at. I thought about the state of my refrigerator at home and decided to head for the Pale Ale.

IT WAS A slow time for Portsmouth tourism, but thanks to Martine's creative menu, plenty of locals were ready and willing to fill the Pale Ale's dining room at lunchtime. Men and women in business suits crowded the dining room, discussing their days and making their deals over salads of crisped pumpkin shreds and wilted winter greens, accompanied by what I presumed was local beer or one of the tavern's signature cocktails.

Sean was behind the bar, hat pushed back on his head. He was engaged in pouring something from a Boston shaker through a strainer and into a highball glass with the kind of concentration normally reserved for brain surgery.

I slipped onto a stool. Sean didn't even look up. He set the shaker down, flicked a stray grain of salt (unless it was sugar) off the side of the glass, garnished it with a sprig of mint (unless it was basil) and set the creation lovingly on the server's tray. The freckled brunette server beamed at him, then saw me. We beamed at each other, more than a little awkwardly, and she took the drink to her table.

"For the record, I did notice you come in," Sean told me.

"I know," I told him. "Busy day?"

"Steady," he said. "Can I get you something?"

My stomach rumbled in a highly unladylike and indelicate fashion. "A menu?"

Sean grinned and handed me one from under the bar. "The special's a delicious beef stew with winter vegetables over fresh noodles. If you're really hungry . . ."

Right on cue my stomach growled again. "You may take that as a yes."

Sean slapped the bar in approval and typed my order into the sales terminal. "How about some warm cider to go with that?"

"Sounds perfect." My hands weren't exactly blue, but they were getting close. Something in my New Englander's bones told me we were in for more snow soon.

I am not a serious drinker of any sort, and Sean knows that, so the steaming mug with the cinnamon stick in place of a straw or stirrer was fresh-pressed cider, not hard. It was, however, mulled with clove, allspice and citrus zest. I sipped.

I sighed and the troubles of the world melted away, at least for a minute.

"Rough morning?" Sean asked.

"Yeah," I admitted. "It really has been."

"Should I ask?"

I stirred the cider restlessly with the cinnamon stick. I also glanced around me. I was the only person at the bar. Everybody else was sitting at their tables, deep in their own conversations or enjoyment of their own lunches. No one was paying attention to me and Sean. Yet, anyway.

"It's kind of a long story," I said reluctantly.

Sean followed my gaze around the dining room and nodded. At the same time, the swinging door behind the bar opened, and a man in a white jacket and apron came out and set a bowl of stew and noodles on the bar. It smelled divine. I reached for my fork.

But not before Sean picked up the bowl and the cider mug.

"Hey! That's my lunch!"

"And this is my break time. Let's go." He jerked his chin toward the swinging door behind the bar.

"But—!"

But Sean wasn't paying any attention. He just carried my lunch through that door without a single backward glance. I followed because I had no choice. The fact that I still had the fork clutched in my fist is not something we really need to discuss.

I HAD NEVER been in the Pale Ale's wine cellar before. It was dim and cool, with arched brick doorways and a flagstone floor. State-of-the-art coolers filled with bottles lined the walls. Beside them stood stacks of wooden crates printed with the logos of local breweries and distilleries.

Sean set the cider mug on the top of a cooler and stood an empty crate on end in the center of the room. He set another on its side and dusted it off.

"Well, you certainly know how to sweep a girl off her feet with the atmosphere."

"Do not mock the man holding your lunch." He gestured for me to sit. I did, fork poised in case I needed to do some actual damage.

Sean set the bowl down on the crate that was taking the place of a table. I dug in immediately. He was right. It was delicious.

"So," I said around my mouthful as Sean put the cider mug on the table. "You always take your break in the basement?"

"Mostly, I go outside, or to our very nice break room in the attic, but it's November and I got the idea you wanted privacy." He pulled a crate up to the makeshift table. "Now. Talk to me, Anna."

I sighed and stirred my noodles and rich broth with my fork. I tried to remember that Sean and I had only just started dating. He didn't need all the crazy details. I was taking this slow. I was still getting over my last (disastrous) relationship. But I looked up in his blue eyes and my resistance wafted away on a cloud of cider-scented steam.

So I told him about searching Ramona's apartment and about Kristen's arrest and about Val. I told him about going to the clinic and my conversation with Rachael that had raised so many more questions than it had answered. I even told him about Mittens, although I glossed over the details of the ritual. But he got the picture.

Sean tugged on the brim of his fedora and blew out a long sigh. I waited for the skepticism to crease his face. I braced myself. He was going to say he needed to get back to work now, because he might like me, but this much weirdness he did not need in his life. I couldn't blame him. At all. Ever. I had known starting to date again was a bad idea. It was better we both found that out now.

But he didn't do any of these things. "So now you think Rachael was taking you for a ride?"

"I don't want to, but I do. She gave me the keys, and she was so insistent that Cheryl killed her mom, and she's not telling me everything she knows. What else am I supposed to think?"

"It sounds bad," said Sean. "But there's a lot of holes."

"Tell me about it. Every time I turn around, another one opens. It's like Kenisha and Julia both said—there are too many pieces here for just one puzzle."

"Well," said Sean, "maybe you need to find the corners."

"Sorry?"

"My grandmother was a jigsaw puzzle fanatic. I spent a ton of Sunday afternoons eating her cookies and working puzzles. She always found the corners first, then the edge pieces, and then she'd work her way to the center. So. What are the corners? Or maybe who are the corners?"

I frowned. "Well. Ramona."

"Right.

"Cheryl and Kristen."

"Right. Who else? Who was there that day?"

"Pam Abernathy, I suppose.

"Okay, so if those are the corners, where do they go? What actually happened on, well . . ."

"The night in question?"

"You said it. I didn't. What happened?"

"Ramona died. She fell, or was pushed, off her balcony onto the rocks." *Pushed.* I scraped my fork along the bottom of my bowl. Somebody'd asked about being pushed. Who was that?

"What else?" Sean prompted.

"Ramona's laptop went missing."

"And?"

"Ruby went missing."

"And?"

"That's the problem. I don't know what else! If I did . . ." I stopped. "Wait. That's not true. There were the phone calls. Kristen and Pam both got phone calls saying something was wrong with Ruby and they should check on her."

"So somebody wanted them there."

"Somebody wanted Ramona discovered?" That was not something I had considered before. "I mean, we were thinking those phone calls were just a run-up to a ransom demand or to somebody claiming the reward." I stopped. "Pam's call."

"What call?"

"Pam got another call. It was somebody asking if everything was clear with the vet. Pam told me it was from her partner, Milo Walsh, but there was something weird about the way she did it."

"So, Pam got a call telling her something was wrong with Ruby, and then she got a call from somebody who wanted to know everything was all right."

"Not so mysterious when you put it that way. She was working late that night. She probably bolted out from the office and Milo called to check on her."

"If he was in the office to see it happen."

"What?"

"Milo's in New York."

"How do you know?"

"He's a regular here. Old-school guy. Drinks Dubonnet when he brings Mrs. Walsh in for Sunday date night. I had to find it specially. He told me he was headed to New York for a week or so."

I swirled the last of my cider with the cinnamon stick. "So, you think that either Milo knew Pam had a meeting set up with Ramona and he called to see how it went. Or Pam lied about who called." I remembered her bout of laughter when she found out how little I'd learned from the phone call I'd listened in on. "But why would she do that?"

"Why would she have a meeting with Ramona and not mention it to anybody?" countered Sean.

"But she can't have done it. She'd have to have gone to the condo, pushed Ramona off the balcony, gone away, set up an alibi and come back." Which was scarily close to what she said when she was laughing at me. "And even then, the police would be able to tell Ramona had died a couple of hours too early for Pam's story to hold water." They would be able to tell, wouldn't they? They always could on the cop shows.

"Okay," said Sean. "That covers Pam, then. What about Cheryl? Where was she?"

I didn't know. I hadn't thought to ask. Which was, all things considered, a little embarrassing. "You're kind of good at this."

Sean touched his hat brim. "You can thank Grandma McNally and her jigsaw puzzles."

I raised my mug. "To Grandma McNally." I drank the last of the cider.

"So, what are you going to do now?" asked Sean.

"I'm going to find out where the missing corners were," I said. "Starting with Cheryl Bell."

❦ 39 ❧

🐾 DECIDING TO TALK with Cheryl was easy. But first I had to find her. Fortunately, when it came to the location of newsworthy individuals in Portsmouth, I had an inside source.

As soon as I got back to the Jeep, I called Frank. Yes, in fact, he did have Cheryl's phone number. Yes, he would give it to me. On one condition.

"What condition?" I asked, maybe just a bit nervously.

"That *Seacoast News* gets an exclusive when you find the cat."

I paused a full ten seconds to make sure I'd heard this properly. "If you can't beat 'em, join 'em?" I asked.

"Yep," he said. "Promise me you still respect me?"

I promised. I probably even meant it. In return, he gave me Cheryl Bell's cell phone number. I wrote it on the front of the sketch pad on my passenger seat and hung up.

"I'M ONLY TALKING to you for one reason."

This was Cheryl Bell's greeting when she pulled open the door to her suite at the Harbor's Rest hotel.

Hello to you, too. I didn't say that. I just followed her as she turned her back and stalked into the suite's living room. The cream-colored curtains were closed, but all the lamps were turned on. Their harsh light showed how carefully Cheryl had made up her face and caught in the highlights in her skillfully dyed hair. She was dressed for business in a tailored skirt suit and two-inch heels. Three different Aldina bracelets clinked and jingled on her wrists. She'd worked on this appearance, on this persona, and she wasn't going to give it up anytime soon.

She sat down dead center on the squared-off beige sofa and crossed her ankles. She did not invite me to sit.

"I need to know what the police are saying," she said bluntly. "Do they really believe Kristen killed Ramona Forsythe?"

This was the very last thing in the entirety of the known universe that I expected Cheryl Bell to ask. To put it mildly.

Unfortunately, my surprise showed.

"I know what you're thinking," Cheryl announced. "You expected me to be breaking out the champagne."

Because you might be the real killer. I squashed the thought. I reminded myself I knew nothing for sure.

She sighed sharply. "Well, maybe this will help move things along. While I know Kristen is guilty of a number of things, murder is not one of them. And, if she goes to jail, I'm going to have a much harder time getting the money I'm owed."

I opened my mouth. I shut it again.

Cheryl Bell tapped her heel restlessly. "Well?"

What could I say? "Yes. As far as I know, the police really do think Kristen killed Ramona."

"What kind of idiot does she have for a lawyer to let things go this far?"

I couldn't answer that. "They also think she was trying to frame you for it."

Cheryl actually looked bored. Okay, I wasn't the first to bring her this particular news. "Did Lieutenant Blanchard tell you that?"

"As a matter of fact, he did. But, quite frankly, I'm a little surprised that you're repeating it." She rubbed her hands together, and her bracelets jingled.

"And I'm a little surprised you're talking to me instead of him."

"Yes, well. Our priorities have . . . diverged recently."

Even though you offered to lie for him if he needed it? I thought, remembering the conversation I'd overhead while looking for my napkin under my table in the dining room.

"Well, now that you're here, you might as well go ahead. Ask it." She glared at me. "Oh, never mind. I'll say it for you. You're wondering if I really did kill Dr. Forsythe."

"Actually I wasn't," I said, which was the truth.

"Then you're an idiot." She drew herself up. "I'm about the most obvious suspect there is in this whole mess. The answer, however, is no, I did not kill her. I had no reason to."

"You did if she wouldn't let you take Ruby," I said.

Cheryl Bell looked at me steadily for a long time. Although her perfectly made-up face didn't shift even a little, I could see her making up her mind. She was deciding what to tell me, and how much, and she wasn't going to be rushed.

Of course, during that whole time, she was watching me, too, and what she saw made her grin. It was not a pleasant expression. In fact, it reminded me a lot of Lieutenant Blanchard. No wonder the two got along so well.

"Oh, dear. The good doctor certainly had you fooled, didn't she?" Cheryl clasped her hands in front of her chest and made her eyes go wide. "The sweet, tenderhearted veterinarian!" She blinked rapidly several times. "Well, let me tell you something that'll wipe the dew out of those eyes. After our little tête-à-tête in her waiting room, Ramona Forsythe contacted me. She offered to hand over Ruby in exchange for ten thousand dollars."

"*She* came to *you*?" It is possible that a tiny bit of shock crept into my voice.

"Yes. Your kind, self-sacrificing veterinarian offered to sell one of her patients."

I knew in that moment that if I opened my mouth, I would only start stammering. Cheryl Bell leaned back in her chair, crossed her legs at the knee and looked at me the way Alistair looks at a fresh can of tuna.

"I suppose you're about to protest that she never would have done such a thing?"

I wanted to, but I couldn't, because I remembered everything Frank had said about Ramona's debts. I also remembered how tense and worried Ramona had gotten when Cheryl had first walked in on me, Ramona and Kristen just a few short days ago. Could that really have been a sign of the guilt she felt about what she was planning to do?

I also remembered my talk with Enoch Gravesend about intellectual property and the Attitude Cat brand, and how the possibility of a fraud and a scandal at Best Petz might threaten the worth of that brand.

"Why would you even bother?" I asked. "I mean, you had to know that Ruby wasn't as important to the Attitude Cat brand. The important thing was how the brand looked to the public."

"You think I'm just making a nuisance of myself with this lawsuit to see how much money I can get out of Kristen?"

"Yes," I said, because sometimes honesty really is the best policy.

Cheryl seemed to agree. "Well, you're right. That's exactly what I'm doing. I thought . . ." She shook her head. "I thought Kristen would settle by now. Or Best Petz would, or Abernathy & Walsh." She frowned. "I can't for the life of me understand it. Settling is the smart thing. The easy thing. Why drag us all through this?" She didn't wait for me to answer. "You know, Ms. Britton, I thought I had my life all figured out. I mean, I was a classic. I was pretty. I had brains, ambition. I'd gotten hold of a little money. I was going to make a new life in the big, bad city. I even landed a rich husband. I thought, 'This is it. I'm good now. I'm safe.' But look at me." She spread her perfectly manicured hands.

"Back in the small time, trying another hustle. But it seems I've lost my touch."

I swallowed. The edge was gone from Cheryl's words. No. That wasn't quite true. This was a different edge. Just as sharp, but with a ring of weary truth I hadn't heard before.

"Why would you tell me any of this?" I asked.

"Because you're in this up to your neck," she said. "Oh, don't look surprised—or innocent. I've been a hustler; I can spot another."

Was that what I was? Maybe. Kind of, anyway. It was not a comfortable idea, but I set it aside. What mattered right now was that Cheryl Bell was at least acting like she wanted to lay her cards on the table. If that was the case, I wasn't about to deny her the chance.

"So what did happen the night Ramona died?"

Cheryl glanced toward the curtained windows. It seemed to me she was making up her mind about how far she was really willing to let this conversation go.

"Ramona called about an hour after we . . . met," she said, choosing her words carefully. "She said she had a proposal and asked me to meet her downtown. I did, and she offered to sell me Ruby. I agreed, and we made our plan. I paid her five thousand up front. She would leave her apartment door unlocked so I could get in. I went to her place and I brought a cat carrier with me. Somebody was bringing in groceries and they held the door. I went in."

I tried to keep my forehead from furrowing. There was something wrong. That ring of truth I'd heard in her voice a minute ago had faded. Now she was almost reciting.

"As she promised, the apartment door was unlocked," Cheryl went on. "So I went in, but the place was empty."

"And you didn't think it was strange that Ramona wasn't there?"

"I thought she was out establishing an alibi." Cheryl laughed bitterly. "Ironic, isn't it? The idea was that she was going to let me take the cat while she was on an emergency call or, well, something. But when I got there, I looked everywhere I could think of, and there was no cat."

My inner Nancy Drew was prodding me. Something was not quite right with what Cheryl was saying or how she was saying it. But I couldn't put my finger on exactly what.

"Where did you look? Was it in the bathroom or under the couch . . . ?" *Or under the bed?*

"I don't remember, exactly. I was getting scared. The longer I couldn't find her, the more certain I got that I was being set up."

"Why would Ramona try to set you up? I mean, if you'd already paid her."

"I assumed that somebody else paid her more to run a double cross."

"Who?"

"Hmm. Let me think. Who was in touch with Ramona Forsythe who would also have an active interest in blackening my name?

"You mean Kris."

"Of course I mean Kris. If she could get it out there that I was trying to buy Ruby from her veterinarian, how is that going to make me look to the judge?"

"But Kris wasn't even in town."

"You don't have to be in town to offer a payout."

I hated to admit it, but she had a point.

"What did you do then?" I asked.

Cheryl hesitated, and I felt the pause all the way down to my bones. Inner Nancy tapped her foot impatiently. "Nothing. I got out of there as fast as I could."

"And you didn't try to call Ramona afterward or anything?"

"Ms. Britton, if you'd just offered to buy stolen property from someone and they stood you up, would you call them back?"

"I don't know."

"Well, I do, unfortunately. So, no, I didn't call. As things turned out, I'm glad I didn't. There." She spread her hands. "Now you know, and you can go tell all your Nosey Parker friends."

That expression dropped so casually made me sit up a

little straighter. "Cheryl . . . did Lieutenant Blanchard warn you about me?"

She lifted one shoulder in a half shrug. "As a matter of fact, he did."

"And he warned you not to talk to me."

"He had a whole list of people I shouldn't talk to. Starting with Frank Hawthorne, but he was too late there."

"So why aren't you listening to him?"

The corner of her mouth curled up into a tight sneer. "It's not my job to make Blanchard's life easy for him. Not anymore."

Inner Nancy was pacing now. I tried to tell her to sit down and be patient.

"So." Cheryl stood. "There you have it. I was a fool and now I'm a murder suspect. And, as it so happens, I have an appointment I have to get ready for. You can show yourself out." This was an order, not a request.

I got up. I picked up my things, but something Cheryl had said was nagging at me. It perched on the tip of my brain, but I couldn't quite make it show itself.

"Ms. Britton," said Cheryl softly, so I looked up at her again. "You seem to be friendly with Kristen, or at least Kristen's friends. You want to see her cleared. So do I, because as little as I like to admit it, I need her."

Which was why her interests had diverged from Blanchard's. Blanchard wanted to see Kristen in jail. That was when Inner Nancy Drew gave up trying to be subtle and gave me a sharp elbow to the back of my brain.

"Cheryl," I said. "When you got into the apartment, did you notice anything strange? Anything you could put your finger on that told you something was really wrong?"

She glared at me. "Beyond the fact that the cat was gone? Nothing. Everything looked perfectly normal, at least as far as I could tell. I'd never been in Ramona's home before."

"And what time was this?"

"I'm afraid I wasn't keeping track. Around seven, I think."

"Thank you."

She nodded without answering.

I drifted through the hotel lobby. The sense that I was missing something followed me all the way through the lobby. It hung in the air while I scratched a forlorn-looking Miss Boots's ears in the lobby. Evidently, Alistair had not been back recently.

"Let him go, sweetie," I told her. "The big galoot will only break your heart."

She sniffed at me.

When I got to the parking lot and my Jeep, I started the engine and sat for a long time with my arms wrapped around me.

Because Cheryl Bell had lied about being in Ramona's apartment. She must have. If she'd really been there, she would have noticed that the balcony door was open. That detail had not gotten into the media reports of the crime—at least, not yet. I knew because recently I'd been maybe just a little obsessed with following the news.

If you'd read only about what was found, or not found, in Ramona's apartment, you wouldn't know about that open door. But if you'd been there, you couldn't miss it. I knew that, too, because when I ran into Ramona's apartment that night, the first thing I noticed was that the place was freezing.

So, Cheryl was lying. But why this particular lie? It was dangerous. If the police believed she was there that night, they might believe she was the murderer.

But then, maybe that was the point. The lie was so dangerous, so potentially damaging, it would seem more likely. I mean, why would anybody make up a story that could turn on them like that?

If Cheryl's story about bribing Ramona and stealing Ruby was supposed to turn away suspicion from any part she might have played in Ramona's death, why tell me instead of the police and her old friend Lieutenant Blanchard?

Reflexively, I tucked my hand into my purse to touch my

wand. I stared out my windshield, trying to remember exactly what Cheryl had said and how she'd said it. I focused on my memories with my artist's eye. I tried to remember her face, the way she'd leaned forward, the arch of her eyebrows and the tilt of her head. She was asking for help. She needed help, but nothing about her said she expected to get it. In fact, from the first minute I walked in, her face and her body expressed nothing but contempt.

She wanted me to tell the story because she didn't respect me. I was nothing but a Nosey Parker. She would have gotten an earful about that from Blanchard. And because she thought I was just playing around, she thought I was sure to miss something important. Something about the story, or the night of the murder, that Cheryl wanted to keep hidden.

What is it? I tightened my grip on my wand. *How do I find out?*

I ran my mind back over the story and forward again. There was nothing in it I could check. It was all Cheryl's word about what Ramona had said and done. Except for that detail about the doors, there was nothing to check and nothing to confirm.

Except. Maybe.

I let go of my wand and dug down for my cell phone instead. There was one detail in Cheryl's story that might have left a hole behind. She said she'd paid Ramona five thousand dollars, half of the ten thousand she'd promised. If that was true, the money had to be somewhere.

It was also the one detail Cheryl Bell didn't know I had a way to check.

I hit a speed-dial number and waited while it rang.

"Anna?" Frank Hawthorne said as soon as he picked up. "What's up? Did you talk to Cheryl Bell?"

"Yeah, I did."

"And?" he prompted. I pictured him reaching for a pencil and flipping open a fresh legal pad.

"Frank, does your friend at the accounting firm owe you any more favors?"

"Not really. But from your tone, I feel like I might be about to owe him one."

"Can you find out if any of Ramona's accounts got a deposit of five thousand dollars recently?"

"Like, how recently?" he asked.

"Like, the day she died."

❧ 40 ❧

🐾 AFTER I HUNG up the phone with Frank, I called Val.

"How'd it go this morning?" I asked her. "Is there any news about Kristen?"

"I gave a statement, but it didn't change anything. They're still holding her." Val's voice was ragged. I suspected she hadn't slept much. I heard Melissa fussing in the background, which couldn't be helping.

"Which means Blanchard thinks he's got something definite." The idea sent a shiver through me. Even if Blanchard suspected Kristen was the one who planted the Aldina beads, that couldn't be enough to arrest her on, even if he did put it together with Kris's old record. Neither would the scratches on the balcony door, or even the fact that Ruby was still missing (as far as the rest of the world knew).

But add in the fact that Kristen had so very deliberately lied about where she was going, and then tried so hard to cover up her movements. All that together might be enough for Blanchard to spin into reasonable-sounding suspicion.

"It's such a mess, Anna," croaked Val. "I don't know how, but somebody must have found out Kristen's staying here.

There are news vans all over the place. There're reporters camped out on the sidewalk. Roger's unplugged the house phones. I feel like we're under siege."

"Take Melissa to the cottage," I told her. "They don't know about me. You can hide out with the cats."

"Thank you! I didn't want to ask, but . . ." Val paused and there was some shuffling and a gurgle of protest. "Have you heard anything from Kenisha?" she asked me abruptly.

"Not yet."

"How about Julia?"

"Not a thing. I take it she hasn't called you either?"

"No," said Val. "I'd go talk to her, but . . ."

"You're under siege. I know. Look, you take care of you and the baby. I'm downtown. I'll stop by the bookstore and make sure everything's okay with Julia."

"You're sure?"

"Yeah. I need to see her anyway." I needed to get this spell off my back before I, and maybe it, did any more damage. Kenisha was right. Magic and law enforcement should not mix.

"Thanks, Anna."

"What are coven sisters for?" I told her. "And don't let Alistair give you any guff."

"I won't." I heard the smile in her voice and felt a rush of relief.

We hung up and I stashed my phone in my purse. I touched my wand once more, for calm and good luck. I did not like the fact that Blanchard wasn't letting go of Kristen. It made me itchy. Maybe he was just playing for time, but maybe he really had something. It might even be something new that none of the rest of us had found out about yet. I just had to hope it wasn't something my magical interference had thrown into his path.

"One thing at a time, Anna," I muttered to myself as I pulled my gloves on and hurried down the sidewalk.

I wasn't the only one out and about today, though. As I was crossing the square, I recognized Zach, Pam's assistant, headed in the other direction, carrying two bags bearing the red-and-white logos of a well-known national sandwich chain. I raised my hand and he raised a bag and made a gesture that I assumed meant the boss was really hungry and he had no time to stop and pass the time of day.

I watched him go and wished that was the extent of my problems.

Within five minutes, I was repeating that wish with extra emphasis. Because when I got to Midnight Reads, I saw a black-and-white cop cruiser parked right across the street, the regulation distance from the fire hydrant. Kenisha sat behind the steering wheel, staring out the windshield, lost in thought.

She was so far gone, in fact, that she didn't even turn her head as I ran up to the car. Not until I pounded on the driver's-side window, anyway.

"Britton!" she exclaimed as she brought the window down. "What's the matter?"

"That's what I was going to ask you! Is Julia okay?"

Kenisha's mouth twisted up tight. "Oh, yeah. She's fine."

"Then what—"

I didn't get any further. "I'm on duty, Britton. You may have noticed the cop car I am sitting in."

"You can't mean Blanchard asked you to stake out *Julia*?"

She frowned up at me.

"Okay. Sorry. I shouldn't have asked. I know that. But . . . I mean, everything is okay, right?" I was babbling, but I had alarm bells sounding in my brain, and that always sets off a babble. "I mean, there isn't a problem with Julia and, you know, anything . . ."

Like she's enchanted someone else? Or sent her familiars on a search-and-find errand that's made more problems, or . . . or you found out about the summoning spell she laid on me . . .

The possibilities kept on mounting the longer Kenisha kept her hard, suspicious gaze on me. I felt suddenly seasick. I had to stop this. Right now.

"Listen, Kenisha, I'm pretty sure I don't want to tell you this, but you should probably know anyway. I've been talking to Cheryl Bell and Rachael Forsythe."

Kenisha's frown deepened.

"Yes. I know. You're right. But Cheryl told me . . . she told me she was at Ramona's apartment the night Ramona died. And she said she was there because Ramona had agreed to sell her Ruby. And she said when she couldn't find the cat right away, she left because she thought it was a setup and she didn't tell Lieutenant Blanchard because it wasn't her job to make his life easy for him." I stopped, out of breath.

Not anymore, she'd said. It wasn't her job to make things easy for him *anymore.*

"But she's lying, Kenisha. She can't have been at Ramona's, because she didn't know the balcony doors were open. So she might be doing it to cover for somebody. And I wanted you to know, because I didn't want you to think I was doing anything behind your back. She also said she'd paid Ramona five thousand dollars for Ruby, but if that's true, then where's the money? And I know you're going to be angry because none of this has anything to do with finding out the connection between Ramona's death and the true craft, and I'm sorry. And I haven't heard anything from Julia all day, and now that I see you here I'm even more worried than I was. So I'm going up to see her, unless you really don't want me to, in which case . . ."

"You'd probably go anyway?" Kenisha finished for me. Her voice was flat, and my heart sank. At least it did until I saw the tiniest curl at one corner of her mouth. It wasn't actually a smile, but it was a start.

"Probably, yeah."

"This relationship needs work, Britton."

"Again, probably, yeah." I paused. "I don't suppose you found those beads on the crime scene photos, did you?"

Kenisha glared at me. "I don't suppose you think I'd actually tell you that we didn't?"

"I know that you would never tell me anything like that."
Because there are some days when I am actually fairly quick
on the uptake.

"Good. Because I wouldn't. Just like I wouldn't tell you
that they're having trouble determining the exact time Ramona died because of the rain, the lousy cold weather, not
to mention the spray off the river."

"There is no reason I would need to know something like
that," I agreed. "Not that you'd tell me."

"No reason at all, because it is absolutely none of your
business that it makes this cover-up story of Cheryl Bell's
even more of a problem and, incidentally, messes with Pam
Abernathy's alibi."

"So, it all kind of makes things worse."

"Yeah, it kind of does." Kenisha sighed.

"Sorry."

"So am I," she muttered. "Look, just . . . go see Julia."
She faced forward again. "And when you do, try to get her
to come to her senses, will you?"

That rush of relief I'd felt dropped away so fast my head
spun. "About what?"

"You'll know when you get in there."

"Thanks loads," I muttered and turned away.

"HELLO, GABRIELLE." I tried to sound cheerful, or at
least normal, as I walked into the bookstore. "Is Julia in
today?"

Gabrielle stopped counting quarters into the cash drawer
and glanced toward the back of the shop. "She is, but . . .
maybe you should wait before you go back there."

"Is something wrong?"

She glanced toward the pair of harried-looking mothers
supervising their pack of kids at the Lego table. "Wendy
Forsythe stopped in."

Oh.

"Okay," I said brightly. "I'll just have a look at how the
murals are holding up, then."

Probably I should have listened to Gabrielle and waited. But apparently today was not one for good impulse control. I did have a look at my murals, which were just fine. They hadn't been up for even a week yet, after all. Then I slowly slipped down the MYSTERY aisle, which I suppose was appropriate, and I came out by the sitting room and the door to Julia's office. The door was open, but Max and Leo stood squarely in the center of the threshold, ears and tails up and muzzles thrust forward. Clearly, Gabrielle was not the only one who thought I shouldn't be going in to see Julia yet.

Wendy Forsythe stood on the other side of the dachshunds. She wore an old-fashioned black dress, and her gray hair was pulled into a tight bun. From this angle, she stood in three-quarters profile, but she didn't notice me hovering (because that's better than lurking), because she was busy trying to stare down Julia.

Julia was on her feet and leaning hard on her walking stick, making sure Wendy did not miss a single hard word she spoke.

". . . Wendy, you were not the one who sat with Ramona for hours while she agonized over paying the bills. You were not the one to listen while she worried about what you would do when you found out how short the money was . . ."

"I supported my sister!" Wendy snapped. "It was my money that started her clinic!"

"And you never let her forget that for a minute. She was terrified of you."

Max whisked around and galloped back to Julia's side. I took a step forward, but Leo wasn't having any of it. He raised his ears, his muzzle and his hackles at me.

"We were sisters," said Wendy, her voice low and intense. "I loved her."

"And because you were her sister, you felt like everything she did reflected on you. You demanded loyalty and discipline from her, just like you did from yourself. Only Ramona had different standards, and you couldn't cope with that."

"I gave her everything she needed!"

"And in return you wanted everything she had," Julia

replied evenly. "But there are boundaries we do not cross, Wendy. Not even for family."

"We look after our own," said Wendy. "That is the first duty of a witch of the bloodline. Perhaps if you'd remembered that, you and your family would still be on speaking terms."

I stared at Leo. I couldn't help it.

"Yip," he told me. Which, of course, got Julia's attention.

"Anna!" Julia edged past Wendy and pulled her glasses off. "Has something happened?"

"Um, well . . . ," I began, but my eyes flickered uneasily toward Wendy. I couldn't help it.

"Oh, no, don't mind me," she said, and the words were so dry and brittle they practically crumbled as she spoke. "I was just leaving."

"We'll finish this conversation later," began Julia, but Wendy turned on her with a gaze as hard and sharp as broken glass.

"No, we won't. The next accusation you or any of your people make against my family will be in court or in front of the Council of Coveners, because I am done with your interference. Do you understand me?"

"I have always understood you, Wendy."

But Wendy was busy turning that glass-hard glower on me. "As for you, Anna Britton, I asked you to stay away from my niece. Now I hear you are egging on her worst instincts—"

"I'm sorry, Ms. Forsythe, but it was Rachael who asked me to search her mother's apartment."

"Did she ask you to invite the police?" demanded Wendy. "Did she ask you to make accusations about someone breaking the wards in order to interfere with the official investigations? Did she *ask* . . ."

Leo's hackles went up. I kept waiting for Julia to pick him up or give him a command to back down, but she didn't do either.

"You will be careful how you speak to *my* apprentice, Wendy Forsythe."

The two women stared old, sharp daggers at each other. Leo and Max stationed themselves at Julia's side. Max's lip curled back, showing a row of white teeth. I was frozen in place. What should I do? What could I do?

"Julia?" called a voice from the front of the shop. "Everything okay back there?"

It was Gabrielle. It was a normal question, asked out of normal concern, but just then it was so sudden and surprising, we all blinked. Dachshunds included.

"We're fine, Gabrielle," Julia called back. "Unless there was something else?" she said to Wendy.

Max growled long and low in his doggy throat.

"I've said all I have to say." Wendy turned and marched out the door, but her anger stayed behind, as strong as any Vibe I've ever felt.

"What was—" I began, but Julia cut me off.

"It was nothing, Anna," she said, and I found myself really sympathizing with Kenisha's hatred of that word. "When you get to be as old as I am, your life develops a great deal of background noise." But even though she was trying hard to dismiss what had just happened, I didn't miss how carefully she lowered herself back into her chair. "I'm assuming you came here because you have some news?"

Where do I even start? I waded gingerly through the dachshunds so I could stand next to her desk. Julia gestured me toward the office chair, and I sat after I removed the pile of paperbacks to the corner of her desk.

I met my mentor's sharp blue eyes. I knew what I had to say to her, but I had no idea where to begin. Max pawed at her skirt and Leo balanced himself on his hind legs, briefly anyway. Julia smiled down and picked them both up to lie across her lap.

She also apparently decided she needed to take charge of this particular conversation.

"I heard," she said, "that Kristen Summers has been arrested. I assume you've talked to Valerie since then. How is she?"

"Really worried."

"I'll call her. We should make sure the rest of the coven is checking up on her and her family."

"I'm sure she'd appreciate that."

"And Kenisha told me that you searched Ramona's apartment."

"Oh. Um." I thought about Kenisha sitting out front in the cruiser, staring out the windshield at nothing. Somehow, I got the feeling that conversation had not gone well.

"Were you able to find anything useful?" Julia prompted.

Now I knew it had not gone well, because if it had, Kenisha would have managed to let Julia in on the important details, just like she did for me.

"Julia . . . ," I began, and I stopped.

I didn't come here to talk about Kristen, or even Ramona. I came here because I'm worried about you and what you're doing, and so is Val, and so is Kenisha, and so would everybody else be too if I'd had five minutes to fire up the phone tree.

"Anna? While I do appreciate a dramatic pause, if you have something to say, I'd much rather you did so."

"Julia." I twisted my hands together. "I'm worried about what you . . . about what we did. I think maybe we should—back away for a bit. Especially on the magic."

"I don't understand you, Anna. You, of all people, cannot be suggesting we should just sit and wait."

"No, of course not. But . . ." Memory jumped to the front of my mind. I was in Ramona's apartment, and Kenisha was ordering me to stand still, to touch nothing.

"Ruby is at my house," I told her instead. "Alistair found her and she's been hiding in my basement. That's why Max and Leo . . ."

"Yip!" Leo, sensing he had become an important topic of conversation, wriggled off Julia's lap and trotted over to sit on my toes. "Yip!"

"Anyway, that's why they couldn't find her, because of the wards on the cottage."

"That's wonderful!" Julia pressed a hand against her chest. "Such a relief."

"No, it isn't," I said. "Because now we don't know where she was, or who tried to steal her, if anybody even did."

I watched the implications of this settle into Julia's thoughts slowly, and I watched her brush them away. My spirits plummeted.

"Yip?" Leo wagged hopefully. I patted his head. Max, not to be outdone, dug his nose under Julia's hands so she had to start petting his head again.

"What is your impression of the situation, Anna?"

"I *think* Ruby was stolen, or cat-napped, or whatever. Alistair doesn't want to let her go." Of course, that may have just been because the furry lunkhead was in love again. It says something about the direction my life had taken that I was getting used to having conversations about my cat's powers of judgment.

Julia didn't even crack a smile. "There is an invocation we could work. We would need several of the others. Of course, we will spare Kenisha . . ."

Spare Kenisha. I could just imagine what Kenisha would think about that.

"Julia . . . because of what Alistair did, because of what *I* did, we've lost any chance of finding out where Ruby really was, or who took her. What if it gets worse? What if we end up shifting things around so much that Kenisha and Pete are never going to be able to fit the pieces all back together again? What if we become responsible for Ramona's real killer getting away?"

"Yip!" announced Max sternly. I ignored him.

"You agreed with me, Anna," said Julia coolly. "You agreed we would make use of your gifts to find out who the witch is who interfered . . ."

"*We're* the witches who are interfering, Julia," I said. "We're getting in the way of the police."

"The police will have to manage their own affairs. If magic was used to harm Ramona, that is our business."

"The two aren't separate! Not where Ramona's death is concerned."

Julia's eyes glittered, hard and unrepentant. I felt a deep

chill rising in me. In the back of my head I saw Kenisha with her arms folded and her eyes narrowed. This was exactly what she'd warned me about. I heard her whispering to me in my kitchen, asking me to keep an eye on Julia, to make sure she didn't go too far.

Of course Julia saw the accusations in my expression. I'd never been able to hide anything from her. Max wriggled off his mistress's lap and ducked behind her full skirt.

I wished I could do the same.

"Julia, does this have something to do with the Forsythes?"

"It has everything to do with the Forsythes," she snapped. "Ramona is dead!"

"I mean with you and the Forsythes." *You and Wendy, or you and Rachael.*

"You've been talking with Kenisha. She's convinced you I'm trying to settle some old score."

"No, that's not it."

Julia waved one hand, tired and dismissive.

"All right, yes, I've been talking to Kenisha. She's my friend and my coven sister, and she's worried because you haven't been talking. To any of us. At all."

"I am talking with you now, Anna."

"Well, then you can listen to me tell you that Rachael said she's the one who broke her mother's wards. She said it was family tradition. She had to undo any spells Ramona might have left in the world. I saw her at the clinic this morning. She was painting over all of Ramona's warding circles there, too."

Julia went very still for a moment. "I hadn't thought about that," she breathed. "That is possible, I suppose. But still, she should have known how suspicious it would look."

I had meant to go on (gently) and talk about survivor's guilt, and how Julia should ask herself whether what happened when her good friend Dorothy died was affecting how she felt about Ramona's death. I wanted to say that maybe it wasn't the best thing to sit alone in her shop or her apartment, brooding. Maybe it was time to call on her coven for help and support, because that was what we were about, right? Guarding and healing. Right?

But I didn't. Because between one word and the next, a new idea hit me so hard it took all my breath away.

There was another way to look at the fact that the books of shadow were missing. Especially when you knew that there were all kinds of old feuds and suspicions in town, just below the surface, and if you knew that there had been an extra, invisible set of locks on Ramona's apartments and they'd been jimmied, just like the balcony doors.

If you had a suspicious turn of mind, like, say, the only witch cop in New Hampshire, you might wonder if Julia Parris had broken in and stolen the books. Julia had the opportunity. She'd at least been near the apartment building the morning after Ramona was killed. She certainly had the means, since she was one of the most powerful witches in New England. She even had the motive, because while she liked Ramona, she very clearly and openly carried a grudge against the rest of the Forsythes. Specifically, against Wendy Forsythe.

And she hadn't called the rest of the coven together. She was working her magic alone, in secret. Like she didn't want her friends and sisters to know what it was she was doing.

I didn't believe Julia had deliberately interfered with a crime scene or an investigation any more than I believed that Valerie had. The problem was, it didn't matter what I believed, or even what Julia and Val were really doing. What mattered was the part of the picture that the police could see. And what the police could see right now did not look good.

Especially if Kenisha decided there really was something strange about Rachael letting me into the apartment in the first place, murmured that unhelpful little voice. I told it to go soak its head.

"Julia, I think you need to take a step back," I said. "I think if you're forgetting details about ritual . . . you've maybe let this become personal."

As it turned out, this was exactly the wrong thing to say.

Julia's face hardened. Leo retreated to her side, at the same time Max reappeared from under her skirt.

But I didn't need hints from the dachshunds to tell me that Julia was angry. Every clipped-off word she spoke made that abundantly plain.

"Before you continue with your accusations, there are two things you should consider. The first is that I found the wards had been shattered the morning after Ramona's death. That is at least a full day before Rachael returned to town."

"I know, Julia, but . . ." But it didn't matter. Well, okay, it did matter because it meant Rachael had to be lying, like she was lying about having Ramona's books of shadow, which was important, but . . .

"The second is that your own Vibe told you there was a considerable streak of greed in the person who murdered Ramona. Greed that could have been for a share of Ruby's fame. It could have been a share of Kristen's business. Or it just could have been money. Like the money a woman might loan her sister to start a business she hoped would turn much more profitable than it has."

"I know, Julia, but—"

"But," she cut me off, "since you feel my assistance is unwelcome, I withdraw it." She lifted her walking stick and touched me on the shoulder with the glass handle. She whispered something too low and too fast for me to hear. I felt a jolt, like static electricity, and a rush, like someone had pulled a blanket off me to let in a burst of cold air.

"So mote it be," said Julia. "The summoning is removed. As you wanted."

"Julia." I swallowed. "It's just that—"

"It's just that you feel you are no longer able to trust my judgment. So, perhaps you should just leave."

"Julia—" I tried again.

"I asked you to go, Anna."

Somebody growled. I looked down at Max and Leo, who'd closed ranks between me and Julia. In the next eyeblink, I got to my feet and scooted out of that office as fast as I could without actually running. I walked through the sitting area and down the aisles and out the front door without once looking back.

Because just for a second, instead of two sweet miniature dachshunds guarding my mentor, I'd seen two full-sized Doberman pinschers.

And they did not look happy.

🐾 WHEN I PULLED into the cottage driveway, the sun was setting in a blaze of red and gold. Alistair was sitting on the porch, bolt upright, with his tail curled around his feet. It was the kind of highly dignified feline pose he adopted only when he was extremely annoyed at me.

"Merow!" he announced.

"So, I take it Val got here okay?" I asked, scratching his ears.

For an answer, Alistair vanished.

"We'll call that a yes, then." Despite all my worries, I couldn't help smiling, just a little.

"Hello, I'm home!" I called as I unlocked the front door.

"Hello!" Valerie called back. "We're in the kitchen, drinking your tea!"

I dropped my purse on the table beside the door and hung my outside clothes on the hooks. When I turned around, Val was there with two mugs of peppermint tea in her hands. Melissa did her best to wriggle in welcome despite being securely confined in the BabyBjörn sling on Valerie's chest.

"Ab-ab-ab!" she told me.

Val handed me a mug, along with an apologetic smile. It didn't take long to see what the apology was for.

"Hi, Anna."

Kristen Summers stood uncertainly on the hallway threshold.

"Kristen!" I exclaimed. "This is great! What happened? I mean . . . I thought . . ."

"Her lawyer got the bail hearing moved up, despite Blanchard's best efforts," Val said. "And honestly, we didn't know where else to go that wasn't surrounded by media."

"No, no, it's fine. I'm glad. Come on into the living room." I went first and pulled the drapes, just in case of overzealous newspersons. As I did, I couldn't help but notice that Alistair was not anywhere in sight, and neither was Ruby. I glanced at Valerie and she shook her head. She hadn't told Kristen we'd found Ruby yet.

Kristen took the armchair by the fireplace, and Valerie took the sofa. I settled onto the window seat and tucked my feet up under me.

"Did you see Julia?" Valerie asked as she lifted Melissa out of the sling and laid her on the afghan beside her. "How is she?"

"Yes. Good. Worried." Which was mostly true. The only problem with having Kristen here was that there was a whole lot of that conversation I couldn't repeat right now. "I also went to talk to Cheryl Bell."

"Am-oom!" exclaimed Melissa.

Now we were all looking at Kristen. She hunched forward with her elbows on her knees, watching the steam rise from the mug she held in both hands.

"What did Cheryl have to say?" she asked. "I mean other than cheering over the fact that I managed to get myself arrested?"

"For what it's worth, she doesn't think you killed Ramona."

"You're kidding, right?" said Kristen, and the surprise was genuine. "I would have thought she'd be turning handsprings."

"Actually, she was worried, because if you were tried for murder, the lawsuit over Ruby would go on the back burner and it would take her that much longer to get the money."

"Now, that sounds like Cheryl," Kristen muttered.

Val and I looked at each other. She winced in sympathy. She also tickled Melissa's tummy, just a little.

"She said something else, too," I told them all.

Kristen grimaced. "You might as well go ahead. I'm already sitting down."

"She said . . . she . . . that Ramona . . . well . . ."

"Anna," said Val sternly. "You're stammering."

"Yeah. Right. Well. Cheryl said that Ramona offered to sell her Ruby for ten thousand dollars."

"What?" Val and Kristen chorused, but then Kristen added, "And you *believed* her?"

"No, actually, I didn't. At least, I believe maybe Cheryl offered it, but not that Ramona took it. But, well, there's a problem . . ."

"Because why would Cheryl lie about something like that?" asked Val.

"Because she's Cheryl," said Kristen wearily. "She lies; it's what she does." But Kristen saw the doubt blossoming on Val's face, and she clenched her hands tight around her mug of tea.

"The problem is, Ramona really was having money trouble," I said. "And apparently her sister, Wendy, was on her case about it. Maybe it got to be too much."

"No," said Kristen flatly. "I won't believe it. Ramona was my friend, and she loved Ruby. She would never turn her over to Cheryl, not for any money."

"Kristen . . . ," Val began, but Melissa kicked her, and Val had to grab that one very wiggly foot and give it a gentle shake.

Kristen set the mug down, carefully, like she was afraid of breaking something. "You're always asking why Cheryl and I stopped talking? I'll tell you." She was breathing hard, like she'd been running. Her face flushed bright pink. "She was trying to get me to steal for her."

"*What?*" shouted Val.

"She knew, about you and me and our racket, and she was trying to get me to fork some of the takings over to her. For her. But I'd gone straight by then, just like you did, and she knew it. I'd been staying with her because I thought maybe I could talk her into getting her act cleaned up. I thought I had," she added in a whisper. "But that night she came to me, and she said that she needed money and that I owed her. I only found out later what she was really up to."

"What?"

"She was informing on . . . people to Michael Blanchard."

That's what she meant. I sucked in a long breath. *When she said, "It's not my job to make Blanchard's life easy for him. Not anymore."*

"He was paying her, and she was feeding him information. She was trying to set me up so she could get more money so she could leave town." Kristen rounded on me. "*That's* why you can't believe her. She uses people and she doesn't care who she hurts, as long as she gets what she wants."

Val picked Melissa up and cuddled her close. "Oh, Kris."

I felt a patch of warmth at my side, and I looked down. Alistair was crouched next to me, his tail lashing back and forth. He was staring so hard at Kristen, his whiskers quivered.

My mouth went dry. This was not something I was looking forward to.

"Kristen," I said, or croaked, really. "This doesn't explain why you've been lying to the police, and us."

Kris swiveled in her seat so she was staring right at Val. "You *told* her?"

"You can trust her, Kris," said Val. "Anna just wants to help, like I do."

"Why'd you go to New York, Kristen?" I asked. "Why'd you lie about it?"

"You can tell us anything," Val added.

"I can't," choked Kristen. Tears welled up in her eyes.

"You know me, Kris. After everything, would I try and pull a fast one on you?"

Kris shook her head. Val got up and went to wrap her friend in a warm hug. They leaned together for a long time, not saying anything. Melissa looked up at Val with a slightly confused expression on her round face and made a concerted grab for her chin.

"Am-oo?"

"Merow," said Alistair, and I swear for a minute it sounded like he was answering the baby.

"Pppbbbttt," she announced.

I sighed. I would think about this later. Right now, we had other problems to take care of. "I think it's time, big guy."

"Merow!"

"No, seriously. Now."

Alistair twitched whiskers and tail at me in a curiously resigned gesture. But he also got up and trotted through the dining room toward the kitchen.

Val and Kris pulled apart. Val furrowed her brow at me. "Anna, what are . . . ?"

"Meow!"

Kris jerked her head up and twisted around in the chair, just in time to see a long-haired black-and-white cat bound into the living room.

"Ruby!" she shouted.

"Meow!" Ruby launched herself into her owner's lap.

"I don't believe it!" Kris gathered her cat up into her arms and cuddled her close. "Ruby! I've missed you so much."

"Maow!" Ruby licked her cheek delicately and batted at her braid. "Meep."

Alistair sat in the doorway of the dining room and washed his tail in a gesture of extreme nonchalance. Despite all our problems, I couldn't help grinning.

"Where did you find her?" asked Kris over her cat's ears.

"I didn't. Lover boy over there did." Alistair switched to washing a front paw.

"Oh."

"Yeah. Oh," I agreed. "But all's well that ends well."

"Definitely." Kris kissed Ruby on top of her head. "Thank you, Alistair."

"Marow!" he declared loftily.

I laughed. "He says you owe him a can of tuna."

"And you wonder why your cat won't eat kibble," said Val.

"Well, he can have a whole case of albacore as far as I'm concerned." Kris hugged Ruby again. "I'd just about given up. But she's home now, and it's all over."

"Except you know that's not true," said Val softly. "And it's not going to be over until you tell the truth."

"I know." Kris sighed and settled Ruby back down on her knees. Ruby turned around several times and curled up, draping her tail over her nose. "You're right. I know you're right. It's just, it's hard to talk about. I don't even know where to start."

"Maybe I can help," I said. "This is all about the Ultra-premium line, isn't it? Best Petz was planning to sell cheap imported stuff and advertise it as organic and natural and all that."

"Oh-om-gah!" announced Melissa. Val tickled her baby's tummy again and was rewarded with a big grin.

"Merow!" agreed Alistair.

Ruby climbed up out of Kristen's arms and settled onto the back of the chair.

"When did you find out?" Val asked Kristen.

"I didn't find out. Ramona did. She heard some rumors when she was working with some of the animal handlers on the set of the new commercials, and she told me." Kristen gestured broadly, like she thought she could grab hold of some kind of answer. "She said she was going to report Best Petz to the FDA, and if the FDA wouldn't listen, she'd take it straight to the media before the line had a chance to be released. She told me I should get out of the way before things hit the fan." Kristen knotted her fingers around the end of her braid and tugged, hard. "*That's* why I was going to New York. I was going to be huddling with a whole team of lawyers and PR people to try to figure out how to keep

Ruby and Attitude Cat Enterprises out of the line of fire."
She snorted. "And you can see how well that worked out."

Val and I looked at each other blankly.

"Okay," said Val, holding up one hand like she was pleading for the world to stop for just a second. Melissa made a
grab for her thumb and missed. "This is bad. But you told
the police, right, Kristen? You explained."

"No," said Kristen.

Val stared at her friend blankly for a second while that
single word sunk in. "Well, you can tell them now." Val got
to her feet, cradled Melissa against her shoulder and headed
for the dining room and then the kitchen to get to the phone
on the wall. "We'll call Kenisha and she can . . ."

"No!" shouted Kristen to her back.

Val turned, and all the steel I knew waited in her spirit
was shining in her eyes.

"No, please, Val," said Kris more softly. "If you tell the
police about this, they'll have everything they need to convict me."

"But how . . . ?"

"If Best Petz goes down, the Attitude Cat brand is finished. Kaput. The second the cops find that out, what are
they going to think?"

But we all knew.

What the police had been missing to convict Kris of
murder was a genuinely plausible motive. When the scandal
about the pet food came out, they'd have that motive. In
spades. They would think that Kristen killed Ramona to
keep her quiet. Then they'd think she stole the laptop to get
rid of the evidence. Kristen could also have easily broken
into the apartment during Ramona's funeral to plant the
Aldina beads under the bed to frame Cheryl.

"Kris," said Val. "I know this is scary, especially because
you're right in the middle of it. But it's really not that bad
in the scheme of things. It's just false advertising, right? And
nothing's even been released yet. So there might be a fine,
and Best Petz will have to issue an apology, but companies

recover from stuff like this all the time. It's not a matter of life and death!"

"Except it is," said Kris.

"What do you mean?"

"Ramona told me . . . she told me that the reason the food was so cheap was that they were using ground-up peach pits as one of the fillers."

There is a feeling you get sometimes, like there's something very big and very bad looming behind you. That feeling closed in on me now.

"I don't understand," said Val. "I mean, peach pits can't be any good for a cat, but . . ."

"Ramona said peach pits can be poisonous," Kris told her. "They've got trace amounts of cyanide in them. It probably wouldn't be enough to make a grown cat sick, right away, but still . . ."

The world froze. Kris was still talking, but I couldn't hear any of it properly.

"Wait, wait! Stop!" I held up both hands. "Say that all again."

Kris frowned. "Ramona told me the food they were importing had—"

"No. Not that. The part about cyanide."

"Peach pits have cyanide in them. Not a lot. But still, it isn't . . ."

I was off the window seat, in the foyer and pulling my phone out of my purse before Kristen finished her sentence.

"Merow!" announced Alistair from the stairwell. "Merow!"

"I know, I know!" My hands shook as I punched up Rachael's number.

"Anna, what on earth . . . ?" began Val, but I waved her away. The phone was ringing.

"Hello?" said Rachael on the other end.

"Hello, Rachael? It's Anna."

"What's happened? You sound like you've been running a marathon."

"Listen, Rachael, is there any chance, any at all, that the kitten who was brought in today ate some of the Best Petz Ultrapremium food?"

"That hasn't been released yet." I heard the frown in her words.

"I know, I know, but you know, maybe she got hold of a special or a prerelease deal or a sample package or something like that . . . ?"

"I don't see how. Why are you asking?"

I looked toward my living room, toward Kris, who hunched in her chair, pale and angry and miserable.

"Merow!" Alistair reminded me.

"Because your mother found out that the new Ultrapremium line wasn't just cheap. It was tainted." And I told her what Kris had told us. Kris and Val, with Melissa in her arms, came to stand on the threshold and listen.

On the other end of the phone, Rachael was quiet for a very long time. "I'll check," she said. "I'll call back as soon as I hear something."

"I'll keep the phone on."

We said good-bye and we hung up.

"Start talking, Anna." Val hoisted Melissa a little higher on her shoulder. "You're freaking me out."

"Me too," said Kris.

"Maow!" Alistair snaked past them and circled my ankles. "Maow!"

I took a deep breath and smoothed my hair back with both hands. "Okay. Yes. Right."

I told them all about going to see Rachael at the clinic. I told them about her reaction to the news that Kristen had been arrested, despite, or maybe because of, the Aldina beads Kenisha and I had found.

Then I told them about Mittens.

"But . . . ," stammered Kris. "It's not possible. The line hasn't been released yet. The only reason we were even waiting was because there were at least three weeks left! How could Mittens's owner have gotten hold of any of the food?"

"I don't know," I said. "But it's a pretty huge coincidence otherwise. I mean, Ramona was investigating the possibility of tainted food, and a kitten turned up, poisoned, right here in Portsmouth. There has to be a connection."

As if to emphasize my point, my phone rang. I hit the Accept button and put it to my ear.

"Anna? It's Rachael. You were right." Her voice was shaking and raw. I wondered if she was crying. "I called Lisa Lewis. She said she had a sample pack of kitten treats from Best Petz. Mittens had gotten into the bag and eaten most of them." She gulped. "She's bringing me what's left. I'm calling a lab I know so we can get them tested as quickly as possible. But . . . oh, my God, if this is true, there's no time to waste . . ."

"But did she say where she got the sample?"

"Pam Abernathy," said Rachael. "Lisa's a client of theirs." She paused again. "I've got to call Pam right now, find out if Pam's given samples out to anybody else . . . Oh, God, Anna. I've got to get this going. I'll . . . We'll talk later, right?"

"Yes. Right. Go."

Rachael hung up without saying good-bye. I slid my phone back into my purse, but it was a long time before I could look up at my friends and our cats.

"Merow?" Alistair head butted my shins.

"I take it that was Rachael," said Val. "What did she say?"

"She says that kitten did get hold of some of the Ultra-premium food. She's calling a lab to get some tests, and then they'll be able to report it. So, hopefully, nobody else will get hurt."

I said this to Kris. She swallowed and walked back into the living room. She sat on the sofa and softly petted Ruby's back.

"How long have I got?"

"Don't worry, Kris," said Val. "You're not going to face this alone. Right, Anna?"

"Right," I said as firmly as I could. My mind was racing, trying to grab up all the separate bits of information that had been dropped in the past few days. It felt very full. "But we are going to have to take it all to the police."

"There has to be something else we can do before then," said Val. "Some way to keep Kristen in the clear. And"—she caught my gaze and held it—"there's still Julia. And Kenisha."

Kristen looked confused, but neither Val nor I elaborated. I understood her. Kenisha still thought Julia had been involved with whatever happened at Ramona's apartment. If we weren't able to answer that question along with all the others surrounding Ramona's death, we risked breaking apart the coven.

"You know there's one more possibility here, don't you?" said Val softly.

"Only one more?" I answered, and if I was a little grumpy about it, I think I get a pass on that one.

"You said Cheryl might be covering for someone."

"Maybe. I mean, we know she lies." In fact, she'd offered to lie for Blanchard. I'd heard her do it.

"But not for free," said Kris. "There's got to be something in it for her."

"Well, what if it wasn't Ramona who offered to sell her Ruby?" said Val. "There was someone else who wanted the money, and had access to the apartment, *and* was in town at the time, *and* who Rachael might feel like she needs to cover."

My mind shuffled through its basketload of facts and slowly brought up the relevant pieces. "You can't mean Wendy Forsythe?" I said.

Val nodded slowly. "I mean Wendy Forsythe. What if she's the one who offered to sell Ruby?"

Wendy. It would explain the broken wards. She could have gotten her sister out of the apartment somehow and gone in to meet Cheryl herself. But maybe Ramona came back too soon, or maybe she never left like she was supposed to . . . and there was a fight, or an accident.

"How would we prove it?" said Kris. "If Wendy hasn't come forward yet . . ."

"She's not likely to," Val finished for her. "And none of us will get her to."

"But there's still something missing," I said. "Even if Cheryl had planned to do something like meet Wendy at the apartment, she never actually got there. I'm sure of it. Something stopped her. But she still feels the need to cover up what really happened. That means she thinks there's still something in it for her."

"Maybe she thinks Wendy still has Ruby?"

I shook my head. "You think Cheryl would let herself be strung along like this without proof? Besides, if Wendy did get her hands on Ruby, she'd be better off trying to claim the reward than selling her to Cheryl."

"Fewer moving parts, less chance of a double cross," said Kris. "You'd make a good hustler, Anna."

I didn't know what to say to that.

"So, what do we do?" she asked.

I bit my lip. The clock was ticking. If Ramona had been killed because she could prove Best Petz was going to release tainted food, we not only had to find her killer; we had to re-create her evidence trail, and do it quickly. Otherwise . . .

I really didn't want to think about what would happen otherwise.

And now there was this. The very real possibility that Aunt Wendy had been in her sister's apartment and had broken the wards, not to get the books of shadow, but to try to cat-nap Ruby and sell her to Cheryl Bell.

On top of that, every day Pete thought Kenisha was hiding something to protect the "book group" was another day Kenisha risked getting into severe trouble and maybe even losing her job. We had to find some way to let everybody know what had really happened. Without accidentally getting the wrong person arrested.

We had to line the pieces up. All of them, and we had to do it fast. But despite everything, there were still too many pieces. And at least two different puzzles, with at least two sets of corners (sorry, Grandma McNally). And at least two sets of motivations.

Well, no, not really. There was only one motive here. Greed. There were just a lot of people who shared it.

Slowly, a plan began to take shape in my mind. I had no way to tell if it was actually a good plan, but it was all I had.

"I think I know what we can do, Val. But I'm going to need help, from both of you," I added to Kristen.

"What is it?" Val asked. "I mean, it seems like we've already talked to everybody who's going to talk to us."

I met my friend's worried eyes. "This is not going to involve talking."

❧ 42 ❧

✿ NINE O'CLOCK THE next morning found me sitting in my Jeep within view of the door to Abernathy & Walsh. I had a portfolio on the passenger seat beside me and a coffee to keep me company. Alistair, still sulking over the loss of his latest girlfriend, had declined to put in an appearance. I'd tried turning on the radio for some background noise but quickly switched it off. The story of Kristen's arrest, and her release on bail, was all over the news. Practically all I heard were exclamations like "Another strange twist in the case of America's most famous cat . . ." and "We've got an update in the Attitude Cat murder . . ."

The good news was that the mobs of media personnel who had been filling Market Square had all decamped for the courthouse and police headquarters. For the first time in days, the narrow downtown streets were as close to navigable as they ever got. Of course, that might change as soon as they heard that Attitude Cat had been found. But Kris was holding on to that particular bit of news for at least another five minutes.

So now I waited on the narrow side street in peaceful

silence and tried hard not to look like I was lurking. Which, to be honest, I kind of was.

Everything we'd found out so far said that Ramona was killed to keep her quiet about the tainted food Best Petz was getting ready to release as its Ultrapremium brand. So the question became, how many of the people involved—the "corners," as Sean had called them—knew about that?

Kristen knew, obviously. It had driven her to sneak to New York to try to get out of her contract with Pam and Best Petz.

Did Cheryl know? She was counting on Attitude Cat being a valuable brand for years to come.

Did Pam know? She had the alibi, sure, but that was shaky now that the time of Ramona's death was in question. Plus, she might easily have spilled the beans to somebody, like Cheryl. They might have worked together to come up with a plan. Those anonymous calls could have been meant as a distraction. That scene in Ramona's office could have been window dressing.

And then came the newest question. Did Wendy know? She was quickly becoming a "corner" person in the puzzles. Wendy was already worried about Ramona's money, or lack of money. Val might have gotten it right. Wendy might have planned to sell Ruby to Cheryl to recoup the money her sister owed her. But, she also might have found out that her sister was planning on blowing the whistle. She might have gotten angry because that would mean the end of those consulting fees from Best Petz.

There might have been an argument, and an accident.

The problem was, Wendy wasn't going to talk to me again. Not after that scene in Julia's office.

Cheryl wasn't likely to talk to me again either, and if she did, she might lie. I'd called Frank last night, but he still hadn't gotten an answer from his friend at the accounting office about whether that five thousand dollars had shown up in Ramona's account. I'd told him that the money might have gone to Wendy rather than Ramona. He said he'd do what he could, but he did not sound hopeful.

Rachael's phone had been sending calls to voice mail since

she'd called me the night before to tell me that Mittens had been given some of the Ultrapremium food. Which probably meant she was still frantically collecting the lab results and other information. So there was no talking to her yet.

But Pam was another story. Pam didn't have to talk to me. She had an office, and that office had files. If Abernathy & Walsh depended on Attitude Cat as much as I thought they did, there'd be signs of it in their files. If I was lucky and had been living right (a big "if" right now), there might be signs of whether Pam knew there were severe problems with the new Ultrapremium cat-food line. There might even be a memo or an angry e-mail from Ramona or from Kris somewhere. If I was really, really lucky, there'd be something indicating a connection between Pam and Cheryl Bell. Because the more I thought about Val's theory that Cheryl had killed Ramona to preserve the Attitude Cat brand, and its potential earnings, the more sense it made.

Now I just had to prove it. And ignore the little voice in the back of my mind that said if this very simple, very straightforward theory had any chance of being true, Kenisha and Pete would have worked it out already and arrested Cheryl.

That same little voice also pointed out that even if I could find a connection between Pam and Cheryl, I'd still have to find a connection between Pam, Cheryl, and some witch or witches unknown to make sense of all the questions swirling around Ramona's death.

I sighed, picked at the crumbs of the corn muffin I'd bought to go with my coffee and wondered why I didn't get the helpful kind of little voices.

What I did have, however, was a surefire way to get Pam out of the office so I could get a look at those files.

My phone made the little whooshing noise that indicated a text message had arrived. I checked the screen.

SHE'S CALLING NOW. V.

I looked up at the door to Pam's building.
Okay, countdown. Ten . . . nine . . . eight . . .

I'd just reached four when the building's door flew open and Pam Abernathy emerged. She hadn't even bothered to put on a coat, never mind a hat or gloves. I ducked down in my seat, but I needn't have bothered. Pam just jogged carefully down the sidewalk in her high-heeled boots with her phone pressed tight against her ear, not paying attention to the cold or anything else around her. Which wasn't at all surprising when you knew that Pam was talking to Kristen Summers, and that Kristen was saying Attitude Cat had been found, and that Pam should come to McDermott's B and B right away.

I grabbed my portfolio off the passenger seat and headed up the stairs. The next step in my master plan involved getting inside Pam's private office without anybody getting suspicious.

Now, despite what you may think, I have only minimal experience breaking into places where I'm not invited. So I'd done what any girl would in this situation. I'd turned to my older brother for advice.

He'd answered on the first ring.

Ted installs home security systems. He's also going to night school to finish his degree in something called "security design." When I asked him—hypothetically, of course—about breaking into somebody's office, he gave me a whole series of expert opinions. Including:

1) Don't do it.

2) No, really, sis, don't.

3) You get caught, and I am not bailing you out.

4) You better not mention this conversation over Thanksgiving dinner. Grandma B.B. will kill us both.

Once we got through several variations on this list, however, Ted did have a few practical things to say. They included the fact that you can almost always talk your way into a place, if you really try. So, my plan for this morning involved a little fast talking, the contents of my portfolio, and a fair amount of luck.

I won't say I missed Julia's spell right then, but I did feel a little nostalgia as I climbed out of my car and climbed the stairs.

"GOOD MORNING, ZACH."

"Huh? What? Oh." Zach looked up from the sheaf of papers clutched in his fist. More papers were scattered across his desk and half the floor. He was the only one in the front office. Today's shirt was a bright green, or maybe it was yesterday's shirt, because Zach had that rumpled and wild-eyed look you get when you haven't been to bed in a long time. "Anna Britton, right?"

"Right. I had an appointment with Pam?" This was not true, but I had been rehearsing my casual tone and look in the Jeep's rearview mirror. "About an Attitude Cat coloring book?"

"Really? I'm sorry . . ." Zach grabbed for a black engagement book, sending a fresh shower of papers down onto the carpet. "It's been . . . a little crazy here . . . some news came in about . . . well . . . about a client last night . . ."

Zach flipped nervously through the planner. I couldn't tell if it was lack of sleep making his hands shake like that or too much caffeine. There were at least four large paper coffee cups mixed in with the crumpled sandwich wrappers in the wire wastebasket by his desk. "I've got nothing here . . . Maybe you can reschedule?" The phone was ringing. "Hang on." He picked up the receiver. "Abernathy & Walsh, can you hold? Yes, no, yes . . . please, can you . . ."

"How about I just go drop the samples on her desk?" I pointed toward Pam's office. Zach waved vaguely in response. I took this as permission, slipped inside and closed the door.

The last time I'd been in this office, there'd been a table

filled with samples and mock-ups for Best Petz's new Ultra-premium product line. Now that table was completely empty. All signs of the new campaign had been tidied—or swept—away.

"Merow?"

I jumped and spun, which is a neat trick, and I don't recommend you try it, especially in heels, because the only reason I didn't end up down on the floor was that I banged up against Pam's desk. I also had to slap my hand over my mouth to keep from shouting.

Alistair watched all this from his position on Pam's much-scribbled-on desk blotter, lashing his tail back and forth. Human acrobatics did not impress him.

"What are you doing here?" I whispered fiercely. "Shouldn't you be helping keep an eye on Ruby and Kris?"

"Merow," he said noncommittally.

"Okay, then, you can watch the door." I scooted around the desk. Alistair turned in a full circle and sat down again, facing the door. On the other side, Zach's voice rose and fell unevenly. It did not sound like his conversation was going well.

I just had to hope that meant it was going to be a nice, long call.

Pam did not, unfortunately, do anything really helpful like leave her laptop open so that I could get in without knowing the pass code. She also did not conveniently leave her personal appointment book lying on the desk blotter with all those hastily written notes (I had to move my cat to check), or anything like that. And she locked her desk.

I glanced at the office door. I should not do this. But then, I shouldn't be in here at all.

I fished the sample coloring book pages (yes, I actually had some; it had been a very late night) and cover letter out of my portfolio and laid them on the desk, except for the one I dropped on the rug. Then I crouched down behind the desk and pulled my nail file out of my pocket.

These days, when people think about office security, they worry about their e-mails and their computers. Desk locks, according to Ted, are like window latches—they get taken for granted and are a lot easier to get into than they should be. I let out a long breath, mentally crossed my fingers, slid my file into the gap between drawer and desk frame and worked it back and forth, very, very carefully.

If there was a clock, it would have been ticking, but not as loudly as my heart was pounding. I was sure the door was going to open any second now. Kris hadn't been able keep Pam at the B and B, and she was coming back now. Or Zach was going to wonder why it was taking me so long to drop off a few pieces of paper. This was a bad idea. I needed to stop this. Right now.

"Merow," Alistair said. I gritted my teeth and wiggled my file.

The latch snapped back and the file drawer slid open. I swallowed a big lump of fear.

Zach's voice paused for three frantic heartbeats before it started up again.

Pam's files were as tidy as the rest of her office. Carefully labeled manila folders filled color-coded hanging files. A good half of the files were related to Attitude Cat. There were invoices, proposals, spreadsheets and memos going back at least seven years. Another fat set of files was devoted to Best Petz. On the surface, these looked like more of the same, until I pulled one invoice out to take a better look and saw the big red note written in stiff block capital letters.

OVERDUE!

There were more of these notes, on more invoices. A lot more.

Out in the front office, Zach's voice had dropped away.

"Merow," said Alistair, which I assumed meant *Hurry up, human!*

I flipped faster. Pam filed her invoices according to date. The most recent ones were not overdue. They were marked PAID IN FULL (in black ink).

Okay. Okay. That told the story of the income for

Abernathy & Walsh. Bills submitted to Best Petz had not been getting paid about a year ago. Now they were getting paid. Right about the time Pam started billing for the development of the Ultrapremium campaign. Which spoke volumes about how important this new line was, not only to Abernathy & Walsh but to Best Petz itself.

Expenses were (of course) in a separate set of files. I pulled one out. I flipped. Pages of multicolored receipts for office supplies, phone bills, bills from hotels and restaurants and . . .

And Dr. Ramona Forsythe.

"Merow!" Alistair told me again. Zach was talking again, more slowly. Things were winding down out there.

The file had at least five invoices to be paid to Dr. Ramona Forsythe for "consulting." And they were not small. Abernathy & Walsh had paid Ramona at least seventy thousand dollars over the past year.

This was what Ramona was going to give up to blow the whistle on Best Petz. Wendy would not be happy. But did I honestly believe she was willing to let innocent animals get sick and die so her sister could keep a lucrative consulting gig? I pictured Wendy's eyes as she stared Julia down. I remembered the greed I'd felt ringing so loud and clear around Ramona's apartment. I heard Val's voice neatly laying out all the reasons it was Wendy, not Ramona, who was behind the plan to sell Ruby. Which would, incidentally, bring Cheryl to Ramona's apartment at the perfect time to make her look guilty of murder.

I shuddered.

A quick shuffle through the rest of the folders failed to turn up any paper copies of e-mails. There were letters from law firms, copies of contracts, and endless, endless eight-by-ten glossy color photos of aspiring cats.

And finally, way toward the back, there was a fat folder labeled ACE/CB.

I yanked it out and flipped it open.

But this was not more invoices or receipts. This was a whole sheaf of densely written legal papers. If the print had been any finer I would have needed a microscope. As it was, I practically had to put my nose to the paper.

"Me-er-ow," muttered Alistair.

"Yes, yes, I know," I muttered back. I couldn't hear Zach, but I was never getting another chance. I had to keep reading.

Since I make most of my money freelancing, I've seen a lot of contracts. These, though, were really different from the ones I was used to, and a lot more complicated.

I should have brought Enoch with me.

"Maow!"

"I am hurrying!" I hissed back.

These weren't contracts for services or consulting. This was a purchase agreement. Specifically, it was an offer from Best Petz to buy Attitude Cat Enterprises for . . . my eyes bulged in their sockets as they skimmed over all the zeros, including the ones on the commission that was going to Abernathy & Walsh for brokering the deal.

Kristen had said she wanted to get out of the Attitude Cat business. These papers said she was doing it in the most direct way possible. She was selling the brand.

It was a great solution. Kristen got to keep her cat, and she made enough money that she was set for life and didn't have to work in a business that didn't make her happy anymore.

At least, it would be a great solution, if a scandal about tainted cat food didn't interrupt the deal.

On the other side of the door, Zach's voice paused again, and my heart thumped. But the tenor rumble started up again. Alistair's ear twitched.

There was one other bundle of papers in the folder. I bit my lip and lifted up the cover sheet.

This I recognized right away. This was a consulting contract, with the new Attitude Cat Brandz, LLC (a wholly owned subsidiary of Best Petz Worldwide). I even recognized the name on it.

That's because the name was Cheryl Bell.

I sucked in a long breath. Okay. I'd come in hoping to find a connection between Pam and Cheryl. Here it was.

Pam had two problems after all. The first was Kristen, who was burning out on being the owner of a celebrity cat. The second was Cheryl. Pam must have realized that even if Cheryl Bell lost her lawsuits, she still could find new ways to make trouble. These contracts were an attempt to kill two birds with one stone. Yeah, I winced at the metaphor too, but it was accurate. As soon as Kristen sold Attitude Cat Enterprises, Pam and Best Petz could turn right around and put Cheryl on the payroll. I bet there was a nice little fee hidden in all these closely written clauses for Abernathy & Walsh's part in negotiating the deal.

One very important detail remained, though. These contracts were originals, not copies, and they were unsigned. The deal hadn't gone through yet.

And now it might not. Ever.

"Merow!" Alistair vanished.

I slammed the drawer shut and dove under the desk. The doorknob turned. I snatched my sample page off the carpet.

"Everything all right, Anna?" Zach leaned in at the same moment I straightened up with the sample page I'd "dropped" in my hands. All as innocent as Alistair over an unattended slice of salmon.

"Yes, sorry, loitering." I laid the page on the desk with the others. "I was hoping Pam might be back by now."

"She might be a while," said Zach. "It's a very important client."

No kidding. I hoped he didn't notice how tightly I clutched my portfolio to my chest, or that my voice was maybe just a little too bright as I asked the next question. "Bet there've been a lot of late nights?"

Zach rolled his eyes. "You have no idea. Even the night Ramona died. We were right here, trying to get the final print and media budgets sorted out."

"That's for the new Ultrapremium line, right? That's a pretty big deal."

"It's an enormous deal. Boss was a little nuts about it. I bet she sent me and Damon out ninety different times for sandwiches and coffee. We even ran out of dry-erase markers at one point." He chuckled. "I've never seen her so worked up. So, you know, you might not be hearing from her about those samples for a while. Are these them?" He picked up a page and squinted at it absently, but his attention was really on the rest of the office. "They're really good."

"Thanks." I made myself keep my eyes on him and keep smiling. At the same time, I had a death grip on my portfolio. Had I left a drawer open? Dropped an invoice? I didn't know. I didn't dare look.

Zach was still looking around. "Something wrong?" I asked, hoping he didn't hear the hitch in my voice.

"No . . . no . . . only I think the job is getting to me. For a second I could have sworn I heard a cat."

43

♣ "SEEMS TO ME we've been here before," said Kenisha.

"Here" was the private dining room at the Pale Ale. I owed Martine big-time. I kept monopolizing her space. And her bartender. Sean was standing beside the table, pouring out coffee and more of the mulled cider.

"Well, you said you didn't want us holding any more secret meetings," I reminded her.

"Me and my big mouth." Kenisha nodded hello to Val and Roger (and Melissa). The Clan McDermott had arrived shortly after I had texted them the all clear from Abernathy & Walsh.

Rachael Forsythe was there too, huddled in her chair, a stack of printouts and faxes on the table and a tote bag resting on the chair beside her.

Kristen, of course, was not there. She was still with Pam, presumably crafting the announcement that Attitude Cat had been found. Frank Hawthorne was not there either. He was at the paper, probably with his hand hovering over the Send key. Because some anonymous source might just possibly have given him the heads-up that Ruby was back safe and sound.

But while Frank was not physically with us, his presence was going to make itself felt. Because just as I stepped out onto the sidewalk, fresh from my little bout of breaking and entering Pam's desk, I'd gotten a phone call.

"Anna?" Frank said. "I've got something you're going to want to hear."

"What is it?"

"That five thousand that Cheryl told you about? That she was supposed to have paid to Ramona? According to my source at the accounting firm, there's no sign of it anywhere in Ramona's bank records." He paused and I heard the sound of rustling paper. "Looks like Mrs. Bell went and lied. Again."

Yes. I had to agree that it did look that way.

"So what's going on?" Kenisha laid her cap on the table and took the mug of coffee Sean pushed toward her. "I thought at the end of the mystery, it was the suspects that all gathered together."

"You know me," I said. "I love to defy expectations."

"Is this all of us?" asked Val before Kenisha had a chance to tell me what she thought of that.

"There's two more."

"One more," said Sean.

Julia sailed through the doorway. None of us actually stood up as she strode to the head of the table, but I'm sure we all wanted to. Sean touched the rim of his fedora like he was thinking of taking it off in front of the lady. He saw me looking at him, and he blushed.

Julia sat and folded her hands on top of her walking stick. I tried not to notice how neither she nor Kenisha had acknowledged each other.

She did acknowledge me, though.

"I am not certain I approve of this plan of yours, Anna," my mentor announced.

"I know," I said. "And I know we need to talk and you're mad at me and I might have to turn in my wand when all this is over. But we're running out of time, and unless anybody's got another idea—"

"Well, good morning, everybody."

Pete Simmons pulled his furry Russian hat off his balding head. He surveyed us all with his perpetually tired eyes.

"Good morning, Detective Simmons," said Julia gravely.

"Hi, Pete," said Kenisha. "Thanks for coming."

"Sure, sure." Pete settled into the chair she shoved out for him and accepted a cup of coffee from Sean. "Always glad to meet with members of the community."

"And we appreciate that," I told him.

"The thing is, it's kind of a busy time right now, so maybe you could tell me what all this is about?"

He was asking Kenisha, but she, and everybody else, was looking at me.

Showtime.

I took a deep breath. "So, Detective Simmons, as you know, we . . . are all members of the Portsmouth Area Ladies Book Group and Bonfire Appreciation Society."

"You are?" said Pete slowly. "I didn't realize the group was so . . . extensive." He looked at Kenisha. Kenisha looked at the bottom of her coffee cup.

"We are a venerable and wide-ranging organization," said Julia staunchly.

Kenisha stared at her and at me. I gave a very small shrug. Valerie adjusted Melissa's blanket. She'd been the one on the phone with Julia, explaining the plan while I was busy in Pam's files.

"Dr. Forsythe was a member as well," I said. "Naturally, all of us in the society were terribly shocked by her death."

"Naturally," Pete replied. Sean, helpfully, topped up Kenisha's coffee cup. And Pete's.

"And, naturally, we've been spending a lot of time talking about what we can do to help the Forsythe family," I went on. "And while we were talking with our members and paying condolence calls, we heard some things that might be helpful to the investigation."

"I see." Pete blew on his fresh coffee and sipped judiciously.

"So, of course, we immediately contacted Officer Freeman, who advised us that the right thing to do was to tell the police immediately."

"Because the PALBGBAS is a civic-minded organization that includes many Portsmouth small business owners," added Val. "And we wanted to be sure to tell you everything at once so as not to waste your valuable time."

Pete cleared his throat. "Well. I see. And I of course would like to thank the members of the . . . I'm sorry . . . ?"

"Portsmouth Area Ladies Book Group and Bonfire Appreciation Society," said Kenisha. "Just like I told you."

"Sure. Right." Pete's mouth puckered up. "Thank you all for your civic-mindedness. I'm sure my lieutenant will say the same when he finds out about this." He looked right at me, and I tried not to squirm. "You don't mind if I take notes?" He pulled his book out.

"Not at all, Detective," said Julia regally. "Whatever you need. We are only here to help."

Kenisha was drinking coffee, which was probably a good thing, because I had the distinct feeling she was in danger of cracking an inappropriate smile.

"Right. Okay." Pete pulled his notebook and pencil out of his jacket pocket and opened it to a blank page. "Ms. Britton, can I assume we'll be starting with you?"

He could. I looked into Pete's mild, drooping eyes, and I started talking.

I told him about Ramona's connection with Pam and with Best Petz. From the patient way he listened, I got the idea he already knew about it.

Then I told him about the tainted food and Ramona's intent to blow the whistle.

Pete stopped writing. "You're sure about this?"

Val reached into her bag and pulled out a piece of paper. "Kristen couldn't be here, but she wrote this out." She pushed the paper toward him. "She's expecting to hear from you, to confirm everything."

Pete read the statement, and took his time about it. When he was finished, he didn't say anything. He made another note.

I told him about how I'd picked up Pam Abernathy's phone the night Ramona died, and what I'd heard. I am pleased to say I managed to keep the stammering to an absolute minimum. I also apologized profusely.

Pete wrote this down without comment. I had the distinct feeling that once again he was not at all surprised.

Then it was Rachael's turn. Keeping her eyes fixed on the tabletop, she spoke quietly about the sick kitten she had treated, about my phone call asking whether Mittens could have gotten hold of any of the Ultrapremium food.

She pushed the stack of papers toward Pete. "These are the lab reports," she said. "And the warnings that were registered about the supplier Best Petz was using."

"Is there something else you want to say, Rachael?" prompted Kenisha. Because Kenisha had been the one who'd picked Rachael up at the clinic this morning to bring her to our meeting. On the way, she had asked about Aunt Wendy and the wards and explained that the only way for Rachael to keep her family safe was to tell everything she knew.

"Go ahead," said Kenisha to her now. "We're all on your side."

Rachael's eyes slid sideways to Pete. But she nodded.

"My mother and my aunt Wendy were . . . they'd been fighting about money," she said. "Aunt Wendy thought Mom should be making way more from the clinic than she was. She . . . got it into her head that Mom was hiding the money."

I sat up straighter. I hadn't heard this.

"The night my mother died, Aunt Wendy broke into her apartment and stole some of her . . . journals." Rachael lifted the tote bag and set it on the table. "I found them this morning. She thought they might show that Mom was hiding some money from her."

I glanced at Julia, who sat as still and silent as a stone.

"And what did Ms. Forsythe have to say when you confronted her?" asked Pete. "I mean, you did confront her?"

Because what else would you do when you found out your aunt had stolen from your mother? Rachael grimaced. "She said she was doing it for Mom's own good. She said . . ."

"It's okay, Rachael," said Kenisha. "We can go over all this with Ms. Forsythe directly. Right, Pete?"

"Sure, sure, sure," he said. "Is there anything else, Ms. Rachael?"

"Yes," said Rachael. "The day before my mother's funeral, I was in her apartment. I was angry. I was sure Cheryl Bell had killed her and I didn't think anything was being done. I decided I'd try to . . . push things in what I thought was the right direction. I'd gotten an Aldina bracelet for my last birthday and I took two of the beads and put them under my mother's bed, and then I asked Anna to go to the apartment. I knew Anna had a . . . reputation for finding things . . . and hoped she would discover the beads."

"And you called us to go in after her?" said Pete. "Just to be sure it all came out?"

"Yes," Rachael whispered. "Am I going to jail?"

Pete turned over a page in his notebook. "I don't think it'll come to that. Interfering with an investigation is a serious matter, but I think we can make a case that there was emotional distress and extenuating circumstances."

The whole room let out the breath we'd all been holding.

"But," Pete added, "it does mean we're going to have to check the rest of the story very carefully. And we'll probably need to be getting some additional details. For instance"—he laid his finger on one particular note—"if your mother found out about the tainted food, why didn't she report it right away?"

"The brand wasn't released yet," I said. "Ramona thought she still had some time."

Pete nodded, managing to convey both his sympathy and the fact that this was probably not the most prudent course of action. Pete was very talented that way.

"There was also a great deal of money riding on the new line, and Attitude Cat," I said, so Pete would be looking at me instead of Rachael. I could tell she was beginning to get frightened again, and more than a little bit angry.

"And, Ms. Britton, you know this, because . . . ?"

"I did some research," I said. I really hoped I wouldn't

have to tell him it involved an overly convenient phone call, a fake coloring-book sample and a nail file. "Pam Abernathy was setting up a deal to sell the rights to the Attitude Cat brand entirely to Best Petz, and when that happened, Cheryl Bell would get a consulting job from them, presumably in exchange for dropping the lawsuit."

"Presumably," said Pete. "You could prove this?"

"You know, Pete," cut in Kenisha. "The lab reports here"—she tapped Ramona's stack—"might finally be enough for Judge Turner to give us a warrant for the Abernathy & Walsh files. It goes straight to working out the motive for the murder. I mean, if Cheryl Bell was due to get a payout when the deal went through and the new line hit the shelves, there ought to be a record of it in the files, right?"

Pete tapped his pencil thoughtfully against the table. "Sure, sure. That might just do it." He checked his watch. "And the judge should be back from lunch just about now."

"Wow," chirped Val. "Great timing."

I may have prodded her ankle under the table. Firmly.

"Well." Pete got to his feet. "I want to thank you for your information." He paused. "You can be sure we'll be taking all this very seriously, but you ought to know that when it comes to an investigation this complicated, well, it doesn't always go the way we think it should. What looks obvious from one angle might turn out to be something quite different when you get the whole picture." He said this straight to Rachael. "And we might uncover a lot of other unpleasant facts in the process."

Rachael pushed the stack of paper toward him. "I know, Detective. I just want to help. These are copies of what we've found about the pet food. The phone numbers are all there if you need to check the findings with the lab."

"Thank you," said Pete. "You've been very cooperative, and that's going to count for a lot. Officer Freeman? I'll see you back at the station? Soon?"

"Right behind you, Detective," agreed Kenisha.

Pete shouldered his way back into his coat and gathered up the papers. Sean held out his hat for him. Their eyes met.

"Ladies Book Group and Bonfire Appreciation Society?" said Pete.

"I'm doing a flaming rum punch for the December meeting," replied Sean coolly. "You should come."

Pete raised both eyebrows at him and walked out without saying another word.

❧ 44 ❧

🐾 VAL HURRIED TO the dining room door and peered out. Presumably to watch Pete leave the premises, because she turned around and let out a triumphant whoop. "We did it!"

"Ah-moo!" added Melissa, who may have gotten slightly sandwiched between her parents as they kissed.

"Maybe," muttered Kenisha.

We all turned to stare at her.

"What do you mean maybe?" I asked. "You heard Pete."

"Yeah, I heard him." Kenisha sighed. "I also know him. He's not sure how much he believes. Maybe none of it."

Rachael got to her feet, her face flushed red. "But he'll figure it out, right? It's all right there in front of him."

"We can hope," said Kenisha. "But between your planting fake evidence and Anna's kind of vague answers about how she got the business details on Attitude Cat, there's a lot of dicey stuff here. If it doesn't play out exactly the way we want it to . . ." She let the sentence trail off.

"But . . . but . . . I just . . . I confessed!" Rachael threw her hands out. "I put Mom's reputation out there, and the clinic's!"

And Aunt Wendy's. She didn't say that, but it shone in her eyes.

"Easy does it, Rachael," said Sean. "We're all worried, but this place isn't as private as all that. You might not want to . . ."

Rachael was not in a mood to listen. "It can't all be for nothing!"

"It won't be," said Julia firmly. "You told the truth. Remember, what you send out into the world comes back to you, threefold."

"And Pete will look into it," said Kenisha. "And I'll back him up with everything I've got. We're just going to have to be patient."

"You don't understand, any of you!" shouted Rachael. "This is going to come out in just a matter of hours. If people don't know what Cheryl was doing, it's going to look like Mom was covering up the tainted food!"

"That's why the next place we're going is the *Seacoast Times*," I told her. "You're going to talk to Frank Hawthorne and get the story out first." I'd been reading up on disaster communications strategies along with probable cause for search warrants.

"And you think that will make a difference?" she said, clearly torn between hope and disbelief.

"I think at this point, it can't hurt."

Rachael didn't answer me. She just picked up the tote bag with the books of shadow and turned to Julia. "I think you'd better take these," she said softly. "Aunt Wendy . . . she might . . . well, the truth is, I don't know what she's going to do next."

Julia took the bag. "I am sorry this has come down on you, Rachael. And I'm sorry I have done so very little beyond make it worse."

"Julia . . . ," began Kenisha.

"No, Kenisha. It's all right." Julia raised her eyes to the room. "I owe you all an apology. I have been hurt and grieving and . . . taking Ramona's loss far too personally. It has led me to . . . intemperate words and actions. I ask for forgiveness, from all of you." These last words she spoke directly to me.

"We've all made mistakes," I said.

"And we're still all here." Val took Roger's hand. "And we're still all a family."

"So mote it be," murmured Julia.

If it had been anybody else, this might have ended in a hug. But this was Julia. It ended in a deep breath. And marching orders.

"Anna, you will take Rachael to see Frank Hawthorne," she said briskly. "Valerie, Roger, I think you had better return home and be there when Kristen and Pamela get the news about this search warrant that will shortly be coming their way. Probably, there will be some upset. Mr. McNally . . ." She turned to Sean.

"Yes, ma'am?" Sean touched his hat brim.

"Do you by any chance know how to mix a sidecar? I need a drink."

"IT WILL BE all right, Rachael," I told her as we climbed into my Jeep. "You'll see."

She folded her arms tightly around her. "I know; at least, I think I do. But you know, Julia talked about family. This is all about my family. And I'm breaking us apart," she added in a whisper.

"No. This is not your fault."

She didn't answer. Not directly. "Maybe we shouldn't go to Frank just yet. Maybe we should wait until after we're sure Detective Simmons's got everything straight. I mean, what if I go public and there's still another shoe waiting to drop?"

I bit my lip. "I understand how you feel, Rachael," I said. I also ignored the highly skeptical look she turned on me. "But Frank—"

And of course, that was when my phone rang. "Sorry," I muttered as I yanked it out of my purse. "Let me just . . ."

I moved to mute the thing, but then I saw the number on the screen.

"Well. Speak of the devil." Or at least the newspaperman. I hit the Accept button. "We're on our way, Frank—"

But Frank wasn't listening. "Anna, that big meeting you were going to have with Pete Simmons, is it still going on?"

"No," I told him. "We just finished, why?"

"Well, you might want to start it up again. I finally heard from my source at the accounting firm."

Uh-oh. "And?"

"He's sorry he took so long, but a police investigation really complicates everybody's access to their records and—"

"What did they find?"

Rachael was looking at me. Of course she could hear only half the conversation, but it was not in any way the good half.

"Ramona Forsythe had an account, opened right at the time of her death, with exactly five thousand dollars in it."

"What?" Oh, no. *Poor Rachael.* I squeezed my eyes shut. This would break her heart.

"But here's the thing," Frank went on. "It looks like Ramona didn't open it. Somebody else opened it in her name."

"You can do that?"

"If you have enough information, you can."

"But who?" Wendy? Cheryl herself? *Oh, please.* My gaze darted to the passenger seat. *Please, not Rachael . . .*

"Pam Abernathy."

❧ 45 ❧

🐾 THE FIRST THING that happened was Rachael sent a text to Aunt Wendy telling her not to worry. Things at the clinic were just taking a little longer than she'd hoped.

The second thing that happened was that I drove us to Ramona's condominium and parked the Jeep a good quarter mile down the road.

The third thing that happened was I turned to Rachael and watched her unbuckle her seat belt.

"Rachael . . . ," I began.

"No. I am not changing my mind," she said in a steely tone that would have done Julia, or Aunt Wendy, proud. "You heard what Kenisha said. Pete already has doubts about what we told him. We go back waving some new scrap of evidence, he's going to think something's fishy."

Especially when Pete now knew that Rachael had already tried once to make a false case against Cheryl.

"Besides," she went on. "Pam . . . Pam is a friend of the family's. I can't accuse her without being sure. Enough people are already going to be ruined by this."

"But we are sure," I told her. "Now we have to let the police do their job."

"Anna." Rachael faced me. Her eyes were dry but red around the edges, reminding me of her sleepless night. "I came out here this morning because you asked me to. I told Pete everything because you said you were sure it would settle all the questions and that we'd be able to put Cheryl Bell in jail. But it's only made everything worse."

"But now we know that Cheryl was conspiring with Pam to cover up the tainted-pet-food scandal. She will go to jail."

"And if Cheryl denies it? She's already set up her story." By telling it to me. I grimaced. "Or what if Pam tells a different story? Then what? The police already don't believe us! And Aunt Wendy . . . I don't even want to think about what she's going to say." Anger warred with the fear in her voice. "I just . . . I just want to be sure it's not all going to be for nothing. Please," she said. "You have to let me talk to Pam first. I have be sure."

I did not like this. And yet, I felt responsible. It was my fault things were as confused as they were. I had been so sure that we would lay everything to rest this morning. But now this new shoe had dropped. And the clock was still ticking down. Fast. And faster.

"You don't have to be there," said Rachael.

"No," I said. "You're not doing this alone." She looked ready to argue, but I didn't let her get started. "If there are two sets of eyes, and two phones making a recording, whatever we end up having to tell the police will be that much more believable."

Rachael clearly didn't agree, but she didn't argue. She just pulled out her phone and hit a number.

"Hello, Pam? Yeah. It's Rachael. Yeah . . . I know. But, Pam, I need you to come over to Mom's apartment." She paused. "I know you're in the middle of things. But there's a big problem. It's about the new Best Petz line," she added, and she looked at me while she did. "I've found something here, and I don't know what to do."

She listened and nodded, like you do even when you know the person on the other end can't see you. "Right, ten minutes," Rachael said, and she hung up.

The next thing that happened was that I went with Rachael as she unlocked her mother's apartment, and I hid behind the curtains.

Well, okay, I hid behind the half wall in Ramona's loft. It wasn't the most secure location in the world, but it would allow for a better sound quality than my first idea, which was me hiding out on the balcony. I climbed the stairs and settled down behind the chest where Ramona kept the tools of the true craft.

"Merow?" Of course Alistair was there, right beside me, running his paws over his ears to show how seriously he took the whole situation.

I sighed. "Okay," I whispered. "But you need to keep quiet."

For an answer, he vanished, then reappeared under the bed, scrunched back so far in the shadows, all I could see were his blue eyes.

Right. Good. That's my guy.

I crossed my legs and generally got myself as comfortable as I could. I laid my wand on my knee. All the Vibes left from Ramona's death were still here. I breathed as deep as I could and focused on my shields. I needed them. There was so much anger swirling out beyond that shimmering mental curtain, it was nearly impossible for me to sit still.

I pulled out my phone, checked the charge level and made sure I had the voice recorder ready to go.

Below, the intercom buzzed, and I just about jumped out of my skin.

Just breathe, I told myself. *Breathe and focus.*

I peered around the corner of the chest. From here, I could see down the stairs to the door. Rachael walked into view and pressed the buzzer to let whoever it was in. She stood right in front of the door, gathering her nerve. A few frantic heartbeats later, somebody knocked.

I ducked back. I also hit the Record button on my phone and set it, carefully, on top of the chest.

"Rachael," Pam sounded breathless. "What on earth's happened? What have you found out? I had to leave Kristen back at the McDermotts'. I can't tell you how badly everything's exploding right now."

I heard rustling. I bit my lip and dug my fingers into the carpet. *You can't look. You can't look.*

Rachael didn't answer.

"Rachael?" Pam's voice broke. "Please, honey, what is it? You know I just want to help."

"You," Rachael croaked. "I found out about you."

There was silence for one heartbeat. Two. I gripped carpet and clenched every muscle in my body. I had to hold still. I had to. The Vibe pressed hard against my shields.

Breathe, breathe, breathe. I clutched my wand.

"What are you talking about?" asked Pam, very, very carefully.

"I know about the Ultrapremium line," said Rachael. "About the tainted fillers they're using in the food."

There was another long, painful pause. "You know?" breathed Pam finally.

I will not move. I will not check to make sure the phone is recording. I will not give myself away. Alistair slunk on his belly to the edge of the bed. I glowered at him. *You won't either, you big galoot.*

"I've been going through the clinic records," Rachael said. "There was enough in the files that I was able to piece the truth together."

Nice one. I leaned the back of my head against the wall. My hand hurt from how hard I gripped my wand.

"Listen, Rachael, I understand this is a shock." I could picture how Pam's face shifted as she pulled on her expression of gentle sympathy. "It's a terrible situation, and it needs to be brought out in the open. If you could give us just a few weeks more—"

Rachael didn't let her get any further. "I had a kitten in my office the other day. She'd been eating the food. She almost died."

"That must have been an older batch," said Pam quickly.

"I promise you, Best Petz has fixed the problem. They changed suppliers months ago."

"Is that what you told Mom?"

That stopped Pam cold. "Rachael, I don't know what you think you know . . ."

"I know enough to make your life very difficult if I decide to."

Pam sighed. I imagined her straightening up and plastering a reasonable expression on her face.

"All right. Rachael, you have as much of a stake in this as any of the rest of us. I was going to be offering you the same consulting contract with Abernathy & Walsh as your mother had. Think about it. It'll be a steady income for you as soon as you get your license. You could get the clinic back on its feet if you wanted. All we need is one more week to finish a little paperwork."

"And after that?"

"After that, Attitude Cat belongs to Best Petz. Cheryl Bell quietly drops her lawsuit, and we all take the profits and go our own separate ways."

Alistair crept out from under the bed. His whiskers were twitching madly. He didn't like this. Neither did I. My shields wavered and I felt the hot anger and cold greed slam hard against them.

"And what if Best Petz lied about changing suppliers?" Rachael demanded below us. "They've lied about everything else just to save themselves some money."

"I've already checked," Pam said soothingly. "I've verified everything. Really. You have to trust me. It's already done."

"Then why won't Best Petz make an announcement? Tell people who might have gotten some of the old samples to throw them out?"

"That's coming, I swear," said Pam. "I've got the press release all drafted. I just need one more week. That's all. Then you can take whatever evidence you think you have about tainted food to the whole world. I don't care. Just give me time to clear myself and my people out of this mess."

"Is that what you told Mom?"

"Rachael, your mother was my friend. She *understood*. She was giving me time."

Alistair was on all his paws, his tail fluffed out. I spread my fingers and braced myself. This was bad. I felt it. The Vibe was churning through the whole room, a whirlwind of feeling. This was wrong. Really, seriously wrong.

"But it wasn't going to be enough time, was it?" said Rachael quietly. "That's why you had to conspire with Cheryl Bell. You offered her the consulting job. You opened the account and put the money in so it would look like Mom was stealing. That way no one would believe she was actually going to blow the whistle on Best Petz."

"Rachael . . . "

"Who did you get to make those fake cat-napping phone calls?"

Pam sighed impatiently. "Zach. I told him it was part of a PR stunt, so don't go blaming . . ." She didn't finish that sentence. "Listen to me, Rachael. We've all made mistakes—"

"This isn't a mistake! This is deliberate fraud! It's criminal neglect! It's perjury and—"

"Don't you think I know that?!" screamed Pam.

Silence fell, hard, thick and heavy.

"What was I supposed to do, Rachael?" Pam said. "I've got people depending on me! I'm a fifty-year-old woman. My firm specializes in pet-oriented branding. Who is going to hire me if they discovered I helped cover up a case of tainted pet food? There is no way to recover from that. I just needed time to erase the chain. That's all. I needed to keep my people safe."

"And yourself," said Rachael bitterly. The tide of anger surged, and surged again. My head lifted; so did all the hairs on the back of my neck.

"Yes, yes! All right!" Pam was shouting again. My shields waved, wobbled and held. Barely.

Alistair crept to my side. He rubbed his head against my hand. I wrapped an arm around him.

Something was wrong. Something was happening, beyond my shields. Something bad was thrumming through the air, catching itself up in the Vibe, strengthening it, pushing on it.

"Mom wasn't going to give you as much time as you wanted, and that's why you killed her. You reminded Cheryl Bell that her consulting job and its big fat paycheck depended on Best Petz and you, so she would help you cover things up afterward."

Something's wrong.

"Rachael, no—"

Something bad is coming.

But Rachael didn't let Pam get any further. "You killed her. Right here. She let you in because you were her friend." While Damon and Zach were out running some errand, getting coffee and sandwiches and dry-erase markers. "You came in and you pushed her off the balcony onto the rocks. Did she die right away, or did you have to go down and smash her head against the boulder to make sure? You must have been so happy for all that bad weather to wash away any extra evidence."

Something's coming.

"Rachael, no . . . I . . ."

It's close, it's close . . .

"What . . ."

Alistair hissed. He was up on his feet, his back arched and all his fur standing on end, a nightmare cat. A split second later, I felt the spell. This was no slow prickling up my hands. This was a wave of anger that hit me like a storm blast. I tried to jump to my feet, but I only sprawled full-length on the carpet. If it hadn't been for my shields and Alistair, I think I might have passed out.

"Rachael!" I shouted, or at least I tried to. "Rachael, stop!"

The only answer was another surge of anger backed by cold, strained magic. My lungs seized up. My heart squeezed tight. It took everything I had, but I forced myself onto my knees.

"Merow!" wailed Alistair. "Maow!"

"Kenisha," I hissed through gritted teeth. "Get Kenisha."

But Alistair didn't move. I didn't have time to argue. I grabbed the half wall and hauled myself upright. The air was so thick with anger and magic, it was like I was drowning in molasses. I willed my shields to harden, to block it out, to cut me a path.

I made it to my feet, but barely. What I saw then almost knocked me right back down.

Down below, Pamela was crumpled against the wall, her breath coming in gasps. Rachael was sitting on the couch, watching with cold and dead eyes.

"Rachael," I croaked.

Rachael didn't move. She stared at Pam. All her focus, all her will and all her magic narrowed down to a single point. The throat. Rachael was going to throttle Pam. She was going to strangle her to death and not leave a mark.

Her family were healers. She was a healer. She was turning that talent against Pamela's body. Pam's lips were turning blue. She shifted her gaze toward me. She lifted her hand.

"Rachael, stop!" I gasped.

"She killed my mother," Rachael answered, her voice flat and final.

"I know, I know." I started for the stairs. Slowly, painfully. I clutched the rail with my free hand. Alistair was right beside me. "But you can't . . ."

"Yes, I can," replied Rachael calmly. Her eyes never flickered from Pam's throat. "I'm doing it."

I was halfway down. Three-quarters. "But this isn't justice, Rachael. This is revenge. The law . . ."

"I don't care!"

I believed her. In that moment, nothing meant anything. My head spun. I couldn't keep my shields up. The trapped anger, rage and greed were leaching into me. In another minute, I wouldn't care either.

What could I do? It took all my strength to hang on to what was left of my shields. I wasn't Rachael. I didn't have a personal gift to turn on her. I needed help. I didn't . . . I couldn't . . .

"Merow!" cried Alistair. "Maaawoooow!" My Vibe surged and strained.

Pam's head lifted, slowly, and her face was a mask of fury. "She deserved it. After all I did for her, and you."

"I told you," said Rachael, her voice as cool and dead as her eyes. "I don't care."

Oh, no. The anger, the greed, the cold horror of it all, pressed against my brain. The apartment walls could barely keep it in. I could barely keep it out.

Rachael didn't blink. Pam's eyes closed. Her head slumped down onto her knees.

"Merow!" wailed Alistair. And I knew. I had a chance. One chance. Rachael had once used her magic to try to influence me. I had to return the favor, and I had one advantage she didn't.

I had way more than just my own feelings to draw on.

I focused. Hard. I had no preparation. But I had my familiar and I had my wand, and I was angry and I was frightened and I had absolutely had enough. Enough of Pamela. Enough of Rachael. Enough of people acting like money was more important than life itself.

In need I call . . .

In hope I ask . . .

Let her feel it. Let them both feel what I feel right now . . .

With all my strength, I grabbed my Vibe, and I threw it hard at Pam and at Rachael. So hard, it exploded in my mind like fireworks.

Rachael screamed. The Vibe—the whole tangled net of dread, fury and desperation—threw itself across them.

Rachael screamed again, and I felt her grip on her magic falter. Alistair jumped up into her lap, thrusting his face into hers, breaking her final thread of concentration. The vibrations and the energies swirled and collided.

And shattered.

I dropped to the floor, like all my strings had been cut.

"Yip! Yip! Yip! Yip!"

There was a banging and an explosion. It was my heart. My heart had burst inside me. I was sure of it. Now my life was flashing in front of my eyes. My life had cops and friends pouring through a doorway.

And, apparently, dachshunds.

❦ 46 ❧

❧ PAMELA ABERNATHY WAS charged with the murder of Ramona Forsythe and was taken away by an escort of police officers that included both Officer Kenisha Freeman and Detective Pete Simmons. They wanted to take Rachael Forsythe as well, so she could be booked for attempted murder, obstructing justice and interfering with a crime scene. They would have, too, but Rachael needed to go to the hospital to be treated for exhaustion and severe dehydration.

No, none of us tried to explain that one.

Cheryl Bell was charged as a coconspirator. Zach quit Abernathy & Walsh the next day to go back to college and get his masters degree in social work.

Kenisha got a commendation from an extremely grudging Lieutenant Blanchard for superior police work. Pete stood at her side during the ceremony, beaming like a proud papa at his daughter's graduation.

Sean and I took a long, leisurely drive up to central Maine and had a wonderful dinner that included lobster macaroni and cheese at a roadside diner. I may have drunk a little too much artisanal vodka and fallen asleep in the passenger-seat side of his ancient station wagon on the way back, but we don't need to go into that.

On the night of the new moon, the full guardian coven and the full Forsythe family gathered on the spiral path in my back garden. In the dark, as the first real snow of winter fell around us, we lifted our voices, our hearts and the power of our craft. Wendy knelt by the fire and asked for healing and forgiveness from the living and the dead. We stood around her and hailed the stars and the memory of Ramona Forsythe. We wished her peace; we wished her a safe journey to the other side.

I felt something, distant but strong, ebbing away, and I knew for a fact that if I went back into that condo, I wouldn't feel anything out of the ordinary.

Except maybe one thing. But I didn't quite know how to bring it up. At least, I didn't until I'd said good-bye to all my coven sisters, and Julia and I were alone in the living room, with Max and Leo curled up asleep with Alistair, in front of the fireplace.

Julia settled herself onto my couch. "You have something you want to talk about, Anna," she said. It wasn't a question.

"Well, yes. No. It's not important."

Julia sat and waited. Julia was good at waiting.

"I think I did . . . I did something unforgivable."

"What's that?" she asked.

"You've . . . we've . . . talked about how you should never use your magic to directly influence another person."

"We have," she agreed.

"But, when Rachael was attacking Pam, I . . . turned my Vibe on her. On both of them, really. I wanted them to know what . . . what it felt like when somebody died."

"You did it to save a life. It was within the bounds of the threefold law."

"You didn't see their faces. You didn't hear . . ."

Julia stopped me. "Are their faces really the problem, Anna?"

I shook my head. "I wanted to hurt her. I mean, I really wanted to hurt them both. I wanted . . . I could have . . ."

"But you didn't."

"I wanted to," I said again.

"And when the moment came, you turned away. You used your power to save, not to destroy." Julia reached over and took my hand. "I am proud of you." She paused. "It was, however, rather sloppily executed. We will have to work more on your focus."

"Yes, Julia," I said meekly.

After that conversation, there was only one other piece of business to take care of. Well, after that conversation, and after I had a good long sleep, and possibly the biggest breakfast ever eaten at the Friendly Toast.

There was a phone call to Sedona, Arizona.

"Anna!" cried Grandma B.B. as soon as she picked up on the other end. "I've heard the news! They've caught Ramona's killer! You have to tell me what happened! Are you all right, dear?"

"I am, Grandma. Really. Promise." I looked at Alistair, who was sitting on the kitchen windowsill. He yawned. He'd heard it all before.

"Oh, thank *heavens*," said Grandma. "I've been so *worried*. You should have *told*—"

"That's what I'm calling about, Grandma," I cut her off.

"I don't understand, dear."

"Telling people what's really going on. I'm going to tell our family that I'm a witch. And I'm going to do it at Thanksgiving so they'll all get to hear it at once, and if Dad gets mad, he can get mad. And if . . . and if he stops talking to me . . . well, that's going to be his decision. I . . . I'm not going to keep this secret from them anymore. Especially not from Ginger and Bob."

"Ginger and Bob?" breathed Grandma.

"Yeah. Grandma, they're having a baby. Have you thought about the fact that this one might be a girl? She might inherit the magic."

Grandma B.B. was silent for a long time, and when she did speak again, it was so softly I could barely hear her. "Yes. I have thought about that a great deal lately."

"So." I tried to gather my nerve. "You do what you have to, but this is my decision."

"Yes," she murmured. "Yes, of course." I heard voices in the background. "Oh, dear. That's James and his brother. They're here to help me with the attic and the mudroom. I have to go, Anna . . ."

"Sure. We're not done, though."

"No, I know that."

"I love you, Grandma B.B."

"And I love you, Anna."

She hung up and I hung up and let out a very long breath. Well, that was done. I just wish I knew what was going to happen next.

"Merow," Alistair said, firmly.

"I know, I know, big guy," I told him. "And, honest, I wasn't going to argue!"

About the Author

Born in California and raised in Michigan, **Delia James** writes her tales of magic, cats and mystery from her hundred-year-old bungalow home in Ann Arbor. She is the author of the Witch's Cat Mysteries, which include *By Familiar Means* and *A Familiar Tail*. When not writing, she hikes, swims, gardens, cooks, reads and raises her rapidly growing son. Visit her online at deliajamesmysteries.com.

Ready to find
your next great read?

Let us help.

Visit prh.com/nextread

Penguin
Random
House